PRAISE FOR AUTHOR JOHN CLARKSON
AND HIS JACK DEVLIN THRILLERS!

"An all-guts hero!"   —*The New York Times*

"The *Death Wish* of the '90s—brutally real, fast as
a heavyweight champion's left hook—
with an unforgettable impact."
—WILLIAM J. CAUNITZ,
author of *One Police Plaza* and *Cleopatra Gold*

"Clarkson's debut delivers what it promises with
smooth authority. Action fans will applaud Devlin's
arrival on the suspense scene."
—*Publishers Weekly*

"The writing is supercharged as Clarkson keeps the
reader on edge with a constant stream of action."
—*The Orlando Sentinel*

"A virile book from a powerful writer."
—Loren D. Estleman,
author of the *Amos Walker* mysteries

"A beautifully paced thriller . . .
a helluva good read."
—Stephen Solomita,
author of *Bad to the Bone* and *Forced Entry*

Titles by John Clarkson

AND JUSTICE FOR ONE
ONE MAN'S LAW
ONE WAY OUT

ONE WAY OUT

JOHN CLARKSON

JOVE BOOKS, NEW YORK

ONE WAY OUT

A Jove Book / published by arrangement with the author

PRINTING HISTORY
Jove edition / January 1996

ISBN: 0-515-11802-8

A JOVE BOOK®
Jove Books are published by The Berkley Publishing Group,
200 Madison Avenue, New York, New York 10016.
JOVE and the "J" design are trademarks
belonging to Jove Publications, Inc.

PRINTED IN THE UNITED STATES OF AMERICA

10 9 8 7 6 5 4 3 2

This one is for Heather Anne.

ACKNOWLEDGMENTS

I'd like to thank Mark Lucas for his advice and assistance, particularly for introducing me to Andrew McMorrin. Andy turned out to be one of those rare people who do what they say they will, and do it better than anyone has a right to expect. Andy made it possible for me to accomplish in days what would have taken me months on my own, if at all. Thanks to Thomas McMorrin for handling transatlantic communications with such ease and aplomb. Thanks to Norm Siegel for guiding me on technical matters. And, of course, thanks to Ellen, the best London companion of all.

ONE WAY OUT

CHAPTER 1

JOHN PETCHEK NERVOUSLY scraped his thumbnail between his two bottom teeth and tasted the bitter sting of acrylic blue.

He thought to himself, I hate doing this. I hate watching them see me sweat. I hate standing here in front of their animal eyes with my hand out. Not knowing what the fuck those baboons are saying with that stupid West Indian sing-song shit they call talking. They love to watch me walk out of here knowing I'm going to be driving the streets of Hackney with enough cocaine to get me sent to jail for five to seven.

Petchek smelled the acrid odor of his fear-induced sweat. It filled the inside of his car, a 1970 rusting yellow Rover with no radio and a thick chain that locked the steering wheel to the floor.

But the money made it worth it.

If the London traffic wasn't too bad, he could make the drive in a little over an hour, from his loft south of the river, over the Tower Bridge, through the crowded streets of the City, north into Hackney.

The Jamaicans processed their coke up in Hackney in an abandoned section of the Frampton Estates just off Mare Street.

Petchek would make the drive, walk onto the estate, and get his consignment. Then he would keep his head down and drive back to his London loft. Skim his take and deliver the rest to Uncle Frank.

He had worked up the weight of his cocaine deals so that this delivery would net him twelve hundred pounds cash. Bang. Right then and there in big, crisp fifty- and hundred-pound notes. Plus he'd make another four or five hundred pounds from selling grams to his artist friends. And Petchek knew there would be more. Much more. Uncle Frank would be building up to a level that Petchek doubted this particularly vicious crew of Yardies could handle. This was just the beginning.

Petchek liked being the middleman fine. Supply Uncle Frank and skim just enough to supply his friends—a fashionable little group of pretentious artists and hangers-on who frequented the latest hot spots in Notting Hill or Soho or wherever.

Petchek enjoyed being the one who had the shit for sale. And he enjoyed looking the part. Tall, slim, with thick dark hair that he let grow long and appear unkempt—a style that went well with his perpetual three-day-old beard, black jeans, and paint-stained shirts. Petchek even managed to make sure there was a bit of paint on his hands and under his fingernails.

He told himself selling cocaine was part of staying outside the reach of normal, square society. Just part of living the life of an artist. But deep down even he knew that was a lie. He did it for the same reason everybody else did it. He did it for the money.

Money that allowed him to live the life of an artist, whether he sold his paintings or not. Money that enabled him to pay for the loft in the up-and-coming Butlers Wharf section of London, and eat out, and send the kid to school, and pay the damn Visa every month. Christ, he thought to himself, we go through fucking money like water. So as much as John Petchek hated this part, hated driving into Hackney to pick up the drugs, he did it anyhow and endured the ritual of fear.

As soon as he pulled into the section of the estate where the Jamaicans had set up their operation, he spotted three of Oliver's bad *bwouys* keeping watch. They tracked him with their vacant eyes from the moment he parked until he reached the building entrance. Petchek avoided their gaze and tried not to think about how easily one of them would hurt him if told to do so by Oliver.

There were always at least three of them in front of that dirty, squat estate building. And no one walked into Oliver's operation without walking past them first.

The place didn't look as if it needed guarding. It seemed to be abandoned. Left for demolition in a section of the public housing estate that was too run-down and decrepit even for

London's poorest. All the windows on both the ground floor and the upper two stories were covered over with sheets of warped, dirty plywood. The building seemed lifeless, but just the sight of it caused a ripple of fear to sweep up from Petchek's scrotum to his throat. God, I hate going in there, thought Petchek.

As he stepped into the dim ground floor of the estate building, Petchek's presence sent Oliver's Doberman pinscher guard dogs into a frenzy of snarling and barking. They were locked up in a small room right next to the stairwell that led to the upper floors. Petchek heard their claws scrape against a scarred red door that separated them from the stairwell. He cursed and quickly raced up the stairs, hoping the dogs would calm down if he moved away from them, but it just made them howl and bark all the louder in frustration.

In order to turn the dogs into killers, Oliver and his men constantly tormented them. They starved the dogs, beat them, jerked them off then kicked them in the testicles before they could come, spit on them . . . anything they could think of to make the animals as crazy and vicious as possible.

Petchek finally reached the second floor and pounded on the thick wooden door that kept out the outside world. A door so thick that even if the police tried to raid the place, they would need several minutes to batter it down.

He pounded twice on the door and waited. It would take a few moments for them to check him and open all the locks.

He inhaled once, quickly, said "Fuck it" out loud. It wouldn't be long now. He'd worked his way up to this. His biggest buy yet.

The door swung open and the bright fluorescent lights hit his eyes like a slap. The sweet sharp smell of ether and alcohol stung his nostrils. He stepped inside as he squinted against the light and handed a small green duffel filled with money to a guard, who took it without comment and slammed the big door shut.

The hip artist who wanted everyone to notice him in Holland Park or Chelsea stood near the door in Hackney trying to be invisible.

But he couldn't resist watching the sight in front of him. Six women and one man dressed like demented doctors in hair nets and surgical masks sat around a long table, cooking, cutting, weighing, and bagging rock cocaine into smaller and smaller packages. The powder and rock were white. The flames of the propane burners were blue and yellow. But the only colors Petchek saw were the beautiful pastels that decorated British pound notes.

How many kilos of cocaine had passed through this room? How many British pounds had been earned here?

But Petchek knew the money generated by this business wasn't the clean, crisp currency he would soon have. These Yardie bastards could only get hard used money grabbed from clutched hands on dirty streets or passed across stinking urinals and toilets. Not like the new fifties and hundreds Petchek would get. Their money would be grubby five- and ten-pound notes collected like dirt from all over London as if brought to them by a huge vacuum cleaner powered by the collective suck of a hundred thousand poor lungs.

Petchek's mind snapped shut when one of Oliver's men handed him back his canvas duffel bag. As he hefted the bag, he allowed himself a smile. Two kilos of almost pure cocaine. Shit, man, I'm pushing some heavy weight now. All of a sudden he didn't mind the nervous, sick feeling. It was almost over. All he had to do was turn around, wait until the door opened again, then get the hell out of there and drive back to his part of London. The clean, civilized part, where he could stop in a friendly pub and down a nice pint of Murphy's and congratulate himself.

But just at that moment, a door opened at the far end of the room and Oliver appeared, followed by Hinton, a man Petchek did not want to see. Ever.

Oliver was a compact, muscular, very dark Jamaican. Top bad bwouy in Hackney. The current Don. The head of the biggest Yardie crew operating in London. His front tooth and the two next to it on the right were capped in gold, but it was Oliver's eyes that gleamed at Petchek. There was a smoldering rage behind Oliver's eyes that seemed to fuel him with more heat and power than any drug ever could. Unlike most of the Yardies Petchek had known, there was hardly ever any laid-back, cool-mon aspect to Oliver. Especially not now. Oliver was moving right at him, with that goddamn Angel of Death, Hinton.

Petchek felt an almost overwhelming need to flee. The urge to empty his bowels hit him so suddenly he had to physically clench his anus shut. He forced a smile onto his face.

Oliver smiled back with a feral grin and said, "Yes, Mistah Petchek, here you are."

"Yes, Mr. Oliver, How are you?"

Still flashing the gold-toothed smile, Oliver answered, "Not good, mon, but lot better dan you."

In the moments Petchek used up trying to figure out exactly what Oliver meant, Hinton slipped behind him. Just like that, he was surrounded. Oliver hot and glowing in front of him, Hinton icy cool behind him. Petchek looked at Oliver, but could feel Hinton behind him. Could almost see the tall man's pockmarked face and deep cold eyes.

Petchek knew that the big door wouldn't open for him now, and his mind raced after a way to stop what was happening. But he wasn't even sure he could speak. How could these guys know I've been skimming? It's too soon. Too little. They have thousands. What do they care what I do? They have their money.

And the money was his last clear thought. Oliver's arm flashed through the air, Petchek heard the slap of Oliver's fist against his cheekbone, everything went black for a moment, and then the pain engulfed the side of his face.

Oliver screamed, "I always be better dan a dirty dog like you, because I don' steal from people."

And then Petchek's fear and confusion were solved. Hinton slammed an eight-inch stiletto into his back. The blow felt like a searing punch. The pointed blade glanced off a rib and ripped all the way through Petchek's right lung and nicked the side of his heart.

Petchek grunted. Staggered forward. Hinton ripped the knife out of him, pulling him away from Oliver and causing even more damage to Petchek's torn muscle and flesh.

The foolish artist/coke dealer dropped to his knees, then forward onto his hands. Blood was filling his lung while the traumatic slash to his heart sent the vital organ into immediate fibrillations. The heart quivered and fluttered in his chest like a huge can of worms.

Oliver knew death when he saw it, and his rage doubled because he thought this man was going to die too soon. Too easily. Oliver kicked him viciously in the stomach. He spat on him, and yelled, "Get up, goddamn ya, get up."

He kicked him again and again. Oliver knew he was running out of time. He reached back and suddenly had a short machete in his hand. He swung it at Petchek. The blade cut Petchek's left ear in half, split apart his cheek, and gouged a long slash in the side of his head. Petchek was on all fours, but instinctively raised his left hand to shield himself. Oliver swung at him again, severing two fingers and cutting through to his skull, hitting with such force that the bone cracked.

Oliver was raging now. Moving around to get a better angle. He screamed, "Open da fucking door."

The big guard fumbled with the locks and bars, terrified that Oliver's machete might swing at him if he moved too slowly.

Luckily, the door was open by the time the short powerful Oliver had dragged Petchek's dying body to the doorway.

But Petchek's brain still had enough blood to keep him conscious. The door was opening. They were dragging him out. Out. A surge of adrenaline kicked his heart. It flexed in a thunderous spasm in his chest. The pain was enough to bend his sternum, but a flash of consciousness pulsed through his brain. His heart thundered, beating now but tearing itself apart and pushing more blood into his chest cavity and lung.

His car! Could he get to his car and make it to a hospital? Sheer, raw survival instinct filled him. Oliver's raging voice was in some dark ringing tunnel.

He felt himself being dragged and kicked toward the door.

And then Oliver stepped into position. Something was grabbing Petchek's hair, pulling his head up off the floor. Hinton held the head. Oliver gripped the machete with two hands and swung with all his strength at the back of Petchek's neck. The blow severed the spine, the tendons, the muscles, but a good bit of ligament and cartilage held. He swung again, and again, chopping, hacking, splattering blood all over the implacable Hinton.

Finally, the head was hacked free. Hinton pulled it away from the body and tossed it out the door. Oliver ran after it and kicked Petchek's head down the stairs. He spat at the bloody, tumbling body part, then turned to grab at the corpse his men were pushing out the door. Hinton shoved the torso over the edge of the top step and Oliver slashed at it with the machete, ripping a wound across the back of Petchek's flopping left leg.

What was left of Petchek rolled and tumbled and thundered down the stairwell. Blood slapped and spilled across the stairs and walls. Oliver reached up and grabbed a chain that ran down to a lock at the top of the red door. The screaming, barking Dobermans were now in a frenzy over the smell of Petchek's blood. Oliver pulled the chain. The door burst open, and three crazed animals exploded into the stairwell, scrambling and slamming into one another as they fought for Petchek's head. And then, suddenly, the torn-apart body slammed into the pack and the dogs went finally, unalterably wild.

A frenzy of snarling, ripping, tearing, and biting boiled at the foot of the stairs. Petchek didn't see or feel or hear the dogs tearing and slashing at him, but Oliver did, and for a moment his seething rage was satisfied. His dark, gleaming, gold-toothed smile returned.

CHAPTER 2

An ocean and a continent away, Jack Devlin stood on the edge of a perfectly burnished cherry-wood veranda. He listened to the delicate trill of wind chimes as he absorbed the serene beauty of the Japanese garden in front of him. Without looking at any one thing, his eyes saw a dozen shades of green reflecting off moss, plants, and ancient bonsai. He felt the solidity of the garden's dark earth and gray rocks, accented with the fluid energy and sound of softly gurgling water. He breathed the cool evening air, lightly scented with pine.

The garden was beyond peaceful. It was a true oasis. A haven, hidden away from the smog-filled busy streets of Los Angeles. And the setting sun bathed it all in a soft golden glow, creating a moment that Devlin decided would never quite be duplicated.

Devlin stood without moving, dressed in the same clothes he had been wearing when he left Honolulu a little over seven hours earlier—gray linen slacks and a burgundy-colored cotton polo shirt. The clothes fit him well. Devlin had the body of a thirty-year-old pro linebacker. Unfortunately, he had the eyes of a sixty-year-old warrior.

Behind him William Chow sat Japanese-style at a low cherry-wood table made by the same craftsman who had fashioned the veranda. Although the house and garden had been built in the Japanese style of architecture, Chow was not Japanese. He was a unique mixture of several Oriental bloodlines: Indonesian, Chinese, Japanese. His connections to the Far East and beyond were as complex and pervasive as his heritage. And as the business of the East had more and more become the business of the West, Chow's sphere of influence had grown and lengthened.

William Chow ran one of the world's premier private security agencies, Pacific Rim Security. He provided information and protection for several multibillion-dollar conglomerates in Hong Kong, Japan, and Korea, as well as for a very small roster of wealthy private individuals. Jack Devlin was one of his most experienced and trusted operatives.

With his impeccable Armani suit, his tortoiseshell glasses, and his graying jet-black hair, Chow had the appearance of a corporate executive. And in fact Chow was carefully calculating a profit-and-loss question endemic to his business. Chow was comparing the value of Devlin's experience and expertise against his liabilities.

Having reviewed Devlin's report on his mission to Hawaii, Chow sat in a trancelike level of concentration trying to calculate the toll this latest effort had taken on Devlin. Unlike most employers, who thought of employees as commodities, Chow had an unalterable commitment to Jack Devlin. Chow fiercely maintained the Eastern ethic that once a man worked for you he was an employee for life. In Chow's mind, his life and Devlin's life would be forever intertwined.

Chow had witnessed firsthand Devlin's career and what it had cost the man. After this last assignment, Chow was convinced that if Devlin were to survive, he needed to step back. To rest and recuperate. To take a sabbatical from chaos. Chow was deeply concerned about Devlin's well-being. But he knew Devlin, and he knew that Devlin's rest would have to wait.

Devlin sensed Chow rise behind him and waited for the older man to step onto the veranda. For a moment the two colleagues stood side by side listening to the twilight sounds.

Chow spoke first. "Hawaii was difficult."

Devlin turned to look at his mentor. "Yes. It turned out to be more than we expected. More than *I* expected."

Chow stepped off the veranda, still deep in thought. Devlin fell into step next to him. Knowing that Chow was struggling with something and not wanting to disturb him, Devlin moved quietly and fluidly alongside the smaller man.

After a short, silent walk, Chow stopped near a small pool of water alongside the garden path. It contained two goldfish that were fourteen years old and had grown to the perfect size for the secluded pool. Their lives completely matched the protected space of water allotted for their existence.

Devlin listened to the sound of a miniature waterfall that flowed over pure white granite rocks before it gently fell into the fishpond.

Devlin was content to listen to the waterfall. Finally, after several minutes, Chow spoke.

"You have recovered?" It was as much a statement as a question.

"Pretty much. Some things will last for a while yet."

"Yes. I'm wondering if we should talk about that."

Devlin turned to Chow.

"If you'd like to, William, of course."

Chow looked back at Devlin, but Devlin deftly suggested, "However, I would say that the discussion will have to be deferred for the moment. It seems I have a personal problem."

Chow simply nodded, then quietly said, "Yes." He handed Devlin the telegram he had been waiting to receive.

Jack, sorry. Urgent. I need your help. I'm still in London. Annie.

A phone number and address were also on the telegram, but Devlin didn't bother to read the numbers. The single word "Annie" was enough of a message. Images of her flashed in his memory. A physical feeling of love and loss hit him so palpably that he realized his breathing had been altered. It had been so many years. Devlin had not expected to hear from Annie. Nor had he expected his reaction to be so intense.

Chow's soft, refined voice interrupted the flow of feeling. "I'm sorry," Chow said. "Messages of this sort rarely bring good news."

"No. They don't. I'm going to have to leave for London."

"I see."

"Thank you, William."

Chow bowed slightly and offered his services. "We are at your disposal."

"Thank you, sir."

"But I'm sorry to admit that in London, we might not be able to do everything we would wish to do for you. As you know, Jack, Western Europe is not in our primary sphere of interests. We have limited resources there."

"I know. I'll be in touch."

Chow extended his hand. Devlin grasped it. Neither of them needed to say more. Devlin held Chow's hand for just an extra beat, and then was striding out of the garden. But after a few paces Chow called his name softly.

"Jack."

Devlin turned. Chow was silhouetted by the setting sun. For a moment in the backlighting, the man who was such a towering presence in Devlin's life appeared somewhat diminutive.

"Yes sir?"

"Try to keep perspective, Jack. Personal matters sometimes affect us with surprising force."

"Yes sir. I'll try."

And then Devlin was gone. And Chow was not at all comfortable with that fact. Chow wanted to know exactly what "Urgent" meant, and who "Annie" was.

Whoever she was, it was apparent Jack Devlin was not going to waste any time answering her call.

CHAPTER 3

As DEVLIN'S JET roared toward London, Hinton gunned the engine of his red Saab and turned a corner onto Coldharbour Lane in Brixton. He revved the engine, downshifted smoothly, and gripped the leather-wrapped steering wheel. Hinton loved his car. Hinton liked the smell of the car and the size of it and the smooth power. Hinton had come to England to get and take things like his red turbocharged Saab.

He continued up Coldharbour under the British Rail tracks and turned into a maze of small lanes packed with row after row of three- and four-story flats. The buildings were in various states of disrepair. Rental laws, the dole, and drugs had taken their toll on these dwellings. There wasn't much profit left in this part of London, so the landlords repaired nothing, the people asked for little, and for many, life in Brixton remained grim.

But not for Hinton. Now, more than ever, places like Brixton and Hackney and Stoke Newington were places for men like Oliver and Hinton and their crew of Yardies. The world of the Yard man revolved around two things: crack cocaine and guns. With crack you made money. With guns you protected the money. And often, with guns you got the money to buy the cocaine that made money.

A third element invariably came into play: prostitution. Crack always produced women who needed to sell themselves for the drug. Oliver considered it a kind of spillover waste product that could be sold somewhere outside the main business to add extra cash to the bottom line. Oliver tolerated his prostitution business more than he operated it. He would not turn his back on the money. Just as long as it didn't cause him too much trouble.

This quiet section of Brixton was perfect for Oliver's

12

whores and their trade. And for his need to have a quiet headquarters.

He needed the space to conform to the rather arcane prostitution laws in England. A flat that contained one woman offering sexual services for money was not a brothel, and the woman was not a prostitute. A flat that contained two women doing the same thing was a brothel, and they were prostitutes. So Oliver used his building to house five separate flats for prostitution—one on the ground floor in the back, two each on the second and third floors. His headquarters occupied the top floor. The whores worked quietly downstairs and made money. Oliver sat upstairs counting it.

Hinton parked his car at the curb. He got out, glanced proudly at the glowing red finish on the bonnet, and entered the building.

He sniffed the smells of the place. Spicy Jamaican food was cooking somewhere. One of the whores must be making a meal for the others, thought Hinton.

The food smells, plus the scent of cat spray and garbage, brought back memories of his childhood in Kingston. Close, but not exactly the smell of his old yard. Maybe it was the lack of unrelenting heat that changed the mix. The perpetual wet cold of London's winters never brought enough sun to beat down and cook everything to the proper ripeness. Or maybe there just weren't enough good West Indian blacks to get the smells right. Too many Pakis and Irish and white yobs mixed in with everybody else. For now, London was home. It would have to do. And whatever it was, London was better than the grinding poverty and increasingly dangerous back streets of Kingston.

Any man who had survived Hinton's life to this point was both more than and less than most others who walked the earth.

Hinton had survived everything the island had thrown at him, including eleven years in a prison where you had to maim and kill in order to live. The strong ate the food, wore the shoes, slept in the beds. The strong sucked the life out of the weak, and survived. Hinton now knew that there were very few things on earth that could be worse than a Jamaican prison. Certainly no jail in England.

Hinton had survived by tapping into the inhuman part of himself. The part that connected with a darker existence than what he saw and smelled and heard. In the dark, dangerous prisons of Jamaica, Hinton had found solace in the inscrutable netherworld of African/Christian gods. The world of Voodoo and Santeria. For him, it was the world of his chosen patron god . . . Chango.

When he reached the top-floor landing, Hinton approached a wire-mesh gate that completely sealed off the landing from the stairwell.

On the landing, two of Oliver's Dobermans moved in a constant circuit along the length of the hallway. These dogs were not the wild curs that Oliver would unleash on police or others trying to attack his drug-processing lab. These dogs were trained. They knew Hinton's smell, so they were content to eye him silently.

Hinton hated the dogs, for he knew that, if given the chance, the dogs would try to kill him. That knowledge made Hinton instinctively want to kill them first.

Hinton pressed the button which alerted Oliver's guard that someone was outside the gate. The motion prompted the bigger of the dogs to walk toward him. Hinton listened to the *click, click* of the big dog's toenails on the hard floor. He stood still until the Doberman was in front of the gate, then hawked a gob of phlegm and spit it right in the dog's face.

The dog was instantly out of control. He threw himself at the wire mesh, barking furiously. The second dog rushed next to him and joined in.

Hinton's blood raced as he bent down and smiled silently at the dogs. He thought about gutting them with his long stiletto blade.

The dogs barked and growled as if they could read Hinton's twisted mind. There was a brutal animal connection between Hinton and the dogs. Hinton fought the urge to pull his knife out and slam it into the nearest dog's belly the next time he jumped at the wire door. Just then the trainer, Eddie, entered the landing and called the dogs off.

Eddie knew better than to say anything to Hinton about tormenting the dogs. Even though the Dobermans were quivering with the killing urge, the trainer managed to snap their leashes on them. He pressed the buzzer and Hinton pushed open the wire door. Hinton stared at the man and his dogs, daring the trainer to speak and the dogs to bark.

He walked to the front door of the apartment. The door opened, revealing a woman who was so large that she nearly filled the doorframe. Hinton stopped immediately and bowed his head.

"Hello, Momma."

The big woman was Lydia Cientro. She was a mix of Haitian and Dominican, but had lived much of her life in Jamaica practicing a strange blend of Voodoo and Santeria. Her hair was covered in a wrap made of a colorful blue and red print material. To cover her big body, she wore a shapeless sack of a dress made from the same material as her headdress. Her arms and hands were adorned in rings and bracelets.

The respect Hinton showed her was instant. But she simply stood at the door examining him without uttering a word for about five seconds. Momma Cientro did not appreciate Hinton's penchant for tormenting the dogs. She did not like the noise. Only when she was satisfied that Hinton was sober, dressed well enough, and sufficiently humble did she extend her hand. Hinton took the large, pudgy hand of the *honsi*—priestess—and kissed it.

Lydia Cientro turned and led Hinton into the main room of the apartment, which had been completely transformed into an altar room for various icons and gods, including Hinton's patron, Chango.

The room was isolated from the outside world. The windows had been painted and covered with drapes. The only light came from a single red bulb gleaming in the middle of the ceiling and several votive lights burning around the altar.

The room was carpeted with many, many rugs scattered about. The walls, like the windows, were covered with drapes. Every fabric was some shade of dull red.

On the altar the effigy of Chango, half man/half woman, an androgynous denizen of hell, glared down at Hinton.

Hinton bowed before the statue and placed his token of worship into a brass dish—a crisp hundred-pound note. It wasn't only the denomination that mattered; it was the newness and freshness of the bill that made it a respectable offering.

Incense burned and clouded the room. The woman priest watched Hinton from behind. She had a scowl on her face, as if she had tasted something bad.

Hinton deferred only to his religion. Momma Cientro was a part of it. She was granted his respect, for Hinton really and truly believed that the power of Voodoo and gods such as Chango existed. And he was convinced that the god of thunder and lightning bolts had saved him from a living hell. How else could he explain his sudden and unexpected release, not only from prison, but into this heaven of opportunity, this soft ripe plum of a city that waited for him to grab and suck.

It was an obvious miracle.

When Hinton rose from his knees, the big woman motioned him toward the hall leading to Oliver's office.

"He's waiting for you."

Hinton nodded and left. He was aware of her displeasure with him. It bothered him, but he didn't have time to deal with it now.

Oliver was talking on the phone when he entered, and motioned for him to sit down.

Hinton looked around the office. It was all glass, chrome, and fluorescent light. It was as if the Yard boss had felt compelled to create the exact opposite of the altar room.

Oliver had little to do with the *honsi*. But he, too, believed in the workings of the primitive religion. So did many of his men. So he had his own church built. It was his insurance.

Oliver listened to the voice on the phone. He was dressed in an expensive dark blue suit and a black silk collarless shirt. Unlike many of his peers who favored large gold "cargo" in the form of chains and other ornaments, Oliver's only affectation was a thick gold chain wrapped around his left wrist.

Oliver spoke in a low, guttural Jamaican lilt that sounded only vaguely related to British English. Hinton knew he must be talking to one of his men.

Oliver had created his powerful crew by gathering men around him who operated with a matter-of-fact ruthlessness. They killed like savages—very easily. In the anarchic world of West Indian gangs, their power and survival was based on their ability to terrorize. But even amidst this group, Hinton stood out. He not only killed easily, he killed religiously. The hard men of the Yard killed without compassion. Some even liked killing. Hinton *believed* in killing.

As he talked on the phone Oliver pulled out small stacks of pound notes from his desk drawer. He divided them into two piles. Oliver paid by the inch.

He hung up the phone and handed a one-inch pile to Hinton. "For you," he said.

Then he handed him a quarter-inch pile.

"And da bonus, mon."

Hinton took the money and rifled through it, getting some idea of how much it was.

Oliver interrupted his counting. He didn't like his hirelings to count money in front of him, felt they should just take what he gave them. "Okay, bredrin, you can stop dat now. We have a lot of business to take care of."

Hinton pocketed the money and looked up.

"First go on over to King's Cross and check on Louis. See if da trash hanging aroun' der be causing any trouble. If so, you take care of it. We cyan let dem kind t'ink they can fuck wit' us.

"Then you find Lionel. Him over in the Wicks by da factory. He finally got a lead on dat white scum we dealt wit'. Also a clean piece for you. You find out da information, take care of it. You know what to do, right?"

Hinton nodded his head and stood up to leave without further words. He was anxious to get started.

"One more t'ing. Very important. We have a meeting tonight with da Yugoslav."

Hinton frowned. "Where?"

"A place called da Yard in Soho. Rupert Street. He thinks he's funny, maybe. Or maybe he's stupid."

"So you going to deal with him?"

"Of course. He got two t'ings I want."

"What?"

"Money and guns. More of it dan anywhere in dis yard, mon. But we first got to sort out some t'ings. So I want you there. Ten o'clock. Finish your business and be there. You take Lionel wit' you."

"You expecting trouble?"

"I always expect trouble. That's why I'm still alive. Maybe I don' kill as quick as you, my fren', but I always be da mon who kill first."

Oliver allowed himself a quick grimace that was his version of a smile.

"Go on, now. I'll see you tonight."

Hinton left the office and made his way back through to the altar room. The big woman was waiting for him. She sat on a well-worn wooden chair with her fat arms folded. She was still glum.

Hinton went down on one knee and asked for her blessing. The woman took his head in her hands.

"Do you believe in the power of the god?"

"You know I do."

"Or do you believe more in the power of your gun and your knife?"

"What have I done to offend you, Momma?"

The big woman looked up at the ceiling as if she could see the sky. Outside it was growing dark. A thunderstorm was sweeping down from the north. It would rain heavily soon. The distant rumble of thunder filtered into the room.

"Be careful, my son. One rainstorm can touch many people."

With that, she extended her blessing. Hinton made the sign of the cross and stood up. He wasn't interested in discussing her cryptic message; it was something she did. All he wanted was her benediction and the protection it brought to him. With it, and with the protection of Chango, he believed he would not die. At least not today.

CHAPTER 4

THE SAME THUNDERCLOUDS that rumbled while Hinton knelt under Momma Cientro's blessing could be heard across the Thames by a little girl age six, who was sitting on her window-sill, feet planted on her bed, looking up at the gray, threaten-ing sky. She was Elizabeth Petchek, and she was waiting for her mom to take her to Ladbroke Grove Grammar School in her old Notting Hill/Holland Park neighborhood.

To keep herself company, Elizabeth began to sing. She knew the whole song, but she enjoyed singing only one line: "It isn't raining rain, you know, it's raining daffodils."

She looked up at the rain-filled sky and sang the line from "April Showers" over and over again.

Elizabeth was the kind of child who made people stop on the street and comment on her beauty. Especially older women. The first words out of most women over fifty when they saw Elizabeth were, "Oh my, what a beautiful child." Almost as if it were a burden of some sort. "Oh my," they'd say. But they always followed quickly with, "She's so sweet," as if to ameliorate the toll they knew the beauty would one day demand.

And beautiful she was. Elizabeth had thick black silky hair surrounding her perpetually animated face. She had soft, dark, engaging eyes that looked very big when she opened them wide. She smiled easily. She had that quick, clipped Brit-ish accent with just enough verve and cheekiness to make her seem both precocious and charming. But the best part was when Elizabeth laughed. When she laughed, even the hardest-hearted person had to smile. As for Elizabeth, she had a good heart. She was much too young and innocent to realize the budding power of her beauty. So, for now at least, she was a little kid who most of the time tried valiantly to please her mom and dad.

Lately, however, an ineffable sadness clung to the small child. Something was wrong. It used to be that her daddy was in and out at odd hours and different times, but lately he wasn't around at all. His absence confused Elizabeth, because no matter how rational her mother sounded when she explained that he was away on business, Elizabeth instinctively knew something was wrong. And Mummy was gone now a lot too. Mummy had to dress up and do something called "appointments." And she seemed about to cry sometimes. And lots of times now, Mummy wasn't able to pay attention to what Elizabeth was saying.

So Elizabeth sang to herself and waited for things to be the way they used to be, and for her mother to come take her to school. At the sound of her mother's approaching footsteps, Elizabeth stopped singing and slid from the windowsill onto her bed. She bounced off the bed to the floor, then turned to smooth the blankets.

Annie Petchek entered her child's room carrying a pair of red galoshes—the kind with one big button and an elastic band to close them.

"Come on, kiddo, we're late."

Elizabeth sort of hopped/ran over to her mother.

"I get to wear my boots today?"

"Yes."

Elizabeth was delighted, and the delight made Annie bend over and hug her daughter tight to her legs. Elizabeth wrapped her arm around her mother and squeezed back. It felt good.

"Okay, hurry up now."

"Yes, yes, Mummy."

The hugging felt good, but the galoshes were too much competition. Elizabeth grabbed them from her mother's hands and plopped right down on the floor to pull them on over her shoes.

Annie smiled at her child. When Annie and Elizabeth were together, it was obvious why Elizabeth was such a beautiful child. Her mother was the adult version of the little girl. Older, more elegant, more sensual. But for the moment, the horror of her husband's death had robbed Annie Petchek of any chance of looking as serene and beautiful as she usually did. She was far from adjusting to the tension and revulsion and fear that dominated her thoughts, much less to the loss. Annie Petchek's world was falling apart, and she was not at all sure that she could prevent it from happening.

Elizabeth was distracted by the galoshes and didn't see how quickly her mother's smile disappeared. Annie felt her brows furrow and noticed that her left eye was twitching again. She rubbed that side of her face and pulled herself away from the dark emotions that were overpowering her. This was no time to look haggard. Jack was coming. It had been too many years since she had seen him, and she couldn't afford to let him see her in such a state.

She ran her hand through her hair. It was the same thick, silky black hair as her daughter's. She wore it almost shoulder-length and seemed to always be running her fingers through it to get it out of her way. But it was one of her best features, and she wouldn't even think of tying it back.

As Annie watched Elizabeth pull on the second boot, she ran the tips of her fingers across her cheekbone and wondered how Jack would look after all these years. She frowned. The years always seemed to treat men better.

She knew her skin was still soft and clear, and that her face still held its somewhat austere, forthright beauty. But at the moment she had little desire to gaze into a mirror. She did not want to examine the loss of youthful radiance, or the fine lines, or the tension.

Well, she thought, even if the face has lost some of its youth, the body is still there. She felt her stomach and smoothed her skirt across her hips and derriere. At thirty-eight and just under five feet nine inches, her weight was exactly the same as it had been when she had first met Jack Devlin. Standing naked in front of him there'd be a difference, but not standing clothed. Another smile rippled across her face. One much different from the kind her child evoked. Men were so predictable. Annie knew she had what they wanted. Long legs, big tits, and a great ass. And Jack Devlin was no different. Yes, he also noticed her graceful neck and wrists and ankles. But Devlin had always appreciated her looks and her body, and made no apologies for it.

She stopped her inventory of herself and turned to go into the kitchen. "I'll make your lunch. Bring your jacket when you get your boots on."

"Yes, Mummy."

Annie walked back through the apartment to the kitchen. For London, it was a very unusual place. The apartment was in a converted loft building in the Butlers Wharf neighborhood. Over the hundreds of years people had lived in London, every structure had been renovated or fixed to accommodate its tenants. But only recently had a wave of renovation transformed the large factory and loft buildings of Butlers Wharf. It was unusual to find such space so close to central London. The large, airy lofts, filled with natural light, had attracted many artists, as well as advertising agencies and design studios. Restaurants and galleries had followed. As had the up-and-coming mix of urban professionals. Annie and John had come into the neighborhood rather early and had avoided the crushing prices of apartments that were now the norm, but the expense of buying the loft and renovating it was the main reason John had turned to dealing cocaine. Nothing else could bring him the quick infusions of cash that he constantly needed.

Annie's loft apartment was one of four on the sixth floor of a converted factory. Each apartment radiated out from a central corridor. Her apartment was set up with the rooms stacked one after the other from front to back. Past the front door was a small entranceway, then a large open living room with a high ceiling, two bedrooms, and a bath, all off the same hallway, and then a very large kitchen. There was a back door off the kitchen that led down a flight of stairs to a fire exit door, which opened directly onto the street.

Annie finished making Elizabeth's lunch and then packed it into a red backpack. The girl's notebook and assorted school supplies were already in the pack.

As Elizabeth came happily clomping down the hallway in her rubber boots, Annie took a small umbrella off the kitchen counter.

"Now listen, honey, I'm going to give you your own umbrella today."

Elizabeth's huge eyes widened. "Really?"

"Yes. But don't lose it. When you get to school put it in your backpack."

The little girl became very serious about this new responsibility. "Yes, Mum, I will. Don't worry."

"Good. Let's get going. We have to walk across the bridge today."

"Can't we take a taxi to school, then?"

"No. We're going to take the Tube."

Annie led her little girl to the back door of the kitchen.

"Mummy, why do we have to go down the stairs? I don't like the stairs."

"It's a shortcut."

"It is?"

"Yes. We come out closer to the road this way."

And we have less chance of being seen, thought Annie.

Elizabeth stood and waited as Annie unlocked the back door. Unlike most London apartment doors which had simple one-piece locks that snapped shut, Annie's back door was secured with a formidable old locking system left over from the days when the space was an industrial loft. From the inside, you had to turn a knob round and round to slide two iron bars into or out of the doorjambs. From the outside, you turned a key. Annie twisted the inside knob a final turn, pushed open the big door, and stepped out onto the dark, dusty landing. She went through the locking process, then she and Elizabeth walked down the six flights of stairs, at just about the same time as Jack Devlin's flight from L.A. started its descent at Heathrow.

CHAPTER 5

As THE BIG jet descended, the change in air pressure woke Devlin. He opened his eyes and in five seconds he was totally alert, but quite surprised. A blonde woman with piercing green eyes was staring at him. And when he looked back at her, she continued staring without apology, except for a quick smile.

She said, "You timed that just right—we're landing."

Devlin sat up and appraised his seatmate. She looked exactly like a beautiful blonde should.

"No," said Devlin, "I should have been up a lot sooner."

The blonde cocked her head and turned the smile up a notch. "Is that a compliment?"

"Yes."

"Thanks. My name is Joan Cunningham."

"Jack Devlin."

They shook hands.

"What brings you to London, Jack?"

"Business. What about you?"

"I'm negotiating a modeling contract. Europe seems to be interested in tall, blonde athletic types at the moment. My acting career wasn't going all that great in L.A., so I figured I'd try this for a while."

Devlin listened for the egoism that one would expect in such comments, but it wasn't there. The woman had relayed this information so matter-of-factly that she didn't sound at all conceited.

"What business are you in?"

Although he had several standard answers, Devlin didn't use any of them.

She reminded him, "You said you were traveling on business."

24

"Insurance."

She waited for elaboration, but Devlin didn't provide any.

"Maybe I'd better give you a little more time to wake up."

Devlin's mind was far from sleepy. This was too good to be true. And as a result, silent alarms were sounding. It wasn't at all impossible for this to be a setup. Many had been done much more artfully than this one. A beautiful blonde who just happened to be assigned the seat next to him in first class on a flight to Europe. A flight that would provide more than enough time to strike up a friendship. Devlin's habit of using planes to catch up on his sleep, however, had significantly reduced the time available to make the connection. Was that why she seemed too intense? Too friendly, too soon? Or was it just that Devlin had become too suspicious after so many years in a dangerous business?

The very fact that he was unsure about what was going on was reason enough for Devlin to worry. He knew that the difficult assignments had piled up too quickly, taking too much out of him. He badly needed rest and respite. He knew it. Did someone else know, too? Was that someone an enemy? And then a very comforting thought struck Devlin: Was that someone a friend? Was this Chow's work? He knew Devlin's flight—his personal assistant, Mrs. Banks, had booked it. Could William have recruited someone so fast?

"I'm awake, now. Wide awake."

This brought back the woman's smile. "So how long will you be staying in London?"

He hadn't said he was going to be staying in London.

"A few days. Maybe a week."

"Well, I'll be here for at least that long. Would you like to have dinner some night?"

My God, he thought, she's not taking any chances.

"Sure. Where can I reach you?"

The blonde dug into her purse and pulled out a card. It bore her name in a script typeface that was supposed to be elegant, and an L.A. address and phone number. She turned the card over and wrote down a London phone number and address.

"This flat belongs to a friend of mine. You can reach me here. Where are you staying?"

"At the Connaught."

"Nice. Call me, okay?"

"I will."

The plane bumped to a landing. Joan Cunningham flashed a dazzling smile to sink the hook as deeply as possible, then began gathering her things for deplaning. Devlin resisted the urge to shake her hand for having completed her mission in time.

Joan made sure to walk with Devlin through the terminal to the baggage area. She seemed more relaxed now, content to let the conversation dwell on insignificant topics . . . how bad British food was, how nice the parks were, how easy it was to get around on the Tube.

Devlin's bag appeared first, and he said a polite good-bye. Joan insisted he share a ride with her into London, but Devlin declined.

"No thanks, Joan. Really."

She stepped back and gave him her most enticing look: head slightly down, blonde hair falling perfectly around her face, eyes gazing up.

Here it comes, thought Devlin.

"Are you really going to call me?"

"First chance I get."

"Where'd you put my number?"

Devlin thought to himself, If this woman weren't so beautiful she wouldn't get away with half this shit.

Without producing her card, he rattled off the phone number.

Blonde Joan nodded. "Well, Mr. Devlin. I'm impressed. Call me if you feel like it. It could be fun."

With that, she sashayed back to the baggage carousel, making sure to give Devlin a pleasant view. He took the time to admire it, then headed for Customs. When he reached the central terminal, he stopped at a pay phone. He punched in the direct-dial code, connected with an outside overseas line, and punched in the required numbers.

He checked his watch and calculated the time difference. When a voice answered, Devlin dictated a message for Mrs. Banks.

"This is a request from Jack Devlin." He took the woman's

card out of his pocket. "Please run a check on a Joan Cunningham. Blonde, about five-eleven, a hundred and thirty pounds. Supposed to be an actress/model." He carefully recited the phone numbers and addresses on her business card and then said, "Please ask Mrs. Banks to verify that information. I just need to know if it checks out. If it doesn't, I'll give further instructions."

Devlin waited for the voice on the other end to repeat the information.

"Good. Also, tell Mrs. Banks I need a list of local freelancers available in the London area approved by the company. Divide them into the usual categories for now. I won't know what I need until later. I'll call you back and tell you where to fax the information. Thanks."

Devlin imagined the reliable Mrs. Banks dutifully executing his requests, and then just as dutifully passing on the information to Mr. Chow. Mrs. Banks was smart, tough, and absolutely loyal to William Chow. The fact that Chow had given Devlin direct access to the formidable Mrs. Banks was a tremendous advantage that Devlin used to its fullest. She was the ultimate conduit to the resources of Pacific Rim Security.

Devlin's next phone call was to Annie's apartment. As he listened to the foreign ring tones, he turned his back on the phone and watched the people moving about the terminal. Devlin was not one to face a wall for any longer than he had to.

He waited for six rings and decided Annie wasn't home and didn't have an answering machine. He terminated the call, walked to the Thomas Cook foreign exchange kiosk, and exchanged five thousand American dollars for English pounds, then headed outside to find a taxi before he ran into Joan Cunningham again.

Hinton, on the other hand, would have liked very much to run into somebody. Preferably somebody who felt like causing him trouble. His encounter with Momma Cientro had left him very much in the mood to inflict pain and draw blood.

He had just emerged from the Underground station at King's Cross. He walked against the tide of harried evening commuters heading into the large train station and crossed

Pentonville Road. His slow, imperious gait contrasted with the rushed footsteps of those around him. People instinctively veered away from him, giving the tall, dark-skinned man plenty of room.

Hinton was headed for a grimy arcade/entertainment center about two blocks east of King's Cross station.

King's Cross had always been a seedy area. But as with most dicey spots in London, a casual passerby could easily miss the nasty business being conducted around them. Londoners tended to move quickly through the area on their way to some other place. They might notice a wasted drunk wandering about and the general disarray and dirt, but rarely would the average person take note of the significant business in drugs and street prostitution conducted almost round the clock near the mammoth train station.

In front of the arcade, a seemingly deranged black man was arguing with a young girl who had the appearance of a street waif wasted on drugs. Another black man, heavily muscled in a tank-top T-shirt, stood waiting for something. A few paces up the block Hinton spotted Leon, one of Oliver's Yardie bad bwouys. Leon fit the part. He wore his hair in long unkempt dreads, sported a scraggly beard, and dressed in matching lime green jacket and pants. Oliver's other bwouy, Pudgy, was around the corner eating in an Indian restaurant which featured an evening special: all you could eat for £3.50, not including drinks.

The riffraff on the street knew that Leon and Pudgy were in the neighborhood to conduct Yard business. And their presence deterred most problems. But if a challenge from a rival group arose, Hinton was the man designated to not just handle it, but to exact a degree of retribution designed to prevent any further trouble from occurring.

Leon ran the string of women who discreetly displayed themselves on streets jutting off the long empty roadway that ran alongside the train station. The women would pick up their johns cruising in cars or on foot, then either walk or ride around to Gray's Inn Road and check in to one of the cheap hotels available for short stays. Either on the way to the hotel or from the hotel, they'd nod to Leon as he stood at his post outside the arcade. Sometimes they would service a hurried commuter in the backseat of his car, but most of the time they would head for the cheap hotels. Every couple of hours Leon's runner, or sometimes Leon himself, would come by each whore's corner and pick up her earnings. The policy was that no whore would stay on the street with an excessive amount of cash. Losing a whore to a violent john or the police was one thing; losing her earnings was an entirely different matter.

The same system applied to the drugs Oliver's crew sold. Pudgy was in charge of those sales. The drug transactions were evenly divided between customers walking on the street and those driving in cars. Pudgy and three or four steerers would make themselves just visible enough to send a customer to a constantly rotating handful of locations: outside the grimy Indian restaurant, the doorway beneath a twenty-four-hour snooker hall, a spot near a strip joint/pub that featured a bevy of worn-out women who displayed their breasts and vaginas for tips dropped into a beer glass.

On a regular basis, a runner would come by and exchange drugs for money. No seller had more than a few hundred quid on him or a couple of dozen rocks of cocaine wrapped in sealed plastic or aluminum foil. The Yardies had yet to adopt the American custom of selling crack in vials.

Again, with the runners constantly collecting cash and delivering drugs, any losses through arrests or rip-offs would be minimal.

The trade was conducted without fanfare. Almost invisibly. But with a never-ending steadiness that caused money to accumulate quite rapidly. To keep the operation supplied and running required enormous effort and discipline. The pressure of it all made Oliver quite ruthless about anything that disturbed his trade. And it made Hinton very happy, because Oliver wanted all matters of conflict to be solved with the most extreme amount of violence possible.

By moving out of the West Indian neighborhoods into King's Cross, Oliver was inviting trouble. He was encroaching on the fluid mix of runners and pimps and crack salesmen who had always operated in the King's Cross area under a free-for-all setup where any piece of commerce was usually negotiated and obtained through a mix of money and muscle.

Oliver hadn't asked anyone's permission. He was running his own, self-contained operation as an open challenge to everyone. And he was ready to fight and maim and kill if necessary until his right to sell women and drugs was no longer challenged. Oliver expected some trouble. Most likely starting at the street level. Hinton hoped for it.

After checking with Leon and Pudgy, Hinton made three circuits around the neighborhood. Each time he started his circuit in front of the arcade. First, Hinton would stand on the street allowing everyone to get a good look at him. Then he would start walking with his nine-millimeter automatic pistol tucked into his waistband, a bullet in the chamber, the hammer of the gun cocked. In his right hand was his stiletto, slid under his watchband up his sleeve, with the front end of the knife cupped lightly in his palm.

Hinton's face tended to scare most people off, even if they did not know how dangerously armed he was. His eyes were deeply set back. His high cheekbones and pockmarked dark skin made him extremely foreboding. As did his almost militarily erect posture. Hinton paid little attention to his dress, but whatever he wore, he looked as if he should be attending a funeral. And unlike most Yard men, who favored plenty of gold jewelry, Hinton's only accessory was a necklace of small red and white beads, the colors of his protective deity.

As he turned the first corner, Hinton looked up the block. He saw the cars, the bum squatting in a doorway, the whore at the end of the block, the broken empty windows, the trash fluttering along the gutter. His eyes took in everything, but most importantly everything that moved.

Hinton, of course, was crazy. He imagined himself some sort of lightning rod or magnet for violence. Within minutes his breathing had turned shallow and his eyes had taken on a glazed look. Hinton wanted someone to try to hurt him. Hinton wanted violence to erupt around him so he could stand and fire his gun, one bullet at a time, precisely, at whoever was trying to harm him. Or, if they were within his reach, he wanted to stab and slash them. Hinton wanted to see how his gods and his hate protected him. Let an enemy appear, he prayed to himself, so he could draw his gun and walk straight toward them and fire until they were killed. Hinton really believed he would not die, would not be hit by one single bullet unless his god wanted him to be hit. And if the god who had already saved him from hell wanted his life, he could have it.

The only thing that worried Hinton was falling into the dark rage where he could become lost and blind. Literally lost in a red haze of rage. It was his only problem in the stalking game of death. And Hinton was sane enough to realize it. He was somehow sane enough to know he lived in an insane state. That state, however, was becoming more and more attractive to him. It was the source of his power. Hinton was beginning to enjoy the game of seeing how long he could survive that way before his mind went completely.

Nothing happened on the third circuit. Hinton returned to the spot in front of the arcade. There was the sweet/sour afterglow of the adrenaline surge. But no killing this time. No blood to offer. No flesh to cut or screams to enjoy.

Hinton checked in one more time with Leon and Pudgy. The two bad bwouys kept their distance from Hinton. They did not want to get too close to him or say anything that might disturb him. Hinton walked away from them, swallowing the sour taste in his mouth. He was unsatisfied. Perhaps akin to a junkie who had missed his fix. He hailed a cab and headed for Oliver's warehouse in Hackney Wicks. He was hungry now. He would eat with Lionel. Hot, spicy Jamaican food. Maybe a curry of some sort. And cold beer. Then he would go on to the next job. Suddenly Hinton smiled. At least that would be satisfying. He'd make sure of that. He checked his watch. He had plenty of time before Oliver's ten o'clock meeting. And if he was lucky, there might be a blood feast at that gathering, too.

CHAPTER 6

DEVLIN HAD TOLD Joan Cunningham he was staying at the Connaught, but he had no such intention. He preferred London hotels that were much less well known and more discreet. He enjoyed the bar and the food at Blakes, and appreciated two of the ground-floor suites there, but Devlin could never quite get over the lavish haute couture decorating style of Anouska Hempel. He always felt that a stay there was better enjoyed in the company of a woman.

For this trip, he had made arrangements to stay at the venerable Draycott on Cadogan Gardens near Sloane Square. He was able to book his preferred room, No. 12, the suite overlooking the back garden. Devlin had always considered London a civilized town. One of the reasons was the plethora of private gardens tucked into every nook and cranny of the city. One such garden was behind the Draycott. The luxury of it in such a crowded city was something Devlin greatly appreciated. The peaceful green park was exactly the kind of buffer between a residence and the outside world that Devlin enjoyed.

As expected, the November weather was gloomy and inhospitable. Rain spattered the taxi windows on the drive in from Heathrow, but the windswept downpour abated just as Devlin entered the hotel.

Stepping into the quiet town house reminded Devlin of how timeless a city like London and a hotel like the Draycott could be. All was peaceful in the small foyer. There were no check-in lines or people moving about in front of the reservations desk. In fact, there was nobody in sight except Vincent the concierge. Check-in was a handshake. Walking into the Draycott was more like walking into a private home than a hotel. Since there were only twenty-five rooms, and the hotel was housed in a discreet town house in a quiet residential neighborhood, most people passing by never suspected that the Draycott was a hotel at all.

Devlin followed the bellman as he walked up, down, and around the convoluted staircases that led to room 12. The older gentleman made the same comment Devlin had heard on his last stay: "Guests of the Draycott have to be in good shape, sir."

Devlin nodded and focused his attention on the leg muscle that had been gouged by a bullet in Hawaii. There was very little pain left. Walking up and down the carpeted stairs actually felt good after having been confined to planes for almost twelve hours.

Devlin unpacked, checked the number of the fax machine in his room, and called it in to Mrs. Banks. After the bellman turned on the desk lamp, he opened the curtains wide and lit the neatly stacked pile of coal in the suite's ornate fireplace. The November gloom and chill disappeared and the room became cozy and welcoming.

The bellman left quietly with a promise to provide Devlin with whatever would make his stay more comfortable.

Devlin hadn't eaten since yesterday's breakfast with William Chow. He checked his watch. Almost four o'clock. Restaurants would be between servings. He dialed room service and ordered a smoked salmon platter, brown bread, and a bottle of mineral water. Fizzy.

And just like that he was back in London. And just like that, ordering food made him think of Annie.

He had met her when she was a hostess for a restaurant/bar called Billy Budd's on Lexington Avenue in New York. It was so many years ago that Devlin no longer had any desire to count them. It was just after he had graduated from the New York City Police Academy, first in his class, an achievement he hadn't sought. It was merely that he racked up so many top scores that it was inevitable. His standing meant he received a good assignment. He was assigned to the 13th Precinct in Manhattan. The one-three. The same precinct where the Police Academy was located.

The precinct covered an area that extended from Fourteenth Street to Twenty-ninth Street, from Seventh Avenue to the East River. It was a clean, quiet section of Manhattan. No really bad areas to speak of, although a few stretches of Seventh Avenue were a little ratty in those days. There was prostitution here and there on Lexington, some gambling, some bookmaking, and a few drug dealers in the expected places, plus the usual spate of burglaries and other petty crimes, but nothing like the intractable, soul-destroying crime that existed in some parts of New York.

And yet within days, Devlin had stepped right into a mean little crew of crooked cops in the precinct who were hustling for payoffs from anybody and everybody they could coerce. His first partner was the leader of a rogue clique who made it known that favors could be had for the right amount of money. Merchants on Third Avenue paid to avoid tickets when their trucks double-parked for deliveries. Gramercy Park landlords paid for extra coverage around their precious park. Bookies and pimps paid so that they would be warned if there was going to be trouble. And everybody kept their mouth shut. Why rock the boat?

Devlin was quietly told he wouldn't get his cut until after six months on the job. That was the routine. Rookies had to wait. And it was expected that he would wait and would take.

At the end of six months, Devlin resigned from the force. It caused quite a stir. He never explained why to any of the brass who hectored him for an answer. It was rather remarkable for a kid just turned twenty to stand up to all the badgering. But he had decided that there were certain things he wouldn't do. He wouldn't rat out a fellow cop, and he wouldn't put money in his pocket that he hadn't earned.

It was just before he quit that he met Annie.

His one luxury in those days was eating dinner out after he finished his tour. He was pulling down his salary, plus he worked weekends at his uncle's bar in Turtle Bay, and there was no mortgage or children to worry about so Devlin had enough money.

The minute he walked into Billy Budd's he noticed Annie. Every man who walked in there noticed Annie. She was tall and dark and literally captivating. Very few people who walked in and saw her, walked out. They were captured by her smile, her looks, her manner. She could have been a hostess in any restaurant in New York. But there she was in a neighborhood joint on Lexington in the thirties—just as stunning to young Devlin as if she had been a movie star.

He enjoyed eating his grilled chicken and drinking his Budweiser and watching her greet and seat the customers. He watched Annie slyly, not wanting her to catch him at it. But even if she had caught him staring at her, he wouldn't have stopped. He enjoyed seeing her work the room. She made everyone, men and women, feel special and welcome. Yet she maintained a certain distance and dignity that prevented any rude advances. Devlin considered her ability to do that quite amazing, because he knew that every man who entered Billy Budd's thought about what it would be like to sleep with her. Devlin knew the first thing two guys talked about after she seated them was what they would give to get her in bed.

That's why Devlin always came to Billy Budd's alone. He didn't want to hear one of his buddies talk about what he would do with her in bed. He did not want to be like everyone else who wanted her.

Two weeks after he started eating at Billy Budd's, Annie introduced herself to him. It was a Monday night. He still remembered every word of that conversation.

She had shown him to his table near the window. She wore a red knit dress that set off her figure beautifully and made her shiny black hair look even richer. It was a warm evening in October. One of those lingering Indian summer days that sometimes grace New York's autumn. The kind of day that makes you think winter will never come.

She handed him the menu and said, "You're getting to be a real regular. I should know your name."

"It's Jack. Jack Devlin."

He put out his hand to shake, almost as if she were a man. He remembered how firm her handshake was, and how big her hand was.

"Anne Turino," she said.

Their hands lingered for just a fraction of a second longer than normal, and at that precise moment Devlin knew somewhere in his head or his heart that they would be lovers.

He skipped Tuesday's dinner, planning to return on Wednesday. He wanted her to miss him. During his Wednesday tour of duty, he thought about how to ask her out. She must get asked out every goddamn night, he told himself. He found it strange to be wondering how to ask her for a date. It was something he had never needed to plan. Girls had always seemed to find him. But this Anne was so much a woman, it was different.

As soon as he was cleaned up and out of the locker room, he was on his way. He had planned to ask her after he paid his check. He would catch her between customers. He arrived primed and ready.

She wasn't there.

The owner, a big barrel-chested Greek named Constantine, was tending bar. He told Devlin that Annie had taken the day off. He called her Annie, not Anne. Instead of eating at a table, Devlin sat at the bar and ate, and drank a little too much.

He found out that she was due back on Monday. That meant the rest of the week and a whole weekend before he could see her again. He finished his meal and determined to put it out of his mind. But as he walked down Lexington to the subway, he couldn't shake the disappointment. And then he became angry at himself for having made this conquest so important.

By the time Monday came, he had jettisoned all the patient waiting, calculating, and·strategizing.

He walked straight into the restaurant. She saw him immediately and went over to him.

"Table by the window?"

Suddenly the thought of eating another Billy Budd's meal repulsed him.

"No, not tonight."

"No? Where would you like to sit?"

"I don't want dinner. I just want to know if I could take you out one night this week. What night would be convenient?"

"Oh."

It wasn't an answer. He had completely surprised her. Devlin suddenly felt awkward. But then she saved him. She smiled.

"Oh, well."

This time the "oh" sounded like an interested "oh" instead of a surprised "oh."

Devlin smiled back at her, and he knew everything was going to be fine.

"I'm sorry. I suppose you weren't expecting that. But would you like to? How about Friday?"

"This Friday?"

"Yes. Would it be all right?"

He wouldn't take his eyes off her until she answered. He willed her to say yes, and she did. She even said it with another smile. "Yes. All right. This Friday."

She gave him her phone number and address. The information seemed like an enormous prize to him. Now he knew where she lived. He knew her phone number. He could actually contact her or see her anytime he wanted to.

They agreed he'd pick her up at seven-thirty. He thanked her and left. And he never ate another meal at Billy Budd's again.

Lying on the bed at the Draycott, years later, not only did Devlin remember the exhilaration he had experienced that night, he still felt a glimmer of it. He'd been so excited that he'd actually had to restrain himself from smiling and punching his fist into his hand as he'd walked down Lexington Avenue.

He had asked the prettiest girl in town out, and it hadn't even mattered where they would go or what they would do on their first date. But he was young and free enough to just set a time and figure it out later. He could quit the police force because it stank. Ask the prettiest girl in town out for dinner. He could do it all. It didn't matter.

Their romance soared. He took her to the Cloisters and City Island and Shea Stadium. She took him to Puglio's, the Museum of Modern Art, and Bloomingdale's. He took her to his apartment in the West Village for lovemaking, and she took him home for dinner in Brooklyn. She was a native Italian New Yorker. He was a native Irish New Yorker. Between them they seemed to know every nook and cranny of a city they had never shared so deeply with anyone.

They introduced each other to so many firsts. He took her

to her first Knicks game at the Garden. She took him to his first opera at Lincoln Center.

He squired her to Chumley's in the Village, and she ushered him into the serene aura of the Bethesda Fountain at dawn.

For a long while the magic was so pure and easy they almost lit up rooms when they entered. People smiled at them. The tall dark handsome Irishman and the striking dark Italian beauty. Together, they sparkled.

Now, Devlin pushed the memories away until the next time he needed them, sat up on his bed, and picked up the hotel phone.

He dialed the phone number he had memorized for Annie. This time it answered on the third double London ring. He was surprised when he heard her voice.

He had to clear his throat when he spoke to her.

They talked for only a few sentences, as if they both wanted to get off so they could compose themselves. She gave him her address. It was in a part of London he had never been in. Across the Tower Bridge on the South Bank. Gainsford Street. Devlin had only a vague idea where that was. She said it would be better to come after eight o'clock when her daughter Elizabeth would be asleep.

Devlin replaced the phone and tried to picture Annie Turino with a daughter.

CHAPTER 7

AFTER DEVLIN'S CALL, Annie hurried to get Elizabeth bathed and ready for sleep. It seemed to take forever to get the little girl settled in bed. She lied down next to Elizabeth and began reading *Winnie-the-Pooh*. The words of the story came out of her mouth, but she was thinking about Jack Devlin. She wanted her little girl to kiss her good-night and be tucked in and fast asleep before he showed up, and she didn't have much time.

She came to a good stopping point, closed the book, and announced, "Okay, kiddo, I'll read some more tomorrow. Time for sleep now."

Elizabeth offered her puckered mouth for the good-night kiss. Annie obliged.

"Good night, Mummy."

Annie liked hearing that British "Mummy" pop out of her little girl. For the moment, for just a second, the horrible dark dread lifted from her life. The nightmare hadn't happened. Her husband hadn't been torn apart and killed like an animal.

But the relief from the nightmare lasted only a few seconds. Then the fear and dread and confusion tumbled in on her again. It covered her like a heavy quilt around her shoulders and seeped into her bones. It made her stomach turn. She had to fight it off like morning sickness, and gather her thoughts for Jack.

How could she explain all this to him? How much should she tell him? What could he do for her?

"Don't forget my night-light."

Elizabeth's request brought Annie back to the moment.

"I won't."

Annie got up from the child's bed, smoothed her skirt, and

brushed back her hair. She walked over and turned on the comforting little night-light stuck in the outlet near the floor.

"Good night, Lizzie. I love you."

Elizabeth had already snuggled into her pillow, and the "I love you, too" came back muffled.

Annie left the bedroom door open a crack and walked to the living room, where she sat down at her desk and took out a piece of writing paper. She folded the paper in half, checked her watch, and saw it was eight-twenty, then started making notes. Single words meant to remind her and organize her thoughts: *John. How long. How much. Uncle Frank. Police.*

Annie was a list maker. She had to make sure she told Devlin her story in exactly the right order, with the right amount of detail.

Suddenly, the intercom buzzer rang from downstairs. He's here already, she thought. She wanted to check herself in the bathroom mirror before she answered the door, but she didn't want to keep him waiting down in the lobby to be buzzed in.

She pushed back her hair, walked to the intercom near her front door, and pressed the talk button. "Jack?"

After a slight pause, an electrified voice answered back, "Yeah."

She buzzed him in, returned to her desk, and slid her notes under the desk pad. She thought to herself, Well, it's been too many years since I've seen him to worry about the way I look now.

The chime ding-donged on her front door. It was the same chime that sounded in millions of apartments around the world. It was the same chime and the same peephole that millions of people looked through. But Annie did not want to see Jack Devlin through a peephole after all these years. She walked quickly to the door, turned the door handle, and *wham!* The door slammed into her, and she was shoved back so hard she hit the wall behind her. And before she was even able to open her eyes, a hand grabbed her by the throat, pulled her forward, and slammed her back into the wall again.

"Ah then, who's Jack?"

It was Hinton.

Annie was struggling to breathe. She clawed at the hand on her throat. He was crushing her windpipe. She couldn't breathe. She twisted away from him to try to gasp a breath of air, but he had her pinned to the wall. The pressure continued. It hurt terribly, the crushing grip on her throat. She couldn't think. It was getting dark on the edge of her vision. Just before she passed out, Hinton released her throat and slapped her hard on the side of the head. She fell to one knee. Everything turned black, then flashes of brightness sparked behind her closed eyes. And then waves of pain pounded through the side of her head and her throat.

She knelt on one knee, desperately trying to pull air into her lungs. Her mouth dripped saliva and blood, but she didn't stop to wipe it away. Air was all she wanted.

But before she had taken three breaths, Hinton grabbed her by the hair and pulled her to her feet. She was dizzy with pain. She was disoriented, but the sudden searing agony of being lifted to her feet by her hair made her scream.

Hinton growled quietly, "Shut your mouth, pig bitch."

Hinton let go of her hair, put his hand on her face, pushed her head viciously back against the wall, and held it there.

The apartment door was still open. He turned to Lionel, who was standing in the doorway.

"Close the door. Stay out in the hall and keep watch."

Without hurrying, Lionel pulled the door shut. And as quickly as that, Annie was sealed in, cut off from everyone—alone with this animal.

The tears began to burn in her eyes. "Stop," she said. "Please, stop."

Hinton sneered and grabbed her by the back of her neck. He twisted his body and flung her into the living room, shoving her with such force that she lost her balance, fell, and slammed against the base of the couch.

The animal was on her in a split second. Again Hinton viciously pulled her by the hair until she was standing.

"You don't tell me to stop, bitch. You don't tell me notting. I tell *you*."

Annie was so terrified and in such pain she thought she would throw up. Her legs felt shaky and weak. She was afraid she couldn't stand. Hinton shoved her down onto the couch.

For a moment, the terror seemed to abate. She was out of his grasp. She was sitting. He had said something that indicated some intention. In the few moments of respite, she suddenly became filled with anger. She was furious that such a crude, disgusting man had somehow gained power over her. How could she have let him into her house? How could she have become so helpless in such a short time? And what about Elizabeth? What if this horror got to her? She buried her face in her hands, partly to stop from seeing Hinton, partly to stop him from seeing her cry. She wanted to get away from him, even if it was by closing her eyes.

But there was no getting away. Suddenly she felt a sharp, searing pain across the back of her hands—like someone had whipped them with a switch. She pulled her hands away from her face and saw Hinton straddling her. He was holding his stiletto switchblade in his right hand. He had slashed the backs of her hands with the razor-sharp tip of the blade.

"Don't vex me now, girl. Get your head up! Look at me."

She forced herself to look at him. Hinton's cold animal eyes were fixed in a deathlike stare. There was a sheen of sweat on his dark face, and an air of arousal about him that repulsed Annie. She tried to look at him without seeing him. She held her hands away from her so they wouldn't drip blood on her skirt. The wounds weren't deep, but enough to cause pain and draw blood.

Now Hinton moved closer. He carefully took a fistful of her rich black hair, and slowly, almost delicately, placed the point of the stiletto under her right eye. He talked very slowly and precisely, but it couldn't hide his Jamaican accent. She recoiled from the sour smell of spices and garlic on his warm breath.

"Now, you fuck with me, I take out your eye and then stick this knife in the hole until you are dead like that pig man who was your husband. You understand? Say 'yes.'"

Annie forced out a "yes."

"That's right. Now, you tell me what I want to know and you get to live. You play with me, girl, you die. And before you die, I cut you up, I fuck you, my friend outside fucks you, I piss on you, and then you die. You understand?"

Annie couldn't control herself. Tears started to trickle down her cheeks. She felt like she was on the verge of diarrhea.

In a soothing voice Hinton told her, "Ah, that's good, sweet t'ing. Cry a little so you wet my knife and it slides in easy."

She forced herself to do something. Anything. "What do you want?" she asked.

"That's right. Now you got it. I tell you what I want, and you goin' give it to me."

Hinton was pleased with himself. He had managed to terrify the woman quickly. He could actually smell her fear. To him it was like an offering of incense to his god.

"Listen to me. Your husband cheated us. Taking for himself what wasna' his. Now we take back everyt'ing. We know how much he took, and we want it back."

Annie knew that was impossible, but all she could do was agree. "Okay." She nodded. "Okay. I'll give it to you."

Hinton asked for money because Oliver wanted it. All Hinton wanted was to kill the woman. And her child. To Hinton money was nothing. He wanted her dignity, her child, her life.

He pushed the point of his blade into the skin under her eye. Just enough to create a small drop of blood that flowed down her cheek like a tear.

"Okay den, where's the cash?"

Suddenly, the intercom buzzer sounded. Annie's senses were so heightened that it sounded ten times louder than it was. She flinched at the noise. Hinton spun toward the door. He realized it must be the one she had been expecting.

"Who is it?"

"It's a friend. A friend of my husband's."

Hinton pulled out a compact pistol, a .44-caliber Charter Arms Bulldog Pug, from the inside pocket of his sport coat. It was a mean-looking gun, with enough caliber to blow away half of Annie's head. It was the clean gun that Oliver had told him Lionel was to give him when they met. Hinton had taken the Charter Arms revolver and given Lionel his semiautomatic. Although he preferred his knife, he could shoot her with this gun and not worry about anybody tracing the weapon.

The gun was fine for dealing with the woman, but not for a gunfight. It had to be cocked for each shot, and it only held five rounds. He had given his 9-mm to Lionel. But there was one advantage to the .44. Hinton knew that if a bullet that size hit anywhere on a human body, that person would be down and out for a long time.

He pointed the gun at her.

"Buzz him in, girl."

She couldn't. It would be like giving Devlin a death sentence. She just sat paralyzed. Hinton didn't have time to force her. He realized he had pushed her over the edge. She was useless now. He grabbed her by the arm and dragged her over to the intercom. He pressed the button, then went to the apartment's front door, dragging Annie with him.

He opened the door and saw Lionel leaning against the wall opposite the door, smoking a cigarette like he was waiting for a bus.

Hinton hissed, "Somebody's coming up. Get out the gun, mon. Wait over there out of sight. When he come here, shoot him."

The hallways in the building formed a four-sided rectangle around a central elevator shaft. Annie's renovated loft was to the right of the elevator at the end of the corridor. It was at the corner where two hallways met.

Hinton closed the apartment door, pulled Annie between him and the door, and shoved her against it. Then he barked at her, "Down," and shoved her to her knees. He placed the hard barrel of the .44 on the top of her head.

"Move or make one sound, I blow your head off."

Annie bowed her head and remained slumped on the floor.

Hinton pressed his eye to the peephole. He had a clear view of the hallway that ran toward the elevator. He could also see Lionel pressed against the wall opposite the doorway, gun raised, waiting for the visitor to come down the hall to Annie's door. When he stepped into view, all Lionel had to do was pull the trigger. While Lionel shot him from the side, Hinton intended to open the door and shoot him in the face.

Suddenly they heard the sound of the elevator stopping at the floor. The door opened and Devlin stepped off. He turned right and started for Annie's door. Then he stopped and looked at the number on a door to his left. He turned around and started walking in the other direction.

Hinton watched him through the peephole. "Stupid," he muttered to himself.

Lionel stood waiting around the corner, opposite Annie's door.

Devlin kept walking casually in the other direction, to the left of the elevator. When he reached the far corner, he turned and suddenly broke into a run.

At almost the same time, it occurred to Hinton that the hallways in this building seemed to go all the way around, in which case, unless Devlin realized the apartment numbers were leading him away from Annie's door and turned to come back, he would eventually come around behind Lionel.

He punched Annie on the top of the head with the pistol. "This damn hallway goes all the way around, right?" he snarled.

Annie grabbed her head and let out a yelp of pain. Hinton couldn't wait for an answer. He viciously shoved her out of the way with his foot and kept kicking her farther back until he had enough room to open the door.

By then, however, Devlin had turned the corner onto Annie's hallway. He was running full speed now, straight for Lionel, who was still standing, facing the other direction, gun ready. Devlin had no gun. British laws were so strict there was no way he could bring a firearm into the country. But Lionel had a gun. And if he turned, Devlin was dead.

The closer Devlin came, the greater chance there was that Lionel would hear him. And in the next instant, he did hear him. Lionel turned, bringing the gun into shooting position. Just before the barrel leveled at Devlin, Devlin's right fist slammed down across Lionel's nose, with all of Devlin's strength and onrushing speed behind the punch. Lionel's nose broke so badly that the septum was shoved all the way to his right cheekbone. Devlin swept the hand that had delivered the punch back across Lionel's wrist, blocking the gun, pushing it off to the side. The block caused Lionel to fire the gun, but the bullet buried itself in the floor. Devlin grabbed the hot body of the automatic with his right hand, twisted it out of Lionel's hand, then pivoted and delivered a shattering upper-cut—slamming the underside of his forearm and elbow into Lionel's chin, breaking the right mandible, and slamming the man's mouth shut so quickly and with such force that he bit through his tongue and cracked three bottom teeth.

Lionel's short shout of agony ended suddenly as his brain circuits stopped firing and he collapsed unconscious against the wall opposite Annie's doorway.

Hinton pulled the door open, raised his gun, and started shooting in Devlin's direction without taking time to step out and aim.

Devlin spun to the wall on the same side of the hallway as the apartment door to get out of the line of fire. Lionel wasn't so lucky. Two of Hinton's rushed shots tore into him. One ripped into his neck, tearing out the carotid artery and the back corner of his broken jaw. The second bullet burst into his chest, hitting the fifth rib, which sent the hot, flattened piece of lead spinning and tumbling through Lionel's chest cavity, tearing through the right lung, ripping apart muscle tissue, and lodging in his spine.

Lionel's terrified heart sent pulses of blood out the torn artery in his neck. Five-foot crimson spurts hit the opposite wall with such force that Lionel was splattered with the back-wash of his own blood.

As soon as he finished shooting, Hinton slammed the door and turned to look for Annie. She was gone.

The first 999 emergency phone call was received at Scotland Yard, phoned in from a panicked downstairs neighbor screaming about gunshots. The emergency operator had to yell at the caller to get an address, while simultaneously tapping into the CAD—Computer Aided Dispatch—system. Once she obtained the address, she alerted the Tower Bridge Division of the Metropolitan Police Force that guns were being fired in their area. Report of gunfire initiated an immediate, high-level, well-orchestrated police response.

While Hinton had been shooting at Devlin and killing Lionel, Annie had managed to get to her feet and run in a crazed, crablike, stumbling dash. She had scooped Elizabeth up from her bed, blanket and all. Elizabeth was stunned and wide-eyed. For a fraction of a second she struggled against her mother. Annie told her, "It's me, baby. It's me." Something in Elizabeth responded to her mother's voice, and she grabbed

Annie around the back of the neck and wrapped her legs around Annie's waist.

Annie, with the power of an adrenaline-filled mother fighting for her child, stood up with the forty-five-pound girl clinging to her and ran down the hall to the kitchen.

Just as Hinton was about to run to the back of the apartment to kill Annie, three 9-mm bullets smashed into the lock and door handle of the apartment door. Seconds after Hinton had slammed the door, Devlin had spun around and fired Lionel's gun.

The three 9-mm bullets not only destroyed the lock, they blew the door back with such force that the hinges bent.

The highest-ranking administrative officer at the Tower Bridge Division station was a deputy inspector, but he was well versed in the procedure required for responding to an armed incident. The first call went out to SO-19—Special Operations—which dispatched a pair of ARVs—Armed Response Vehicles—called Trojan Units, each under the direction of a highly trained Special Operations inspector. The next calls were to notify the proper chain of command at the Tower Bridge Division, which in this case meant an inspector and a chief inspector. Every division in London was simultaneously alerted via the CAD system, and the entire operation was monitored by Scotland Yard headquarters.

Hinton had no idea of the armed police response that was about to descend on him in no more than twelve minutes. His concern was the man shooting out the front door. Hinton backpedaled away from the door and shot back until the five-shot Charter Arms revolver was empty.

Devlin's ears were ringing from the gunshots, fired in an interior space, but he knew the pause in gunfire probably meant the shooter's gun was empty. He wanted to move fast, before his enemy had time to reload, but he had no idea how many men were in the apartment or what he would find on the other side of the door.

Hinton, even in the heat of the killing fever, stood in the apartment hallway calmly reloading his gun, one cartridge at a time.

Annie was at the back door, desperately fumbling with the rotating knob on the old door lock. Hinton's slashing cuts had drawn enough blood to make her hands slippery with it. She could not get a firm grip on the locking knob. The weight of holding Elizabeth kept her off-balance. She could not get the door open.

Hinton had finished reloading, but instead of shooting at Devlin, he turned to walk to the back of the apartment. His first job was to kill Annie. Then he would kill whoever had interfered with his offering to Chango.

Devlin knew he had to get into the apartment quickly. He looked at the gun he was holding. It was a compact Beretta. As Devlin remembered, the gun could hold either a thirteen-clip magazine or an eight-clip. But whichever clip it held, there was no guarantee the magazine was full when he'd twisted it out of Lionel's hand. He could have as many as nine shots left or as few as none. He popped the magazine out of the Beretta. It was the eight-shot clip. He pushed down the first cartridge in the magazine to try to estimate by feeling the tension how many bullets were left. It felt like there were at least three bullets in the clip.

Devlin looked at Lionel. He was looking in the eyes of a dead man. Devlin shoved the clip back in, took a breath, pushed himself off the wall, and spun into the doorway. He fired one shot into the ceiling of the apartment while he dove behind a couch in the living room area.

Hinton stopped walking toward the back of the apartment, turned, and pulled off three shots in the direction of the main room. The shots cracked into the wall behind Devlin and off to his right.

Devlin looked for a target to shoot at, but Hinton was too far back into the apartment hallway to be seen.

In the kitchen, Elizabeth screamed at the exploding gunfire. Annie held her tighter and finally, finally twisted the lock the last notch. She started to pull the big iron door open.

Hinton stood motionless in the hallway. He had no idea there was a back door to the apartment. He still wanted to kill Annie, but he did not want to be shot while he was doing it. He thought perhaps he should kill the one in front of him first. Yes, he said to himself. And quickly, for he knew all the gunfire must have alerted the police by now.

Then he heard the sound of a door slamming somewhere behind him.

He cursed quietly, forgot about whoever was in the living room, and started to run back to the kitchen. A white heat of rage surged in his head. He could not let this woman escape. This whore wife of a thief. She was for Chango.

Devlin heard the footsteps pounding down the hall. He jumped up and ran to the doorway that separated the hall from the living room.

Devlin was mentally dividing the apartment into segments of advance and cover. The apartment door to the couch, the couch to the hallway. Now, he would have to turn into the dark corridor and dash past a gauntlet of doorways, each of which could be concealing the shooter.

Thinking time was over. Do the first move, now!

He dashed to the first hallway door, Elizabeth's bedroom—turning into it gun first—just as Hinton reached the back door.

Hinton wrenched open the door, expecting to see Annie fleeing down the stairs. An image of a bullet blasting into the back of her head seized him. Hitting her hard. Slamming her forward as her head popped and blood sprayed.

But she wasn't in sight, so he threw himself down the first flight of stairs. He was growling with rage. He howled as he ran down the stairs. She must be just ahead. Just out of sight. He could almost hear her whimpers as she ran from him.

And now he heard the police sirens wailing in the distance. If she made it to the street he might not be able to shoot her. He jumped down the remaining section of the stairway and landed hard. He turned the corner and took the next flight down two stairs at a time. Where was she?

Back in the apartment, Devlin had made it to the kitchen. He saw the blood on the door. He knew now that he was alone in the apartment. Whatever was going to happen would happen on the other side of that door. Another fucking door, he thought to himself.

He gripped the knob, held the Beretta in position. He pulled open the door and stepped out with the gun aimed and ready to fire.

Just as he hit his firing position, Annie, stilling carrying

Elizabeth, stumbled onto the sixth-floor landing. Devlin spun, ready to pick his spot and shoot. When he had to pull back from firing, the jolt to his taut nerves was horrible. He grunted and barked out in anger, "Goddammit."

He dropped his arm and slowly stood up. Annie could do nothing but stand and hold Elizabeth.

Her trick had worked—she had run up the stairs instead of down. When she heard Hinton pounding down the stairwell, and estimated he was far enough away, she had hoped to carry Elizabeth back into the apartment and lock him out. But the adrenaline had burned off. Her strength was gone. All she could manage now was to stand there holding Elizabeth. She could not take one more step. When Devlin appeared, for a split second she thought it was Hinton's henchman, Lionel. She was ready to die right then and there, but it wasn't Lionel, it was Devlin.

He moved to take Elizabeth out of her arms, but the child was clinging too tightly. Instead, he put his arm around Annie, supporting both of them, and guided her back into the kitchen. He slammed the door behind them and twisted the lock into place.

Near the bottom of the stairwell, Hinton heard the door slam, and realized that Annie had tricked him. He looked up the stairwell, not making a sound. Not screaming or cursing. But his cold, dark eyes closed to a slit, and he made a vow to his god that he would kill that woman. Slowly if he could. Quickly if he had to. He vowed that he would not live unless she died. He would tear her heart out of her chest and offer it to his god. He envisioned the bloody organ in his hand. He felt the warm wetness of it. But then the image was suffused by a blood red rage that filled his mind completely.

Finally, the insistent two-tone wail of police sirens penetrated into his consciousness. He turned and walked down the last few stairs. At the exit door he shoved the hot revolver into his coat pocket, kicked the release bar, and walked out onto the narrow street. He didn't look around to get his bearing, but immediately turned to his left and started walking away from where he stood. At the corner he turned left again and disappeared from Annie's street.

CHAPTER 8

DEVLIN LOWERED ANNIE onto the kitchen chair with Elizabeth still clinging to her. He didn't try to speak to Annie. She was too much in shock. And he didn't try to take the little girl away from her. He let Annie simply hold Elizabeth and stroke her hair, even though she was streaking it with blood.

He unloaded the Beretta and placed the clip and the empty pistol in a kitchen cabinet.

With that done, he sat next to Annie and gently took her bloody hand away from Elizabeth's head and held it in his own.

"Annie?"

He waited until she turned her head to him.

"Annie, the police are on their way. Do you understand?"

For a moment, Annie's eyes were blank. Devlin watched her struggle to focus. When he felt she could hear him, he told her, "I want you to tell them exactly what happened. You don't have to leave anything out. If I talk, don't interrupt me, or contradict me. Okay?"

Annie nodded. She was about to speak, but Devlin kept talking. "Good. Now they're going to come in here with their guns drawn. Don't be afraid. Don't scream or make any sudden moves. Hang on to your daughter. I'll talk to them first."

Again, Annie nodded. But Devlin was not sure she was able to completely understand him. Then she slowly pulled her hand free from his and laid it against Devlin's cheek. It seemed to break her spell of silence. He was real. He was here in front of her, and he had driven away that disgusting creature who had hurt her.

"Jack."

"Yes."

"Jack. You're here. Are you all right?"

"Yes. I'm fine."

But Lionel Williams was not fine. He was dead. And he was a mess. When Special Ops PC Eliot Holstrom angled his extendable mirror out the elevator to view the corridor and saw Lionel's blood splattered all over the walls, he knew this call was for real. He quietly placed the mirror on the floor and reached to his right shoulder. He pressed the send button on the personal radio microphone and quietly announced, "We have wounded. Good amount of blood in the corridor. I can see an arm and a hand. At least one down. We will proceed in that direction."

Holstrom's words were heard by dozens of listeners, most importantly his driver in the ARV, who was the point man on all missions. His name was Mark Kelly. He had driven their V-8 Rover 827 at an average of sixty miles an hour through the crowded London streets to arrive at target in just under eight minutes.

Chief Inspector James Waldron of the Tower Bridge Division, Metropolitan Police Force, was also listening to Holstrom's broadcast. Waldron was in command of all patrols in the division. He was the highest-ranking police constable on duty when the first calls came in. Waldron had called in Special Ops, and now stood outside Annie's loft on Gainsford Street waiting. He would take over when Special Ops gave the all-clear. Waldron had neither the training nor the inclination to be anywhere near armed villains. In fact, despite being a member of the Met for fifteen years, Waldron had never owned or fired a weapon.

Back in the loft building, Holstrom turned to his partner, John Greene. Both men wore Kevlar body armor reinforced with ceramic shields. Greene carried a bulletproof shield as further protection. Their weapons included personal-issue Smith & Wesson revolvers and Heckler & Koch MP5 carbines. Greene handed the portable shield to Holstrom. He then placed his revolver in its holster and swung his H&K into position. Holstrom would advance with the shield and his cocked revolver. Greene would back him up with the H&K. The machine gun held thirty rounds, but Greene's magazine held only twenty-six bullets so that there would be less tension on the spring and less chance for the high-powered weapon to jam. If either man fired his weapon, the shots would be dead-on accurate and aimed to kill instantly.

The Special Ops PCs edged out of the elevator and walked slowly down the corridor, tight against the wall. Within ten steps, Annie's bullet-ridden doorframe came into view. The absolute quiet in the hallway lessened the tension somewhat. Holstrom had the feeling that whatever had happened here, it was over. He continued step by step toward the door. He wanted to be a bit closer before he announced his presence. He looked carefully at Lionel's bloody arm and hand to see if there was any motion at all. His primary concern was that the man might be only wounded, just waiting to turn and fire.

Holstrom turned once more to his partner. It was a good feeling to know that if he went down, Greene would unload his magazine at whoever was responsible. Holstrom nodded to Greene. Greene nodded back. Holstrom shouted out, "This is the police. Put down your weapons and come out slowly. Keep your hands up and in view. Now."

In the kitchen, Devlin turned to Annie and told her, "All right. Remember what I said. You stay here. Don't move. Don't worry. I'll handle it."

Devlin walked to the front of the apartment, but stood back in the hallway. He yelled to the open door, "There's no one in here with weapons. The man who shot the guy in the hallway is gone. There's a woman and child in here. The woman is injured. She needs a doctor. I'm coming out the front door and I'll bring you in. Don't shoot. It's over."

Holstrom yelled back, "Keep your hands where I can see them."

"Right. I'm coming now."

Holstrom aimed his revolver at the door. Greene aimed the H&K. They were ready to kill in less time than it would take to breathe just once.

Devlin put his hands in front of him, then walked into the living room, out the front door, and into the hallway. He yelled, "I'm coming around the corner. Hands first."

Devlin leaned forward so his empty hands came into view. Then he stepped into the corridor. When Holstrom saw that Devlin was white, unarmed, and well dressed, he stepped away from the wall and approached him. Greene shifted to a spot where he had a second angle of fire, then relayed what was happening into his microphone. Both men heard their commander's voice through their radio earpieces, telling them to go slowly.

Holstrom kept his revolver pointed dead center at Devlin's chest.

Devlin didn't like that, but he stood his ground, hands raised over his head. When Holstrom was four feet away he said, "Please turn and face the wall, sir."

Devlin did as he was told.

"Hands on wall then."

Devlin leaned forward, but kept his eyes on Holstrom. As Holstrom advanced, Devlin said, "Mind the blood on the floor, Constable. I don't want you slipping with that cocked revolver."

Holstrom stopped and looked down. He wasn't sure he appreciated receiving advice from the man in front of him, but admitted to himself that whoever Devlin was, he was right. He had been concentrating so much on Devlin that he had been about to step into Lionel's blood. Holstrom frowned at the idea of falling on his ass and firing his weapon as he hit the ground.

"Bollix. Bloody fucking mess you've got here, mate."

"As I said, I didn't shoot him. You might want to radio in a description of the man who did, in case he's in the area."

"That'll be done by the regulars. First we secure the area. Give me your right hand and we'll get to it."

Devlin frowned and lowered his hand behind him. In one quick move Holstrom slapped a cuff on his wrist. Devlin felt an instant sharp pain as Holstrom twisted the cuff slightly and asked politely for Devlin's left hand. It didn't feel at all like a conventional handcuff. Devlin turned to look and saw that it wasn't. Instead of being joined by a chain, these cuffs were connected with a solid piece of hardened plastic. It was a simple, yet extremely effective innovation. The person doing the handcuffing attained tremendous leverage once either wrist was cuffed. A simple twist dug deeply into the skin. A hard twist would probably crack a bone.

"Nasty little tool you've got there," Devlin said.

Holstrom grunted and cuffed Devlin's left wrist. He turned

Devlin toward the apartment and told him to go ahead. It was not lost on Devlin that he was positioned to block any shots that might be fired in Holstrom's direction.

As Devlin entered the living room, he stopped and said, "One other thing."

"What?"

"There's an unloaded gun back there in a kitchen cabinet. Let the woman come out with her child first. The gun belongs to that dead fellow in the hall."

"Christ, who's in charge here, then?"

"You are," said Devlin. "I'm just suggesting."

Holstrom thought for a moment. "All right. You call her out. We'll get another team up to cover you while my partner and I check out the rest of the place."

"Fine. Thanks."

"Don't thank me yet."

CHAPTER 9

OLIVER SAT IN the backseat of his black BMW 735i, fuming. The big car was parked on a small side street in Soho. Oliver was waiting for Hinton. And Hinton was late. Oliver knew the longer he waited, the longer the Yugoslav had to wait. Which was only going to make a difficult meeting worse. But this was one meeting Oliver did not want to have without Hinton.

The Yugoslav had said the purpose of the meeting was to find a way to do business without Petchek. Oliver knew the real purpose could just as easily be to revenge Petchek's murder. His problem at the moment was not knowing which thing Mislovic wanted more.

Besides the fact that it was dangerous, Oliver had little desire to meet with Mislovic for another reason. He wasn't West Indian. He wasn't even English. Not even Western European.

Ivan Mislovic was not looking forward to the meeting either. And as Oliver suspected, the extra waiting was making it worse. And the fact that Mislovic was sitting with a man even more impatient than he didn't help. His bodyguard and chief enforcer, Zenko, was ready to leave, now.

Next to Zenko, Mislovic appeared calm. He was dressed in a quintessentially British three-piece suit and a white silk shirt buttoned to the top. The clothes were expensive and fit him perfectly. Mislovic was well built, and slim. He didn't carry the extra twenty or thirty pounds most middle-aged men acquired. Although his Slavic face was a bit broad for his physique, he was a handsome man with hair that had turned steel gray.

If Mislovic was an aristocratic Slav, Zenko was a peasant. He was short, broad, and powerfully built. Zenko wore a rumpled, baggy, dark suit. Its best feature was that it fit loosely enough to cover the Grendel P-30 machine pistol strapped under his right arm.

Mislovic appeared to be enjoying his glass of Armagnac, but his mood actually hovered somewhere between bemused and furious that he was meeting with this dark savage who had cut off a man's head and fed it to dogs. He glanced at his watch and thought about the fact that he was actually waiting to sit at the same table with him.

Oliver checked his watch for the third time. He'd give Hinton five more minutes, then go ahead without him.

Oliver watched his driver, Louis, come out of the restaurant where Mislovic waited. He walked to the car and slid into the driver's seat.

Oliver asked, "So?"

"Looks normal," said Louis. "He is drinking. One guy at the table wit' him. Their car cyan get in that street wit' all dem market stalls. It's waiting aroun' on Brewer."

"How many in the car?"

"Two."

"Any others?"

"Maybe one or two back in the bar area. I don't think there are any on the street."

"Too many damn guys. Who have we got?"

"Leon is in da place. We got four others outside. Two watchin' their car. One at each end of the block."

"Everybody start shooting now, there be one goddamn mess. Where's dat bloody fucker, Hinton? Somet'ing must a gone bad wit' him."

Oliver pulled open a storage compartment built into the back of the seat in front of him and took out a compact 9-mm Uzi machine pistol. The gun was small enough to shove into his waistband and hide under his jacket, yet held a twenty-round magazine and could spray bullets fast enough to kill a roomful of people very quickly, even if Mislovic did have three men with him. With Hinton, Oliver was sure they could kill them all. Where the fuck was Hinton?

Oliver's question was answered by the sound of a car door slamming. He looked across the street to see that Hinton had just gotten out of a London cab and was crossing over to the BMW.

He motioned him into the backseat.

"What happen', den?"

"Trouble. That woman had protection. Some hard guy. He shot Lionel. I couldna' get close enough to kill her. This gun is a piece of shit."

Hinton pulled the five-shot Charter Arms pistol out of his pocket and dropped it on the floor of the car.

"Every damn shot you had to cock it. Stupid Lionel only brought a handful of extra bullets."

"Lionel dead?"

"Yah, mon."

"I guess da mon was stupid. Who was it shot him?"

"I told you, the guy with that damn bitch."

"Who was he?"

"Next time I see da mon, I be sure to ask him."

Oliver knew Hinton wasn't telling him everything. But now wasn't the time to push it. The list of people who could supply the woman with protection was a short one, and Mislovic's name was at the top of it.

He turned to Hinton. "Was it the cops?"

"Hell no. No cops in this damn city gonna shoot some guy for the likes of her. But they showed up damn quick when the guns went off. I got out through the back. There were stairs in the back."

It had to be Mislovic. That stupid white boy who stole from him was his nephew or some kind of relative. Did Mislovic feel an obligation to protect the wife and child? If that was true, then a war had started.

"Fuck!" Oliver spit on the black velour carpeting. Killing Mislovic would not be easy, but if the man was out for blood, better handle it right now. Except Oliver didn't want to kill him. He wanted the man's money and guns. And was the man crazy enough to hit them in public like this?

"What dat restaurant look like, den, Louis?"

"You walk through a small door on the street. Go on back for about ten feet through a gangway. It opens onto a court-yard. That's why they be calling it the Yard, mon. The only part be inside is da bar."

Oliver pictured it. Far back. Isolated. Not a bad place for a hit.

Oliver leaned forward and told Louis, "All right, bwouy, listen to me now."

"Yes, boss."

"I want you to go into the restaurant, and tell dem bastards I don' feel good, and I don' want dinner. Tell him I invite him to the pub across the street for a drink. Tell him Mr. Oliver requests—*requests*—that he come alone. Be polite."

"Yes, sir."

"Hinton and I will be in the pub. You come back and pull across over der. You got all that?"

"Yeah."

"Okay. When ya come out, tell the others 'bout the change. Den be ready to get us the hell out of here if we come out the damn pub fast. Okay, go."

Oliver turned to Hinton. "You sit at the bar in der. I'll sit at a table." He handed the Uzi to Hinton. "Keep this one near your hand. There's twenty fast shots in it, brother. Not like any damn revolver for a woman. You got your other piece?"

"I gave it to Lionel."

"He shoot it?"

"Not so it did any good."

"Fuck it. If dat white bwouy make any move, or if any of his guys try to come in der, shoot him first, den shoot everybody else. Try not to shoot me, but keep popping until we be out of da place."

"I will."

Hinton had that weird bloody look in his eyes. Oliver didn't know if that was good or bad for right now, but he knew that in the long run it would be good. The shit was happening now. Blood had been spilled. He didn't know how or why, but he knew it would continue until he was either dead or on to the next level of the game.

Both men got out of the BMW and walked across Rupert Street. A few doors west was a run-down pub on the corner. There were entrances on both sides. Like many pubs in London, it had been occupying the same spot unchanged for decades. The pub had a small bar area in front and tables, chairs, and stools that ran along one side. There were a few stools empty at the bar. All the tables were occupied except the last one at the back of the room. The pub was messy, dreary, and smelled of stale beer and whiskey. There was the usual batch of old alcoholics sipping their pints and slowly smoking their harsh, hand-rolled fags, but most of the place was filled with the working-class people of Soho. No tourists or upscale fashionables for this place, which was fine with Oliver.

Oliver and Hinton made a few heads turn when they walked in. It wasn't the first time they did that. Hinton sat down quickly on a vacant stool and Oliver took a spot at the table in the back. He sat facing the front door.

Hinton was pleased to see they had Red Stripe on tap and ordered a pint. He sipped his beer with his left hand while his right hand held the 9-mm Uzi pistol under his jacket. There was no waitress service, but there was coffee behind the bar. Hinton told the bartender, an overweight Irish alcoholic with thinning hair and a fuck-you-mate attitude, to bring his friend a cup of coffee with a double shot of rum.

By the time Oliver got his coffee and rum, Mislovic was leaving the restaurant and walking across the street with Zenko and his two men. Zenko walked in front like a big, suspicious bulldog who was smelling something bad. The other two were local tough guys Mislovic had hired. They walked on either side of the aristocratic Yugoslav, looking like bouncers who had gone to seed, which is what they were. Mislovic had brought them along for their size more than anything else. He didn't expect any real trouble. But he didn't know about the blood that had been spilled at Annie's.

When he reached the front entrance to the pub, he told his men, "Stay out here."

Zenko assumed that did not mean him and started to follow Mislovic into the pub.

"No, you too, Z."

"I go with you."

"No. I want you here. If they come out first, you shoot them."

This mollified Zenko, but not much.

Mislovic started to enter, then stopped and pointed to Louis sitting in Oliver's black BMW. "And shoot that one, too. That clown walked in and out of the restaurant looking at us two times. They have no manners, these people."

The moment Mislovic entered, Oliver knew it was him. He didn't fit into this working-class Soho bar any more than Oliver did, but it didn't seem to faze him. Mislovic entered with a smile, looking directly at people who scowled at him. Despite the fact that Mislovic was meeting with a West Indian Yardie he considered to be less than human, in a smoke-filled dump that was crowded with people who instantly disliked him, he looked genuinely pleased.

As Mislovic approached, Oliver stood up and stepped forward with his hand out, ready to shake. Mislovic looked at the short, dark man and decided Oliver hadn't been out of the jungle for very many generations. Despite that, he smiled and shook Oliver's hand. Mislovic was surprised at the lightness of Oliver's grip. He had the immediate impression that Oliver was a man who completely rejected society's rules. And that no authority influenced him in the slightest. He was his own authority, ready to kill or die in a second. Mislovic admired that. And a twinge of discomfort passed through him because he knew he had lost that capacity years ago.

"Mr. Mills, I'm happy to meet you."

"Yes, Mr. Oliver. Thank you."

"Please sit."

"Thank you."

"What would you like to drink?"

"I'm not sure."

"Cognac?"

Mills looked around and peered at the bar's stock and said, "Just coffee will be fine."

Oliver raised his voice to ask the bartender for another cup of coffee, then shrugged his shoulders as if to comment on the lack of service.

Oliver asked, "You sure you don' want somet'ing to go wit' the coffee?"

Oliver's Jamaican accent made it difficult for Mislovic to understand him. He leaned forward and concentrated. He didn't quite understand Oliver's "don' " instead of "don't." So he just said, "Uh, no."

"Maybe later?" asked Oliver.

Mislovic understood that. "Yes. Yes. Maybe later. What about you? What happened to your appetite? You don't feel good?"

"I lost it."

Mislovic looked at him for a moment, gauging Oliver's remark. "Really?"

"Yes. I found out a friend of mine was killed a little while ago."

"Tonight?"

"Yes. So I don' feel like eating."

"You say you don't feel like eating because a friend was killed?"

"Yes."

"How?"

"How what?"

"How was he killed?"

"I heard he was shot, mon."

"Oh. I'm sorry to hear that."

"Are you?"

"Yes. Why not?"

Mislovic watched Oliver looking at him, and suddenly realized he was being accused here. He felt a flash of anger, mixed with fear. It occurred to him that this black savage sitting across from him was ready to shoot him. The thought of being shot in this stinking English pub by a Yardie infuriated Mislovic. It was ridiculous.

Oliver asked, "Why should you be sorry?"

Mislovic leaned forward and looked right in Oliver's eyes. "Why shouldn't I be?"

"You tell me, mon."

"Wait a minute. Are you thinking I am responsible?"

"Somebody is."

"Who is this that was shot? Where did it happen?"

"Your nephew's apartment."

"My nephew? What are you talking about?"

"I sent two men up der to clean up loose ends. Dat bitch wife of your nephew had protection. One of my guys was shot. Now who could have supplied her wit' protection?"

"Why are you sending people over there? Haven't you done enough feeding that man to your dogs? It was me he was stealing from, not you. Is this your custom, to continue to kill his family?"

"The money he gained wasna' his to keep. Da family cyan profit from dat. He stole my drugs for himself."

"The drugs were mine once he bought them from you. Don't you think I'm capable of handling these things in my own way?"

"I don' know what you be capable of, Mr. Mills. All I know is that anyone working with me cyan steal. Period. I know that John Boy for years back from da Notting Hill days. That's why I deal wit' a white boy. Otherwise you won't get the goods from me. But look what happen. I deal with da white man and I got problems."

"Look, I'm not going to argue with you. I have more important issues to deal with. Let this go now, or we will have to reconsider working with you."

"I cyan let this go. One of my men was killed because of dat woman. I let that go, I soon be dead."

Mislovic frowned.

"All I need to know right now is if you were the one protecting her."

Mislovic looked directly at Oliver and said, "No. If I was protecting her, *both* of your men would be dead."

Oliver smiled at that answer. "So you don' know notting about this?"

"Only what you're telling me."

"It's very strange, den. Who is dis guy shooting my bredrin?"

"I don't know. But I'm going to find out."

"You will?"

"Yes. I will. Listen, I don't agree with your vendetta against the woman. But I'm not making it my business. Her husband stole. He paid for it. That should be it. I'm not interested in any of it. If you are, that's your business, but I suggest you take care of it quickly and discreetly. It will only serve to harm both of us. My interest is putting back together our business. There's much more to gain working together than in fighting each other. If your main interest is getting back a few dollars from some widow, then tell me, because I have other things to do."

Oliver took a moment to make up his mind, then answered, "What do we have to gain working together?"

Mislovic spoke quietly and directly.

"All right. I've been here for a little over six months. I have set up my operations to a certain extent and have discovered the situation here. What have I seen? Mostly the same chaos and insanity I thought I left behind in my home country. Everybody fighting everybody else. If you don't mind me saying so, the business you run in London is primitive. You have no organization. No cooperation. No future. There's too much fighting. Too much raiding your competitors.

"Look how the Triads here work. The Chinese run heroin. They do it quietly. They are very well organized."

Oliver interrupted, "They never grow, either."

"Correct. It's a small business, but it's stable. Maybe they make less, but they make it year after year. Your type burns out after one or two years. Then the next gang is in control. The Chinese don't have to worry about dying tomorrow. You do."

"That's da only way for a Yard mon. We got to take what we can get."

"Then learn how to take more, more efficiently. Your people run the cocaine. It has the potential to be a large business, a huge business, but honestly speaking, it's a mess. You are constantly fighting each other for money and customers. Every little group that gets a few guns goes out and robs the other group. The most vicious group holds sway until somebody more violent comes along. For the moment, that's you. But no one is safe, so no one can prosper. You have come out on top for now. But let's be honest: It's only a matter of time before a few of your key people are shot and you are on your way down.

"Look at your associates in America. They are working with Colombians in Miami, Mexicans in Los Angeles, Dominicans in New York."

"So I should work with you."

"Yes. You've never gone out of your community. The West Indian community. So you've never had a chance to expand."

"Expand where?"

"Europe. Eastern Europe. Do you have any idea of the markets opening there? The borders are sieves. We can get anything in and out of there we want."

Oliver sipped his coffee and listened.

"What I have to know is how much you can supply me."

Oliver raised an eyebrow. "Nobody can get you more than me."

"Your supply is from where?"

"That's my business and my bredrin'. You want it, I can get it for you. And I'm not talkin' 'bout two or three kilos every month like wit' dat white boy you was using."

"Forget about him. If we do this quietly, correctly, I'm talking about ten times that amount now, and a hundred times that soon."

Oliver kept his poker face on, but the profit potential was not lost on him.

"You have dat kind of cash?"

Mislovic smirked. "Why do you think I'm in London, my friend? This is one of the easiest places to launder money in the world. We're talking amounts you have no idea of. We're pulling money out of the East that was hoarded by governments and old Communist party leaders. I can't let this money lie stagnant. It has to be invested. I'm buying whatever you have to offer."

Oliver paused for a moment and looked at Mislovic.

"Money isna' everyt'ing, boss."

Mislovic leaned back. "No. It's not. But it can *buy* just about everything."

"You first have to find the seller."

"What is it you want?"

"I want more than nine millimeters out on the street. We start moving those amounts you're talking 'bout, I need more firepower. Money not the only t'ing coming out of your part of da world."

"No, it's not."

"What can you offer me?"

"More than you can handle, Mr. Oliver. We have access to the contents of whole garrisons, my friend. You need Kalashnikovs, we have them."

"I want them."

"Anything can be negotiated. Arms control is a very sensitive issue. If I make you too powerful, you will become a problem. But if you are my ally, you cannot be weak. It's just a question of finding the right balance."

Oliver smiled his gold-toothed smile. "I t'ink we can work together."

"Then that's the first step. Let's find out if we can do that. The rest will come."

"What's the first step den, mon? Now that we dealing direct, there should be no problems."

"Let's talk price."

"I will always be under da market, no matter who is selling."

"All right. As you say, we're dealing without the middleman. I expect the best prices."

"What do you have in mind?"

"We'll talk specifics when the time comes."

"Fine. Just let me know how much and when."

"For the time being, let's think in terms of doubling my last order. At the minimum."

"Okay, give me a day or two, I'll set it up. How can I contact you, Mr. Mills?"

Mislovic said, "Give me your phone. I'll program a number in it. Call it when you're ready."

Oliver handed his cellular phone to Mislovic. As he punched in the numbers, Mislovic said " 'Simplicity' is my favorite English word, Mr. Oliver. Make our transactions simple. I don't want any of this switching cars and all that complicated bullshit."

"Like gentlemen, huh?"

"Something like that."

Oliver looked at Mislovic's coffee. He hadn't touched it.

"You want that drink now?"

"Some other time, Mr. Oliver. Frankly speaking, I'm not really comfortable in this place."

Oliver shrugged. Mislovic stood up to leave. It seemed to him that it was over without bloodshed. The beachhead had been established. Now the maneuvering and planning and setting of deadly traps could begin. But first, he had to get out of the pub.

Mislovic knew too many men who had walked out of a successful negotiation and been shot. He'd used the trick himself to lull an enemy into letting his guard down. There was nothing more pleasurable than making an enemy think he was your friend before you killed him.

"Call me when you're ready," he told Oliver.

"I will."

Time for the next move, thought Mislovic. He put out his hand to Oliver and said, "Why don't you let me help you clean up your problem with the woman."

Oliver was surprised at the offer. "What do you have in mind?"

"Well, for now, you're going to have a hard time getting close to her. At least I can help you locate her. Find out who this person is who's shooting your men."

Oliver shook Mislovic's hand. "Dat would be appreciated."

Mislovic smiled. "We don't need messy loose ends. We have much to do, my friend."

Mislovic turned and started the long walk to the front door. If they were going to try something it would be now, before he reached the street.

He knew Hinton was the one who would pull the trigger, but he would not give them the satisfaction of looking at him as he passed.

Hinton gripped the Uzi pistol. He was convinced this man was their enemy. It was so hard for him to let Mislovic walk out that he started grinding his back teeth.

Finally, Mislovic felt his hand land on the front door. He pushed it open and stepped outside. He looked to his left and saw Zenko flat against the outside wall of the pub with his hand under his jacket.

As soon as he saw Mislovic, Zenko slipped his arm into his boss's and led him quickly into the small side street that ran toward Wardour.

"We go now, Ivan. These Africans have men all over the street."

"They call themselves Yardies, Z. And they're not African. They're Jamaican."

"Come. It's all the same shit."

The two heavyweights fell into step behind the Yugoslavs, and all four men faded into the Soho crowd.

CHAPTER 10

ELIZABETH WAS FINALLY asleep. It has been almost two hours since the police had responded to the shooting at Annie's loft apartment. She sat on her living room couch with Devlin next to her. Devlin's wrists were still encased in the uncomfortable one-piece handcuffs.

The police constable in charge, Chief Inspector James Waldron, sat across from them. The Special Operations people were just finishing their information-gathering and debriefing. Two homicide detective inspectors were conducting an investigation of the deceased victim. Morgue personnel were organizing the removal of the body. Pictures were being taken. Someone was talking on a cellular phone with the Crown Prosecution Service regarding charges that might be filed.

As with any death in a large city, a complicated bureaucratic process would begin to spew out an enormous amount of paperwork. It was as if the civilized part of the city could survive if enough paper were produced to cover the murder and sop up the blood and muffle the hysteria.

Devlin watched Waldron talk into Annie's telephone. He could barely hear the chief inspector, but he knew what Waldron was talking about. Waldron was talking about him.

While the police worked, Devlin and Annie sat quietly, establishing a pocket of stillness amidst all the activity.

Annie was now physically and emotionally exhausted. She had entered a state of enduring repose. All the muscles in her face were relaxed. She had a calm, mysterious look about her. A Madonna amidst murder. Paramedics had tended to her cuts and wrapped her hands in gauze and adhesive tape. The cuts weren't deep, but the bandages made them seem severe. The coverings added to her aura of vulnerability.

Devlin was no more than a foot away from Annie, yet he

68

felt her physical presence on his arm and shoulder. Outwardly, he matched her calmness. Inside, however, his tension and discomfort grew. Occasionally, he would glance at her, stealing a quick dose of her beauty for himself, but that only added to his unease. The handcuffs prevented him from touching her. The situation prevented him from speaking to her. So he kept to himself, waiting, keeping his growing irritation from turning into anger. Devlin did not want to antagonize Waldron to the point where he would be arrested. Devlin knew that London police constables were given a tremendous amount of leeway in deciding how a case should be handled. The officer in charge had the authority to decide whether or not a crime had been committed, who should be arrested, and what the initial charges would be.

For the moment, Waldron controlled Devlin's fate, and therefore, Annie's. Waldron was a lean, intense man who looked more like a lecturer at a good university than a chief inspector in charge of uniformed personnel at a London police division. Devlin shifted uncomfortably. He had the feeling that if he played this wrong with Waldron, the typical British reaction would set in. Waldron would become officious and formal, following procedure that would lead to his arrest. And Devlin was in no mood to be arrested.

The one advantage he had at the moment was how skillfully Annie had handled the situation. She had managed to give the police only the minimum amount of information without antagonizing them. And even more amazing, she seemed to have elicited their sympathy by deftly playing the role of victim.

If Annie had not contacted him from halfway around the world, Devlin would have almost believed that she knew nothing more than what she had told the police.

She was smart enough not to lie but to reveal only the truth she wanted revealed. She told Waldron and the others her husband had been dealing in cocaine. Selling to his friends. Yes, she'd had her suspicions, but he had kept it from her. For some reason, the people who were supplying him had killed him. She was still having trouble believing it had happened. And now, tonight, someone associated with the people who killed him had come to her house to terrorize her into giving back money her husband had allegedly stolen from them, money which she did not have. Mr. Devlin was an old friend who had come to assist her family in this terrible tragedy.

Waldron was not naive enough to believe an old family friend could disarm a villain, drive away another armed man, and not suffer a scratch in the affair, but he could not for the life of him come up with a crime that Devlin might have committed. The gun retrieved was not Devlin's. The dead man appeared to have been shot with bullets of a larger caliber than the gun Devlin claimed to have taken from the victim.

Finally, Waldron replaced the telephone receiver in its cradle. He shook his head, as if he were about to talk to himself. But before he spoke, he leaned forward and took the handcuffs off Devlin. He leaned back again, pursed his lips, said nothing. Waldron looked as if he needed to give his brain more time to catch up with all the information he was processing.

Finally, he looked at Devlin for a moment and spoke. "You get around, don't you?"

Devlin did not answer.

Waldron looked at Annie and said, "Mrs. Petchek, how did you say you know Mr. Devlin?"

"We met many years ago. In New York. We were quite fond of each other, but perhaps too young to know it. We've kept in touch on and off throughout the years."

"You know his background?"

"Just generally. I know he has experience in law enforcement."

"And you thought he could be helpful?"

"Yes."

"Perhaps serve as a kind of protector?"

"Yes."

"Well, you're in good company. Your President Carter made the same choice."

"Yes. I know Jack worked for the Secret Service."

"Mmmm. As well as the New York City Police Department, the U.S. military, and a private security company known as Pacific Rim. Mr. Devlin is a man of wide experience in security matters."

Waldron turned to Devlin. "Of course, Mr. Devlin, you

realize you have absolutely no license or authority to work in the United Kingdom."

"I'm not working. I'm here to help a friend. I know less about this than you do. I only arrived a few hours ago."

"Hmmm, and look how much trouble you've managed to cause in such a short time. Quite extraordinary, I'd say."

Devlin didn't respond.

Waldron scratched his head, rubbed the back of his neck, and conceded that he wasn't going to find out any more tonight. "This is going to take quite a bit of sorting out, I'm afraid. Where are you staying, Mr. Devlin?"

"The Connaught. Although I haven't had time to check in yet."

"You won't be staying there tonight?"

"Perhaps. I haven't even had a chance to talk to . . ." Devlin hesitated, then said, ". . . Mrs. Petchek."

"I'd feel a bit more comfortable if I knew exactly where you were between now and tomorrow at eleven."

"What happens tomorrow at eleven?"

"You and Mrs. Petchek will appear at my office, which conveniently is only a few blocks away. As is the Magistrate's Court so we'll be able to confer with Her Majesty's Prosecution Service. My instincts are to arrest you right now, Mr. Devlin, but honestly speaking I don't know what to charge you with. If it turns out that gun belongs to you, we'll have a good place to start."

"It doesn't."

"Yes, and for your sake, I'm hoping the bullet wounds in the body outside don't match the bullets in that gun either."

"They don't."

"Well, we'll see to it. I have to confer with my colleagues to make sure the physical evidence matches your stories. Mrs. Petchek, I also must coordinate your case with your husband's murder case, which by the way is assigned to the Wembley Division. Which is where they found . . . the . . ."

"I know what they found."

For the first time that night, Annie's voice had taken on a hard edge.

"Yes, I'm sorry . . . well." Waldron abruptly stood up and walked over to talk to one of his men, an older, horse-faced man, Sergeant Reilly, who looked as if the only thing he wanted to do was leave and get some sleep.

Devlin turned to Annie and said, "It should be over soon. Are you okay?"

Annie turned and looked at him a moment before she answered. "Yes. Mostly just tired now."

Waldron returned and placed his card on the table between them. "Here's my card. Be at that address tomorrow at eleven. I suggest that you arrive on time—I don't want to come looking for you."

Waldron stood up to leave, but Devlin said, "Can I ask you a couple of questions?"

Waldron dropped back in his chair. "Why not?"

"After these men finish, are you going to leave somebody here in case the man who did this decides to come back?"

"I wouldn't imagine he'd be crazy enough to do that."

"Just in case."

"Well, that's not quite the procedure we follow. Assigning police personnel for private security is not our charge. I should think that would be more your responsibility, Mr. Devlin. I suggest a more worthwhile course would be to call a twenty-four-hour locksmith and get the front door repaired. And don't answer it unless you know who's on the other side."

"What about a constable until then?"

Waldron thought about it for a second. "Interesting how someone who might be charged with murder or at least illegal possession of a firearm has the cheek to ask the police for a security detail. And again, you're supposed to be the one supplying security, Mr. Devlin."

"But as you said, I'm not allowed to work in this country."

Waldron stood up quickly. "I'm not interested in sparring. I'll leave a man until you get the door fixed. Be in my office tomorrow. Eleven o'clock."

Devlin watched Waldron give final orders to several police personnel, then leave, taking the horse-faced sergeant with him.

Annie turned to Devlin. He said, "We have to talk."

"I know, I know. But please, not before I take a hot shower and clean myself. Then I'll tell you everything you want to know."

Devlin's frustration cranked up another notch, but he didn't force it. "Okay."

Annie stood up and headed for the back of the loft. She walked awkwardly at first, but by the time she reached the hallway, she was steady again.

Just before she left the room, she turned back.

"Dev."

"What?"

"How did you get to the one that was waiting in the hallway? Why didn't he shoot you when you came to my door?"

"I didn't come to your door. I went the other way."

"Why? Did you know he was waiting for you?"

"Yes."

"How?"

"I was suspicious that you had just buzzed me in without asking who it was. I figured if you were in enough trouble to ask me to come here, you'd be more careful about who you let in. When the elevator opened, I smelled him. Cigarettes and garlic. It didn't smell right."

"Literally."

"Literally. When I came around behind him and saw the gun, I was just lucky to get to him before he could shoot."

Annie nodded. She stood where she was, thinking about it, picturing it. She nodded once more and walked into the hallway.

Devlin watched her leave, then picked up the phone. His first call was to Ludwig, the night manager at the Draycott. There was a fax in his room, and he needed the list of names, now.

CHAPTER 11

ACROSS THE RIVER in a tough Irish neighborhood, Ben Johnson surveyed the remaining balls on the snooker table in front of him. He was at the Kilburn Snooker Centre. The sign outside offered eleven championship tables and a fully licensed bar. The possibility of anyone actually playing a championship match in the dark, dingy snooker hall was nonexistent. And the fully licensed bar consisted of a shelf with a few bottles of whiskey and a cooler chest filled with two brands of beer. But since the place was open twenty-four hours a day, and because the management allowed him to maintain a locker on the premises, the snooker parlor served as Johnson's twenty-four-hour answering service, storage facility, and place of recreation, which meant it served many of his needs.

His need at the moment was to figure out a way to sink the last three colored balls in this game of snooker.

A nineteen-year-old mulatto named Tyell who fancied himself a tough guy and a shrewd pool hustler was Ben's opponent. He smoked a spliff of half tobacco/half marijuana as he impatiently watched Ben line up his next shot.

Tyell considered himself skilled enough to easily take this big stiff. But for some reason he had lost three out of the last four games. They were playing for five quid a game, plus twenty to the first to win four out of seven. It was time to turn it on and take this chump, and Tyell was anxious to do it.

Tyell squinted his eyes and stared at Ben, and then at the table and balls. He thought Ben Johnson looked just too big, too slow, and too stupid to be beating him. The man kept his head down as he walked around the table. He had a big gut. He grunted instead of talked. He shouldn't have been winning.

Tyell watched the big man, but he didn't really see him. If

he had really looked, he would have seen that the 260-pound man was as hard as a weathered oak. He had a big stomach, but it merely went along with everything else big on him. Big wrists, big hands, big head. Ben Johnson was all big, much of it big muscle. The muscle made him much lighter on his feet than he appeared to be. And though he kept his head down, his eyes were always looking—up, down, across the table, around the room. Ben missed very little. Right now he enjoyed watching the kid watch him shuffle. Johnson knew that the mulatto would soon catch on that he was being hustled, for Ben would have to make a very good shot right now if he wanted to keep winning. And that's when the fun would start.

Ben sank the little yellow ball and was moving around to shoot the orange when the manager called out from behind his counter.

"Hey, Ben. Phone call."

Ben took his time and sank the next shot. The cue ball rolled into perfect position to sink the final ball. He was one shot away from winning it all.

Ben left the table to answer his phone call. He walked toward the desk. He didn't say a word or turn to look at the kid, but he knew he'd left Tyell fuming. By the time he picked up the heavy receiver from the snooker hall's old-fashioned desk-model phone, he knew Tyell had finally admitted to himself what had really been happening all along.

Tyell frowned at the cue ball. He thought over the last few shots of the game. Snooker was not an easy game. Luck went only so far. His frown turned into a sneer. First, he was disgusted. Then he was mad. Very mad. That big oaf had hustled him. Tyell was so mad he actually became self-righteous. How could that fucking yob cheat him? The fact that Tyell would rob, lie, steal, and cheat anyone who was within sight of him didn't matter. He immediately decided that what Ben had done was unfair.

Ben talked into the phone, but watched Tyell pimp-walk away from the table to the toilet in the back of the hall.

"Johnson," he said into the receiver.

Devlin was on the line, calling his first choice from the list Mrs. Banks had faxed to him at the Draycott.

"Ben, Jack Devlin. I'm in town. Are you available to work?"

Ben knew Devlin through Chow's organization. He had worked with him on one job and had been recommended by Devlin for another. Both jobs had gone smoothly and had paid well.

"I'm available, Mr. Devlin."

"Good. Let me fill you in. This is not for Pacific Rim, but I am using their resources. It's *my* job. We have to protect a woman and child. The people after her are definitely lethal. My plan is to see if I can alleviate the situation for her and/or get her out of country as soon as I can. I need backup to guard her while I'm making a few moves. Are you still interested?"

"Yes, sir."

Tyell emerged from the toilet. He strolled casually over to a table that was near the exit. Past the exit door was a straight double flight of stairs that led down to the street. He leaned against the table railing and watched Ben. Ben knew what would happen next. He picked up a cue ball from the racks of balls stacked on the manager's counter and continued listening to Devlin.

"I'm estimating no more than three or four days. It should be over by then."

"All right. When do you need me?"

"Right now, I'm afraid."

"Okay, where are you?"

Devlin gave him the address on Gainsford Street.

"What equipment do we need?"

"I'd like you to supply me with a nine."

"Yes. No problem."

"I'd suggest something heavier for yourself."

"I understand."

"Whatever your rates are for the equipment is fine."

"Right."

"How long do you estimate before you can get here?"

"I have what I need right here. Within the hour."

"Good. Thanks. See you."

Devlin hung up the phone, but Ben didn't. He continued listening to the dial tone.

Tyell shifted uneasily, like a fast rookie deciding whether or not to steal second base. Ben thought for a moment the kid might not do it, but he was wrong. Tyell suddenly moved swiftly toward the exit.

In a sweeping, fluid motion, Ben sent the cue ball flying toward the mulatto's head. It missed by about a foot and crashed into the wall by the exit door. There were six other people in the snooker hall, plus the manager. They all turned to see what had happened. Nobody said a word, nobody but Tyell. He yelled at Ben, "What the fuck you doing, you bloody yob?"

"Don't leave."

"Fuck you, don't leave."

There was no way the big oaf could catch him, thought Tyell. He straightened up tall and pointed at Ben and yelled, "Who you think you are, throwing that shit at me?"

Ben hung up the phone, but didn't step away from the counter. Tyell kept talking fast, laying down a barrage of curses and empty threats, but all the while he edged toward the exit.

Now Ben moved. Fast. Tyell was in mid-sentence, and the shock of seeing Ben move so quickly added a second to the time it took him to bolt through the exit door. Before the door had closed, Ben was in full stride. Tyell was out the door and down the first few stairs, not bothering to look behind him. If he had, he would have been amazed to see Ben place his hand on the corner of the last table between himself and the exit and vault over it as if it were something he did every day.

Tyell was just hitting the second set of stairs when Ben burst through the door and bounded down eight stairs in two giant steps, hitting the first landing with such a thud that the entire staircase shook. Tyell had barely made it to the bottom of the stairs. He didn't have to turn around to know he was trapped. How the fuck did that big son of a bitch get there so quickly?

"Shit," he muttered.

He turned to see Ben towering over him on the first landing, about ten stairs above him. But the wiry mulatto had guts. He pulled out his wing knife from his back pocket and made the appropriate flourishes, ending up with the six-inch blade pointing at Ben.

"You stay the fuck away from me, bigfoot, or I cut you up."

He kept the knife pointed at Ben and backed up toward the door.

Ben stared at him from above. The arrogant threat made him angry. Ben told him, "Put my money on the stairs and I'll let you go. You owe me thirty-five quid."

"You didn't win the last game."

"I would have if you'd stayed."

Tyell would have gladly put the money down. Unfortunately, he didn't have it. He turned to run out the door.

Too bad. Ben had another cue ball in his hand, and threw it with such force that when it hit Tyell in the back it cracked two ribs. Tyell fell forward and smacked his head into the exit door.

Ben walked slowly down to him, picked him up off the floor by his belt, kicked open the door, and threw Tyell onto the street. Tyell landed on the pavement with a thud, scraping the skin off his shoulder, one side of his face, and a knee. To his credit, Tyell still had the knife in his hand. He turned over and swiped it at Ben, who paused just long enough to avoid the tip of the blade, then kicked Tyell's arm so swiftly that he cracked Tyell's radius bone, just above the wrist. The knife flew into the street.

Now Ben picked up Tyell and slammed him down onto the trunk of a car. He grabbed the front pocket of Tyell's jeans and pulled the entire pocket off. No money came out. He went to the next pocket. Same thing. Tore it off the pants. No money.

He flipped Tyell over and was about to tear off his back pockets when the mulatto screamed, "Come on. I ain't got no money."

Ben stopped.

"Then you shouldn't be gamblin', boy."

"You hustled me."

"Shut up."

Tyell closed his mouth.

Ben flipped him back over so he could see him. He stuck a large finger in his face and said, "It's not just the money that pisses me off, boy. It's you. And all the crap on this earth like you. I don't ever want to see you again. If I do, I'll figure you're sneaking up on me to kill me, and I'll kill you first. Now git the hell out of here."

Then Ben slapped Tyell across the face hard enough to bloody his nose, pushed him back onto the trunk of the car, turned, and walked back to the snooker hall.

CHAPTER 12

DEVLIN FINISHED HIS last phone call and checked his watch. It was almost two A.M. He sat in Annie's living room letting some of the tension drain out of his body. The jet lag and the events of the evening were taking their toll. He was beginning to run on reserve. All the police personnel had gone, except for a young constable sitting near the front door. Devlin pictured what would happen to the young man if the people who were after Annie decided to come back. His entire weaponry consisted of a rubberized six-inch truncheon and his one-piece handcuffs. Devlin didn't think he could ever become accustomed to the concept of an unarmed police force. It was obvious that the police who were armed were very well trained, but who could possibly afford to wait ten minutes for guns to arrive? A minute was an eternity in a gunfight. Ten minutes was death.

Devlin heard the bathroom door open. Annie was finished with her shower, but Devlin knew there wasn't enough hot water in the world to wash away the terror he had seen in her eyes.

Devlin started to walk to the back of the loft, but paused to tell the young police constable, "Son, don't think about catching any sleep. If they come back you might get shot, but hopefully not before you can call in those guys with the guns."

The constable looked at Devlin and frowned.

Devlin left the room and headed down the hallway, almost bumping into Annie as she came out of Elizabeth's room. They stepped back from each other, feeling awkward at treating one another like strangers.

Annie was dressed in a pale blue terry-cloth robe. Her thick black hair was wet and piled on top of her head, revealing all of her beautiful face. She smelled of soap, and all traces of her makeup were gone.

Devlin said nothing for a moment. He was content to just look at her. She had been a beautiful, magnetic young woman when he had met her. She was still a beautiful woman. Still magnetic. But now there was a strength and stature about her that age had gracefully rendered.

Devlin didn't apologize for staring at her. Annie accepted his gaze without comment.

They were standing very close in the narrow corridor, and she had no clothes on under the robe. If Devlin hadn't thought about it at first, she could tell that he was thinking about it now. To break the tension, she held up her hands and showed him her wet bandages. "Does it matter if I got these wet?"

Devlin squinted at the bandages in the low light. "I'd better change them."

He led her back into the bathroom. It was still warm and steamy from the shower. Devlin was surprised at how large the room was, but then realized that this must have been old factory loft space that was recently renovated. The tub and sink were black porcelain. The walls were white ceramic tiles with decorative strips of smaller black tiles. The space that wasn't covered in tiles was covered in mirrors.

Devlin motioned for Annie to sit on the closed toilet seat. She sat and leaned forward to place her hands over the sink.

Devlin looked through the medicine cabinet over the sink, but he couldn't help but look down at Annie as well. Her skin was so smooth, so perfectly white as to be nearly flawless. Her robe had opened, exposing one thigh. From his standing position above her, he could see deep down into her cleavage.

At that moment, sitting on her closed toilet, dressed only in the robe, her gleaming black hair still wet from the shower, Annie seemed both powerfully alluring and heartbreakingly vulnerable. This sudden unexpected intimacy so soon after the fight for survival nearly disoriented Devlin. He remembered that between them there had been an instinctive, open, free sexuality. They had never held back, and doing so now was distinctly uncomfortable. But it was obviously inappropriate to allow any sexual attraction to blossom between them at the moment. Devlin found himself saddened by the chasm the years had opened between them.

He looked away from her and concentrated on finding a pair of scissors in the cabinet. He found a small pair and carefully started to cut the bandages off her hand, forcing himself to look at her hands instead of her face or the rest of her body. But even her hands seemed beautiful to him.

And then he pushed all of that away and asked her, "What the hell happened, Annie? How did you get into this mess?"

She didn't say anything for a moment. She had to push away her sadness and frustration with a shake of her head before she could speak.

"Christ, I don't know, Dev. I can't believe I was almost killed tonight. What if you hadn't come?"

"What happened, Annie?"

"I don't know everything. We needed money, and my husband started selling coke to his friends. I didn't think that much of it. Doing lines of that shit had been part of his scene ever since I knew him."

"You don't get killed selling coke to your friends."

"He got in over his head."

"How? Who are these people he was dealing with?"

"He was buying from Jamaicans. Yardies. They don't normally deal with whites, but Johnny knew the head guy from way back. He lived in Notting Hill years ago when a lot of Jamaicans lived there. So that's why this guy would deal with Johnny."

"What guy?"

"A man named King Oliver. He's apparently the head of a big group of Yardies. He controls a lot of the drug trade in London, I hear."

"So why did they kill him? If he was selling to friends like you say, he couldn't have been dealing that much."

"That was the problem. He got into something way out of his league. Johnny was Yugoslavian. When all the troubles started a few years ago, there was a steady stream of relatives that were coming out of there. A lot of them ended up here."

"Yes?"

"Most of them were in pretty bad shape. Johnny kind of avoided them as much as possible, but one of his family was an officer in some Croation army battalion or division, I don't know which. This guy started fighting early on. I guess it got pretty crazy over there with the different groups. Serbs, Bosnians, Croats, Muslims. Johnny once told me that some of these guys had Velcro insignia on their uniforms. They'd stick different insignia on for different battles. It sounded crazy to me. More like a bunch of armed gangs than armies fighting each other. So, about six or eight months ago, this uncle of his defected with some of his soldiers. He goes by the name Frank Mills, but his name is Mislochek or something like that. I think he was a colonel or a major. I don't know. It was way beyond me."

"What does that have to do with dealing cocaine?"

"Hey, these guys are killers, Dev. They don't walk into the West and apply for corporate jobs. They're basically outlaws. Nobody has real control of them. So when Uncle Ivan Mislo-something up and left, he apparently took a lot of money and arms with him."

"And he set up shop here in London?"

"Here. Western Europe. I'm sure they're starting in the U.S., too. You'd be amazed at the number of criminals and thugs flowing out of those countries. The old Communist governments are gone, so they have no need for them. Their militia and secret police forces are being disbanded. There are no state-run programs of terror anymore. They're looking for new places, and we're it. Russians, Georgians, Serbs, Czech, East Germans. Uncle Ivan is one of many."

"How do you know so much about these people?"

"Johnny talked about them all the time."

"So his uncle wanted to get into the drug business?"

"Johnny said he had a lot of money to invest. I think it was only one of his interests."

"Where is he?"

"Ivan?"

"Yes."

"He has an office someplace in Soho. I seem to remember Johnny saying it was on Berwick Street."

"And he used your husband as a source for drugs."

"Johnny wouldn't tell me all the details, but yes, he was the middleman. There's no way the Yardies would deal directly with Yugoslavs, so they used Johnny."

"Why did they kill him?"

"I don't know. They must have figured he was cheating them somehow."

"Was he?"

Annie frowned. "My husband was reckless. He was capable of anything. You know, artists these days are involved in a lot of things they call art, but which are just crazy. I don't think Johnny had a very solid sense of reality."

Without warning, Annie started crying very quietly. The tears just appeared, without sobs, almost without emotion.

"It makes me so goddamn mad, Dev. Half the time I don't know why I'm crying. It was so stupid. And what they did to him was so disgusting."

"What did they do?"

Devlin was still holding her hands as he cut off the last of the wet bandages, so he was able to feel her shudder. She gripped his hands as she told him.

"They cut off his head, Jack. They beheaded my husband. They mutilated him with a machete and fed him to a pack of dogs. The police wouldn't even let me see his body."

Devlin thought about what kind of people would use a steel machete on another human being, but found himself shutting down the image in his mind before it could form completely. He held Annie's hands and told her, "Don't think about it."

"I can't stop."

Her voice rose in pitch. For a moment Devlin thought she might lose herself to hysteria.

"You don't know what that man did to me tonight. What he said. It was horrible, Jack. Fucking horrible. It makes me sick every time I think of it. You've got to help me. You have to stop them. Get me out of here. They're going to kill me."

"No they won't. We'll take care of it. They won't hurt you, Annie."

"I have to get out of here. Take me home, Jack."

"It'll be all right, Annie. We'll see the police tomorrow and take care of what we have to do, and then we'll get you someplace safe."

"What if the police won't let me leave?"

"Don't worry about that."

"They're going to kill me, Dev. They're going to kill me and Elizabeth."

Annie squeezed Devlin's hands. The bandages were off, and he could see the pressure of her grip make the blood seep out of the cuts. Devlin saw the terror in her. She held him so tightly it was almost as if the fear in her was being pressed into his own hands. He thought for a moment that her voice might keep going straight up until she was screaming at him.

"That man was horrible, Dev. He wanted the money Johnny was supposed to have stolen, but I know he really wanted to kill me. They sent him to kill me. He wasn't human. You have to help me."

Devlin allowed her to cling to his hands and knelt in front of her. "I will, Annie. I will. Just take it easy. It's over now."

But she wouldn't stop, and Devlin didn't know what to say, and all he could think about was that he was kneeling on one knee holding her hands as if he were proposing to her.

"No, you don't understand. You didn't see him. His eyes. He's crazy. You'll have to kill him to stop him, Dev."

Finally, Devlin shouted, "Annie, stop it!"

And suddenly she did stop, her terrified remembrance of the past hours suspended by Devlin's shout.

"I'm not killing anybody, Annie."

She looked at Devlin kneeling in front of her as if she didn't know how he had gotten there.

She leaned forward and asked a soft "What?"

"There's been enough killing, Annie. I'm not going to kill anybody."

"But they aren't going to stop, Dev."

"You're not at their mercy. They can't hurt you if we don't let them."

"You didn't see that man, Dev. He'll never stop."

"I don't have to see him, Annie. I know all about them. Forget about them. I'm here. Forget about killing people. It'll be all right. I promise."

Annie took her hands away from Devlin. For a moment, her beautiful face was twisted with disbelief. "I thought you would understand. If I could, I'd kill every one of them."

Devlin's voice rose in anger. "And afterwards you'd feel even more haunted. Believe me."

Annie sat on her toilet and bowed her head. Then she looked up. She knew without doubt or equivocation that if she ever saw Hinton and she had a gun, she would shoot him in the eyes with it, but she calmly looked at the man in front of her and said, "I'm sorry. I can't tell you to kill someone for me. But unless you kill that man, Jack, you'll be dead, too."

And then she slowly placed her hands back into Devlin's. He took them, and wrapped them in fresh bandages.

CHAPTER 13

By THE TIME Annie finally crawled into her bed, she was exhausted. But she nevertheless woke at her normal hour, seven A.M. She listened for Elizabeth, and decided the child must be still sleeping, then rolled over and tossed and turned until just before nine, when she finally gave it up and opened her eyes, ready to stay awake.

The apartment was extremely quiet, and for a moment Annie's mind drifted into a peaceful reverie. For two or three seconds, last night had not happened. The days before had not happened. The horror of her husband's death, Hinton's attack, Devlin's coming . . . none of it had happened.

Then, in the silence of the morning, it all came rushing back. She closed her eyes tightly at the pain of the memories, but none of it went away. And then the quiet engulfed her and terrified her and drove her out of bed.

She shrugged on her terry-cloth robe, left the bedroom quietly, and walked to Elizabeth's room to check on her. The child was still asleep. Next she wanted to find Devlin. The loft was stuffy, and it felt strange to be there so late in the morning. Assuming Devlin was sleeping on the living room couch, she went to find him.

As she arrived at the doorway, a huge man stood up quickly from a chair in which he had been sitting near her boarded-up front door. He was wearing what looked like a long canvas overcoat that reached almost to his ankles. But it wasn't just canvas. The long coat was lined with bulletproof Kevlar. And in his hands was a very brutal-looking Mossberg Model 500 bullpup shotgun.

Even though her mind told her this man must be on her side, she was so startled and frightened by him that she couldn't speak and her brain couldn't assemble an explanation of how he might have gotten there.

Then, in the midst of her paralysis, a rather gentle, raspy voice spoke to her in a strange accent that sounded to Annie like a mix of southern American and British cockney.

"I'm sorry, ma'am. Mr. Devlin hired me to look after things here. We didn't want to wake you. He said it would be all right to introduce myself when you woke up. My name is Ben Johnson."

Annie just stood staring at him. She had never seen a man so rugged-looking. His gray hair was cropped short. His face was lined and creased, and there was a scar that split his right eyebrow into two parts. He was clean-shaven, and seemed almost military in his bearing, but he looked too scrabbled and rough to be in any modern-day army.

Ben stood waiting, patiently letting her reaction to him take its course. He was accustomed to the way some people stared at him, and he was wise enough to just let it pass.

And then, of course, the reality that this man-mountain was guarding her door swept over Annie, and she smiled in gratitude.

She walked straight toward him with her hand extended, and he gave her such a frank and warm smile in return that she suddenly felt released from the terror and dread that the morning had brought to her.

He allowed her to take his hand, then carefully closed it around hers. Annie tried to grip Ben's hand and shake it, but it was so big and meaty that she couldn't begin to get her fingers around it. She gripped what she could and did her best to shake it, looked into his face, and noticed he had piercing blue eyes amidst the deep creases and lines.

"I'm very happy to meet you, Ben, and I'm glad you're here. I feel much better."

"Thank you, ma'am. Mr. Devlin told me he'll be back in time to take you to the appointment with the police at eleven."

"That's right. I almost forgot about that. Well, have you had breakfast?"

"As a matter of fact, I helped myself to a bowl of your cereal."

Annie wondered if there was any left.

"Oh, that's good. Would you like coffee?"

"Yes."

"Milk and sugar?"

"Black."

"Okay."

Annie looked at her front door and saw that a half-inch plywood sheet had been bolted onto what was left of it and that a lock had been rigged up.

"Did I sleep through that repair?"

"I guess so. The man was just finishing when I got here. He seems to have done a pretty good job."

"Well, I'll get your coffee."

"Thank you."

Annie turned to walk back to the kitchen, stopped, and turned back.

"Is that a shotgun?"

"Yes."

"Are you supposed to have that?"

Ben nodded once. "Yes, ma'am."

CHAPTER 14

WHILE BEN WAITED for Annie to get him his coffee, Mislovic was finishing his—a large cup of cappuccino.

Mislovic enjoyed the morning ritual. It was the first public activity of his day, and took place in his Soho headquarters. At least a few of his employees had to be present for it. And, of course, he had to look the part. This morning, he was dressed for the role in a dark blue silk and wool double-breasted Savile Row suit, a custom-made white Egyptian cotton shirt with French cuffs, and discreet gold cuff links in the shape of ovals. The shirt was buttoned at the collar, without a tie.

Mislovic sat in the back room of a small import-export company on Berwick Street in Soho, his headquarters. The company was called Witmans, and the sign facing the street announced that Witmans featured merchandise which included T-shirts, sunglasses, badges, baseball hats, buckles, and alternative fashion accessories. There was no sign announcing the other merchandise Mislovic dealt, such as drugs, stolen currency, and smuggled arms.

Along with a still thriving porno industry, chic bars and restaurants, and many legitimate businesses, Soho had long been a venue for various criminals, many of them ethnic groups, particularly the Chinese and Vietnamese. Mislovic had little trouble finding a cooperative West End real estate company that would lease him the store with no questions asked and a hands-off policy.

In the front room of the Berwick store were scattered boxes filled with legitimate goods and a long counter that separated the front from a storage area. After the storage area, there were two offices, side by side, then a large room containing four tables with wire legs and wooden tops, matched by chairs in the same style.

In the big room there was a makeshift bar along one wall. On the bar were several bottles of liquor and a coffee machine. A large muscular man named Roland stood behind the bar. He didn't do much except stand there, since the cappuccino Mislovic drank came from the Italian restaurant down the street at the corner of D'Alby and Berwick.

Roland was one of Mislovic's soldiers. He was just under six feet four inches and just over 240 pounds. Roland was the strong, silent type, mostly because he spoke very little English.

Roland wore a loose-fitting knit sweater that hung outside gray slacks and thick gold chains on his neck and wrist. Roland felt gold jewelry was a prerequisite for a Western criminal.

In addition to Roland, Mislovic was flanked by Zenko and a local criminal named Jimmy Atlas, a fast-talking gambler and bookmaker. Also in the room was one of Mislovic's workmen, a congenial, overweight fellow named Josep Petrov who answered to the name of Pete. Pete could be counted on for just about anything from a night of congenial eating and drinking, to murder.

The final member of the club that morning was a slightly retarded boy named Bobby. Bobby was a local misfit whom Zenko had taken under his wing. Bobby's jobs were various. Sometimes he could be found selling hot dogs at the Lambeth Street market, or hustling theater tickets in the West End. At other times he'd clean up the back room at Witmans or run for cappuccinos to the Italian restaurant.

Bobby was a strange-looking lad. He was rail-thin. He cut his own hair with a worn-out electric clipper, so there were inevitably spots that were gouged out to the bare skull. His ears stuck out. He usually had a weird, lopsided grin on his face. If you discounted a primitive cleverness that was part street smarts, part survival instinct, Bobby was a modern-day version of the medieval village idiot.

While Mislovic read the morning edition of the *London Times,* Zenko talked on a cellular phone.

When he'd finished his conversation, Mislovic asked, "Did you find someone who could help?"

"Yes. One of our contacts is working on it."

"Working on it?"

"Yes."

"What does that mean?"

"He's looking for a police in that neighborhood."

"Where her apartment is?"

"Yes."

"Where the shooting was?"

"Yes."

"Why?"

"They get the case."

"Ah. But he doesn't know anything yet?"

"Just what he see over police computer."

"What's that? What does it say?"

"Not much. The call. Where. Someone shot."

Mislovic said, "Give me the phone."

He dialed a number from memory. When the person he was calling answered, he talked very quietly.

"Did I wake you?"

Annie answered, "No."

"What are you doing?"

"Why are you calling here?"

"I want to know what you're doing."

"What are *you* doing?"

"Nothing."

"That's right, nothing. And those animals you deal with are over here trying to kill me. What am I supposed to do, just sit here?"

"Why did you bring this person into this?"

"I need protection for me and my daughter."

"Who is this guy?"

"Someone I know from New York. He has nothing to do with you or Johnny."

"Get rid of him."

"Don't be ridiculous."

"What's his name?"

"Devlin."

"You don't need him. Don't cause trouble."

"Then tell those animals to leave me alone."

Mislovic did not respond.

Annie waited another moment and said, "That's what I thought. Good-bye. Don't call here again. I have enough problems already."

Mislovic shut off the phone. He asked Zenko, "Your man doesn't know anything?"

"He just follow the reports coming over computer. But from what he said, I think the black Yardie lied to you."

"Oliver?"

"Yeah."

"Why?"

"It don't say Devlin shoot their man. I think Oliver's own guy shot him."

"My God, these people are animals. They shoot each other instead of the enemy?"

Zenko shrugged. "Sometime it happens. You know that."

"There's no excuse."

Zenko shrugged again. "No excuse. But sometime it happens."

"Does your contact know anything else?"

"No. But he find someone he can buy."

"For how much?"

Zenko shrugged. "We negotiate."

"All right. It's a start. I doubt if that savage Oliver will believe we had nothing to do with this, but for the moment we are not totally ignorant."

"You think Oliver believe you send the bodyguard?"

"He did. I don't know about now. Christ, this woman is complicating things."

"We should kill him."

"Who?"

"The black. Maybe her, too."

"And what? Start all over? I don't have time for that. For now we have to work with him. If we have to, when we have enough information and contacts, we kill them all and start up our own operation."

Zenko frowned, but didn't argue.

"They're all pigs, Z. All savages. One is no better or worse than the other."

"What about the woman?"

Before he could answer Zenko, Mislovic was interrupted by

Bobby, who walked into the back room and announced that there was someone outside who wanted to see Mr. Mills.

All the men turned to Bobby. Mislovic asked, "Who wants to see me?"

"A man outside."

"A man outside. Did he tell you his name?"

Zenko and the others watched the exchange. Jimmy Atlas felt like taking bets on whether or not Mislovic would be able to understand what was going on.

"No," Bobby answered.

Mislovic was patient. "What did he say, Bobby?"

The boy squinted once, quickly, and remembered the answer. "He said, he's a friend of Anne Petch."

"Who?"

"A friend of Anne Pets."

Mislovic looked at Zenko. Zenko widened his eyes. Mislovic turned to Bobby and told the boy, "Very good. Now I want you to go outside and tell the man to wait right there. Then you go somewhere and come back tomorrow. Understand?"

Bobby nodded.

"You've done enough for today, Bobby. Tell the man to wait, then you go home."

Bobby nodded again and left.

Mislovic turned to Jimmy Atlas and said, "Make sure he tells him, then you take off, too."

Atlas stood up to leave.

Zenko asked Mislovic, "You think this is the fucking New York guy?"

"Sounds like it."

"You think she send him over here?"

Mislovic shrugged. "She's capable of almost anything."

"Is she crazy?"

"Who knows."

"It must be her. How else he would find you so fast?"

"I'll ask him."

"What are you going to do with him?"

Mislovic thought for a moment, then responded. "I'll give him to Oliver."

"To the Yardie? Why?"

"It will accomplish two things: teach that bitch she can't pull nonsense like this, and convince Oliver I am his friend. We will be helping him. They will be in our debt."

"They have no honor."

"They'll have nothing by the time I'm done with them. For now I want them to think we are willing to help them.

"So, Z, go out there and check this fellow. If it's this Devlin, you go over him from top to bottom and then bring him in here. He must have a lot of balls to come down here looking for me."

Zenko said, "Maybe not. Maybe she tell him we are friends."

"Could be. Just make sure he's clean. I don't even want a nail file on him."

"Okay."

On the way out, Zenko gave Roland and Pete orders in Croation. They both stood up and left the back room.

Out on the street, Devlin calmly leaned against a parked car, looking as if he belonged in Soho. He wore slacks and a sport coat, but no tie. He shirt was unbuttoned to the second button from the top and he wore a thick chain around his neck.

Zenko came out and asked him, "Who are you?"

"I'd like to see Mr. Mills."

"You have appointment?"

"Not yet. How's his calendar?"

"His what?"

"His calendar. His schedule."

Zenko stared blankly at Devlin.

Devlin decided those words were not in the Slavic man's vocabulary.

He asked, "Is he busy?"

Zenko waved Devlin toward him and said simply, "You come."

Devlin pushed himself off the car and followed Zenko inside the store. When they reached the offices near the rear, Zenko stopped and motioned for Devlin to step into the office on his right. Devlin stepped inside and saw Roland sitting at a desk holding a Grendel P-30 auto pistol. Roland raised the barrel slightly until it was pointing at Devlin's chest.

Devlin stared at the machine pistol while Zenko calmly said, "Put hands on desk. Don't move. You move, he shoots."

Devlin leaned forward and placed his hands in front of Roland. Then he turned to Zenko and said, "Stay close to me. If he shoots that thing there should be enough bullets to hit you, too."

Zenko grunted and slowly checked Devlin for weapons. He was very thorough. He even ran his fingers through Devlin's hair and checked his shoes.

When he was satisfied, he told Devlin to follow him into the back room.

Mislovic was sitting at his table, calm, relaxed, reading his *London Times*. Unfortunately, the cappuccino cup was empty, so Mislovic could not sip it slowly like a gangster in a *Godfather* movie.

When Devlin entered with Zenko, Mislovic looked up and appraised him in the same way he evaluated all men: He compared Devlin with himself.

Devlin was bigger than he, maybe as good-looking, obviously stronger, but Mislovic had no doubt that he was smarter than the man standing in front of him. It couldn't be a smart man standing there. A smart man would not have come anywhere near Ivan Mislovic.

He told Devlin, "Sit down."

He nodded at Zenko to close the door. Zenko motioned for Pete to stand guard outside with Roland, then closed the door and stood behind Devlin, blocking his exit.

"You're Devlin?"

"Yes. How did you know? We haven't been introduced."

Mislovic shrugged. "Who told you to come here?"

"No one. I came on my own.

"Anne Petchek told you about this place and me?"

"Not really. She just told me who you are and that you had a place in Soho. And that you were working with her husband."

Mislovic shrugged again. "So how did you find me?"

"Frank Mills the Yugoslav isn't hard to find. I just asked around."

"Asked where?"

"In the neighborhood. There's no big mystery here. You're not invisible. It took about twenty minutes."

"But she didn't tell you to come here?"

"No. In fact, I assumed she would have told me *not* to come here."

Mislovic had to think about the complicated verb tense, but did not want Devlin to explain it to him. Instead he asked, "Then why are you here? What do you want?"

"I want you to help her."

"Help her do what?"

"Stay alive. I want you to tell the people you are dealing with to leave her alone."

"What people?"

"The people you buy your drugs from."

Mislovic frowned. "You must have the wrong Frank Mills."

"I'm sure that's possible, but I still want you to tell those people to stay away from her."

"Why?"

"Why what?"

"Why should I?"

"Because the people who killed her husband are trying to kill her, too."

Mislovic leaned back in his chair and talked quietly. The more intense a situation got, the more he liked to assume a relaxed, nonchalant style.

"What does any of this have to do with me?"

"You were working with her husband, weren't you?"

"Her husband?"

"John Petchek. Your nephew."

"My nephew?"

"Yes."

"John Petchek?"

"Yes."

"Her husband."

"Yes. Are you being intentionally dense, Mr. Mills, or is there some difficulty with the language. What's the problem?"

Mislovic bristled. "Do you think I had anything to do with what happened to him and his family?"

"I didn't say you did."

"That idiot brought the troubles into his own family. Not me."

"But he was still family, wasn't he?"

"And that means I have to take care of his widow?"

"I didn't say take care of her. I just asked you to tell the people who are after her to stop."

Mislovic paused for a moment, then asked, "Have you ever been divorced, Mr. Devlin?"

"No."

"You know, it's a big problem. Even where I come from. I see it a lot. And I'm willing to admit, most of the time it's the husband's fault. Men like to fuck around, you know."

Devlin didn't respond.

"You know what I mean? Men can't stay with one woman. That's usually what happens. Or maybe they drink too much. Or fuck up at work. You know? There's always problems. Regrets. Crying. It's very hard on the women. And they get a lawyer and complain and complain and complain. 'Help me, help me.' And you know what the professionals have to tell them?"

"What's that?"

"They tell them, 'Hey, you married that son of a bitch, not me.' She married that piece of shit, Mr. Devlin. Not me. If those people have a problem with her, it's not my problem."

Devlin stared at Mislovic, then said, "You took all that time to tell me it's not your problem?"

"What?"

"Is that your answer? 'It's not my problem'?"

"Working with him was my mistake. I was the one he cheated, Mr. Devlin. I should have killed him myself. I'm not interested in prolonging my mistake."

Devlin pressed. "Would you have gone after the wife and child, too?"

"Don't be ridiculous. I'm not an animal like them."

"But you don't care if they do?"

Mislovic waved Devlin off as if the subject were beneath him.

"Or maybe you don't *mind* if they do?"

"You know, Mr. Devlin, you don't look like a stupid man, but you are stupid. Don't insult me with this shit. This conversation is over. This whole problem is over for me—you and the woman, all of it."

Mislovic picked up his cellular phone and punched in Oliver's number, then watched Devlin as he listened to the phone ring. When it was answered, he watched Devlin as he talked.

"This is Mr. Mills. I have someone here who wants to see you. Someone your associate ran into last night, but didn't have a chance to meet."

Mislovic smiled at Devlin. "Yes. I'll make sure he's here for you. But hurry. He might not want to wait."

Mislovic turned off the phone and smiled at Devlin. Actually it was more of a smirk. It was not the right thing to do.

Devlin asked, "Who was that?"

"The people who are giving you so much trouble. You have a problem with them, why not deal direct, huh? You're American. Isn't that the way Americans like to handle these things?"

Now it was Devlin's turn to lean back in his chair.

"I see. Let me ask you something, Frank."

"Yes?"

"Do you consider yourself an intelligent man?"

Mislovic shrugged.

"I mean, would you go so far as to say you're smart? With it? In the know? Clever?"

With each word Devlin became more insulting.

"Am I going too fast? How about savvy? Slick? Do you consider yourself any of the above, Frank?"

Mislovic was frowning now. He knew he was being threatened, but he had never been threatened by someone speaking in such a casual tone.

"Well if you're so goddamn smart and savvy, Frank, how could you be so stupid as to call those people and so idiotic as to wear a three-piece suit that is so out of style it looks like somebody played a bad joke on you?"

Now Mislovic was sitting straight up in his chair. But Devlin wasn't done.

"I thought I'd give you a chance here, but all you are is a bunch of dope-running DPs sitting around doing a bad imitation of a Mafia movie. I mean, are those actually cappuccino dregs in that cup?

"Are you getting this, Frank? If not I'll speak more slowly."

Now Devlin leaned forward, and now there was no mistaking the tone of his voice. "Listen carefully to me, asshole. If anything happens to Annie Turino and her child, if anybody touches her, *anybody,* you will pay. You will wish you were back in that nineteenth-century, third-world, feudal nation of yours getting shot in the ass by your cousin in some tribal war fighting for obscure reasons nobody even remembers."

Devlin stood up to leave. "Now even though you look like a joke sitting there in your pretty clothes, I know your English is good enough to get the general idea, Frank, so you translate that for your fat little friend over there with the wandering hands."

Mislovic was so mad, his normally excellent English became mangled as he spit out, "Sit down. You not going anywhere."

"Yes I am," Devlin quietly told Mislovic. "And it isn't 'You not going anywhere,' it's 'You're not going anywhere.' "

Mislovic snapped. He lunged for Devlin across the table. Zenko started to pull his Grendel out and move toward Devlin from behind. Both men wanted to smash him. They already had a vision of Devlin on the floor as they kicked and beat him.

But Devlin was ahead of them. He had been waiting for them to snap at the bait. He leaned back as Mislovic lunged, then stood up, and in the same motion shoved his chair back with his right foot. The chair flew into the onrushing Zenko. There was a brutal crack as the chair hit both his knees. Zenko fell with a grunt and a curse. For the moment, he was too hurt to get back on his feet.

Mislovic shoved the table at Devlin, trying to knock him down, but it did nothing except bang into the muscular part of Devlin's thighs. Devlin tossed the table aside like it was made of cardboard.

Mislovic rushed at Devlin, grabbing for his throat. Devlin took one quick step to the side, gripped the back of Mislovic's neck, and shoved him forward while he kicked his feet out from under him. Mislovic fell hard, flat out on the floor.

Zenko finally struggled to his feet, at the same time wrenching his gun out of an armpit holster, but now Mislovic was between him and Devlin. In this moment of confusion, Devlin slipped off the chain he was wearing around his neck. It wasn't a piece of jewelry; it was a custom-made weapon based on a Japanese fighting device called a Manriki Gusari—a chain with weighted ends that in the right hands could be devastatingly effective.

The chain extended Devlin's reach by three feet. In seconds he had it spinning so quickly it was almost invisible. Zenko heard the whipping sound, then felt the sudden impact and sharp pain as the chain's weighted end smashed suddenly into the back of his hand.

Zenko's hand split open, the fingers splayed, and the machine pistol clattered to the floor.

Devlin reversed the arc of his swing and whipped the chain around Mislovic's neck as the Yugoslav began to pick himself up off the floor.

As the chain wrapped around Mislovic's neck, Devlin grabbed the free end with his left hand and lifted Mislovic onto his feet.

He shifted quickly and moved behind Mislovic. He grabbed both ends of the Manriki in his left hand and tightened his grip. Mislovic felt as if his throat were being slowly severed. He choked and grabbed at the chain, but he was helpless.

The commotion had drawn Roland and Pete from the other side of the door. Roland was the first one through. He had his machine pistol in hand, ready to fire. Pete was behind him, holding a Russian-made 9-mm Makarov in his right hand.

But Devlin was now behind Mislovic, twisting the chain even tighter, using Mislovic as a shield. Mislovic tried to strike at Devlin's head to knock him away or loosen his grip. Devlin ducked the blow, pulled back sharply on the Manriki chain, and stepped forward, slamming his right knee into Mislovic's kidney. Even choking, Mislovic had to grunt in pain. His resistance ended. He slumped forward, but Devlin held him up with the chain. Zenko and the others watched their boss begin to choke to death in front of them.

Zenko was recovered enough to go for his gun on the floor, but he knew Devlin could easily crush Mislovic's windpipe before he could get the gun and shoot him, so he stood where he was, trying to decide whether or not he could rush Devlin and try to break his grip before he killed Mislovic.

Roland and Pete aimed their weapons, but knew they couldn't shoot Devlin without hitting Mislovic.

For his part, Mislovic desperately tried to shout out a command. He was trying to say, "Shoot him, shoot him," but only a muffled croak came out.

Devlin, however, spoke clearly and calmly. "Don't move. Put down the guns, or I kill him right now."

Devlin watched the men hesitate. He twisted the chain just slightly, completely cutting off Mislovic's air. Mislovic's eyes began to bulge grotesquely.

Devlin barked out the order once more. "Put down the guns."

Zenko yelled back, "Okay, okay! Stop."

But Devlin kept the pressure on Mislovic's neck, until his tongue began to protrude from his contorted face.

"Put 'em on the floor and walk out of here."

Zenko screamed, "Stop it."

Devlin held the chain tight, still waiting for the guns to fall. They had to believe Devlin would kill Mislovic, even though he knew that doing so would certainly mean he himself would die.

Mislovic began making a sickening croaking sound. He was losing consciousness and was about to collapse. Devlin held him up with the chain. It was now cutting through his skin. Mislovic's lips were turning blue.

Finally, Zenko turned to the others and yelled, "Drop guns. Now!"

The guns dropped. Devlin continued to hold the chain tight.

"Walk away from them," Devlin ordered.

They quickly moved away from the weapons on the floor, and Devlin finally released enough pressure on the chain so that Mislovic could breathe. Devlin was afraid that Mislovic might be too far gone, but the Yugoslav suddenly reared back and emitted a horrible rasping sound as he sucked in enough air to stay alive and conscious.

While Mislovic sucked in air, Devlin stepped to his right and picked up Zenko's machine pistol. He straightened Mislovic up and pressed the barrel of the gun into the side of his head while keeping a firm grasp on the chain.

He pulled Mislovic over to the other weapons, then kicked the Makarov and the second Grendel toward the back wall.

Zenko was already walking backwards toward the front of the ground-floor office while wrapping a handkerchief around his bleeding hand.

Mislovic was recovered enough to hear Devlin snarl in his ear, "All right, tough guy, walk out of here slow and easy. I'll blow your head off and shoot my way out the second you give me trouble. I'll kill all of you if you give me one reason to do it. Tell them to keep away, unless you want to commit suicide."

Mislovic did as he was told. At that moment his hate for Devlin was so intense he had to struggle with himself to keep from turning and trying to tear Devlin's throat out before he could pull the trigger. Dying now was one thing; the indignity of what Devlin was doing to him was worse. Mislovic could not bear seeing his men look at him like this. Tied up, a gun to his head. Like a worthless hostage.

When they reached the front room, Mislovic's men stood just inside the door waiting for orders. Mislovic took charge immediately.

"Don't anybody shoot this bastard. Don't do anything. I am going to kill him myself. If you shoot him or try anything, I will kill you, too. Get back. Stay out of my way."

Devlin watched them move away from the door. He pushed Mislovic forward. Just before he reached the door, Devlin swung Mislovic around so he was facing his men. Devlin walked backwards out of the door, pulling Mislovic with him onto Berwick Street.

It was mid-morning, so there weren't many people on the street. If they were watching the scene, Devlin didn't look at them or pay attention to them. He kept his eyes on Zenko and the other two men standing in the doorway. He had no way of knowing if any of them still had a weapon. He turned Mislovic around and walked forward, still looking back at Zenko and the others. When Devlin was about ten yards away from the entrance, Zenko and Roland stepped out onto the sidewalk. Devlin had the feeling the third man had run back into the office to get their discarded guns.

Mislovic stopped walking for a moment. Devlin pulled hard

on the Manriki and said, "Don't make me jerk your chain, tough guy. Walk. Let's go."

Mislovic said, "Devlin, even if you get away, you're still dead."

"Wait a minute. Did you think of that line just now? That's amazing. Do they say stuff like that in Yugoslavia, too? I mean I've never heard it quite like that before. You know, with the Slav accent."

Mislovic would not rise to the bait this time. He simply said, "You're dead."

Devlin dropped his sarcasm and said, "Well, then I guess I'd better shoot you right now. I mean, that's the only logical course of action, since if you live, you'll want to kill me."

Mislovic stopped talking.

They were halfway down the block. Zenko and the others were now following them from a distance.

Suddenly, a red Saab came around the corner and passed Devlin and Mislovic. Then the car screeched to a halt. Hinton and Oliver's driver Louis jumped out of the car.

Devlin and Mislovic were now almost at the corner, Hinton and Louis in the middle of the block, Zenko and the others behind them.

Devlin spun Mislovic around so that he was facing Hinton. Devlin locked eyes with Hinton and knew who he was immediately. Hinton did not hesitate for a moment. He seemed to glide toward Devlin, his gun in his right hand, held against his leg, pointing down. He came right at Devlin and Mislovic. Devlin knew he was trying to get in range for a shot, but he also knew that no matter what the distance, it would be almost impossible for Hinton to take him out without killing Mislovic.

Hinton advanced straight toward them up the narrow sidewalk. Devlin stood his ground. He and Mislovic watched Hinton come closer. Devlin stepped a little farther behind Mislovic and loosened the Manriki Gusari chain a bit, but kept the machine pistol pressed firmly into Mislovic's head.

Devlin spoke softly into Mislovic's ear, "As dumb as you are, Mr. Mills, I want you to watch what your ally is doing. You try to help them out by turning me over, and look how they repay you. You know he's going to shoot you to get me, don't you?"

Mislovic wouldn't give Devlin the satisfaction of an answer, but he was infuriated, both that Devlin was right and that Hinton was ready to shoot him to get to Devlin. Hinton raised his gun. Devlin stayed right behind Mislovic. Mislovic forced himself not to cringe as Hinton took aim. But just before Hinton could pull the trigger, Zenko threw himself at him and grabbed him from behind in a fierce bear hug. Roland stepped in front of Louis and put a big hand up. Louis slapped the hand away, and in seconds they were brawling.

Hinton knew that Zenko had taken away his chance to shoot, so he did not resist. But he kept his gun ready in his hand and resolved to shoot Zenko the moment he was able to. Roland was having a surprising amount of trouble subduing Louis.

Devlin allowed Mislovic to watch the fighting for just a few seconds, then calmly turned him around, walked to the corner, and hailed a taxi.

Mislovic was preoccupied enough with how close he had come to being shot by Hinton that he went along with Devlin and stepped into the taxi.

The two men sat back in the roomy London cab. The driver had his head out the window to watch the fight taking place back on Berwick Street. Devlin tapped on the Plexiglas partition and said, "Let's go, driver—unless you're planning to get out and mix it up back there."

The driver pulled away quickly and asked, "Where to?"

Devlin said, "Leicester Square."

In the taxi, Devlin pulled off his jacket and draped it over his left arm, hiding the machine pistol. When they reached the square, Devlin paid the fare and pulled Mislovic out of the cab.

They walked through the wide-open space of Leicester Square, Devlin close by Mislovic, with his coat over the Grendel and the machine pistol pressed firmly into Mislovic's ribs. Devlin looked around at the large movie theater marquees.

"Feel like a movie?"

Mislovic didn't answer.

Devlin said, "Oh, I guess not—no Yugo subtitles."

Devlin steered Mislovic toward the center of the square and headed for a subground comfort station.

"Come on, Mr. Mills. In case you messed your pants back there, you can clean up downstairs."

Devlin marched Mislovic down into the men's bathroom. He dug out a twenty-pence piece for Mislovic and shoved him forward as the pneumatic gate winked open. This put Devlin on the other side, but he simply told Mislovic, "Go ahead— make a run for it. Let's see if I can shoot you before you get into a stall."

Mislovic stood where he was, glaring at Devlin, while Devlin picked out a coin for himself and walked into the large underground bathroom. For a public facility, it was clean and well kept. There was a long row of sinks and urinals on the left and toilet stalls on the right.

There was one man at the urinal finishing up. Devlin ignored him. He pushed Mislovic backwards and said, "Pick a stall."

"What are you going to do?"

"What do you care? No one is going to see what I do to you. Step in."

Devlin shoved Mislovic into a stall and stood blocking the open door. Mislovic faced Devlin, glaring at him. Devlin looked back at him with a blank expression. Suddenly, before Mislovic could even see it, Devlin delivered a fast, dead-on-target front kick right to the Yugoslav's solar plexus.

The kick sent Mislovic tumbling over the toilet and banging into the wall behind him. He was paralyzed. Unable to breathe. It was a knockout blow. Mislovic collapsed like a deflated balloon and crumpled down between the porcelain bowl and the wall. Devlin looked at the man who would have allowed the first woman Devlin had ever loved to die at the hands of people who used machetes on humans. For a moment, he thought about how easy it would have been to twist the chain just enough to sever his trachea. Then Devlin pressed the flush button with his foot and walked out.

CHAPTER 15

THE BRAWL BETWEEN Mislovic's men and the Yardies did not last long. Pete came running out with Roland's machine pistol and yelled that they should get the hell off the street before the cops showed up. The warning and the machine pistol convinced Hinton and Louis to cooperate.

Zenko grabbed Hinton's gun and hustled everybody into the back meeting room. They searched Louis. He was unarmed. Zenko declared that no one should move until Mislovic returned, or until they found out he was dead. He took the Grendel from Pete and pointed it at Hinton and Louis.

Zenko was ready to shoot someone in the face, particularly Hinton, and the Yardie knew it. But even with the threat of death, Hinton had a difficult time holding back from fighting his way out. He knew that it was only a matter of time before Devlin would get back to the woman and hide her. The tall one who had beaten these fools would certainly go to her now.

But Hinton calmed himself. He told Zenko, "Take it easy, mon. Point the gun someplace else."

He sat down at one of the tables and placed his hands on the flat surface. He would wait a little longer. He himself wanted to know if the Yugoslav leader had been killed by the tall one.

Mislovic was not dead, but he was hurting. He regained consciousness in less than a minute, but he was so disoriented and confused that it took him almost a full minute to pull himself up from between the toilet and the wall and remember what had happened to him. His sternum felt as if it had been cracked, and his neck hurt so terribly that his first thought was that someone had slit his throat and left him for dead. But when he looked down at his Egyptian cotton white shirt, he didn't see any blood. He felt his neck where the chain had been. There was only a smear of blood on his fingers. Devlin's chain had done little more than break through the skin.

Mislovic finally staggered out of the subground toilet, just as Devlin was switching trains at the Embankment station to head for the Tower Bridge stop.

Mislovic came out in the middle of Leicester Square. He gave up trying to find a taxi and decided to walk back to Witmans. It was all coming back to him now, and he was ready to kill.

Just about the time Mislovic walked into his headquarters in Soho, Devlin finally emerged from the Underground at Tower Bridge. The Underground ride had taken a total of eleven minutes, but he knew he didn't have much time. He looked around quickly to orient himself. He couldn't quite see Tower Bridge, but there was the Thames, flowing past the Tower of London. Devlin had always been amused that the squat little fortress in front of him was named the "Tower" of London. The towers bordering the old redoubt were the lowest structures in the area.

He quickly made his way through an underpass and came up on Tower Hill Street, the wide avenue that led to the bridge. Annie's loft was a long walk away. He was on the wrong side of the river, and it had already taken too much time to get this far.

He still carried the Grendel machine pistol under his coat. He was walking too fast, attracting attention from tourists as well as locals. Devlin cursed to himself. He looked for a taxi, even though it was not what he really needed. As he came upon the bridge, he saw his chance. There was a Vauxhall van waiting at the traffic light. It was painted a deep green with ornate lettering on the sides and back that said: Frank Wiley & Sons, Purveyors of Fine Meat and Foods.

Devlin guessed the van was delivering provisions to the string of restaurants across the bridge at Butlers Wharf. Just as the light turned green and traffic started, he stepped into the street, opened the passenger door, and jumped into the moving vehicle.

The driver was an older man, Devlin estimated in his sixties, dressed in a white coat and a leather cap. He turned to Devlin, more surprised than angry, and said, "What?"

Devlin held up a hand and said, "Are you going over the bridge?"

The man responded in a cockney accent made less comprehensible by his anger and surprise, "Bloody hell, what you think you're doing?"

Devlin pulled back his coat and held up the gun. "Sorry. No time for discussion—just head across there and I'll explain what to do. Be careful. Don't say anything or I'll have to do something nasty like shoot off a kneecap. No kidding now. Just drive."

The man clamped his mouth shut and looked forward.

Devlin asked, "You have a wife? Just nod, yes or no."

The man nodded yes.

"Kids?"

Yes.

"Grandkids?"

The man nodded yes vigorously.

"Do what I tell you and you'll see them tonight. Maybe even this afternoon. It'll be an adventure instead of a tragedy."

They were halfway across the bridge and Devlin wished he had a map.

He asked the driver, "Where's your book of maps?"

The driver pulled out a well-worn copy of *London A to Z*. It was the large size. Devlin took it from him and said, "Thanks."

They had reached the other side. Devlin said, "Go straight and find a place to pull over after that traffic light."

The driver drove across Tooley Street and managed to pull out of traffic and stop about ten feet past a bus shelter. He turned to Devlin, who had just located the neighborhood in the book of maps.

Devlin didn't look up, but kept the Grendel out and pointed at the driver.

"Just sit there, Dad. Don't be nervous. Don't do anything."

Devlin continued to study the map.

"London. There isn't one goddamn numbered street in the whole town, is there?"

The driver didn't answer.

"Okay, here we are. I've got it. If they don't all run one way the wrong way."

Devlin looked back at the driver, who was clearly worried.

"Look, I'm sorry about this. It's truly an emergency. I may have another five minutes to save a woman and her baby. Now I'm going to give you one hundred pounds. And one pound. You put the hundred pounds in your pocket and go sit at that bus stop for about ten or fifteen minutes. Or twenty if you don't mind. Then take the one pound, get up and walk to a pay phone, and call your boss. Tell him what happened. You might want to consider forgetting what I look like, but I leave that up to your conscience. Tell him I'll call and let you know where you can get the van. Is the phone number painted on the side?"

"Yes."

It was the first word the driver had spoken since Devlin had told him not to speak.

Devlin handed him the money.

"Are you all right then, sir?"

"Yes," the driver said.

"Okay. Get out and go sit down."

Devlin watched the man do exactly as he was told, then moved into the driver's seat on the right side, awkwardly shifted the van into gear—he was not yet accustomed to shifting with his left hand or driving on the left side—and jerked the truck into traffic.

He looked back behind him for a moment and saw that the van was loaded with various cuts of meat packed in boxes and hanging from the ceiling of the van, iced boxes of poultry and fish, an assortment of institutional-size canned goods, and bags of rice and potatoes. He wasn't sure there would be enough room for his passengers without dumping a good deal of the food on the sidewalk.

As Devlin struggled through the unfamiliar London streets and streaming traffic, Mislovic walked into his headquarters on Berwick Street.

The minute he appeared, Hinton jumped up and headed for the door. Louis stayed exactly where he was. Hinton didn't even turn around to see if he was coming. Zenko lifted the pistol at Hinton, but Hinton came right at him. When Mislovic reached out and pushed the Grendel down, Hinton deftly and swiftly reached inside Zenko's coat and pulled out his nine-millimeter.

Mislovic told Zenko, "Let him go."

Louis bolted for the door and had to run to catch up with Hinton.

Devlin jumped the curb at Gainsford Street and stopped the van right in front of Annie's lobby door. He had made it to her loft in three minutes, but only because he'd turned the wrong way down a one-way street.

He jumped out of the van, stepped into the lobby, and quickly pressed the intercom button three times.

Up in the loft, Ben calmly swung the Mossberg into position as he crossed over to the intercom. He pressed the speak button and said, "Yes?"

"Ben, it's me. I'm coming up. Tell Annie to get Elizabeth ready. We have to get out of there. Now."

Ben turned to see Annie entering the living room. She had heard the message. She stood unmoving. Ben told her in a firm but kindly way, "Best hurry, ma'am."

For a moment, she thought maybe she was late for the appointment with the police, but quickly dismissed that as silly. Devlin's voice told her something was wrong. She hurried back to Elizabeth's room. The little girl was just finishing getting dressed.

"Come on, Lizzie, finish up."

Elizabeth was wearing a plaid skirt, white socks and sneakers, and a white undershirt. She was just wiggling into a white blouse that buttoned up the front. Annie knew the buttons were going to take some time, but didn't want to upset Elizabeth by suggesting she wear something else.

"Okay, hurry up then."

Annie ran on to her own bedroom.

The elevator arrived, and Devlin hurried toward the loft. Ben had him in sight through the peephole and opened the repaired door for him.

"Ben, get your equipment. Load that shotgun with the

heaviest gauge you have. Downstairs there's a green van right in front of the building. Set up in the rear so you can protect the back. And make room for Annie and the kid."

Without a word, Ben walked back to the chair he had been sitting in and grabbed a large leather bag. He placed the Mossberg shotgun in the bag and headed for the door. Devlin ran to the back of the apartment.

Annie met him in the hallway.

"What's the matter? What's happening?"

"Pack some clothes. Take whatever money you have and your passports. Just take what you can get in one bag. One bag. Where's the kid?"

"In her room. What's wrong? What happened?"

"I'll explain to you on the way. Is she all right?"

"Yes. Where are we going?"

"Wherever the next flight out of here takes us. Come on."

Annie hurried into her bedroom, opened her top dresser drawer, reached into the back, and grabbed a tight roll of bills. She fished around and found her passport and Elizabeth's. Then she rushed to her closet and pulled a large nylon carryall down from the shelf and started stuffing it with clothes.

Devlin leaned into the bedroom and told Annie, "Come on, that's enough. Leave some room for your daughter's things. Let's go."

Devlin checked his watch. It was nearly eleven. He found Waldron's card in his back pocket and rushed out to the living room to call and tell him why they were missing their appointment.

Annie stopped packing and followed Devlin out. "I wish you'd tell me what happened."

"I found out you have more enemies than you think. It's stupid to stay here. We'll get to someplace safer, then sort it out."

"What about the police?"

"I'm calling them now. Let's go."

Annie tried to keep her hands from shaking as she shoved a few of Elizabeth's stuffed animals into her bag along with underwear, jeans, and shirts. She finished by pushing a pair of sneakers into the bag and told the child they were going on a trip. She was surprised when Elizabeth did not ask any questions except when they were coming back.

"Oh, in just a few days, honey," Annie said.

"What about school?"

"You'll be back on Monday, dear. It'll be all right."

Devlin stood at the phone waiting for someone at the division to pick up. Finally someone answered, but when he asked for Chief Inspector Waldron, they put him on hold. He waited almost a minute, then slammed the phone down.

Devlin ran back to Elizabeth's room, leaned in, and said, "Okay, time to go. Now, Annie."

Elizabeth had no idea who Devlin was. He smiled and tried to appear calm and friendly, but the little girl became unnerved and confused.

"Mommy, who's that?"

"That's Jack, honey. He's helping us."

"Why?"

"Because Daddy's not here now. He's a friend."

Elizabeth began to cry.

"Where's Daddy?"

"He's away. Don't worry about that now, honey. Come on."

Elizabeth pointed to the buttons on her tiny white blouse. She had only managed to close three out of five.

"But I'm not dressed."

Devlin reached over and took the carryall out of Annie's hand. Annie reached down and picked up Elizabeth.

"Come on, honey. Don't worry. We'll dress in the car."

On the way out of the loft, Devlin grabbed coats for both Annie and Elizabeth and held the door for them. Annie carried her daughter in her arms and walked quickly to the elevator. Devlin slammed the door and followed them.

When the three of them reached the street, Ben was in the back of the Vauxhall van smashing out the rear window with a tire iron he had found in the van. Little Elizabeth flinched at the noise of the shattering rear window.

Inside the van, Ben had stacked up several cartons of canned goods to form a seat near the rear window. There was barely enough room in the small European-size van for Ben to sit at the back window without hitting his head on the roof.

He had also managed to clear out an area in the middle for

Annie and Elizabeth. Devlin noticed that Ben had stacked the foodstuffs right up to the ceiling.

Devlin helped Annie and Elizabeth climb into the back, then handed them their coats and ran around to the front. He climbed into the driver's seat, started the engine, and pulled away from the loft building.

Devlin had only a general idea of how to get to Heathrow from the south side of the river. He picked up the *A to Z* map book and pressed the spine down to keep the front spread open. It only took him a moment to figure out that M4 would take him to Heathrow.

He yelled back, "What's the quickest way to Heathrow? M4?"

Annie responded, "Yes. Go on Tooley to Kent and look for A3. It'll be a left. Follow the signs."

"Okay, sit tight."

Ben wedged himself into his corner and watched the back window. He was wrapped in his Kevlar long-coat, loading heavy-gauge shot into the Mossberg. The shells were specially packed to disperse the shot in the widest spread. Ben looked like a grizzled old wrangler riding shotgun, which is pretty much what he was.

Behind him, Annie and Elizabeth huddled on the floor between the meat and produce cartons. Elizabeth was so distracted with riding on the floor of a van that she had stopped crying. And the sight of Ben seemed to mesmerize her. She stared at him and clung to her mother.

Devlin pulled up and stopped the van. He looked quickly at his map and realized he couldn't get back onto Tower Bridge from Shad Thames, so he wrenched the wheel and turned left. There was barely room for one car on the narrow road. Just as he made his turn he saw the red Saab speeding his way.

Devlin edged over to the left and covered his face with his right hand, hoping that Hinton would not see him as he passed. He turned to Ben and yelled, "If that Saab comes back, shoot it."

Ben looked through the back window and rested the front edge of the Mossberg's barrel on the window frame where he had punched out the glass. The Saab sped right past them and braked to take the turn back onto Gainsford. But as Hinton made the left turn, the broken back window and the tip of Ben's shotgun barrel caught his eye.

In the same breath, Hinton cursed and thanked his god for having guided his eye. The street was too narrow for a fast turn, so he shoved the car into first gear and roared off toward the next corner and turned left. This put him on Afone Street parallel to Curlew, traveling in the same direction as Devlin's van.

Hinton was driving the wrong way down a one-way street. Louis was in the passenger seat yelling for him to watch what he was doing. Hinton's response was to shove his foot onto the accelerator so hard that he almost lifted himself off the driver's seat. The tires squealed and the car fishtailed down the street. An oncoming car lurched onto the sidewalk to avoid him. Hinton swerved to his side and smacked into a set of "Bottle Bank" containers used for recycling. They looked like color-coded giant thimbles turned upside down. The Saab cracked into the first round container and split it apart. There was an explosion of bottles and glass, but Hinton never took his foot off the accelerator. The car bounced off the next two containers and kept on going.

On Curlew, one block over, Devlin was stuck behind slow-moving traffic. There was nothing he could do. Iron stanchions had been sunk into the sidewalk along the entire block to protect the buildings from traffic. He growled in frustration and pounded the steering wheel. If the Yardie hadn't seen him, he'd soon know that Annie's apartment was empty, and then he'd be back on the street.

Devlin checked his side-view mirror for sight of the red Saab.

Hinton raced through a stoplight and turned left on Jamaica Street, heading back toward Devlin. He took the turn too fast and slid into two parked cars. Sheet metal scraped and banged, glass shattered, and the side-view mirror on the Saab was ripped off, but Hinton just kept on going. He reached the Curlew intersection just before Devlin pulled up to the stop sign. He wanted to block the intersection, but he was going so fast that even though he slammed on the brakes, he skidded across the intersection and smashed into a streetlight on the corner. His car hit the base, bounced up and knocked over the streetlamp, then dropped back down onto the base. Hinton shoved the gearshift into reverse and tried to back off the base, but all he succeeded in doing was tearing off his transmission cover and destroying a section of gears.

Devlin finally made it to the intersection. He had heard Hinton's car bang into the street pole, but was surprised when he saw the red Saab hung up on the pole's base. He wrenched the van into a sharp right turn and accelerated. Hinton shoved his door open and jumped out of his car, gun in hand. As the van spun around the corner, he fired at it. Ben immediately returned fire with three blasts from the Mossberg. The shotgun fire inside the van sounded like a series of small bombs. Hinton dove back over the hood of his car and crouched down low. Heavy-gauge bursts of double-aught pellets raked across the body of the Saab, smashing it like a succession of giant fists. The Saab's right rear tire blew; the trunk lid exploded off its hinges; the rear window shattered. Safety glass and shotgun pellets sprayed the inside of the car. Louis had smacked his head into the windshield when Hinton hit the streetlamp and was too dizzy to get out of the car. His head and face were splattered with shot. The wounds were superficial, but he had pulled away from the blasts so abruptly that his head hit the passenger-side window with enough force to break the safety plate glass.

Devlin had the van straightened out and now accelerated hard to put distance between himself and Hinton. Inside, boxes of meat and crates of vegetables tumbled down on Annie and Elizabeth. Annie had covered the child with her body, but she in turn was covered by the meat and produce.

Hinton was insane with rage. Nothing could have stopped him except a direct blast from the Mossberg. He jumped up from behind the car and emptied the rest of his bullets at the rear of the fleeing van. Ben spun away from the window and sat back in the corner, waiting for the gunshots to end before he returned fire. Most of Hinton's shots hit the van. Several bullets ripped through the back windows, smashing into meat and canned goods, sending splatters of beef, bones, chicken, and tomato sauce throughout the interior.

Devlin thought he still might be able to get away, but before

he was even halfway to the next intersection, two cars
screeched to a halt and blocked it.

All eight doors of the cars flew open at once. It was Mislovic with his crew, armed and ready to kill.

Devlin slammed on the brakes. Ben came tumbling off his
boxes, flying toward the front, plowing into a stack of meat,
almost landing on Annie and Elizabeth.

Mislovic and his men had everything . . . machine pistols,
automatic handguns, and a Kalashnikov. They ran around and
crouched behind the two cars, shooting as they did so.

Calls once again started pouring into the Tower Bridge Division, which was just two blocks away. The constable on duty
in the CAD room could hardly believe a second shooting incident was erupting in the same neighborhood the morning after the first incident.

Inside the Vauxhall, Devlin yelled, "Stay down!" He pulled
out the Grendel and wrenched the steering wheel all the way
to the left; keeping the wheel turned, he pushed the accelerator down and crouched below the windshield. As the van
turned away from them, the Yugoslavs continued firing at it.
Most of the shots were absorbed by the side of the truck, and
the stacks of meat and canned goods and foodstuffs, but the
windshield was blown out and glass sprayed through the van,
along with more meat, blood, bones, and exploding cans of
sauces and soups. It looked as if a food processor had erupted
inside the van.

Devlin was protected by the engine and fire wall. Annie and
Elizabeth were under a load of meat and food. Ben had his
Kevlar greatcoat. They were still alive.

Devlin shoved the machine pistol out through the busted
windshield and held the trigger as he put the van into reverse
to get enough room to turn back down the street. His shots
sent Mislovic and his men ducking behind their cars. Devlin
shoved the van into first gear and started a sharp turn. As he
struggled to straighten the van out, Ben somehow managed to
get back on his feet. Devlin finished the turn, and Ben stood
up and wedged himself between the floor and the roof and
started shooting out the rear window again. The blasts
sprayed into Mislovic's men and cars. Shotgun pellets tore

into sheet metal, exploded tires, and ricocheted off the street. Mislovic's men went down and stayed down.

Devlin knew the only way out was back past Hinton, who had started to run up the street when he saw that Mislovic's men had blocked Devlin's escape.

Devlin peered over the dashboard to get his bearings. Hinton was standing in the middle of the street, directly in the path of the van, aiming his gun, now loaded with a fresh clip. Devlin ducked down, but kept going straight on. If Hinton stood his ground, so be it.

Hinton stepped to the side to avoid the oncoming van just as Mislovic's men started firing again. He wanted to shoot into the driver-side window, but the hail of bullets coming from up the street forced him down between two cars for cover. Devlin sped past him in what was left of the van. Hinton tried to shoot into the driver-side window, missed, then stood up and unloaded his gun at the battered Vauxhall.

Both rear tires were blown, so the van was spinning on torn-up shreds of rubber and iron rims. Sparks were spraying back from the rims as if they were Roman candles. The radiator had four holes in it, and steam was pouring out. The engine was cracked and losing pressure, but Devlin kept it revved and in gear. He looked up just in time to angle for the small opening between the rear of the wrecked Saab and the corner. He steered as well as he could without rear tires, but smacked into the Saab's rear bumper. The van careened and bumped through the intersection and headed for Abbey Lane. Police sirens were screaming toward the location. Devlin hoped he could get out of the area soon enough to avoid them.

Mislovic and his men slowly stood up from behind their cars, which had both been damaged by Ben's shotgun blasts. All the tires facing the van were flat. Uniformed police constables were already coming up toward them from the Tower Bridge Division around the corner. Two of Mislovic's men had run after the van, and he told the four men still on the street, "Get out of here. Now."

They shoved their guns under their coats and took off in separate directions down the narrow streets surrounding the ambush.

Devlin pushed the dying van for five blocks until the engine finally seized. He guided it to a curb and shut off the ignition. The Vauxhall was dead.

Devlin turned and saw Ben reloading the Mossberg.

"Ben, get them out."

Devlin shoved open the door on his side and stepped out into the middle of the street. Ben shouldered open the rear door of the van. He turned back and grabbed Annie around the waist and lifted her off the child. Annie clutched Elizabeth, and with Ben pulling them out of the mess, they struggled onto the street. Ben held Annie for a moment to make sure she could stand on her own. He looked her over quickly, trying to discern if there was any blood mixed in with the mess of food stains on her clothes and face. She did not seem to have been hit by any bullets.

The traffic light had stopped a line of vehicles at the intersection, and Devlin ran up to the biggest car on his side of the street. It was a late-model Rover, driven by a woman in her sixties. Devlin pulled open the door. The terrified woman desperately clutched the door handle inside and was pulled halfway out of the car.

Devlin removed her hand as gently as possible from the handle, lifted her back into the car, and yelled, "Move over. Please!"

The woman could hardly stop him. Devlin lifted her out of the driver's seat and dropped her in the passenger seat. Her foot came off the brake and the car jerked forward in gear and the engine stalled. He reached into the car, turned off the ignition and pulled out the keys, and pulled back the emergency brake.

Ben was half carrying Annie and Elizabeth to the Rover with one hand; in the other he held his big leather satchel and Annie's nylon carryall. He opened the back door of the Rover and guided Annie and Elizabeth into the backseat. Elizabeth, who had been covered by her mother, was fairly clean, but Annie was a mess.

The woman who owned the car was yelling at Devlin, but he was standing with one foot on the street, watching Ben and checking to see what was behind them. Two of Mislovic's men were coming toward them from about three blocks away. Hinton was nowhere in sight.

Ignoring the woman did not help quiet her. She started pounding the dashboard and demanding her keys back.

Devlin finally turned back into the car, grabbed her shoulder, and shook it hard, once. "Stop!" he yelled.

She was shocked into silence.

"Don't move. Don't talk. This is an emergency."

She froze. That was good enough for Devlin.

Devlin popped the trunk. Ben threw the bags in and turned with the Mossberg pointing down the street at Mislovic's men. He was ready to stand and cover their escape.

"Forget them, Ben, Get in!"

The big man shoved himself into the backseat. Annie picked Elizabeth up onto her lap so he could fit into the car. The next wave of traffic was upon them, beeping their horns. Devlin restarted the car, and they were off.

Back at the scene of the shooting, it was chaotic. Many of the people who worked in the art galleries and design firms and other businesses located in the area had come out into the narrow streets. The aftermath looked like a strange auto accident with no victims. People kept staring at the cars and looking for blood and broken bodies. They had mistaken the sound of exploding weapons and bullets cracking into sheet metal for the sound of colliding cars.

Police were surrounding the area, but did not have much of an idea as to what to do with the rather peaceful crowd of people milling about.

Two armed Trojan Units had arrived and were trying to decide with their commanding officers whether to stay on the scene or search for fleeing shooters. The incredible number of spent cartridges on the street and the obvious devastation to the vehicles prompted the cops to keep looking for bodies or shooters that simply weren't there.

Mislovic and his men were several blocks away. Hinton was already calmly walking across the wide expanse of the Tower Bridge. He hadn't bothered to reload his gun or look back at his wrecked prize car. He had no idea if Louis or anyone else was dead or alive, and he didn't care. All he knew was that once more he had failed to kill the tall one and the woman.

Mislovic, too, knew he had missed his opportunity, even though he had taken the ridiculous chance of waging open warfare on a London street. Zenko, sweating and mumbling curses in a mix of Croation and English, still carried his machine pistol under his jacket. The heat of the muzzle didn't help cool him off.

Mislovic told him, "Put that gun in a trash basket. We can't take a chance getting caught with it, and you smell of gunpowder enough as it is."

Zenko reluctantly did as he was told.

Mislovic continued walking until they reached the promenade along the river.

"Come," he said. "Let's eat. We can sit outside so we don't stink up the place."

"I think we should get out of here."

"And risk running into all the cops crawling around? No. We'll sit and have a civilized lunch, just like the businessmen do. I need a drink, anyhow; my damn throat hurts and my chest feels like it's cracked."

"We must kill that man. Now."

For the first time in a long time, Mislovic raised his voice to Zenko. "Where is he? Do you see him?"

Zenko frowned.

"Do you know where he is?"

"We should find him."

"After my goddamn lunch."

Mislovic led Zenko toward the tables set up on the outside terrace of the Butlers Wharf Chop House. The overcast weather was slightly chilly for al fresco dining, but by the middle of the lunch hour, every outside table would be full. The Chop House was one of those determinedly stylish restaurants that practically demanded people patronize it, if for no other reason than it had a marvelous view of London back across the Thames.

Mislovic made an effort to appear relaxed and waved over the host, a stylish young man dressed in a three-button black suit, white shirt, and black tie. Mislovic compared the cut of his now-rumpled three-piece suit with the host's. His did appear to be out of fashion. Another thing to stoke his anger. For perhaps the tenth time that morning Mislovic envisioned shooting Jack Devlin, but he put the idea out of his mind, forced a smile, and said, "We'd like a table for lunch. Out here."

"Certainly, sir."

The host seated them away from the best view in a row of tables all the way over by the French doors that formed the restaurant's north wall. Mislovic was too furious at what had turned into a horrible morning to bother protesting. He sat down and mollified himself with the fact that the bad seat would at least hide him somewhat from the rest of the lunch crowd. Before the host left, Mislovic ordered a pint of Theakston's Bitters and a shot of whiskey. Zenko grunted, "Me also."

The host smiled and said, "Your waiter will be right with you."

Mislovic said, "That's fine. But don't let the waiter come to this table without our drinks. Do you understand?"

The host frowned at Mislovic.

"Is my English clear?"

The host took a closer look at the two men sitting in front of him, smiled, and decided to say, "Certainly, sir."

Mislovic smiled back and imagined putting a bullet in the host's left ear as he walked back into the restaurant.

CHAPTER 16

DEVLIN LOOKED INTO the rearview mirror. Annie's hair and clothes were stained, much of it the color of blood. Her face was rigid with tension and fear. She sat in the backseat, holding Elizabeth, not moving. Because there was no moaning or crying, Devlin assumed the stains were from the foodstuffs and meat rather than their own blood. Even if she and the child were in shock, the pain would have been hitting them by now. Ben, on the other hand, was unmarked, but if he had been shot, Devlin knew he wouldn't utter a sound. Devlin asked, "Were you hit?"

"No, sir. But something caught you on your head there— you're drippin' some."

Devlin felt around the crown of his head and found the cold, wet spot. There was a small sharp sting when he touched it. Something had creased his scalp above his right eye. He wondered why he hadn't felt the blood seeping out. Now he had blood on his right hand, and because he didn't want to stain the steering wheel of this borrowed car, he held the hand up.

The woman who owned the Rover looked at him, then opened her purse and gave him a white handkerchief trimmed in a delicate filigree.

Devlin rubbed the handkerchief between his fingers to clean the blood, then pressed the soiled cloth against his wound. He told the woman, "Thank you. I'm sorry to involve you in this, but . . ."

"What are you going to do with me?"

Devlin saw that they were approaching the entrance to the M4. He looked at his watch. It had taken them much too long to get this far.

"We're going to drive your car to Heathrow Airport. You

might as well stay with the car. You'll drop us off and be on your way with money for cleaning and gas. And my apologies for the inconvenience. I'm sorry, but I had no choice."

The woman stared straight ahead. She was a trim lady, very neatly dressed in a gray suit that buttoned up to her neck. She had regained control of herself and calmly answered Devlin without looking at him. "All right." She smoothed her skirt and sat primly in her seat, looking out her window.

Devlin glanced quickly at her and noted that her mouth was pursed. The proverbial stiff upper lip?

After a few minutes on the highway, Annie finally spoke from the backseat.

"What did that police say when you called?"

Devlin glanced at his watch again. "I didn't get through to that guy who wanted to see us. I'm hoping we can get out of here before he shuts us down."

Chief Inspector James Waldron, however, was doing everything in his power to shut Devlin down. In less than twenty-four hours Devlin had created more pressure on Waldron than he had experienced in his entire fifteen-year career with the Metropolitan Police.

There were nearly thirty thousand men and women on the London Met, but on this particular morning it seemed as if the entire attention of the command staff was focused on James Waldron.

Because the Tower Bridge Division was a rather small station house, its highest-ranking officer was a superintendent, one command level above Waldron's rank. Most other divisions in the city had a chief superintendent. The next ranks up included a deputy commissioner, an assistant commissioner, a commander, and finally the commissioner, who was answerable only to the home secretary.

The Devlin affair had reverberated all the way to the commissioner's office, leaving in its wake every commanding officer down to Waldron either scrambling, fuming, or hiding. It was becoming painfully clear that more gunshots had been fired in the last twenty-four hours in a small area of London than had been fired in the last twenty-four years. The London Police Force did not take kindly to running gun battles, even if they occurred on an out-of-the-way street in the Tower Bridge Division.

Waldron's commanding officer, Superintendent Thomas Fenton, had no intention of having his career ruined because of someone in his command. For self-preservation, he had not informed his superiors that Jack Devlin was supposed to have been sitting in the divisional interview room that morning at eleven o'clock, instead of driving a stolen van and firing a Grendel P-30 machine pistol at armed villains shooting more automatic weapons back at him than an IRA terrorist brigade.

However, Fenton had made sure to tell Waldron that if Jack Devlin and the woman Anne Petchek were not apprehended and in his office by the end of his shift, the crucifixion of Christ on the bloody cross would look like *Noddy's Day Out* compared to what he would do to Waldron.

Waldron knew very well that Fenton considered him his only competition in his plans for career advancement. He knew that no matter what Fenton said, he was going to use this mess as a means to ruin him. Waldron was determined not to make it easy for him.

Waldron was using the most powerful weapon in his arsenal: his phone. He had already called in an All Ports Warning, which automatically notified every police officer and Customs official in the country to detain and question anyone fitting the descriptions of Devlin, Annie, and Elizabeth. The warning was given first-rank attention because a child was involved, and because Waldron had specifically noted that Devlin and Annie were considered to be armed and dangerous.

Waldron had then personally contacted the commanders of the BTP—British Transport Police—at Heathrow, Gatwick, and all the London train stations. The Metropolitan Police held the BTP in low regard, usually referring to them as "Drain Runners," but Waldron knew that if they were alerted and made to feel as if a mission were important, they could provide invaluable service at transportation centers in and around London.

Waldron had then exercised his authority as chief inspector to personally tap into the PNC—Police National Computer—and put every constabulary in England on notice to be on the lookout for Devlin, Annie, and Elizabeth. Again, he had specifically entered an armed-and-dangerous notification.

Finally, Waldron had begun to call his personal contacts in Special Branch to elicit their help. This group was established in the 1890s to gather intelligence and handle the Irish problem. Special Branch had contacts in every police force in the U.K. as well as many contacts throughout Europe. Locating and apprehending people for questioning was one of its specialties.

By the time Devlin finally pulled into Heathrow, the net had already tightened around him considerably.

Devlin had decided to fly out on either a domestic or an European Economic Community destination flight, figuring there would be much less security for those flights.

The traffic into the domestic terminals at Heathrow was bumper-to-bumper. Devlin looked at his watch. He knew his escape window was closing rapidly.

Devlin fought the traffic and juggled possibilities. He decided to avoid British Airways, even though it probably had the most flights out. He eliminated Aer Lingus, too. The police communications to those subsidized airlines would probably be the most direct. He avoided the German airlines—too thorough and officious. He decided they should get to the Continent and make their way to the U.S. from there. He spotted the terminal where Alitalia was located. It was big enough to have a good number of flights to faraway locations, and perhaps disorganized enough to neglect checking every passenger carefully.

He pulled the Rover to the curb and turned to the woman he had just made into a car-jacking victim.

"Madam, again I apologize. I just want you to know that you've helped save the lives of this woman and child."

Devlin waited for her to turn and look at Annie and Elizabeth. He would have liked for Elizabeth to begin quietly crying at that moment, but the child looked so bereft and confused that Devlin decided they might just get away with what they had done to this lady without Elizabeth's tears.

He remained silent until the woman finally turned away from looking at Elizabeth.

"Now, you can certainly go to the police and report what

has happened, but I must warn you that you're going to be involved in long hours of questioning. The people who are after this woman and child have caused a great deal of trouble. They have already killed two people that we know of. So if you decide to go to the police, be prepared for that.

"On the other hand, you can take this money for gas and whatever cleanup you have to do, along with our deep thanks, and just drive to where you were going when we unfortunately had to borrow your car."

The woman took the hundred-pound note Devlin held out and said, "Just tell me one thing, young man."

"What?"

"Have any of you committed any crimes? Don't lie to me, because I will know if you are lying."

Devlin said, "No, ma'am. Not in this country."

The woman gave Devlin a look that indicated she was sure it would be just a matter of time before he did commit a crime in England.

"Are you leaving the country?"

"As soon as we can."

"All right then. Keep your money and go."

"Thank you."

"And take care of that dear child. She's the reason I'm listening to your foolishness."

Devlin knew when to quit. He said, "I will," and got out of the car. Ben opened the door for Annie and Elizabeth, grabbed the bags, and followed them into the terminal.

During the ride Annie had wiped her hair and face clean of the most obvious stains. When she got out of the car, she took off her coat, folded it, and stuffed it into a trash bin, but the front of her blouse and pants were conspicuously stained.

Devlin said, "You'd better find a rest room and clean up and get rid of those clothes. You've got a change of clothing in the bag, right?"

Annie nodded.

"I guess Elizabeth here could do with a little cleanup, too."

The little girl nodded at Devlin. Somehow the insanity she had just been through had not terrified her. Devlin thought it might have been because she was underneath her mother's body throughout most of the attack. Whatever the reason, the child was calm and seemed to have grown accustomed to whatever this activity was that involved her mother and these two very large men.

Ben had made sure to stand apart from Devlin and the mother and daughter. But as Annie and Elizabeth made their way to the rest room, the big man followed them without needing to be told.

While Ben discreetly took up a position outside the women's toilet, Devlin headed for a bank of pay phones. He reached into his breast pocket and extracted an electronic address book. It had a 64K memory. It held close to a thousand names, phone numbers, and other bits of information. Devlin punched in the name "Braithwhite, T."

Annie and Elizabeth emerged from the rest room before Devlin had finished his phone calls. Annie had changed clothes and even managed to wash out the worst of the stains in her hair. She had changed Elizabeth's top and cleaned her up, too.

As they walked toward the phone banks, Ben fell in behind them. Elizabeth kept her eyes on the big man. It was clear to her that Ben was protecting them, and she had every intention of keeping him in sight.

Ben motioned them over to a set of seats. They sat and waited for Devlin to finish his phone conversations.

There were crowds of people moving through the terminal. Families with piles of luggage. Young people with backpacks. The elderly with their rolling luggage carts. Ben sat with his large leather bag on the seat next to him and somehow seemed to fit in with the general hustle and bustle that surrounded them.

Finally, after what seemed to Annie like several calls, Devlin hung up the phone. He came over to the others and took the seat next to Annie. She could tell by the look on his face that he was trying to figure out their next move.

"What happened?" she asked.

"I called a contact I have in British Customs. It took a while to get through. Seems like our police friend Chief Inspector Waldron has most of the western hemisphere alerted to keep us from leaving the country."

"What do you mean?"

"We're on all the computers. There's already an All Ports Warning on us. And that's just for starters. I don't think we should try leaving now."

"You sure?"

"Yeah. If we didn't have the kid, I'd chance it. Maybe. But even when these airline personnel are busy, they check out passengers with children very carefully. Too many kids being snatched by feuding parents these days."

Without warning, a question burst out of Annie.

"What did you do this morning? What the hell was all that back there?"

"I went to see your husband's uncle."

"Who?"

"His uncle. Frank Mills."

"Good Lord, why?"

"I thought he might be of some help. After all, those people killed someone that was working with him."

"How did you find him?"

"Asked around Soho."

"What happened?"

"He tried to turn me over to the bad guys."

"Oh my God. I can't believe this. This is insane. How many people were shooting at us this morning?"

"I counted at least five."

"We should be dead by now."

"We probably would be, except we had Ben with us."

"Jack, I can't take this. This is crazy."

"Maybe you haven't told me everything that's going on here, Annie. That kind of weaponry, that kind of shooting—it just doesn't happen here. What's going on?"

"I don't know, and I don't care. I just want out of here. Mislovic knows where I live. He knows my phone number. He called me this morning asking about you."

"Mislovic?"

"Mills. Mislovic."

"He called you?"

"Yes. What happened when you saw him?"

"He tried to turn me over to the Yardies. What did he want from you this morning?"

"He tried to turn you over?"

"Yes. Why did he call you?"

"He was angry that I had help."

"What did you tell him?"

"I basically told him to go to hell. He's not protecting me, why shouldn't I try to protect myself. So what did you do when they tried to turn you over to the Yardies?"

"Did he know my name?"

"When he spoke to me?"

"Yes."

"I think so. Yes, I think he did know your name."

"But you didn't tell it to him."

"Of course not. What did you do when they tried to turn you over?"

"I didn't let them."

"So were they after you this morning, or me?"

"Both, I'd say. Mr. Mills, I think, was mostly after me. The Yardie assassin was mostly after you."

"Listen, Jack. I don't want to get killed. Why don't we try to leave. What's the worst that can happen? If the police catch us, at least they'll protect us."

"I'm not so sure about that."

Annie had not expected Devlin to say that.

"Why not?"

Devlin heard the panic seep into her voice.

"What do you mean? Why shouldn't the police protect me?" she asked.

"They'll try. I'm just not sure they will be successful at it."

"Why?"

Devlin again heard the fear in her voice. He decided that she had been exposed to enough for one day. He wanted to keep her calm.

"Annie, just take it easy. I don't want you to be in a bad position. If the police arrest you now, you won't be able to control it. There's more to be considered. The first thing I want to do is get you and Elizabeth someplace that's safe. Then we'll deal with the police and everything else. We can't do this while we're running. And we can't sit in this airport for much longer. These places are filled with surveillance cameras. The British police are using them more and more."

"What are we going to do?"

"I've made a few arrangements. That's why I took so long on the phones. We're going to walk out of the terminal, you and I and Elizabeth. Ben will be somewhere close. We'll look like a family. We'll get onto the Budget rental-car bus and pick up a minivan. I've made the reservation in a name they can't trace. It'll be a fairly large job tracking every car that was rented at Heathrow, and I'm figuring they won't know we're here anyhow, unless someone has spotted us."

"My God, do you always have to figure all this out?"

"Yes."

"We're driving somewhere?"

"Only to a hotel. I picked one near the airport where we can get a couple of adjoining rooms."

"Why not drive someplace farther away?"

"Because the next few hours are going to be the hours when the most police will be looking for us, when it will be uppermost in their minds. Before they find us, I'd like to try to get the police to stand down on this thing. If I can."

"So for now, we're going to just hide in a hotel?"

"For now. Ben will pay for the room. You stay in the car until he gets the keys. We'll look at the layout of the hotel. Hopefully you can enter without going through the lobby. I'd rather that no one notices a mother and child."

"All right."

"Good, then let's go. Now."

Devlin looked over and noticed that Elizabeth had fallen asleep next to Annie.

"You carry your bag. I'll get her."

He stepped across Annie and gently picked up the child. Devlin realized he hadn't held a young child in a long time. He tried to remember how his young nephew Adam felt in his hands, but then realized first that he was a boy, and second that he was older than Elizabeth. The girl felt so tiny, almost unreal. Devlin's big hands fit nearly completely around her chest. He had the feeling her ribs weren't much bigger than the bones in his fingers.

He quickly placed her against his chest, holding her in the crook of his left arm. He'd hoped the child wouldn't wake, but she did almost instantly. She had that confused, where-am-I expression that young kids get when they wake up in strange places at strange times.

Devlin patted her gently on the back and said, "Don't worry, Elizabeth, Mom's here. I'm just going to give you a ride. Go back to sleep."

Elizabeth looked silently at her mother, then squirmed around in Devlin's arms until she spotted Ben. She stared at him until he looked back at her. The big man and the tiny girl made eye contact, and then and only then would Elizabeth settle back into Devlin's arms.

Devlin looked at Ben. The old warrior's face was absolutely expressionless, but Devlin was almost sure that one of the toughest men Devlin knew in a tough business was blushing.

CHAPTER 17

DEVLIN SAT IN the driver's seat of the rented minivan and watched Ben lead Annie and Elizabeth into a side entrance of the Post Truste Hotel. Ben had checked in, then returned to bring Annie and Elizabeth into the hotel through an entrance where they would not be seen.

The hotel was well suited to Devlin's purpose. It was ten minutes from the busy airport, and it catered to travelers checking in at all hours, mostly for short stays. A couple with a child would not attract undue attention. For now, they would be safe.

Ben and his charges would stay put, but Devlin had to keep moving. He needed to deal with the police. First, however, he needed to sleep. The last time he had slept had been on the flight from Los Angeles. The Yardies were looking for him. The Yugoslavs were looking for him. And every police force in England was looking for him. But no one was going to find him until he slept.

Devlin drove the rented minivan away from the airport and along M4 to Cedars Road and made his way through a maze of streets, his *London A to Z* on his lap, until he found the Chiswick Park Underground station. He picked that station because he knew there would be less police surveillance and because it was on the District Line, the line that went to Sloane Square without any transfers.

He parked the minivan in a residential neighborhood and in ten minutes was riding the Tube toward the Draycott. Devlin looked at his watch and calculated how many hours he had been in London. Not even twenty-four. Amazing how much trouble Annie had gotten them into in less than twenty-four hours.

When Devlin reached his room he called the Tower Bridge

Division and left a message for Chief Inspector Waldron that he would be calling back at four o'clock. He hung up quickly and checked his watch again. He'd get about three hours' sleep. It would have to do.

He gazed out to the peaceful back garden that buffered his room from the noise and bustle of busy London. There would be no enjoying a peaceful moment in that garden. Not this trip.

Devlin lay down on his bed. He had been pushing so hard for so many hours that he knew it would take a few minutes to wind down. He used the time to review what had happened. An extraordinary amount of trouble had occurred in a short amount of time. There had to be more to this mess than Annie had told him. It simply wasn't possible that two crime groups would go to such extraordinary measures to eliminate the wife of a low-echelon drug dealer. Annie was caught in the middle of something much bigger than she had let on. But did the Yugoslavs respond the way they had because of Annie, or because of what he had done to Mislovic? Did Annie know what she had gotten herself involved in? Or was she truly a victim of unusual circumstances?

Too many unanswered questions, thought Devlin. He closed his eyes. He knew if he wanted to keep opening them, he'd better find out the answers.

Mislovic felt like taking a nap of his own. His meal was over. His throat hurt less. He was beginning to relax.

He'd ordered baked salmon, a large salad, and another pint of bitters. Zenko had ordered the exact same thing, which slightly annoyed Mislovic. Zenko couldn't be bothered with trying to figure out the English menu. And for Zenko, food was food.

By the time they finished their meal, the weather had turned too chilly to continue sitting by the river, so Mislovic and Zenko agreed to the waiter's suggestion that they move inside for coffee and dessert. Mislovic assumed that over an hour outside had sufficiently aired out the smell of gunpowder from their clothes. But when they took their table, he lit one of his Silk Cut cigarettes just in case.

Along with coffee, he ordered Armagnac. Zenko settled for

his third pint. Throughout the lunch Mislovic had dispatched Zenko to the pay phones near the men's room to work on finding a police informant in the Tower Bridge Division. Mislovic's military career had thoroughly taught him the need for good intelligence. The lack of it was one reason he had left the brutal internecine Yugoslav battles. There, he'd rarely had accurate information. And he'd quickly found out how disastrous it could be to do battle while not knowing the strength of your enemies, or in some cases even who they were. Which at the moment exactly described the situation regarding the mysterious Mr. Devlin.

Zenko's mood had calmed down considerably as he ate, drank, and made progress developing an information source on the Met Police.

One of Zenko's contacts knew a bailiff working in the Magistrate's Court next door to Tower Bridge Division on Tooley Street. The bailiff was well connected with the police personnel at Tower. By the time Mislovic finished his coffee and Armagnac, the connection had been made. A simple deal. Money for information. The informant did not need to deal with the Yugoslavs directly; everything would be done through the bailiff. The informant wouldn't even need to dial an unfamiliar phone number to pass the information, since people in the Tower Bridge Division often spoke to court personnel. By the time Zenko ordered coffee and dessert, everything was in order.

Now Mislovic decided he would call Oliver. He felt confident that he would soon have something to offer his ally.

He dialed the number and imagined holding a gun to Oliver's head and telling him he was an ignorant black savage, but when Oliver came to the phone, Mislovic calmly told the Yardie boss that he wanted to meet with him. They agreed to three-thirty that afternoon, just inside Hyde Park near the Prince of Wales Gate. That would put Mislovic near his next appointment.

As he walked back to the table, Mislovic entertained the idea of inviting Oliver to tea. Three-thirty was the right hour for it. It might be amusing to see the Jamaican sipping tea in a posh hotel that didn't particularly want to serve either of them.

Mislovic was actually in a good mood when he returned to the table. Except for having had to watch Zenko shovel his food into his mouth, the meal had been very pleasant. The salmon had been excellent, not overcooked the way it was in many British restaurants.

Zenko was wolfing down a generous slice of chocolate mousse cake. It looked so delicious that Mislovic ordered one for himself along with more coffee and the check.

Out on the street, police constables were interviewing people, examining wrecked cars, counting bullet holes, and collecting an extraordinary number of shell casings.

Finally, Zenko came out with it.

"Who we kill first?"

Mislovic's relaxed mood evaporated. "I want to kill that idiot John Petchek."

Zenko grunted. "Too late."

"It's not too late to kill his wife."

"You want kill your niece?"

"Teach her not to recommend idiots to me."

"The Yardies will kill her anyhow. Don't bother."

"Damn savages."

"Why we work with them anyhow?"

"Because Dragan wants our money invested. Nothing makes more money than drugs. And no drug makes more money than cocaine."

Zenko grunted. He had heard much of this before. Mislovic continued.

"We invest our money here because London's banks make it easy to bring money in. Two, three transactions, and it's clean. Once it's clean, we have to put it to work, and London is close to the markets of Eastern and Central Europe. Result: We deal with savages for the moment."

Zenko gave Mislovic another of his Slavic shrugs.

"What? What's that supposed to mean?"

"Sleep with pigs . . ."

"We only sleep with them long enough to fuck them. Once I start buying in real quantities their source will come to me. In six months we'll be dealing directly with their U.S. suppliers, then directly with the cartels after that. We'll kill off these fucking black Yardie savages and be done with them. And we'll take over their fucking business, too. This will be a playground for us. They don't have the men or the weapons to fight us. Nor does this police force. How long did it take them to show up after we started shooting today? Ten, fifteen minutes?"

Mislovic sneered at the thought. "Give me one platoon of our fighters armed with Kalashnikovs and we'll slaughter these Yardie pigs and grind their bones in the dust. There will be enough blood to satisfy even you, Zenko. It'll be over before these idiotic police even answer their phones. The West has no idea the kind of havoc we can create here. But for now, we're new. We start where we can and move on. That's it."

"Pardon me, but maybe we start with the wrong person."

Now it was Mislovic's turn to shrug. "Maybe."

"What do you know about your niece?"

"How much can I know? My sister got out in the forties, before the Eastern Bloc closed. When I found out her daughter had been living in London, I contacted her. I knew her father was connected with Italians in New York. Believe me, that part of the family is not lily-white by any means. I find out her husband dabbled in dealing cocaine, but she said his connection was the top guy in the business. She sounded knowledgeable to me. The way she described the situation with these Yardies has turned out to be accurate."

"Meaning?"

"They're a bunch of idiots. They can't organize themselves. Whoever is willing to shoot the most people gets on top. They don't have decent financing. They don't work anything out. Half of them raid the other half for money and drugs. It's anarchy."

"But they control the cocaine?"

"Yes. For cocaine and marijuana it's the Jamaicans. For heroin it's the Chinese. The Chinese are more civilized, but they won't even talk to an outsider. The Yardies don't want to deal with outsiders either, but they make exceptions. Her husband knew Oliver from a long time ago. It was an opportunity. I took it."

"And he cheat you. He didn't know who you are?"

"Apparently not."

"The wife did not tell him?"

"I don't know what she told him. Maybe it was her idea."

"Then we should kill her."

"Don't be tiresome, Z. We'll give her to the blacks."

"Why?"

"Because it will strengthen our hand with them. Look, we gave them a chance at this Devlin guy. In the same way, I'll give them my niece if they want her. I don't give a shit about her. Her husband cheated us. As far as I know, she could have been the one telling him to skim. She was probably in on it, too, so to hell with her."

"Who is this damn bastard Devlin? What the hell she doing bringing someone like that in here?"

"She knew she couldn't come to me after her husband cheated us. And she had to know the Yardies would come after her. So she hires a professional herself."

"There was more than just him shooting back at us. He was driving. Someone else in back was shooting the shotgun."

"You're right. We have to find out exactly who this man is, and what his resources are."

Zenko said, "I'll get details. Our informant is assigned to her case."

"Is that so?"

"Yah."

Mislovic nodded his congratulations. "Good work, Z. How did you find him?"

"Just keep asking and offering money."

"What can he tell us?"

"Whatever the police find out."

"Good. We have to know how to find the woman. And her new bodyguard."

"Yah. Do you think she send him to us?"

"Maybe. Or maybe she just put the idea in his head and he did the rest by himself. If she's anything like her mother, she's a devious little shit, and she'll do whatever it takes to survive this."

"How does your niece know a man like this Devlin?"

"I have no idea."

"We did not expect this."

Mislovic leaned forward. "That's the problem, isn't it. I thought she was working for herself. Maybe not, huh?"

"I would like to know."

"So would I."

"She tell Devlin that you are the dead husband's uncle, not *her* uncle."

"That's what it sounded like this morning."

"Why?"

"So she can appear to be the innocent victim, I suppose."

Zenko laughed. "Maybe we don't kill her. Maybe we hire her."

Mislovic laughed back. "No. She's already dead. If we don't kill her, the Yardies will. If they don't, the police will get her. She's not the only one who is going to die, either."

"Devlin?"

"Yes. Devlin. But for now we have work to do."

"What?"

"We have business with your friend Oliver."

"He not my friend."

"Today he is."

"I think about killing him with a smile then."

"Good enough."

"Tell me Hinton be there so I can think about killing him, too."

"Don't think too hard, Zenko. Right now just think about making sure they don't kill us first."

This was the second meeting with the Yugoslavs in as many days. Oliver thought about it. Every meeting meant walking into a situation where someone could pull a trigger. But he was fairly certain it wasn't going to be pulled today. Mills had tried to deliver Devlin to them. And Hinton said that Mills and his men had fired on the vehicle Devlin had been driving. It seemed obvious that Mills had decided to work on Oliver's side. So once again, Oliver had agreed to a meeting, but not without sending a man to check the entire area of the park before he walked in and took his seat on the bench.

He had given the job to Alexander, a painfully thin, strangely intense young man from Oliver's hometown of Kingston.

Alexander hardly ever spoke, and he walked so quietly and with such little exertion that he appeared to be floating. He had drifted ghost-like along the path that bordered South Carriage Drive, then into the park toward the Serpentine, along the wide sandy bridal path, and back toward the Prince of Wales Gate.

The area of the park where they would be meeting was open and spacious. There was little foliage. The ground was flat. It was within view of the street. The benches were spaced widely enough so that people could talk to each other without being overheard.

Oliver would be able to see anyone approaching from many yards away. He supposed Mills could have a shooter with a rifle hidden far off out of sight, but he doubted it. Mills might try to kill him eventually. But not today.

After Alexander returned from his reconnoitering and reported that the park area was clear, Oliver still positioned four men throughout the area, and kept Hinton close by him. By quarter after three, everyone was in place.

Oliver sat and waited and thought over exactly how he had arrived in this park, out of his Yard, thinking about killing people and being killed.

Oliver found it almost amusing that Mislovic dared to think he could stand up to him.

He sat on the bench, watching a proper English woman canter her horse along the bridle path. She was dressed in an impeccable riding outfit: boots, jodhpurs, red jacket, and whip. So civilized. So English. He felt like taking out his gun and shooting her. Or even better, just shooting the horse. That would cause more outrage among the simpleminded British. Oliver sneered. These people had no idea how close they were to losing it all.

Then it became very clear to him why he was there. He wanted the power, the money, and the guns necessary to destroy anybody who stood in his way. Mills meant money and maybe guns. And if it meant dealing outside his normal realm to get them, so be it.

They promised money. They promised weapons. And Oliver knew from his last conversation that Mills was going to promise more things. Probably the woman and her bodyguard. It was time to see if the Yugoslavs could deliver.

And there they were. Mislovic and Zenko appeared at the

park entrance. They walked directly to Oliver's bench. Mislovic sat on Oliver's left, Hinton on Oliver's right. Zenko sat across from them on another bench. Without a word, Hinton stood up and crossed over to sit next to Zenko. Oliver watched it all. Now the chessboard was set. Zenko could shoot Oliver, Hinton could shoot Mislovic, and then they could shoot each other. The next phase of the game was about to begin.

CHAPTER 18

ACROSS THE RIVER on the South Bank, Superintendent Thomas Fenton was about to begin his game with James Waldron.

Fenton had read all the reports generated by the first shooting, and had scanned the initial reports on the second shooting incident. This was turning into a bloody mess. This was going to be great fun.

He reached for his desk phone and punched in the internal dialing code for Sergeant Patrick Reilly. "Reilly, your presence is requested in my office."

In less than a minute, the gaunt, gray-haired cop entered Fenton's office. Fenton said, "Talk," and Reilly immediately began a tale of how badly Waldron had botched the case. Exactly what Fenton wanted to hear.

Fenton had one of the four private offices in the division headquarters. It needed painting. The building that housed it was old. There was room for his desk, one extra chair, a computer table, and for one person to stand. But Fenton sat amidst the modest surroundings as if he were the ruler of a major corporation.

Reilly stood. Reciting. Fenton ate it up like his morning oatmeal.

Fenton took great pleasure in listening to Reilly's snide remarks and slurs.

What a perfect little sniveling stool pigeon this Reilly is, thought Superintendent Fenton. And what a fine steaming pile of shit that nance Waldron had stepped into.

This was a good one. There was already one dead body. Too bad it was just one of those Yardie bastards. But not to worry, Fenton told himself: At the rate these maniacs were shooting, there would be plenty more soon. Yardie violence was always good for news coverage, outdone only by IRA terrorists, but since the cease-fire there had been nothing from that quarter. But lo and behold, he thought, now we have Eastern European villains standing up to take their place. With plenty of automatic weapons which never ceased to terrify the public and shake up the police commanders. Too bad they didn't use bombs. Bombs were the best, thought Fenton. But lots of bullets flying out there wasn't too shabby either, was it? The press was already swarming.

Then, of course, there was the extra added attraction of drugs. And the best one of all, not just cocaine, but crack cocaine, Yardie crack. Lovely. After murders and kidnappings, drugs were the best. And don't forget the juicy bonus—there was a woman involved. Now if the woman could be horribly murdered, that would be absolutely fantastic.

An absolute corker, all right. Right here in the quiet little Tower Bridge Division on the wrong side of the river. The biggest thing to hit England since those two beastly little wankers killed that little toddler, Fenton thought with a chuckle. Yes, yes, yes, and who let the only two material witnesses in the case slip away? Who? Why, Chief Inspector James Waldron, that's who.

Glory be to God in the highest, they were lost and gone, and now, thought Fenton, so was that insufferable man's career.

Fenton once again congratulated himself for assigning Reilly to Waldron, because absolutely any mistake that Waldron made would become known to him almost immediately—giving him all the more ammunition to once and for all kill Chief Inspector Waldron's career.

Reilly finished his discourse. Fenton smiled and said, "Thank you very much, Sergeant."

Reilly smiled back and watched Fenton mull over his next move.

"Well, we're really in it now, aye, Sergeant?"

"Yes, sir."

"Got to think of a way to help you fellows out if I can."

"Yes, sir."

"Tough situation. Really bad break, I'd say."

Reilly nodded.

"Any leads on getting this Devlin character and the woman back in here?"

"Not that I know of, sir."

"Hmmm. Damn shame. Hope you won't get too tarred by the same brush, Sergeant."

"Well, sir, that's not important. It's getting these damn villains off the streets that counts, sir. The public has to be protected at all costs."

"Oh, absolutely. Good form, Sergeant. But, we can't underestimate the severity of this problem."

"No, sir."

"No indeed."

Fenton pursed his lips and rested his chin on steepled fingers, striking a pose of concern and deep thought. Soon Waldron would be here and he could torment him for a few minutes. After that, he would call a few of the slimiest newspaper reporters he knew, men who would write just about anything for a few inches of ink they could call their own. He had to fight off the smile. That would just about do it for the day. Then home to the cottage in East Ham, pat the dog on the head, have a tot or two of Jameson before dinner and puds, watch the news, and off to bed. Maybe, thought Fenton, I'll even give a few good pokes to the old woman before I nod off.

Just at that thought, the intercom phone buzzed and Fenton's administrative assistant, Ethel Hornseby, announced that Chief Inspector Waldron was outside waiting to see him.

"Wait exactly one minute, dear, then send him in," intoned Fenton.

He told Reilly, "You sit over there and look browbeaten and penitent. Don't speak until you're spoken to."

Reilly took his seat, and Fenton picked up a sheet of paper from one of the reports and pretended to be interested in it. He heard Waldron walk in, but continued gazing at the page.

After the appropriate amount of time, he looked up at Waldron and said, "Oh yes, sorry, James, I've just been reading your report and taking Sergeant Reilly to task for allowing such an ungodly mess to develop."

Waldron didn't respond.

"Quite a bollix. What in God Almighty's name possessed

you to let these people wander off into the night while you toddled home for your beauty rest?

"A judgment call on my part."

"And what exactly did you judge the situation to be?"

"It was late. I didn't see much good in dragging the woman and her child out into the night."

"Not even for her own protection?"

"We're not in the habit of providing security to every person who feels threatened. And she did have her own personnel for that."

Fenton looked down at his notes. "Ah, yes. This character, Devlin."

"Yes, sir."

"He seemed like the competent type to you?"

"Yes, sir."

"Reliable?"

"Yes, sir. I did a background check on him before I allowed them to remain out of custody."

"What did you find?"

"He had an extensive background in law enforcement. Specializing in security work."

"I see. I see. Well, how do you explain the fact that he didn't show up this morning?"

"Apparently he was fleeing for his life, and the lives of the woman and child."

"Yes, well. Now what?"

"I have every reason to believe he will show up."

"Why is that?"

"Just my judgment, sir."

"Oh, well. Then I guess all is well. Your judgment has been unfailingly correct up to this point."

Waldron did not rise to the bait.

Fenton saw that his gibes were wearing thin. "Well, James, all I can say is that I hope you're correct. For your sake and Sergeant Reilly's here. You know damn well I can't keep the wolves away for much longer. I'll do what I can, but no promises. This mess is one step away from dropping on the desk of the home secretary. Once that happens, their first response will be to clean house. You know that, don't you?"

"Yes, sir."

"I'll be perfectly honest with you, Chief: If this ends up where I think it will, it's going to be every man for himself. I won't allow this division to go down with you. When the proverbial shit hits it, the name 'Waldron' will be invoked. Waldron, Waldron, Waldron. It's on your head. I'm warning you now."

This time Waldron just nodded.

Fenton turned to Reilly, who had remained in his seat with a look of mortification etched into his hangdog face.

"And you, Reilly, I'm surprised at you. A man of your patrol experience, a man from the ranks through and through. Didn't you have more sense than to let Waldron allow these witnesses to scamper off into the night?"

Reilly stared at the tops of his scuffed cordovans.

Fenton raised his voice. "Well!?"

Reilly lifted his head just long enough to mutter, "No, sir."

"Waldron here may have spent too much time behind a desk instead of out in a Panda learning the streets, but you, sir . . . I expected more."

"I'm sorry, sir."

"Of course you are, but what good does that do us now? None, I'd say. Now, Sergeant, I understand how difficult it is to buck the decisions of your commanding officer, but we're all in this together. You have to give Waldron here the benefit of your experience."

"Yes, sir."

Waldron found himself clenching his teeth at the insulting game Fenton was playing, but it helped him keep his mouth shut.

"Well, there's no point in belaboring this. The two of you better get on with it. I want this solved quickly. You get those people in here and get the job done. Go."

Waldron didn't nod, didn't say anything, didn't even bother to look at Fenton. He turned and walked out of the office. Reilly had to stand up and move quickly to catch up with him.

When they reached the outside corridor, Reilly spoke first. "Well, himself really is into it now, isn't he?"

Waldron turned and looked at Reilly. It seemed to him as if he were seeing the man for the first time. His stringy, dirty hair. His dull horse-face. The dingy white shirt hanging on him, with the same stained red tie Waldron had seen hundreds of times, the same blue double-knit blazer, the same crease-less gray slacks.

Waldron had always felt that Reilly was an annoying weight that Fenton had strung around his neck just for spite, but now the man seemed somehow worse than that. Somehow more fundamentally bad. Waldron felt as if he could almost smell the decay in the man. And now something he'd known all along hit his attention with more force than usual. He knew Reilly was Fenton's snitch, but it had never really bothered him because he realized there were many ways Fenton could have found out what he was doing without Reilly's help. It wasn't that; it was something else; something worse.

It disgusted Waldron, and it angered him, and it made him commit a rare mistake. Until now he had never told Reilly anything of consequence. Waldron didn't want to give Fenton the satisfaction of finding out anything significant from Reilly. But this time he wanted to put both of them in their places.

He stuck his finger in Reilly's chest and told him, "Get an unmarked car ready downstairs at four o'clock. Not one of those shit little Mini-Metros. Get a Sierra or a Rover with a fucking engine in it. You be in it with a set of radios. Make sure their batteries are charged. Make sure they work. And you be ready to drive like shit over a shovel when I tell you, because at four o'clock I'll know where that bastard Devlin is, and I want you ready to go with me and get him."

Reilly had never seen Waldron so intense or so angry. He stood mute.

Waldron yelled, "Understand?"

Reilly flinched. "Yes, sir."

"Good. Now go back in there, or pick up your snitch phone, and tell that washed-up idiot Fenton who hasn't yet figured out that this isn't a fucking game invented for his amusement exactly what I just told you."

Waldron didn't wait for any protest or answer. He turned and walked away.

Reilly stood right where he was in the corridor until Waldron turned a corner and was out of sight. Then Reilly's un-pleasant face turned ugly and mean. Nobody talks to me like that, he thought. Fucking wank. I'll call all right, you smart-ass prick.

Reilly ducked into the robbery squad's room and picked up the nearest phone. He dialed the number of a bailiff at Magistrate's Court. He told his contact very clearly, if his people wanted Jack Devlin they should be ready to come get him at four o'clock or shortly thereafter. And be prepared to come quickly, very quickly.

The bailiff passed the word to Zenko's contact, who in turn called the backroom office at the Soho headquarters, but Zenko was not there to receive the call. He was sitting on a bench in Hyde Park watching the man sitting three feet from him. Hinton didn't seem to be watching anybody. His eyes were half closed, and he was silently humming something to himself. Zenko didn't even try to make out the words. His struggle was to refrain from pulling out his Grendel and shooting enough bullets into Hinton's neck to sever his head from his body. As Zenko sat looking at Hinton, he actually pictured the sight of Hinton's head falling off.

On the opposite bench, Mislovic and Oliver, for their part, pretended to be having a congenial conversation.

Oliver had even stood up and shaken Mislovic's hand when they greeted each other, and called him "friend"—although with Oliver the word had sounded so strange that Mislovic did not quite get it at first. In fact, he had to admit he really only caught on to about half of what Oliver said. The West Indian accent mystified Mislovic. Oliver had lived in London for the last twenty years; why, wondered Mislovic, did he sound like he'd just stepped out of some backwater town in Jamaica?

The Yugoslav sat and listened to Oliver's singsong voice. He heard him, but he wasn't really listening. Instead he was thinking about the indignity of Devlin's having put a gun to his head and gotten away with it. Followed by the outrage committed by the crazy one across from him, the one Oliver called Hin-tohn. He had the nerve to aim a gun at him and, worse, had actually been willing to pull the trigger and shoot him in order to get to Devlin. And now, here they were, sitting in the park as if they did it every day, with Oliver calling him "friend."

Mislovic interrupted the Yardie boss and said, "Mr. Oliver, it seems we have a problem."

"Wha' problem?"

"The woman and Devlin."

"No, no, Mr. Mills. *We* don't have a problem. *I* have a problem. You got notting to do wit' dis guy or da woman, or any of it."

"Yes I do. It all traces back to me. And I don't appreciate being threatened in my own place of business and used as a hostage."

"I understand. You cyan let a man show you such disrespect. But I take care of him. Me."

"Well, then let's do it quickly. We don't need these complications."

"Fuck da complications. You should have shot him in the face and be don' wit' it when you had him."

"I was trying to do you a favor. I thought you wanted him. Next time I'll remember that."

"One lickle pull of da trigger, mon, and it'd be over wit'. But der won' be a next time. Next time I'll take care of it."

"Or I will."

"No, no, no, no. Oh no, my friend, we be da ones now who do da shootin'. We shoot him, an' da woman, an' anybody else t'inks they can get in my way or da way of my business. All you have to worry about is our business."

"I see."

Mislovic felt his anger rising and consciously settled himself into a quieter mood.

"But, of course, Mr. Oliver, this fellow has made it very difficult to do business."

"Maybe."

"I don't think it's in our interests to be running around on the streets trying to shoot him."

"Maybe not."

"So in the interests of our business, and as your *friends*, I've taken the responsibility of finding Mr. Devlin and the woman, and helping you eliminate them."

"What you goin' find out, den? Who goin' to tell you, Mistah Mills?"

"We have informants."

"Who?"

"With the police."

"Is this what you brought me here for? To tell me dis?"

"Yes. I did. I expect to have information on where you—we —can find them very soon. I would look forward to delivering Mr. Devlin to you again."

"Fine. I would appreciate that. As friends."

"And as business partners."

"Fine."

"And about our business . . ."

"What?"

"It's time to put our business on another level. I'd like to substantially increase my order."

Oliver hesitated for just a moment. Mislovic was pushing him now, but in the direction he wanted to be pushed.

"No problem. Tell me when and how much."

Mislovic continued, "Let's say ten kilos. As soon as you can get them."

Oliver was silent for a moment. He had never dealt in such a large quantity. "We move dat much, we gonna need a few t'ings from you."

"What? Besides money."

"I'd like to feel a lickle more secure, den. What can we work out wit' you providing me weapons? Assault rifles. You said you can do dat."

"How many do you need?"

"How 'bout one for each kilo. Do it barter. I cut da price per kilo by seven percent for each rifle."

"Meaning?"

"You get da powder for ten-five."

"British pounds."

"Of course."

"Make it ten even and we have a deal."

"Don't be dat way, Mistah Mills. You cyan ask me to pay twelve hundred for one gun."

"Rifle."

"Rifle. Da goin' price is seven-fifty."

"Where? One at a time. I'm ready to supply ten."

"I buy in quantity, den da price should be less."

"No. Not with arms. Arms are power, Mr. Oliver. I'm ready

to give you enough firepower to make you unbeatable on the street. That's worth more than the going price."

Oliver thought about it. He knew Mills was right. He would try to beat down the cost at the other end.

"Okay, Mistah Mills. Dis ain' da time to get into a philosophical argument. Ten even for ten. I like the sound of it."

"Good. Done, on one condition."

Oliver frowned immediately. "I don't like conditions after da price is made."

"You'll like this one."

"Wha'?"

"The deal goes forward, at the agreed price, when Jack Devlin is dead. I can't do business with that wild card running around. The man is dangerous. He's already involved us in gun battles on the street. He's generating too much heat."

Oliver could hardly refuse this condition. But accepting it meant that Mislovic was controlling the deal, and Oliver hated that almost as much as he hated Devlin's interference.

"I don't like conditions. Any conditions."

"He has to go before we do business. If you don't want to do it, I will. But I'm not doing business while Devlin is on the loose."

Oliver boiled over. "I'll put da man's bloody fucking heart in your lap. I'll—" Oliver stopped himself. "All right, da hell wit' it. You want to wait until he dies, fine. You wait."

"I guarantee you we won't be waiting long. My information is reliable."

"Fine."

Oliver stood up. Mislovic remained seated. In a perverse sort of way, he suddenly found himself rooting for Devlin. Get lost. Get down. Stay away. Make this Oliver lose his balls. I'll taunt him with it until he's ready to kill me, then I'll enjoy killing him even more. Now Mislovic felt the old fire. This was the game he loved. War, chaos, hate, and death.

Then Oliver spoiled the moment.

While standing in front of Mislovic he said, "I hear da mon shoot up your car."

It was then that Mislovic noticed the car keys in Oliver's hand.

"I got you another one. A red one." He pointed toward

Knightsbridge Street. "I had to buy one for Hinton. So I got one for you, too. Nice red Saab. Double-parked over der, mon. Enjoy. Consider it a kickback on da first deal."

Oliver let out a hearty laugh and tossed the keys to Mislovic. They hit his chest and fell into his lap.

"Nah. Don't t'ank me, fren'. Just a lickle sign of my affection."

Oliver turned and walked away. Hinton followed. Alexander appeared from behind a tree about twenty yards behind Zenko's bench. Then three more men walked into view from various hidden spots.

Oliver's patronizing act of replacing Mislovic's car was insulting enough, but his childish display of strength made the Yugoslav's heart pound with rage. Mislovic, however, would not give Oliver the satisfaction of displaying his anger. Instead, he took a deep breath and remained quiet and motionless. Well, thought Mislovic, my affectionate "fren'," enjoy your "lickle" games now. Mislovic didn't care what Dragan wanted to do, or how badly he wanted to establish connections in London's drug market; he was certain now that he would kill this Oliver, and as many of his men as possible, very soon.

And so for the next five minutes, Mislovic sat and thought about that. Zenko came across to his bench and sat with him. He knew it was not the time to speak. Or move.

After a while they left the park, and Zenko finally dialed his cellular phone to find out if there were any messages for him.

CHAPTER 19

WALDRON WAS WAITING for a phone call, but not from Zenko. The phone rang only once before Waldron grabbed it and spoke into the receiver.

"Waldron."

"Devlin."

"Devlin, where the hell are you?"

"Sorry we missed our appointment. You must have heard why."

"What the hell is going on?"

"Too many people want my friend dead, that's what's going on."

"You must get in here, now. Both of you. This can't continue."

"You and I have to talk first."

"About what?"

"About why I can't come in."

"Why? What are you talking about?"

"Not on the phone, Waldron. In person."

"Stop this nonsense, man. I'm not tracing this call."

"I'll tell you why when we meet."

"Meet? Where?"

"The Burger King restaurant. Piccadilly Circus. The one rather ironically located underneath the big neon McDonald's sign."

"Why there?"

"I like crowds."

"Well, for God's sake, let's meet someplace decent. There's a perfectly pleasant restaurant across the circle. The Criterion."

"No. Let's enjoy the American experience. I'll be there in fifteen minutes."

"Why are you running me around? Get in here where you'll be safe."

"Don't come with the troops, Waldron, or you'll never see me. Come alone. First we talk."

Devlin hung up before Waldron could argue. The chief inspector slammed the phone down and moved fast. In less than two minutes he was checked out of the division and sitting next to Reilly in a green Rover 1600 heading for Piccadilly Circus.

"What's there?" asked Reilly.

"Devlin, if I'm lucky."

Reilly drove across Tower Bridge, hands sweating, head hovering over the steering wheel, intent on moving through traffic. Waldron had turned on the siren and set the flasher on the dashboard and growled at Reilly to drive faster, but Reilly's main concern was how to get word to his contact. He scraped his brain for an excuse to stop and make a phone call —to his wife, his doctor, his priest; Christ, to anybody—but it was ridiculous. Waldron would hardly let him brake, much less stop for a phone call.

After Devlin had hung up on Waldron, he'd stepped away from the pay phone and walked around the block to the Tower Records store, across from the Burger King. He headed up the stairs to the second floor. The signs over the stairwell said "Classical" and "Jazz," but when he walked through the glass doors American country music was blaring out of four JBL speakers hanging at odd angles from the ceiling. The store was filled with sound.

He kept walking until he was behind a set of casement windows that filled the arches which fronted the store. A rack containing CDs blocked half the window, but Devlin still had a clear view of Burger King across the street.

His three hours of sleep and a shower had brought him almost back to normal. The country music was tough and sharp. He felt energized.

He picked up a CD of gospel music and pretended to read the label. He checked the selection in front of him: country, folk, blues, gospel. There was even a section of Scottish bagpipe and Celtic music. Devlin wondered what the bagpipes would sound like, but was happy with the hard-edged country playing.

Eighteen minutes after he had hung up on Waldron, he saw the green Rover stop in front of Burger King. Waldron got out and turned to say something to the driver. From his second-story view, Devlin watched Waldron go into Burger King while the green Rover continued on to Shaftesbury, edged into traffic, and turned left onto Denman. Devlin lost sight of the Rover, but had no doubt that the car stopped somewhere close by.

Devlin looked around the busy area. There must have been a couple of thousand people around Piccadilly Circus, and the street traffic was bumper-to-bumper with cars, taxis, and double-decker buses, but he was fairly certain he did not see any cars taking positions that suggested they were being driven by police.

Devlin left his perch. On the way out he asked the clerk at the counter what was playing, and was told it was the Mavericks. On impulse Devlin bought the CD, *From Hell to Paradise,* and slipped it into his jacket pocket.

He crossed over to Haymarket, skirting away from the Burger King so Waldron would not see him if he was looking. He walked to Shaftesbury and headed for Denman. Denman was a narrow street that curved back around to Glasshouse. The green Rover was parked up on the curb just past the corner in front of a pub called the St. James Tavern. The driver was just exiting the pub. If he'd had a drink, it must have been a quick one, thought Devlin.

Reilly had tossed down a double Jameson in one swallow while he used the pub's phone. The drink and the phone call made him extremely pleased with himself. He had been able to call in the exact meeting place: the Burger King on Glasshouse Street, Picadilly Circus. Reilly realized that without the exact location, Devlin's enemies would be running around blind in the jumble of stores and mass of people that surrounded Piccadilly. Now, if they hurried they could get Devlin, completely screw Waldron, and Reilly would not even be there. He'd be safe and sound, following orders, parked away from the scene.

Devlin recognized Reilly as one of the cops who had been at Annie's loft the night of the shooting.

Reilly headed for the Rover. Devlin hung back in the crowd and waited until Reilly reached the driver-side door, which was conveniently on the sidewalk side. Devlin timed his move perfectly. As Reilly slipped into the car, Devlin, crouching low, came up to the passenger-side door and quickly slid into the front passenger seat. Reilly never saw him until Devlin was seated next to him. The moment of complete surprise was all Devlin needed to press the gun he had taken from Zenko hard between two of Reilly's ribs. The pressure made the old cop wince.

Reilly croaked out one word: "Caw."

In twenty-seven years, no one had ever pulled a gun on Reilly. He just wasn't up to realizing what that could mean. His response was not appropriate.

"What the bloody hell?"

Devlin said, "Take out those clever handcuffs you guys use."

"Fuck you say?"

Devlin pushed the gun into Reilly. "Hurry up."

"Get out of this car. I'm a police constable."

Devlin looked at Reilly. "What's the matter with you? Are you stupid?"

Then he banged the butt of the machine pistol down onto Reilly's kneecap.

Reilly grunted in pain.

"Don't make any more mistakes. Take out the cuffs."

Reilly pleaded, "Don't."

"Look, I just want to keep you in this car while I meet with Waldron. I can either cuff you to the steering wheel or shoot off a kneecap. It's your choice."

Reilly's eyes started to bug out of his face.

Devlin continued matter-of-factly, "You know, it's not just the limp you end up with for the rest of your life. If I shoot through a pair of dirty old pants like you wear, so much fabric and junk gets in the wound you get terrible infections. I've heard about some people even dying from the infection."

Reilly reached behind his back and pulled out his one-piece handcuffs.

Devlin slapped the cuff on Reilly's left wrist and turned it slightly. Reilly grunted in pain and moved to try to accommodate the twist.

"These things work great, don't they? Hurts like a bitch, doesn't it? Ever since you guys used them on me, I've wanted to try them."

Devlin pulled Reilly's left hand to the steering wheel.

"Okay, put your right hand underneath."

Reilly did, and Devlin quickly snapped the handcuff over his right wrist. Reilly was attached to the steering wheel.

Devlin checked Reilly's pockets and found his badge and wallet. He looked at the black leather case that held Reilly's badge and ID.

"Is this your badge?"

Reilly nodded.

"It looks like shit. Is this thing plastic?"

Reilly wouldn't answer.

"I never knew London police had such crummy little badges. They don't give you guns at least they can give you a decent-looking badge."

"You can't do this."

"Why do you keep saying that? I've just done it. Sit here quietly for ten minutes, and I'll give your stuff to Waldron. Be stupid enough to yell for help, it all goes down a sewer, along with your career."

Reilly kept his mouth shut.

Devlin looked around the car and found an *Evening Sun* in the backseat. He opened it up and laid it across the steering wheel so that it covered Reilly's cuffed hands. A guy sitting in his car reading the newspaper wouldn't attract much attention.

Devlin picked up Reilly's police radio, got out of the Rover, and walked around the corner to Burger King.

He stood outside the entrance looking inside until he spotted Waldron sitting glumly near the front of the restaurant, as far away from the din inside as possible.

Devlin tried to figure out what the restaurant's decor was trying to portray. He finally decided it was supposed to be some sort of spaceship motif. There was something that resembled a robot near the entrance, a corrugated-board construction that looked like a high school version of a *Star Trek* transporter room, and a bunch of bad plastic flying saucers hanging from the ceiling. Horrible synthesized music pounded out of loudspeakers somewhere. Devlin found the attempt at creating a futuristic environment appalling. Yet practically every seat was filled. Waldron had to share a table with a Pakistani couple in matching stonewashed jeans and blue sweatshirts. They seemed quite content. Waldron seemed quite miserable.

There was an empty seat across from Waldron, but Devlin could not force himself to walk more than two feet inside.

Waldron spotted him, and Devlin waved for him to come out.

"You're right," Devlin said. "I'm sorry. It's terrible in there. Where did you want to go?"

"Back to the division. Now."

"No. We have to talk."

"All right." Waldron pointed to the other side of the circle. "Over there. The Criterion."

The two men hustled through the pedestrians and traffic and stepped into the restaurant. It reminded Devlin of a large Parisian bistro, but at this odd hour between lunch and dinner it was quiet and serene. The floor consisted of white tiles, the ceiling was high and arched. Mosaics in muted colors decorated the walls. The furniture reminded him of something you might see in a Toulouse-Lautrec painting.

A tall woman in a beige silk suit smiled at them and said, "Good afternoon. Would you gentlemen like a table?"

"Please," said Devlin.

She led them to the middle of the room, where they took a table near the wall to their right. Devlin sat facing the entrance. Waldron sat across from him.

"Does it really cost all that much more to come in here?" asked Devlin.

"Much more than what?"

"Burger King."

Waldron said, "Of course."

The waiter appeared at the table and Waldron ordered tea. Devlin said, "For two."

Waldron lit a cigarette and told Devlin, "You should have listened to me and come here straightaway."

"You're right."

"And you should have come in this morning with the woman. I gave you a break, and now where are we?"

"Worse off, I'd say."

"Exactly. What are you doing? Come in with me now and let's clear this up."

"Not now."

"What makes you think you have a choice, Mr. Devlin?"

"Let's just say it's my choice until you get those nasty little handcuffs on me again."

Waldron frowned, but did not rise to Devlin's challenge. He took another tack.

"Look, you must realize that if you and the woman stay out there you both stand a good chance of being shot."

"I'm afraid your side isn't all that great either. I can't bring her in and take the chance that you might arrest her, or me."

"Why?"

"She needs me to protect her. I can't waste time in jail."

"If you have to be detained, we'll protect her."

"No you won't. People on your side are working with the people who want us dead."

"That's absurd. What are you talking about?"

"This morning I went to see the uncle of Annie's murdered husband. He goes by the name of Frank Mills, but his real name is Mislovic. Ivan Mislovic. He's the one who used her husband to get into the drug trade."

"I know the name from the file."

"Yeah, well, Mislovic knows a few things, too. He knew more about me than he should have. The information had to have come from your side."

"What information? What did they know?"

Instead of answering, Devlin asked, "What do you know about him?"

"Who?"

"Mislovic."

"I don't know about him specifically, but we're getting reports about Eastern European groups who are coming into Western Europe and the U.K. They're very well financed and well armed. This is where they see the opportunities. He's apparently one of them."

" 'Them'? Who's 'them'?"

"Gangsters, former secret police employees, some ex–military men. They all need new jobs."

"Why here?"

"We're not quite as restrictive as some countries. France and Germany are certainly worse. And we happen to be a primary financial center. London is an easy place for them to bring their money."

"Where's the money coming from?"

Waldron shrugged. "Lots of places. Communist Party funds that were pulled out before the party was overthrown. Government funds that were stolen. When things change, the people in power take care of themselves. But what has all this got to do with the woman?"

"Her dead husband was a relative of Mislovic's. A nephew. Mislovic wanted to get into the drug business. Johnny Petchek knew some Yardie who deals coke. He made the connection. He was the middleman."

"It sounds plausible. That's what they're doing—investing their money in legal and illegal businesses. These are dangerous people you're talking about."

"I know that."

"Why do you say the police are working with them?"

"It may be just one person. Or just a few. But they're getting information from your side. I can't put Annie in your custody if you can't control the information that gets out."

"What information? How do you know it's coming from us? How much did they know?"

"They knew my name. They knew that one man had been shot. They might have known more than that."

"That information goes out over our CAD system. It shows up on screens in every division in the city. Hundreds of police personnel could have seen that information. It's not really restricted. The press has access to it. Lots of people could have found out what you say he knew."

"Five hours later? Not that quickly, Waldron. Mislovic got it from somebody on your side."

"Why the hell did you go see him?"

"I wanted to find out if he would help keep the Yardies off Annie. Whoever it was they sent after her last night, he terrified her. I thought if Mills was doing business with them, he might be able to call them off. Tell them to leave the widow alone."

"And?"

"And it turns out he couldn't care less about the widow. He's pissed off about his nephew cheating him. He thinks he deserved to die, and now he's dealing with the Yardies directly."

"Sounds like you were looking for honor among thieves, Mr. Devlin."

"Stranger things have been known to happen. I thought it was worth a shot. I figured the worst he could do was say no."

"It appears that was far from his worst."

"Yes—he tried to turn me over to the Yardies. Then he joined in the shooting."

"What is going on with these people? This is unheard of. There must have been two hundred rounds of ammunition fired on the street this morning."

"I'm a little surprised myself. That Yardie assassin is after Annie. I think after last night he's taking this personally. As for the Yugoslavs, it's me they want to kill."

"Why?"

"I did not treat Mr. Mills gently when they tried to turn me over to the Yardies."

"What did you do?"

"Don't worry, Waldron, I didn't kill anybody. And I don't intend to. Did your tests show the bullets in that body came from a different gun?"

"The tests aren't in yet."

"You'll get the results you want."

"I still need you to come in."

"I told you I can't risk it."

"You have no idea the alarms this is causing. We don't allow gun battles on the streets of London."

"I think you'd better start getting used to it."

"That will not happen."

"It *is* happening. Do you have any idea how well armed these guys are?"

"Yes. Do you have any idea how many arms are coming out of the former Soviet Union and Eastern Bloc countries?"

"What are you going to do about it?"

"Why aren't you cooperating with us? Why are you convinced Mislovic got his information from us?"

"He knew who I was. He knew what happened last night. He knew more than anyone but you and I know."

"Wait a minute. Are you implying that *I* talked to Mislovic?"

"Did you?"

Waldron stared at Devlin, taking a moment to make sure that the question was serious. "All right, Devlin. I've had enough of you. I tried to be civil with you. I gave you and the woman a break that may very well cost me my career. I took you at your word, which proved to be of very little value."

"Why don't you just answer the question, Inspector?"

"*Chief* Inspector. And now you come in here with this absolute shit about me working with some Eastern Bloc gangster so he could kill you? Who the hell do you think you are? Put your damn hands on the table. I'm arresting you. Now."

Devlin sat where he was, listening carefully to Waldron. Evaluating the man. He didn't move his hands.

"Are we going to do this hard or easy, Mr. Devlin?"

Devlin frowned. "Waldron, that's the oldest line in the book. 'Hard or easy'? You're not going to even think about arresting me unless I let you. So drop the bullshit. Are you leaking information to these bad guys or not? Answer me."

But Waldron couldn't stop himself.

"You're not the one giving orders here. You are under arrest."

Waldron took his police radio out of his pocket and started to call Reilly in. Devlin pulled Reilly's radio out of his pocket and laid it on the table. Waldron heard his own voice over it and stopped talking.

Devlin spoke quietly. "Don't bother, James. It's just you and me."

Waldron stared at the police radio on the table. For just a moment he looked as if he were going to go for the arrest by himself, but somehow Devlin had disarmed him. Was it being called by his first name? Was it the calm tone of voice? Whatever it was, Waldron felt his anger ease away.

"You really think I might be speaking to criminals?"

"I'm beginning to not think that."

"Well don't, for God's sake. It's a fucking insult."

"All right, I'll take you at your word. But don't think I shouldn't have asked."

Waldron stared at Devlin for a moment, and Devlin took advantage of the pause.

"Look, Waldron, you have a bigger problem than me. I'm sitting here talking to you—you know what I'm doing. You don't know who's sitting back there on your side talking to your enemies. I can't come in to you."

"You'll have to eventually."

"Can you guarantee her safety? What kind of witness protection program do you have?"

"Assuming she'll agree to testify."

"Assuming you have bad guys she can testify against."

"I guarantee you whoever was shooting at you on the street this morning will be found and arrested. And we can arrange excellent security through the Crown Prosecution Service. If she agrees to testify."

"Fine. But you have to clean up your side first. If you put Annie in protective custody and information leaks to the bad guys, she can be hurt—maybe even more easily than on the street. We can't come in until you find out who is passing information."

Waldron leaned forward.

"Why do you assume the information came from us? Who else had that information? Your client is connected to those people, not us."

The question stopped Devlin. He tried to think of a reason why Annie might be the source. It didn't make sense. She hadn't even known he was going to talk to Mislovic.

Just then, as if on cue, Devlin heard tires screeching on the other side of Piccadilly. Waldron heard it, too. He turned around, and Devlin leaned to his right so he could see out the front door of the restaurant. Both men watched as Zenko and four others stormed into Burger King.

Devlin's face turned hard.

"You're good, Waldron. You really are."

"What are you talking about? Who are they?"

"You know who they are."

"Who? The Yugoslavs?"

Devlin didn't bother to answer.

"Dammit, man, they didn't find out about our meeting from me. You've got to believe me."

Devlin simply frowned at Waldron. "If not you, who?"

"I don't know, but believe me, I'm going to find out."

"You do that, Chief Inspector. And if you want me to believe you, go across the street and arrest those men. They're the shooters from the street this morning. They probably still have the same guns with them. If you don't think that's a good idea, get some of your armed cops and go arrest them at a place called Witmans on Berwick Street. You don't even need the car—you can walk over there. Or arrest that Yardie bastard who tried to kill Annie. Do something to prove whose side you're on, and then we'll talk."

"I need you as witnesses. As complainants. I have nothing on these people without you and the woman."

Devlin dropped Reilly's badge, car keys, and handcuff keys on the table and stood up.

"And next time I ask you to come alone, either do it or don't come."

"You won't survive out there."

"You get the bad guys, we'll testify."

Devlin stood up to leave, but Waldron grabbed his arm. "Wait."

Devlin turned to him and said, "Don't do that."

Waldron had enough training to take down the average man. Probably even the above-average man. But he could feel the strength in Devlin's arm, and see it in his look. Waldron knew he was out of his league. He slowly released his grip.

"All right, Devlin. All right. You find a hole and hide in it. I can't stop the police personnel who might be looking for you now; it's being run from above me. And the All Ports Warning will stay on. But I'll see what I can do to call off some of the heat. Don't try to leave the country. Just promise me you'll be in contact with me. My career is already close to being over. If I arrest people and can't make a case, it *will* be over."

"All right, but you won't know where I am, Waldron, until I believe you."

"Fair enough. It's not me, Devlin. If it were me, we'd still be sitting across the street."

Devlin thought about that and nodded.

"I logged out my destination at four. I had a request for a car in at three. Only a handful of people could have known where I was going. There's a good chance only two of them knew why."

"Find your leak and plug it. Arrest the bad guys. I'll be in touch."

Devlin pulled out the CD he had purchased, dropped it on the table in front of Waldron, and turned to walk out.

"What's this for?"

Devlin turned back and said, "Keep it. I was thinking about breaking your nose with it."

Waldron picked up the CD. When he looked up, Devlin had disappeared into the crowds and traffic of Piccadilly Circus.

Across the street, Zenko stood in the doorway to Burger King while his men checked the upstairs and the various seating areas on the ground floor. All four men returned shaking their heads.

Zenko stared at each person in the restaurant as if he could turn one of them into Devlin. The strange-looking squat man with the bulldog face stood at the entrance with his men gathered around him. He didn't say a word. He didn't move. It seemed as if everyone in the crowded restaurant just sat and watched him, none of them having any idea of what to do about him.

Finally, he turned and walked back to the car, his men following close behind. If anyone had blocked his way, Zenko would have shot him. James Waldron stood near the traffic light on the opposite corner and watched the Yugoslavs climb into a red Saab and drive off.

CHAPTER 20

IT WAS ALMOST eight o'clock when Devlin returned to the airport hotel. Ben had told him the room numbers when he had come back for Annie and Elizabeth in the minivan. Devlin parked and entered by the same side door off the parking lot they had used. He found the rooms on the fourth floor, occupying a corner at the far end of the building. They were a little farther from a stairway than Devlin would have liked, but otherwise well situated.

Devlin knocked twice on the first door. Ben opened it and stepped aside for Devlin to enter.

"Everything all right?" Devlin asked.

Ben nodded.

Devlin looked around. The connecting doors between the two rooms were open. Each room had two double-size beds. Opposite the beds was a long cabinet/dresser/desk. Under it was a half refrigerator with drinks and snacks. On the far wall was a small round table with two chairs by a double window. There were large closets by the entrance, and around a corner a bathroom with double sinks outside and shower, toilet, and tub inside.

This was on the high end of mid-priced hotels. Not luxurious, but good enough, and just right for the anonymity Devlin was seeking.

Through the connecting doors, Devlin could see that Annie was sitting on one of the beds with Elizabeth, reading to her. Elizabeth was dressed in an oversize T-shirt decorated with a map of the Underground. She was tucked in for bed.

Devlin noticed that two empty pizza boxes had been carefully folded and placed into the small plastic trash pail near the desk in Annie's room. There was no room service, which was good. And he was sure Ben had made them deliver the pizza to the front desk so the delivery people wouldn't know their room numbers. He also noted that Ben had the Mossberg shotgun cradled in his arms while he sat in a chair positioned so that he could cover the front doors in each room.

Devlin hung back in the room so as not to disturb Annie and Elizabeth. He sat on the edge of the bed.

Ben asked him, "You get done what you wanted to?"

"Yeah. Pretty much."

"You have a moment?"

"Sure."

In his raspy, Okie-Brit voice, Ben said quietly, "I'm thinkin' this situation here is turnin' pretty sour on you, Mr. Devlin. I figure there's at least two sets of bad guys after you-all. The Yardies, some of who're 'bout as crazy for killin' as they get. And what is it, Eastern Europeans? I don't know much about those folks, but they are heavily armed. Much more'n usual for this part of the world."

"You talked to Annie?"

"Some."

"What did she tell you?"

"Just who they were. Not much more. I didn't press it."

Devlin nodded.

"And on top of all that, you're hiding out from the police, too."

"I've got the police mostly off our backs for now. But to be accurate, it's a little worse than two separate groups after us. The Yugoslavs and the Yardies are working together."

Ben muttered quietly, "Hellfire."

Devlin asked, "You want out?"

"Only a fool wouldn't want out of this, Mr. Devlin. Don't you?"

"That's not an option for me."

"A wise retreat should always be an option. You're real close to gettin' hurt here, sir. No way one or two men can hold off all those people for very long."

"I don't intend for this to last long."

"Well that's good, 'cuz it ain't. Not with all these players. Now you did tell me this wasn't through the agency, that it was your own affair. But this isn't a business matter of yours.

This is personal. If it was just business, you'd've gotten out right about now."

"You're right. It's personal."

"That's what I thought. It's personal." When Ben said "it's," it came out "hits."

"Ben, if you want out, there's no hard feelings."

"We'll see about that. Mainly I want to know for now what the hell you got planned to save the little girl. I don't know about her momma, but I know for sure she doesn't deserve to get shot up out there."

"No, she doesn't."

"So what's the plan, Mr. Devlin?"

"The plan is to hide deep enough so no one will find us for the next few days. Hide somewhere we can get to without public transportation, because the airports and trains are going to continue to be too risky.

"We're going to have to work with the police, but not until the time is right. When, and if, I think it'll work, I'll make a deal with the police for Annie to come in. I'm looking to get her and Elizabeth into a protected witness program."

"The police here ain't always very good at that business."

"The Crown Prosecution Service does it?"

"Sometimes. Sometimes the Met will set something up with their own people. But you should go through Crown Prosecution, and you'd better make sure they have Special Operations handle it instead of the regular Metropolitan Police."

"Okay. If I think it looks right, that's probably the way to go. If not, I'll find a way to get Annie and Elizabeth out of the country. Either way, I'm not going to wait long. For the moment, I have to give the police time to do their job. Or at least try to. Once they make a few arrests, Annie can be protected through the trial. If she's lucky, they might get most of the people after her."

"You think they will?"

"I don't know yet. But I do know that enough hell has been raised that the police see how bad this one is. I think they'll want to move pretty strongly against these people. Particularly the Yugoslavs. They're new on the scene here, aren't they?"

"Yep. And they're bad news.

"What do you know about them?"

"Like I said, not much. But they don't appear to be playin' by the usual rules."

"How many men do they have?"

"Don't know. They don't need many. They're armed up to military specs. And from what I hear, if they need more people, they got the money to hire local muscle."

"Know anybody who's worked for them?"

"A couple."

"Have they heard of you?"

Ben shrugged. "Mebbe. So the plan is to stay down until the police clean it up?"

"Yes. You worried about reprisals?"

"My tracks are covered."

"Anybody know your real name, Ben?"

"Not that I know of."

Both men lapsed into silence, thinking about what had just been said. Devlin thought about Ben and how this job might affect him. It depended on how well he could stay hidden afterwards. Nobody knew very much about Ben Johnson. And, of course, Ben Johnson was not his real name.

Nor was the name he had used to enlist in the Korean War. Ben was sixteen at the time, and he needed a birth certificate that said he was eighteen. But even at sixteen, Ben was bigger and tougher than most grown men.

His age didn't stop him from being a soldier. Ben fought from the Inchon landing to Pork Chop Hill, earning enough battle ribbons to cover about five inches on his chest. He left Korea a master sergeant, one of the rulers of real war. He stayed in the army, serving in the 77th Special Forces unit and the 101st Airborne.

He remained in the army until 1964, another eleven years. He probably would have stayed there if he hadn't approached the point where he was eligible for retirement benefits.

It was then that a computer in Washington kicked in and stirred up a serving of facts that looked right, but did not quite fit together.

Ben's social security number didn't match his age or his place of birth. A dedicated little bureaucrat started to sniff and scratch into Ben's existence and found that many of Ben Johnson's numbers didn't make sense.

School records, medical records, fingerprints, social security number, birth certificate . . . the more the bureaucrat looked, the more he found a mess of inconsistencies.

Most of the facts on Ben's original enlistment papers had been made up. In the rush of enlisting men for the war, no one had bothered to check. But when Uncle Sam was later called upon to pay someone an earned benefit, that was another story.

Ben was unceremoniously pitched out of the service. He was told to be thankful he didn't have to spend time in Leavenworth for falsifying army documents.

The big man blinked once at his commanding officer, turned, and walked out of Fort Dix wearing a very unfamiliar civilian suit with three hundred dollars in one of its pockets. The money had been hastily collected from his army buddies. It was much like leaving prison.

But whether Ben was inside or outside the service didn't seem to matter a great deal to him. Ben had a list of names provided by former officers and friends in the army. There wasn't a man among them who didn't consider Ben invaluable in war.

Ben was an expert in all small arms, explosives, field weapons, survival in the wild, and hand-to-hand combat. He was extraordinarily strong and fit. He could march all day and all night carrying over a hundred pounds if need be. But most important, Ben Johnson was absolutely fearless. It wasn't a question of overcoming fear—he wasn't frightened in the first place. Fear just didn't register in his brain the same way it did for most men, just as greens and yellows don't register in the brain of a man who is color-blind.

Within three days of his discharge, Ben was hooked up with a group of Canadians on their way to join Mad Mike Hoare's mercenary troops operating out of the Kamina Base in Katanga, Africa. After that, he fought all throughout Africa, Malaysia, Indonesia, and the Philippines. It was in the Philippines that he became known to William Chow's network of resources. By then he was freelancing on his own. He could handle the demands of war, but found he didn't want to handle the vagaries of the men who hired him.

For Ben, there was more likelihood of being cheated or

abandoned by those who hired you than there was of being killed by those who fought you. He now only worked for people he knew by reputation or experience.

London became his base. Ben Johnson had practiced his profession, living day-to-day, still hidden from the official network of driver's licenses, social security numbers, credit cards, and phone listings. Whatever cushion he had against the world derived from the cache of money, forged documents, and weapons that he kept in various places, and from his belief and trust in a small network of people. One of whom was Jack Devlin. If Devlin knew very little about Ben's history, he did know that Ben was one of the few reasons he could expect to stay alive against the killers who were after him.

Both men remained silent with their own thoughts. Silence was no stranger to Ben. He was perfectly comfortable with watching Devlin watch Annie put Elizabeth to sleep.

Through the connecting doorway, Devlin could see Annie, but not Elizabeth. The dim light in the other room was kind to Annie. The shadows softened the worry lines around her mouth and eyes and obscured the tension that seemed to be a constant part of her. For the moment, it was a quiet, intimate scene, a loving mother tucking her child in at night.

But the moment didn't last long for Devlin. He found himself calculating the odds that they would be found and rousted out into the dark night.

Devlin turned back to Ben and interrupted the silence.

"If we stay out of trouble until the cops do their job, assuming they nail these guys, we should be all right. And so should you."

"What about you? Cops know who you are?"

"Yes."

"Then the bad guys will, too."

"That's not your problem, Ben."

"Have you got more planned than you're lettin' on, Mr. Devlin?"

"I usually don't look too far out. Just commit to the next two or three days, Ben, and we should be okay."

The big man sat hunched in his chair, cradling the shotgun and thinking over everything Devlin said. After a few moments, he shook his head as if unable to dismiss a nagging thought.

"If they come back at us, you'll have to kill a good few of them Yardies before they figure you ain't worth it. They generally go at it pretty goddamn hard when they get worked up. And that guy shootin' at us this morning is even worse. He's no typical Yardie. I think that guy is Dominican. Maybe even Cuban. Some mix of somethin' else in there."

"How do you know?"

"I saw a Santeria tattoo on his shooting hand. Those boys don't usually last too long. He looked like he has a coupla years on him. If he's still at it, he must have some grit."

"I suppose. Are you going to hang in, Ben?"

Devlin wasn't interested in hearing how hard this was going to be. He already knew that. Ben grimaced once and answered.

"All right. It's damn foolish, but I'll do it. That little girl has gotten under my skin. I usually frighten away anything that small, but she's got heart, that one."

"I know."

"I'll just say this one more time and then I'll shut up. You-all better get those coppers to act fast, 'cuz there's too many sons o' bitches tryin' to nail us. It's only a matter o' time before they find us."

"I know."

Devlin stood up and walked toward the connecting door. He knew that having agreed, Ben would stay on the job until Annie and Elizabeth were out of danger. Then the big man would melt back into his underworld, until the next phone call.

Devlin watched Annie give Elizabeth a final kiss and stand up. She seemed surprised when she saw him standing in the other room. She hadn't heard him come in. His conversation with Ben had been too quiet to be overheard.

Annie walked over to him and hugged him quickly, then let go and told him, "I'm glad you're back."

The quick moment of physical contact took Devlin by surprise. The feel of her lush body against his, even for just a moment, felt so intense that Devlin was too preoccupied to respond to her comment.

Annie filled the silence. "Are you all right?"

"Yes. I'm fine. Everything here okay?

"Yes. I've actually stopped shaking. Did you eat? We had pizza."

"No. I haven't had a chance."

"Do you want to order some food?"

"No. I think I'll go out."

"Let me come with you."

"All right."

Just like that, he had agreed. Why? It was reckless. Had it been the hug? The small flash of physical contact after all those years? They'd been in two gun battles together, but they hadn't really touched until now. Could she make him reckless just by pressing her body against his and holding him?

He turned to Ben. "Stay with Elizabeth. I'll seal the double doors so you don't have to watch two entrances."

Ben nodded and stood up from his comfortable chair with his usual surprising quickness. He lifted his big black bag and silently ambled into the other room. Devlin knew he would set himself up in the room and guard the child until dawn. And all through the next day, if required. Devlin also knew that they had just silently drawn the lines of responsibility. He would look after the woman. Ben would look after the child.

Devlin closed up the double doors connecting the rooms and motioned for Annie to follow him outside.

They walked in silence to the rented minivan, Annie staying close enough to Devlin that their arms brushed. They parted and each entered the van by their own doors. Devlin reached under the floor mat and picked up the ignition key. Leaving the key there meant he wouldn't have to look for it or fumble in his pocket if they had to make a fast getaway.

He started the van and drove quietly out of the car park.

He asked, "Do you know anyplace to eat around here?"

"No. This isn't exactly my neighborhood. I guess if we drive around we'll find a pub or something."

"Okay."

"So what happened in town?"

"I tried to get the cops off our backs."

"How?"

"I met with Waldron."

"Didn't he want to arrest you?"

"Sort of."

"But he didn't?"

"No."

"What did he say?"

"He wants us to come in."

"Are we?"

"Not until I think it's safe."

"Why isn't it safe?"

"We'll talk about that later."

"When is it going to be safe?"

"When he arrests the bad guys and sets up the right kind of protective custody arrangement."

"For who?"

"You. And Elizabeth."

Annie was silent.

"You agreed to bring me in to testify?"

"Only if I think it will be safe."

"Isn't it my decision whether or not to testify?"

"Yes. I haven't decided anything for you. I just set up what I see as one option you should consider. You have to decide if you want to take that option. Unfortunately, you don't have a lot of choice."

"Why? What do you mean?"

Devlin didn't answer. He concentrated on finding a place to eat.

"Jack, what do you mean I don't have any choice?"

Devlin spotted a well-lit pub decorated on the outside with hanging plants and flower boxes. There was a small car park on the side of the pub. He pulled the minivan in and parked.

He rolled down his window and let the cool night air fill the van, then turned to face Annie. He could tell she was holding back from saying all she wanted to until he had finished explaining himself.

"I didn't say *any* choice. I said *much* choice."

Devlin paused before he continued.

"I want you to know what's going on here, Annie. That is, if you don't already."

"What do you mean by that?"

"I really don't know how much you know. How deep you

are into this thing. What makes these people want to kill you? Why are you so important to them?"

"What people? As far as I knew only the Jamaicans were after me. They think I have John's money."

"Do you?"

"No. Except for about a thousand pounds he gave me a couple of weeks ago. And I only have about half of that left. That's it. Whatever else Johnny got out of them he either hid somewhere I don't know about, or he spent it. Knowing him, he probably spent it. Who else is after me? The Yugoslavs? Are they after me or you?"

Devlin watched her carefully in the dim light. He suddenly had the urge to get her somewhere he could see her more clearly. Somewhere with more light so he could see whether or not she was lying. Or was it that he just wanted to see her?

"Come on. We can talk inside."

"No. Answer me, Jack. Do the Yugoslavs want to kill me, too? What am I supposed to have done to them?"

"I don't know what you've done to them."

"Then why were they shooting at us this morning? Was it us, or you?"

"It was definitely me. Problem is, they don't care if they kill you in the process. But it's worse than that."

"Why?"

"They want to do business with the Yardies. If the Yardies want you dead, so do they."

Annie sat across from Devlin without moving or talking. Devlin watched her. He watched the fear disfigure her beautiful face. Suddenly, her right hand was covering her mouth. She seemed to be having trouble breathing. Devlin reached out and placed his hand gently behind her neck.

"Are you all right?"

Annie struggled for breath. Devlin watched panic overcome her and slowly take her away. He quickly stepped out of the driver's seat and hurried around to her side of the van, then pulled her door open and gently helped her out.

"Come on, Annie. Walk. Walk. Stop thinking. Just hold your head up and look at the sky and walk. Hold my arm. Don't think about anything."

Annie did as she was told. She took shallow breaths, barely holding on, looking resolutely at the cloud-swept London sky.

She thought to herself, Let me see a star. Any star. Or the moon. Anything. She felt like screaming. But she held it in, even though all she could see above her were the scudding clouds. All she could hear was the clicking of her heels on the asphalt parking area. She looked down and saw her feet. Then she looked straight ahead at the pub's sign. She felt Devlin's strong hand on her arm. He was leading her to the restaurant. Other people would be in there. She would have to appear normal. She wanted to know how her uncle could do that to her. How could he turn her over to those animals? How could he?

Somehow she made it inside the pub. Devlin had them seated in a quiet corner. He sat facing the room, and she sat opposite him. All she had to look at, to worry about, was Devlin, but she knew strangers were behind her, and the thought of losing it in front of strangers made her stifle the fear and anger and disgust she was experiencing at hearing that someone who was part of her own family would turn her over to people who used machetes and dogs to kill.

The waitress came over. Annie ordered a double vodka and asked Devlin to pick a wine.

"Are you going to eat?" he asked her.

"Just a salad. Get whatever wine you want. I just want to keep drinking while we talk. I don't think I'm going to like this conversation."

CHAPTER 21

WHEN WALDRON FOUND Sergeant Reilly in the unmarked squad car, trying to hide his cuffed hands underneath the newspaper, he thought he might just leave the despicable man sitting there. Waldron hadn't experienced an overwhelming urge to hit anyone in years, but he did now.

Waldron knew that Reilly was the source the Yugoslavs were using. Just as he knew that Devlin hadn't lied to him when he told him Mislovic had known too much, too soon. He hadn't needed to see the Yugoslavs running into the Burger King to believe Devlin. But it was undeniable proof of betrayal, and here was the betrayer, cuffed to the steering wheel of his own car. This horse-faced, useless traitor had turned against a fellow cop. Cops everywhere committed evil. There was too much opportunity. You could take a bribe. You could lie on the witness stand. You could make a deal with criminals. But even the worst cop wouldn't work with criminals in a way that could hurt another cop. But that was what Reilly had done. He was the worst of the worst.

Waldron forced himself to remain impassive. He reminded himself that revenge was a dish best served cold.

He opened the door and unlocked Reilly's cuffs without a word. Reilly's barrage of curses and threats against Devlin filled the air around Waldron. A smoke screen of pseudo-rage. Waldron didn't respond. He handed the man back his badge and radio.

Reilly looked at Waldron for support, but all Waldron said was, "Let's get back, Reilly. Stop talking about it now."

Reilly kept right on cursing and threatening.

And then Waldron snapped.

"Shut up," he yelled.

It was so startling that Reilly's head jerked back. He had never heard the chief use that tone.

"Just drive back to the division, Reilly, and don't make another sound."

Reilly drove.

Waldron sat back in his seat, suddenly enervated by his own anger. But he pushed aside the fatigue, because he knew there was a tremendous amount of work to be done. He began creating a list in his head. There was the paperwork necessary to obtain the warrants for the arrests of Mislovic and the Yardies. He had to organize a stakeout on the Berwick Street headquarters. He had to contact the Crown Prosecution Service and begin negotiations and arrangements for a protection program for the woman and child. And on and on and on. And he had to do it all without Reilly knowing about it or getting in his way. *And* he had to do everything fast enough that Fenton didn't have a chance to stop him first.

Once all that was done, Waldron promised himself he would get the evidence he needed to prove that Reilly was the traitorous bastard he was. No one else would know about it. No one else would be involved. He would do it. And do it so well, and so thoroughly, that when it was over Sergeant Patrick Reilly would be forever gone.

Reilly had remained silent for ten minutes. It was a major achievement for him. Finally, he blurted out, "So what did you do with that bloody bastard Devlin?"

Waldron stopped his ruminations and looked over at Reilly. "What?"

"Devlin. What happened with Devlin?"

"Nothing. He dropped your belongings on my table and told me to come alone next time."

"Then what?"

"He walked away."

"And you just let him go?"

"No. I went after him. We had words. We reached an understanding."

"What kind of understanding?"

"We'll set up protection for the woman, and then they'll cooperate."

"Protection?"

"Isn't that what you do for witnesses?"

"Who's she going to testify against?"

"Against criminals, Reilly. Isn't that whom they usually testify against?"

"So how long did it take you to make a deal with him?"

"I wasn't looking at my watch."

"It took you long enough."

"I didn't come right back to you."

"Why?"

"Letting him catch you like that did not make me happy, Sergeant. It didn't exactly put me in the best position to negotiate. I thought if I came back to the car before I calmed down I might beat you senseless."

"You what?"

"I walked into the record store and bought a CD."

Waldron pulled out Devlin's purchase.

"What did you say?"

"Like the title: *From Hell to Paradise*?"

"What?"

"Maybe it should be: *From Paradise to Hell.*"

"What are you talking about?"

"Never mind."

"When are they coming in?"

"Soon."

"The woman is going to testify."

"Isn't that what I just said?"

They were coming over the Tower Bridge now. Waldron knew he would be working most of the night. But first he had to get rid of Reilly.

Reilly persisted, "How could you let the man just walk away after what he did?"

"Yes, it was really thoughtless of me. Next time I'll sit in the car and get handcuffed to the steering wheel, and you bring him in."

"Bloody hell if I won't, next chance I get."

"Yes. Absolutely, Sergeant Reilly. If you can find him before I do, you bring him in. Definitely. I'm sure you're well motivated now."

Reilly stopped the car in front of the entrance to the division. Waldron opened the door, but turned to Reilly before he stepped out.

"Check the car back in and go home to supper, Sergeant. Your shift is almost over. Rough day, I imagine. Perhaps you'd like to relax and take a drink or two. Might do you some good. Start fresh in the morning."

Waldron got out of the car.

Reilly shouted after him, "Is he coming in or not?"

"Oh, I'm sure he is. One way or another. Keep an eye out then. I'll see you tomorrow."

Waldron walked into the division.

Reilly spit out the window in Waldron's direction and drove to the nearest phone booth. He left a message for Zenko. The message said he wanted to meet personally. He gave the name of an Italian restaurant in Soho. He told the bailiff to tell his man to look for someone sitting at the bar with his tie undone.

By the time Zenko arrived at the restaurant, Reilly was on his third double Jameson.

Reilly had told himself there was plenty of reason to have a goddamn drink. Even get drunk if he felt like it. That sodding nance Waldron had no idea who he was playing with. Nobody dismissed Patrick Reilly like that. He was bracing bad guys before Waldron was old enough to jerk his little weenie. Fucking bastard. And why hadn't Zenko nailed Devlin this afternoon?

Reilly was just about to convince himself that he would find Devlin and shoot the man on his own, when Zenko's arrival broke his brooding internal whiskey rant. The maitre d' showed Zenko to a table. While a waiter went to fetch his drink, Zenko stared at Reilly until the old cop made eye contact. Zenko nodded at him and Reilly fingered his untied tie and nodded back, very pleased with himself. He finished his Jameson and stood up to go to the toilet.

But Reilly stood up off the bar stool too quickly. He teetered for a moment. He was light-headed and short of breath. He reached out to steady himself on the bar. His head cleared a bit, but he still felt woozy. He pushed himself away from the bar and headed for the toilet, concentrating on finding the door with a top hat and the word "Men." But he still felt nauseous and sweaty. Christ, he thought to himself, what the hell is happening to me? What am I doing meeting with this criminal in person? No. I have to. I'm not playing around anymore. I'll find out what happened today. Waldron will be sorry he ever told me to shut up.

Three minutes later, Zenko entered the small bathroom looking for Reilly, but all he could see were Reilly's battered cordovans underneath the stall door.

Zenko curled his nose. "Hey, light a match, goddammit. You gotta do that knowing I come in here after you?"

"I had to go."

"So go at home, dammit."

Inside the booth Reilly reached into his pocket and pulled out one of his wrinkled cigarettes and lit it. He dropped the match between his legs, just missing the head of his lank penis.

"Shit!"

"Yah, shit. That's what it is. So you the guy working with us?"

"I'm the guy."

"What happen at that Burger King? Piccadilly."

"That's what I wanted to ask you. What happened?"

"Nobody there. No Devlin."

"He was there."

"How do you know? You not there either."

"I was there, dammit. I was around the corner in my car. My chief was supposed to meet him alone, so I waited outside. How long did it take you to get there, for God's sake?"

"You know he was there for sure?"

"I saw the man."

"So why you not arrest the son of a bitch?"

"I told you, I was waiting outside. I thought my sodding boss was going to arrest him, but no, he ended up making a goddamn deal with him."

"Deal. What deal?"

"Devlin agreed to come in if Waldron gets the woman into a protected witness program."

"Witness program? What's that?"

"They set up protection for people testifying against people who might kill them."

"Shit. Who she going to testify against?"

"I would imagine you and your boss."

"Bullshit."

"Yeah? Watch her."

"When does he bring the woman in?"

"I don't know. Yet. If you'd have gotten there in time and shot both of them we wouldn't be worrying about this now, would we?"

"More damn trouble. What your name, Policeman?"

"What do you need my name for?"

"I want to know what to call you."

"Reilly. Patrick Reilly."

"We work together now, Reilly. Direct, right?"

Reilly flushed the toilet and stepped out of the stall. They looked at each other. Neither one offered a hand to shake.

"Right."

Reilly walked to the sink and gave his unshaken hand a fast rinse. Zenko watched him and waited until he started to wipe his hands on the men's room towel.

"So we on same side, Policeman Reilly?"

"Only temporarily."

"So you better find Devlin and the woman for us. If the woman testifies, there will be trouble for everybody. Including you."

Reilly felt better now. The Irish whiskey had kicked in. He wasn't going to let this fucking alien push him around.

"Listen, you."

"Zenko. My name is Zenko."

"Right. Zenko. I delivered him to you once already, Zenko. You know how much chance I have of doing that again? If you wanted the man so damn bad you should have gotten there sooner. He was right there. If you can't do the job, I'll shoot the bastard myself."

Zenko reached into his pocket and pulled out a wad of bills. He peeled off two one-hundred pound notes from the inside of the roll and tucked the bills into Reilly's shirt pocket.

"You don't shoot him. Too much trouble for you, Policeman Reilly. We shoot him, no trouble. For anybody. Go back outside and have more drinks. On me. Give us another chance at Devlin. We take care of everything. We get him. We get the woman. No problems. Everything business as usual. Okay?"

The money mollified Reilly. He imagined putting one of the hundred-pound notes down on a decent bar instead of the little service bar in this wop joint. Now wouldn't that feel good.

"All right, Mr. Zenko. But if we get another chance, don't blow it, you hear?"

"Yah, we don't blow it."

"And in the meantime, I suggest you keep your boss out of sight for a while. Now that my chief has a witness, the next thing he'll be looking to do is arrest your boss."

"Okay."

"I'll be in touch."

With all the swagger he could muster in the small bathroom that still stank from his cigarette and excrement, Reilly pushed open the door and left.

Zenko stood at the sink. He would give Reilly a few minutes to get out of the restaurant before he returned to his table. He turned on the water and adjusted it to the right temperature and carefully washed his meaty hands.

He thought about the Caesar salad that waited for him at his table and wondered what the odds were that this old cop would come up with another chance at the American. Maybe they would get lucky.

The woman, however, was another story. They would not need so much luck with her. If she was to appear as a witness, she would have to come out of hiding. She would have to meet with police, the prosecutors, lawyers. Once that happened, Policeman Reilly could lead them to her. And if they knew where she was, they would know where Devlin was. Use the Yardies to kill them, or maybe even do it myself, thought Zenko. And maybe Policeman Reilly, too. Would be nice to kill him, too, thought Zenko. Then I would only smell his shit one more time, when he messed his pants just before I shoot him.

After the meeting with Mislovic, Oliver drove to a small, seemingly abandoned warehouse located on the north edge of Hackney near a canal called the River Lea. In a city packed with cars, double-decker buses, taxis, bicycles, and a dense underground network of trains and subways, most people for-

got that there were miles and miles of navigable canals twisting and turning throughout the urban sprawl of London. It
was possible to travel virtually anywhere via those canals. It
was easy for an experienced person to disappear into the watery maze.

The canal was why Oliver had located his warehouse there.
The barge traffic was very light, but it was not unusual to see a
commercial or residential barge meander past at any hour of
the day or night. The canal provided Oliver with a method of
quietly bringing goods in and out of his warehouse, virtually
unseen.

While Oliver had gone to the warehouse, Hinton had gone
straight to Lydia Cientro's Santeria/Voodoo chapel to take his
place before the statue of Chango.

Oliver knew that Hinton would work himself into a strange
trance and stay there for hours until he received some kind of
sign or confirmation from his god about the woman. Hinton
was determined to kill her and her bodyguard. Oliver had very
little doubt they would both die. It was only a matter of time.

Oliver didn't know why, or how, but he knew that whatever
Hinton was into, it worked for him. It certainly made Hinton
believe he would succeed. If Hinton's gods could lead him to
the woman, so much the better, thought Oliver. The sooner
Hinton satisfied his blood lust for her, the better. He needed
him to protect his business as it expanded outside of the black
neighborhoods in Hackney, Brixton, Stoke Newington, and
Harlesdon. He needed him for the war that was surely coming
against Mislovic. He needed him to keep order in his own
ranks.

Oliver sat in a makeshift office on the second floor of the
warehouse, brooding over the task of obtaining ten kilos of
cocaine for Mills. It would be his largest single sale. It would
deplete most of his finances. But if successful, it would raise
him to another level. A level beyond the local drug trade.

He walked out of his office and looked down into a large
open area that formed the main floor of the warehouse. The
second-floor mezzanine where he stood circled the open area.
On the mezzanine were a few old offices and storage spaces.
On the ground floor at the front of the building was a rolling
steel door big enough to allow entrance for two cars or a large

truck. It was shut tight. Oliver rarely opened it. Nothing big enough ever went in or out of the warehouse that necessitated bringing a vehicle inside. Also at the front was a metal door that gave entrance into the warehouse when the big door was shut.

On the back wall of the warehouse were opaque windows reinforced with wire mesh. There was also a metal door, bolted shut and locked with an iron crossbar. That door gave access to an overgrown area filled with weeds and grass and debris that hid much of the warehouse from view. A barge passing by or the rare person who walked the towpath on the far side of the canal wouldn't look twice at the old warehouse obscured by tall grass and weeds. But Oliver's men had cleared a narrow path to the canal. Shipments were quickly delivered back there and walked into the warehouse out of sight.

Oliver looked at two of his men sitting by a battered desk near the south wall. From now until his shipment arrived, there would be at least two men in the warehouse at all times. The shipment was due sometime within the next three days.

Oliver stepped back into his office and began a series of phone calls. Money had to be obtained. Transportation arranged. Schedules agreed upon. Guarantees given. The business of his drug trade was done in a singsong patois using confusing code words that anyone but Oliver and his colleagues would find extremely difficult to understand.

There was much to do before the deal with the Yugoslavs was complete, including killing the American and the wife of the thief who had stolen from him.

Annie watched Devlin eat his dinner. He watched her drink. She waited for the food to satisfy his hunger. He waited for the alcohol to calm her down.

She had finished the vodka quickly. Now she was sipping her second glass of wine. They hadn't spoken to each other beyond commenting on the food, but the alcohol had relaxed her. The tone of her voice had dropped a level, and she was staring openly at Devlin with her deep dark eyes.

When the coffee came, Devlin asked, "Are you all right?"

"You mean for a woman alone who everybody wants to see dead?"

"You're not alone."

"Yes. You're right. I'm sorry. I'm not alone. Thanks to you."

"Did you have any doubt that I would come?"

"Doubt? I was so anxious and worried I didn't allow myself to get to doubt. I just concentrated on hoping you'd arrive soon. I was hardly able to imagine it—imagine seeing you again. And then you were suddenly there."

"Are you going to be able to handle this?"

"I don't know. I guess I'm doing a Scarlett O'Hara thing. I keep putting off really thinking about it. I'll think about it tomorrow. At least I'm better now than I was in the parking lot. What the hell was that back there?"

"A panic attack."

"What do people do for that?"

"Take Valium. Or drink."

Annie raised her wineglass. "Well, in lieu of Valium."

"That should do it."

"Yeah."

After a moment Devlin said, "We're going to have to talk about the police."

"What about them?"

"Do you want to talk now?"

"Yes."

"You'll have to think about this now rather than tomorrow."

"Okay."

"You've got two choices, as I see it."

"Go ahead."

"You can work with the police. Hope they arrest the people who are after you. Agree to testify against them. And hope they protect you adequately while they put them away."

"Why do I hear the word 'hope' so much?"

"Because there are no guarantees. I'm not sure of any court systems anymore, and particularly the British courts."

"Why?"

"I've heard too many judges here described as senile old fools."

"So even if they arrest them, and I testify, there's no guarantee they'll be out of my life."

"Correct. But at least some of them will be stopped, and you will be given an opportunity to create a new life for yourself. Maybe with a different name. Certainly in a different place."

"What's the second choice?"

"One more thing."

"What?"

"We haven't gotten into this part much, and I don't think we should, but if there's anything the police might have against you, any crimes they might want to lay at your door, if you cooperate and testify against the bad guys, they'll have to forget all that."

" 'All that' being crimes I might have committed."

"Or they think you committed."

"I didn't commit any crimes, Jack, but as with everything else, that's no guarantee I won't be charged with any."

"Right."

"Okay, what's the second choice?"

"Get the hell out of the country and hope the Yugoslavs and the Yardies don't have a long enough reach to get to you back home. Or wherever you decide to go."

"Is that likely?"

"That they can go after you someplace else?"

"Yes."

"Of course. All it takes is one person who kills for money. It all depends on how badly they want to hurt you. Or how badly they want what you have."

"I don't have anything they want."

"They seem to think you do."

"I know. But I don't."

"Then you'll have to evaluate how far they want to follow you."

Annie sipped her wine and thought for a few moments.

"So that's it. Either I stay and hope, or run and hope."

"Something like that."

"Is this what they call a Hobson's choice?"

"No, actually, I think that's when you have no alternative. You do."

"Neither alternative sounds like a real way out of all this."

Devlin didn't respond.

Annie continued, "And either way my whole life changes."

"I'd say that's already happened."

"If I run, whatever I have left is gone. My friends. My work here. Elizabeth's friends. Her school. It's all gone."

"You can build it up again."

"Will it ever be safe for me here?"

Devlin paused. "Anything is possible. But probably not. Maybe in some other part of England."

Suddenly Annie's face turned hard. "I wish I could kill them all. All of them. That animal they sent after me and my—"

She stopped herself, and Devlin asked, "Your what?"

"Eliminate all of them and all my problems."

Devlin watched Annie struggle to get on top of her emotions. Was she surprised at the fierceness of her own anger? he wondered. Was she trying to steer away from her fear?

"So," she asked, "what if I decide to just get out of here? Just leave? Can we get away?"

Devlin didn't answer right away. He was still busy observing her. Then he said, "Well, it won't be easy. But it's certainly not impossible. I would lay low for a while until things calm down a bit more. Put some time on this All Ports Warning. Then perhaps take the ferry over to Calais. Once we get on the Continent we can go just about anywhere. The problem with that is you leave everything behind. And you leave your enemies free. As I said, I don't know how far these people would go to get you."

Annie sat in silence. She looked at him. He looked at her. Devlin knew there was way too much being left unsaid between them. Too much time had passed for them to be open and connected after just one dinner together.

Finally, Annie blurted out, "How long will you stay with me?"

Devlin didn't answer. He heard a voice inside him say, "Forever." It had come from somewhere inside him that he had long ago given up on. He was so surprised by the reaction that he could not hide the look on his face.

Annie saw his expression and asked, "What's the matter?"

He looked up at her. "Honestly?"

"Yes, honestly. God, Jack, this isn't the time to be dishonest."

"I'm surprised at how I might answer your question."

"How long you'll stay with me?"

"Yes."

"Why?"

"I didn't realize until this moment how strongly I still feel about you."

Now it was Annie's turn to look at Devlin for a moment before speaking.

"Is that good?"

"I don't know."

"Why?"

"Why what?"

"Why don't you know if your feelings about me are good or not? Or maybe I'm assuming something you don't mean."

"When I say I feel strongly about you?"

"Yes."

"I mean what it sounds like."

"Then why isn't that good?"

"Because right now you don't need a lover or a replacement for your husband. You need a professional who can protect you."

"It seems to me you'd protect someone you loved, or cared about, more than you would someone you don't care about."

"Well, you'd certainly want to. But you might end up making more mistakes."

Annie nodded. "I understand. So maybe I shouldn't be asking you what you think I should do."

"Does it seem like forever since we were together?"

The question stopped her. She smiled.

"Yes and no. Do you ever think of me?"

Devlin paused before he answered.

"For a long time, I thought of you every day."

"Every day?"

"Several times a day. Every day."

"How long did that go on?"

"For years."

"Years? Come on."

"Years."

"And now?"

"Now I don't allow myself to think much about anybody."

"Why?"

Devlin shrugged. Annie could see he wasn't going to answer that question. In fact, she felt that if she pushed him too much he might not answer any more questions.

"So what happened to us, Jack? Why didn't we stay together?"

Devlin looked at her, but no words came out.

"Come on. Come on, dammit, tell me. Don't I have the right to know after all these years? Before I die?"

"Did you think of me?"

Annie looked down at the dregs of her red wine, then looked up. "I was obsessed with you. I don't think I ever forgave you for not marrying me."

"I'm sorry."

A quick frown distorted her face. And then it was gone. Replaced by a toughness that Devlin realized was what had kept her together throughout whatever disappointments and difficulties the years had brought to her. A toughness that was going to keep her together through whatever was coming.

"Forget it. It's over, Jack. Whatever happened, whatever the reason, I know it wasn't because you were mean or thoughtless. You just couldn't. I knew it then; I know it now. It's not helpful to talk about that. It's past us. That particular dream is over."

Devlin nodded.

"I've got other things to think about, right?"

"Yes. You do."

They sat silently for a while, Devlin letting Annie think. And Devlin letting himself think about things he had told himself he shouldn't.

And then he said, "Whatever you decide, I'll help you."

"I know you will."

"Do you know what you want to do?"

"Of course I know. I've always known. I'm going to stay and fight. I'm going to do everything I can to eliminate my enemies. Isn't that what you would do?"

Annie's answer didn't surprise Devlin. He knew that despite the panic, despite the fear, it had always been there.

"Yes," he admitted. "That's what I would do."

"And you think the police are the ones who can help me do that, if I agree to cooperate?"

"I'll say I think they are the best possibility."

"Then that's decided. What do we do next?"

"We'll have to give the police a little time to make arrests. So for now we should find a place away from London where we can stay out of harm's way."

"Some little hotel or something?"

"I'd prefer to avoid hotels. I'd prefer something more private."

"Any ideas?"

"I've been thinking about it. One thing is for sure: I want to move on tomorrow. I want to keep moving."

"All right. I'll think about it, too. So tomorrow we travel."

"Right."

"And tonight?"

"Tonight, we sleep."

Devlin caught the brief smile that softened Annie's face for just a moment, but neither of them commented on it.

Devlin paid the bill and they drove back to the hotel.

They entered the room quietly. Devlin knocked softly on the connecting door. Ben opened it. Devlin motioned him into his room. Ben walked in, and Annie slipped into the adjoining room where Elizabeth was sleeping.

Devlin said to Ben, "You want to stay up for the first shift, or you want to sleep?"

"You sleep. I'm up."

"All right. I'll be up in three hours. You can get three or four hours' sleep and then I want to get out of here."

Ben nodded and turned to go back into Elizabeth's room, but had to step aside as Annie returned with her carryall bag. Ben let her pass, stepped into the other room, and closed the door behind him.

Annie looked at Devlin and said, "I'm sure Ben is a nice fellow, but I'd rather not sleep in there with him. You don't mind, do you?"

Devlin sat down on one of the beds and watched Annie gather toiletries and a nightgown from the big bag.

"No. I don't mind."

With her belongings in hand, Annie looked at Devlin.

"This feels a little strange."

"I know."

"It's funny. Even with all the talk in the restaurant, I didn't anticipate this."

"Anticipate what?"

"Anticipate I'd have to think about sleeping in the same bed with you."

"There are two beds, Annie."

"That means I have to choose. I have to think about it."

"If there were only one, you'd still have to decide what to do once you were in bed."

"I know. Well," she said, "as I recall you used to shower at night."

"So did you."

"So who goes first?"

"Go ahead, Annie."

"No."

"Okay, I'll go."

"No."

"What then?"

"Together. Let's shower together."

Before Devlin could respond, Annie walked to the sink area outside the bathroom and placed her toiletries on the counter. She hung her nightgown on the back of the door, then turned away from Devlin and slid her top over her head and stepped out of her slacks. For some reason Devlin found himself surprised at how brief and sensual her sheer lace underwear was. She turned to him and held out her hand.

"Come on. Come with me."

She motioned with her fingers and walked backwards toward the bathroom.

"Come on."

Devlin stood up and undressed, dropping his clothes on the chair by the window.

Annie left the lights off in the bathroom. Outside, one small light burned over the sink. Devlin walked into the bathroom and stood behind her as she adjusted the shower spray. From behind, her body looked wonderful. Her dark hair fell across her bare back. Her rear end looked tight and toned under her lace panties. Devlin had a fierce urge to run his hand over her backside and down her long, sleek legs.

She bent over and stretched to adjust the faucets in the shower. Devlin smiled. He enjoyed the sight of her, although he felt a little foolish just standing there and watching.

But then she turned to him and slipped out of her bra. She slipped her panties down and kicked them into a corner, tossing the bra after them. Steam began to fill the small bathroom. She stepped close to him, close enough so that her full breasts pressed into his chest and her pubic hair brushed against his hardening cock.

She put her hands on his shoulders and looked up at him. And then she smiled ruefully and said, "Dev, there's nothing I'd rather do than sleep with you one more time. Especially since, let's face it, I don't know how much time I have left. I loved you then, and I love you now. In fact, I've always loved you. But how do we make it seem like something more than a cheap fuck in a nondescript hotel?"

Suddenly, Devlin laughed. "Shit, Annie, I don't know."

"Ridiculous, isn't it?"

"Yes. You have no idea how glad I am that you said that."

"Well, it's true. This is the cliché of all times. Two old lovers meet and go at it once more for old times' sake."

Devlin leaned back against the wall and Annie settled into him. He held her close.

"Yes, but how could I not want you here with me like this, naked, right up against me, with that beautiful smile of yours. It's like we've fooled time and circumstance, Annie. Another chance at each other—who could pass that up?"

Annie flipped on the lights and stepped back.

"Talk about time. Look at you." Annie gazed at Devlin's lean, muscular body. "You're down to the essence, Dev. You always had the best body of any man I ever knew, but now you're leaner, more ropy, or muscular. Something."

"Either you're better, too, or I forgot how good you looked."

"Bullshit. Bullshit on both counts."

"No. I like the way you look now, even better than when we were young. You're more sensuous."

"You don't remember me when."

"Sure I do. I've compared every woman I've ever been with to you."

"How come when you say something like that it doesn't sound like complete bullshit?"

"Because it's not."

Annie slapped him playfully on the shoulder and said, "Yeah, so how many thousands have you compared me to?"

"Not thousands."

"Hundreds."

Devlin shrugged. "Only dozens."

"You pig."

"This is a high school conversation, Annie. Even naked."

She shrugged. "It's cute, though, isn't it. Better than mooning at each other naked in the dark."

"So how many men for you?"

"Since my husband? None."

"None."

"Well, one. But he didn't count."

"Why?"

"Never mind."

Suddenly Annie became serious. She had begun to notice the healed scars and old wounds that marked Devlin's body. She saw the livid red slash on his thigh from the bullet in Hawaii. Its presence made the dangerous life Devlin lived intrude between them, and reminded Annie of what had brought Devlin back to her.

She pointed and said, "You didn't have those on you when you left me, Jack."

She stepped forward and touched some of the scars, then stepped closer still and held him in her arms and kissed his shoulder and his neck and his cheek.

"My God, Jack. You should have stayed with me. I would have taken care of you."

Devlin held her and allowed a rush of feeling to overtake him. The sudden and ineffable sadness he experienced surprised him. He felt such an overwhelming sense of loss and remorse that he automatically steeled himself against the pain. But the feelings continued to pour through him. The pain and damage and death. The anger. The evil. The years that would never be lived again. The turns in his life that could never be undone. He felt it all. She had somehow pulled the feelings out of him with her words and her looks and her presence. He held her, and she held him back, stroking his shoulders and his neck.

She spoke softly into his chest and said, "It's all right. We did what we had to do. You were never bad, Jack. You were a good man. You are. You'll always be my man, no matter what."

And then she stepped back from him and wiped a tear away and nodded toward the shower.

"You go first," she said. "I'll turn down the bed and floss or something. We old ladies have lots to do at night. Take your time."

Devlin stood in the shower and let the warm water wash away some of the pain inside. Afterwards, he slid naked between the sheets and lay on his back, finally relaxing, finally feeling comfortable in the nondescript room by the airport.

Sometime later, when he was half asleep, Annie joined him in bed. He felt her unbelievably smooth skin and warmth and softness cover his left side as she nestled in next to him. He put his arm around her, and she laid her head on his chest. Somehow the years between them had melted away. She reached down and patted his growing cock as if to say, Take it easy, Jack, just go to sleep. Devlin smiled. He rolled toward her. He knew there was no way he could have this woman sleep naked next to him and not make love to her. And Annie knew it, too. She kissed him quickly, then slipped away from him and slid under the blanket on the other bed.

Devlin rolled back and let it go. He smiled to himself. Annie Turino. Still the one that got away.

CHAPTER 22

WHILE DEVLIN AND Annie slept, Waldron worked.

It took him two hours to write up his forms with the right blend of hard information, exaggeration, and evasion. According to his report, Devlin had finally appeared for a police interrogation, during which time he indicated that Ms. Anne Petchek would testify, once assurances were made that she would be accepted as a protected witness. It was adjudged that her testimony would be helpful in prosecuting the following crimes and criminals, including blah, blah, blah. The severity of crimes was so on and so forth. The likelihood for successful prosecution was adjudged to be such and such. Etc., etc., etc.

Waldron was very proficient at officialese. He finished his report knowing that, for the moment, it would serve as a paper barrier that would keep Fenton off his back.

Next, Waldron hit the phones. He had to jury-rig a group of men to work the surveillance needed to find Mislovic. It had to be done outside the regular work schedules so that Fenton would not know what he was doing. Which meant that instead of simply ordering the work details, he had to spend an hour on the phone bribing, trading favors, juggling schedules, and dealing sick time, overtime, and double time. But he finally managed to assemble the bodies he needed: six men on two-man shifts, eight hours each day for two days.

He hoped that would be enough time to nail Mislovic. The Yugoslavs were his prime target. Waldron considered them to be far more dangerous than the Yardies. Making a case against Mislovic would be difficult, but it would mean stopping one source from putting automatic weapons onto the streets of London. No matter what happened, no matter how many lies had to be told or regulations skirted, Waldron knew that if he got Mislovic, at the end of the day his superiors would know that something significant had been accomplished. And he knew that no one would question too closely how it had been done.

The next job was getting Annie into the protected witness program. He started by calling a colleague in the Crown Prosecution Service office, Milt Reisel. Reisel had just arrived home after watching a football game. He was drunk on postgame shots of Scotch and pints of stout. In the background, Waldron could hear Reisel's wife complaining that he was pissed and demanding to know who was calling him at eleven o'clock at night.

Neither his drunkenness nor his wife's harangue stopped Reisel from talking to Waldron. Reisel liked Waldron. They had grown up in the same village outside London. They had attended the same schools until college. And Reisel was the kind who was amused by his wife's yelling at him.

After a bit of prodding, Reisel agreed to wangle an appointment with someone in the Crown Prosecution Service who might be able to let Annie into the protected witness program.

"Listen," Waldron said, "you're pissed, Milt, so don't forget this conversation."

"Don't worry, old man. It's as good as done. Call me if you have any problems."

"Who won the game?"

"Haven't a clue. Couldn't give a fuck either. Ta."

And finally, Waldron had to tighten up the net he had strung to keep Devlin from bolting. He knew Devlin could still decide to cut free and run with the woman.

He checked in with all the commanders on duty for the British Transport Police, and emphasized he was still on the lookout for Devlin and Annie. He reissued his All Ports Warning, sent another bulletin through the CAD system and the PNC.

And finally, there was the pile of pages needed to enable him to continue his investigation. Time sheets. Incident reports. Schedules. Estimates. Waldron often found solace in the solitary work. He actually enjoyed filling in the forms with carefully typed, precisely selected words. Waldron knew that the words had very little to do with the truth. The reports weren't true. They existed to protect the police and to prosecute the criminals. And Waldron had spent years learning how to bend them to his will.

When he was finally finished, when he could do no more, he looked at his watch. The readout said 5:22 A.M. His left ear was puffy and sore from the phone. His legs were cramped. His back was stiff. And he felt the fatigue that had been masked for hours by his nervous energy. He knew he would soon be very tired.

Waldron also knew he had to walk now. To get up and move and try to unhinge his cramped arms and legs. He knew where he would go. Out onto Tooley Street, turn right, and continue on to the bridge. He would walk over Tower Bridge until he was halfway across. Then he would stand in the cold early-morning air while suspended high above the gray, sluggish waters of the Thames. He would smell the mix of salt and air and look out over the old city. His city. He'd look past the ancient walls of the Tower of London, the old jail where so many members of royalty were imprisoned and executed, out across the city with its jumble of old and new and forever. And he wouldn't think about the mean and dangerous people that were trying to kill the London he had known. He'd let his eyes rest and his nerves settle down. He'd watch the river and absorb the city; then he would go back to his cubicle office and continue.

Waldron planned his walk out beforehand, like he did most of his moves. He planned it so that he could enjoy it and let his mind think about the next thing he had to do, and the next, and the next, until he had Mislovic arrested, had Devlin and the woman and child in custody, had Reilly destroyed, and had it all done before Fenton or the rulers above him stepped in and stopped him.

He stood up and walked out the front door of the Tower Bridge Division, took a deep breath of the morning air that would be fresh for maybe another hour, and started walking.

Mislovic was starting his morning routine, too. Today he would not wear any of the stodgy Savile Row suits he had depended on for status. Today he would dress casually. And today the *London Times* and cappuccino would not be enjoyed on Berwick Street.

Zenko had called Mislovic right after the meeting with Reilly and warned him that the cops would be looking to arrest him at the Berwick Street headquarters.

Waldron's first surveillance team arrived there at eight. Mislovic didn't.

Mislovic walked out of his flat near Dorset Square and saw Zenko waiting for him in the red Saab that Oliver had given them.

Mislovic looked at the car and frowned. Everything the car represented grated on him. He felt like getting in the back and making believe the Saab belonged to a car service sent to pick him up. And on this morning Mislovic looked like someone who might be taking a car service to work. He looked very much like an executive who worked in one of the glamorous legitimate businesses whose highly designed reception areas fronted the streets of Soho, instead of an ex–military killer turned drug-dealing gangster operating out of a dingy Soho back room.

In his gray wool slacks, black cashmere polo sweater, and brown Bally leather bomber jacket, Mislovic could have been an advertising creative director, or maybe a film production company director. And not just some upstart newcomer. Mislovic looked as if he could be an older, experienced executive. With his steel gray hair and mature features and expensive clothes, Mislovic looked as if he could be one of the deal makers he often saw in the trendy bars and restaurants of Soho. The facilitators in slick, glamorous, fast-paced businesses that somehow gleaned extra panache from being located amidst the sleaze and porn of Soho, the come-on girlie bars, the peep shows, and the stinking single rooms off dingy corridors where junkie whores breaking down from disease and age jerked off men who walked up dirty stairways to hire "models" for thirty minutes. But then, it was all business, wasn't it?

Zenko leaned over and opened the passenger-side door for his good-looking boss.

"What are you doing with this nigger car, Z?"

"I use it until they stick one of those damn boots on it or tow it away."

Mislovic got in and closed the door. He looked around the inside of the car. "How many miles has this thing got on it?"

Zenko squinted at the odometer. "A little over three thousand."

"The prick gives me a car that's not even new. Probably stolen. Let's go."

Zenko pulled away from the curb and headed north, then turned east.

"Where are we going?"

"Marla's."

"Okay."

Mislovic relaxed. Marla's was a small cafe near Portobello Road. It was owned by a Rumanian named Isaac Czmenceau, who was part of the loose network of Eastern European criminals that Mislovic maintained contacts with. Marla was the name of his daughter. Czmenceau owned several cheap restaurants, a strip bar near King's Cross, a used-car lot, a junkyard, and three rooming houses that he filled with women who had been shipped out of Rumania, Russia, and East Germany and locked into prostitution. Some were there by choice, most against their will. The women had been promised jobs in the West, but Czmenceau and his pimps knew how to force them into selling their sex for money, a combination of addicting them to drugs and physically threatening them. Czmenceau was one of Mislovic's customers. He used the crack to enslave the women. Mislovic planned on supplying many men like Czmenceau.

Going to Marla's allowed him to believe he was not hiding from the police. That he was still around. Still in town. Just not on Berwick Street.

And Mislovic enjoyed the ride. He felt comfortable talking in the car. He didn't have to worry about police or competitors monitoring his phone calls. Especially calls on the damn cellular phones. Even that stupid Princess Di had discovered that voices over cellular phones were thrown out into the air where with the right equipment anyone could listen to them.

Suddenly Mislovic asked Zenko, "You check this thing for microphones?"

"Yah. I had Jake do a sweep. Nothing."

"Good. So, when is your policeman going to find out about the American?"

"Soon, I hope."

"Can you trust him?"

Zenko shrugged. "Who knows? We have no choice. It's just money. He say the cop in charge made a deal with the American. He tell police to arrest somebody your niece can testify against, then she come in as a witness. They will protect her if she testifies."

Mislovic smirked. "They can't protect her if we know where she is."

"I know."

"So you've got this bum in the police working. Who else?"

"Czmenceau say he knows somebody who work in the court system. The prosecutor's office. He says maybe they will see the papers they have to file to get her in protection."

"Really?"

"Yah."

"Which will tell us what?"

"Everything we need. I think."

"Good. But I want to get her *before* she gets into the hands of the police. Otherwise, we lose the American. And we have to get him first. Once she is in, too many people have to be shot."

"I don't care how many we kill."

"No, Zenko, take a lesson. We have to be businessmen now. We don't want a war with the authorities. We only kill them if they try to stop our business. Otherwise, we stay quiet and make our money. That's why I want the woman before they get her. We have to get her on the way in. Or before."

"Okay. Last night I put the word out. I make a lot of calls. People we know working hotels, in the railroads, restaurants, pubs, everywhere. I put some money out. Also offered money."

"Good. Maybe we'll get lucky."

"Maybe the Jamaicans can get people to look for them, too."

"I suppose so. Anything else?"

"Like what? What more do you want?"

"I want as much as I can get. What about that ex–cop guy we use to hire muscle. Maybe he can sniff around and find out who the other shooter was in that van. Devlin was not alone. He hired help. Somebody local. Somebody who can stand and shoot a goddamn shotgun while people shoot back. Must not be too many guys like that in this town."

"Yah, good idea. I'll call him from Marla's. Anything else?"

They were just pulling off the A40 flyover onto the local street leading to Portobello Road.

"I'll think of something," said Mislovic. "Don't worry. In the meantime, Dragan wants to meet with us this afternoon. He's going to want to know where we are on this thing, so I want to get in touch with the Yardie and keep the deal moving, even if we don't know where Devlin is yet."

"You have to call Dragan? You know where he's going to be?"

"I'll call him. He'll be in some big hotel. He loves those fucking hotels."

Oliver was, in fact, keeping his part of the deal moving. He was expecting the barge with the cocaine before the end of the morning.

He had left word with Momma Cientro that Hinton should come to the warehouse. He wanted Hinton there when the delivery arrived.

The assassin had spent the entire night in the Santeria/Voodoo chapel. He had smoked spliffs of marijuana and tobacco all night long, sinking deeper and deeper into himself under the influence of the ganja. The first hours, Hinton had spent exorcising the anger and frustrations of the days before. He relived the gunfights with Devlin and meditated on his deep hatred for the man. The fact that this arrogant white American could deny Hinton and his god Chango what was rightfully theirs infuriated the man.

In the middle of the night he had gone so deep into himself, had absorbed so much smoke into himself, that he lost track of where he was. Hinton's hold on reality was tenuous under normal circumstances. But in the Voodoo chapel, with the red lights and the statues and other figures, after hours of smoke, Hinton was not really there any longer. He had concentrated so intensely on connecting himself to the androgynous statue of his god Chango that he believed he could see what Chango saw, feel what Chango felt. He vowed loyalty, vowed to never waver, vowed to bring blood to Chango. He conjured up such a twisted attachment to his god that he began to feel absorbed into the statue. Hinton felt a surge of bloody rage in his head, and the power of death. He lost himself for hours, alternating between promising and begging, between demanding and expecting.

As dawn light crept over the city, Hinton began to come down and pull back into himself. He smoked a lightly mixed spliff to revive himself and clear his head. He drank black coffee. He became more logical in his thinking. He found himself able to follow a fairly rational line of thought. His mind stopped flying from one obsessed bloody idea to the next. A deadly cunning began to take over. Hinton was now convinced his enemies would come to him. All he had to do was give Chango signs of his loyalty. Offer gifts to his god, and the woman and the tall one would be his.

At ten o'clock Momma Cientro interrupted Hinton and reminded him he was wanted at the warehouse when the shipment arrived.

Hinton stood up from his vigil and turned to the priestess. She saw the far-off look in his bloodshot eyes and knew that Hinton had traveled to another world during the night. He was back now, but not in the same mind as a normal man. She instinctively stepped away from him. At that moment, she did not want Hinton to touch her. Lydia Cientro was afraid that he might transfer something to her that was so evil it could overpower even her. She stepped back away from him and simply told him, "Go."

Thirty minutes later, Hinton walked through the warehouse front door at exactly the moment the boatman was tying up his narrow canal barge out back.

One of Oliver's men who had been watching for the barge came to the office and told him the shipment had arrived. Oliver was about to receive the largest shipment of cocaine he had ever dealt.

The cocaine had been flown from Colombia into central Mexico. From there it was trucked to a warehouse in south-west Texas. It had been processed and packaged, then driven to Montreal. From there it had been placed in smaller packages and given to human couriers, who had flown into Brussels and Madrid and Antwerp. More couriers brought the goods into England, where it was divided among various boats, one of which had brought twelve kilos to Oliver's warehouse.

The boatman, a young Belgian named Maurice Trek, had run the canals alone, steering his longboat for the last twenty-four hours. He had eaten and eliminated in the same spot near the stern of his boat. He knew what his cargo was, and he wanted it delivered as soon as possible. That's why he had traveled nonstop.

Trek eased the barge to the old piling behind the warehouse and threw a line around it, letting the momentum of the boat pull the line tight. He deftly jumped off onto the overgrown canal bank and tied off the bow.

Oliver was standing there waiting for him, with Hinton behind him and to his right.

Trek had jumped onto land before he was really prepared to do so. His muscles were too stiff from sitting and steering the boat over the long soft river miles. He bent and stretched and tried to get back his land legs.

Oliver and Hinton watched him and waited. Trek did not want to look at Hinton. He knew very well who Hinton was, and what his job was.

Oliver asked, "So how was the trip, den, mon?"

"No problem, chief. But getting out of that fucking harbor was a bitch."

"Why? What harbor? Dinya not pick up da load at Canary?" Oliver asked.

"No. They fucked up. I had to go up north and get the boat at Kings Lynn."

"Why?"

"Johannes was sick."

"You went from Kings Lynn?"

"Yeah."

Oliver and Hinton exchanged a quick look, but nothing was spoken.

"So where da stuff?"

Trek pointed to the boat.

"I have bags of fertilizer and plants going to Little Venice."

"Where?"

"Little Venice. From there they unload and take the plants to Regent's Park. Then I dead-end a load of building materials for Paddington station."

"And mine?"

"Tell your guys to count sixteen bags in from the stern. Yours is inside bags seventeen and eighteen. It's sealed in bags mixed in with the fertilizer."

Oliver looked at the two men who had walked over to the barge. They weren't too happy at the prospect of unloading and then reloading it.

"Unload da stuff neatly. Get our bags an' bring dem inside. Put his stuff back in the way you took it off."

Oliver turned to Trek. "Come inside, brother. We'll settle up."

Trek followed Oliver back to the warehouse, Hinton falling in step behind them. Somewhere in Trek's consciousness he realized he was caught in between the men, but he didn't allow himself to think about it. Behind him, Hinton was smiling. Everything was being brought to him and shown to him, Hinton thought. It was the power of his god on earth.

Oliver asked, "So wha' happen after you finish da run?"

"I'll tie up under the highway near Little Venice. From there I walk to the railroad station and go home."

"Somebody else come in and get da boat?"

"Yes, sir."

"Take it where?"

"Down to Canary, I guess. I'm done."

Oliver nodded. "Get a good rest, den, huh?"

"Yes, sir."

They walked without speaking further into the warehouse and up to Oliver's office on the mezzanine.

Oliver dropped into a seat behind his desk and opened a bottom drawer. He pulled out a large metal box and flipped the lid, then started dropping packets of bills on the desk. Trek kept looking at the stacks. His fee was two thousand pounds.

"So who told you to go up to Kings Lynn and get the boat?"

"Wilkins told me to bring it down from there."

"You met him at the boat?"

"No. We met in that garage outside of town and drove it down to the dock."

"You loaded up der?"

"Yeah. The boat was ready, except for your shipment."

Trek wasn't really thinking about Oliver's questions. He was watching the stack of bills on the desk. But Oliver wasn't counting out his money. It was all there, waiting, but Oliver was just sitting back in his chair. Trek wanted to ask for the money, but he knew that he shouldn't. He would have to wait for Oliver to hand it to him. He waited, looking at the bills. He was tired. He wanted to get the hell out of there, but he knew it would take Oliver's men some time to unload the cargo, take out Oliver's shipment, and reload. He thought about sitting down. But there was no chair for him. It was then that he looked around and realized that Hinton was standing there, too. Standing right behind him.

Suddenly the air in the room seemed to die. Trek looked at Oliver. The look in Oliver's eyes made him look back at Hinton. The killer was standing behind him. Trek couldn't believe this.

"Hey, what's the matter, man?"

Oliver shrugged. He looked at Hinton. Trek turned to look, too, and in a split second Hinton's knife was plunged into his throat. There was no time to think, to plead, to scream. The only sound Trek made was a gurgling, coughing choke. And then Hinton stepped aside as Trek retched violently and coughed out a spray of blood. Trek tried to inhale, but he couldn't. He bent backwards and grabbed the handle of Hinton's knife. He managed to grip the handle, but he could not summon the strength to pull the knife out.

Hinton stood where he was, staring right at Trek, waiting for the death convulsion to start. He wanted to pull the knife out and stab him again and again, but he held back, waiting for Chango to bring death into the room at the right moment.

And then Trek dropped. He turned to Oliver with his right hand still on the knife. Oliver watched him dying, and almost to himself he said, "Wilkins fucked you up, mon. He shou'na brought you up north. That means you know da whole chain from there to here. You cyan know dat many links in da chain, brother."

Trek's ears began to ring. The pain in his throat and chest was so terrible he wanted to die. But he would not die for at least a few minutes. Hinton knew that, and squatted down near the dying man to watch death take him. The blood coming out of his mouth mixed with a foamy white liquid that had been retched up out of his lungs. Trek's mind was fading into darkness. The pain was ebbing away. It wouldn't be long now. The oxygen was rapidly being depleted in his brain, but there were still organs living inside. A heart beating its last convulsive beats. Hinton watched.

For Oliver, the death simply meant complications. Fucking blood sprayed all over his office walls and seeping out onto his floor. Now he would have to find a new boatman who could finish the run. Now he had problems. Hinton was in his killer state. Oliver was simply angry.

The phone suddenly rang, interrupting his anger.

He snatched the receiver off the cradle. "Yeah?"

It was Mislovic. "How's our deal going, partner?"

Oliver's anger didn't make him any nicer. "It's going. All da way. I be ready tomorrow night. Price as agreed. Don' forget my equipment, too. You remember all parts of da deal, den?"

"Of course."

"Good. I'll call you and tell you where by six o'clock. Give me a phone number."

Mislovic was standing at the pay phone in Marla's. He read the number off the phone and had to grit his teeth not to tell Oliver to get some fucking manners.

Oliver's impatient voice asked, "What about da woman and her fren'?"

"We're working on it."

"Work hard, den. It's you who said it must be done. I'm ready tomorrow at six. You want da goods, tell me where to solve your problem."

"Right."

Oliver slammed the phone down. "Asshole."

He jumped from his chair and stormed out of the office and down the stairs to the warehouse. He wanted to see those bags. He wanted those kilos in his hands. They were his stepping-stones. Enough to buy off Mislovic and get the weapons he needed. Enough to bring in the power and money he needed to tell some people to fuck themselves and to kill the rest. His time had come. All that stood in the way now was Devlin and the woman. It was time for them to die. Now.

CHAPTER 23

ANNIE WOKE UP naked and cold. And alone. For a moment, she didn't know where she was. She closed her eyes again and remembered. She opened them and looked toward the window at the far end of the room. The shade was still pulled down, but she could see a mix of gray predawn light and the yellow glow from the high-intensity lights in the car park.

She looked over to see if Devlin was still in bed. He wasn't. She rolled over and pulled the thin hotel blanket around her, trying to stave off the chilly air in the room. She realized at that moment how much she wanted Devlin in bed with her. How much she wanted him inside her. Inside her. It was clear to her in that predawn moment how little she had loved her husband for the last few years. She wanted Devlin to end her post-marriage virginity.

But right now her bladder was full and she was hungover from the drinking and she was cold.

She pulled the cheap hotel blanket over her and recalled how it had felt to be naked next to Devlin. He was big. And solid. She compared Devlin with Johnny. Johnny had a good body, lean with well-defined, smooth muscles—but not hard muscles like Devlin's. And then the pain of loss seized her, and in the next second she thought to herself, Oh God, what the hell is happening to me? What did I do with Devlin? Running around naked like that. Did I go too far? I should have kept it businesslike. And then she made a face at how ridiculous that thought was. Who was she kidding? She knew that the bond between them was deeper now. And she knew that was exactly the way she wanted it.

She thought about telling him all of it. No. Not now. Why kill the feelings from last night? And finally, she wondered if her skittering mind would ever leave her alone.

She slowly eased out from under the blanket and sat up in bed. She stayed there for a moment, getting her bearings, holding the blanket around her. She pushed her thick, shiny hair back over her head.

She stood up, dropped the blanket, and walked quickly on bare feet to the bathroom. Thinking she would look like hell in the mirror, she avoided looking as she passed by her reflection. She didn't need to see the lines and the dark areas under her eyes.

She grabbed her nightgown from the back of the bathroom door and slipped it over her head, then sat on the toilet, pushed the door shut with her foot, and emptied her full bladder. She rubbed her shoulders, her arms, her breasts, and her stomach. She was proud that everything was solid. Her face might be showing the years, but not her body. Her skin was flawless, and there was no unsightly fat anywhere.

Standing up brought out the dull headache from the vodka and wine. A vein throbbed painfully in her right temple. She decided it was worth it. The cold vodka had helped reduce her nervousness at being alone with Devlin. And the wine had relaxed her. She had been surprised how shaky she had become when she heard the news that Uncle Frank was willing to kill her off to further his own ends. She had calculated that he would remain her ally. That's why she had sent Devlin to him. It hadn't taken much. Just a comment, a nudge in that direction, and Devlin had gone to him to plead her case. But the bastard had crossed Devlin and her. And Jack had reacted accordingly. She had underestimated Devlin. He must have done something to Mislovic that had completely set him off. To come after him and her like that. On the streets with all those men and guns. It had been crazy.

Mislovic was crazy. And in his own way, Devlin was too. She realized she would have to handle Devlin very carefully. She realized she was not accustomed to being with a man like him. It hadn't required a great deal of effort to move Johnny in the right direction. Johnny had been an adolescent compared to Devlin. He had had a wild side and a certain toughness that made him dabble at being a bad boy. But Devlin was a different story. You could not point him in a direction and control him. The police hadn't. Neither had Uncle Frank. She would have to be very careful with him.

Then she put everything out of her head except the shower she would take to revive herself and the work she would have to do to fix her hair and moisturize her face and do her makeup. Not too much makeup. Just enough to hide some of the obvious flaws.

You're trying to make yourself look good for him, aren't you, Annie? Aren't you? Of course I am. Why not? And why won't my mind just leave me alone and let me get on with it?

When she came out of the bathroom, dressed only in her bra and panties, with her hair wrapped in a hotel towel, she felt good. She felt sexy and wanted. She imagined Devlin still in bed waiting for her. Now would be the time to make love—suddenly, without warning or comment, fucking him hard, with total abandon. But the lights were on in the room and Devlin was dressed. He looked as if he had been awake for hours. He was talking quietly on the phone. Devlin looked up and saw her standing there looking at him. He stared right at her in her clean white lace underwear.

She smiled at him and said, "You're up."

"Yeah. I relieved Ben. He needed a few hours of sleep. Elizabeth is still sleeping. They make quite a pair in there. She's so small you can barely find her in her bed; he's so big you can barely see his bed."

Annie smiled. "I'd better get dressed."

"Right."

"So," she said, "how are you?"

"Fine. How about you?"

"Fine."

Annie said, "Interesting night, huh?"

"Yeah."

"When was the last time you let a naked woman out of your bed?"

"I can't remember."

"Probably never."

"But I'll tell you one thing, Annie."

"What?"

"If you keep strutting around in front of me dressed in your bra and panties, you won't get the rest of your clothes on."

He said it with such a straight, solemn face that Annie couldn't soften the comment with a joke or a smile. There was nothing casual about it. The way he said it, the way he was looking at her right now, made her feel both sexually desirable and embarrassed. She wanted to say she was sorry, but she didn't. She didn't say anything. She just walked into the bathroom.

She emerged a few minutes later in blue jeans and a loose-fitting sweater. The sweater covered her in a way that announced there was a lot to cover. The jeans fit a long-legged, graceful woman exactly the way they should have.

When Devlin looked at her, he realized how sexually attractive and powerful she was. Even when she intentionally tried to keep her sexuality low-key, as she was doing now, the effort came back around to make her more appealing. It was clear to Devlin, now more than ever, how much he had wanted this woman, and how much he wanted her now. And it was clear to him why he had left her. Some youthful survival instinct had forced him away from her. He wondered if he were old enough and tested enough to survive her now.

"I have an idea," she said.

"What?"

"About a place to hide out."

"What's your idea?"

"I have a girlfriend. She teaches at Cambridge. In one of the colleges there. She's on sabbatical in France, working at restoring a monastery or something. Her place is empty."

"What is it? A house?"

"It's a little farmhouse. Outside of the town. Closer to a place called Grantchester, actually. Near the River Cam. Very quiet. The place was restored from a ruins a long time ago."

"How far is it from here?"

"Oh, maybe three hours' drive."

"How would you get in?"

"There's a key hidden under the back porch. I know where it is. If it's not there for some reason, we could just break in. She'd understand. And nobody would see us. There's nobody around it for maybe a mile or so."

"Any houses within sight?"

"Yes, but barely."

"Would anyone be suspicious if the place were suddenly occupied?"

"I don't think so. You know, it's a university area. Everybody coming and going. Students. Professors. We could be friends coming in for a lecture series or something and borrowing the place."

"How close is it to town?"

"There are three little villages in the area. Barton, Grantchester, and Trumpington. Then the town of Cambridge to the north a couple of miles. It's mostly back roads, then a spot with a pub, a store, a few shops, and a post office. Then more roads and another spot with about the same."

Devlin was silent for a moment. She watched him think it over.

"Okay, it sounds fine. You're sure there won't be any problem getting in, or being there without your friend?"

"I've done it before when she's away."

"And this friend of yours is in France?"

"Yes."

"All right. Good."

By nine o'clock they were on the road. Devlin skirted around London to the west on the M25 and picked up the M11 headed north. He had no desire to drive through London.

Ben rode in the backseat with Elizabeth. The child had fallen asleep within minutes after they were on the road. Her tiny head was propped against Ben's substantial thigh. Ben thought about putting a hand on her shoulder so she would be held in place, but he was worried his hand might be too heavy on her, so he sat with his hands in his lap, watching over her, ready to catch her if there was a sudden stop.

Annie sat next to Devlin. She felt the barrier he had erected to keep her away, so she simply looked straight ahead, saying nothing, but thinking about how crazy it was that she had such a strong desire to reach over and hold his hand.

They traveled north on the M11 until they reached a town called Harlow. Annie finally broke the silence. It was the first word spoken in over two hours.

"Are we stopping for something in particular?"

"Yes."

Annie waited for Devlin to tell her what it was, but he didn't.

"Should I shop for the house?"

"Yes. Of course. I won't be long."

Devlin drove slowly down the town's main street until he spotted a shop that sold electronic equipment. There was a market across the street. He angled into the space. He went into the store, and Annie crossed the street to the market.

Stopping the car woke Elizabeth. She seemed quite relaxed despite the fact that they were in a strange place. While Devlin and Annie shopped, Ben sat in the back of the minivan, his big black satchel on the floor beneath him and Elizabeth on the seat next to him, chattering away about which dolls she had left at home and which she had brought with her, and why.

Ben thought about which guns and boxes of ammunition he had brought and which he had left behind. And why.

Neither of Oliver's men had any idea why Hinton was so worried about how they carried a dead man. Hinton did not want the dead body bruised.

Trek's remains had been rolled up in a large, clear plastic sheet. He looked like something a giant insect might have encased in a cocoon.

They carried the sagging body down to the canal barge.

Hinton pointed to the open area by the stern and said, "Lay it down, slow. Right there."

Trek's blood had smeared the inside of the cloudy see-through plastic. Whatever was inside the plastic was clearly dead, and Hinton had told them to put it in a place where it could be seen. Neither man argued with Hinton. They simple laid the body down and stepped off the barge.

Hinton started the engine and waited for them to cast off the tie lines. He wasn't going far. Just about a half mile back along the canal to a shut-down industrial incinerator located behind a huge brick building that was an abandoned electrical plant.

Hinton's face was expressionless, but inside he was ecstatic. He was convinced that the opportunity to kill had been a response from his god. So quick, so satisfying. Such a clear answer to his night of prayer. He was deeply grateful, and now he would demonstrate his gratitude to Chango.

Hinton reached his destination and steered the barge over to the bank. His ten-minute ride down the canal had been completely hidden from view.

He tied up the barge and jumped back into the stern. He straddled the body, squatted down, and carefully lifted the dead man, making sure not to let the head bump on the deck.

Hinton managed to slip his right arm and then his left under the body and lift it. He stepped off the barge and carried his offering to what looked like a large steel box six feet high, eight feet wide, and four feet deep that formed the base of a yellow brick smokestack which rose almost sixty feet into the gray, windswept sky above Hackney.

Inside, at the bottom of the rectangular steel box, was a three-foot-long oval gas ring protected by a steel grate. Almost half the front of the box was a door that opened with a pressure latch and swung out wide enough so that refuse and garbage could be shoveled into it.

Hinton wanted Chango's favor and intercession to bring him the woman. If he did not kill her soon, he believed, he would become weak and vulnerable. He would become easy prey for the many people who would revel in his death.

Now his enemies seemed like children to him. He looked at them like little boys dressed up and playing at being tough. They had no real power. None of them. But they had guns, and like children playing with guns they could always shoot and kill you if you lost your power. So Hinton would do everything he could to keep his power.

He laid the body in front of the box and gathered up several wooden skids littering the yard where the incinerator sat like a squat metal house. He broke the skids apart and carefully stacked the wooden slats inside the incinerator until he had a pyre built up about two feet high.

While he worked, he thought about the fire that would bring the skin, soul, and aroma of his kill to the realm of the gods.

Carefully, he unrolled the body from the plastic. He did not want the flesh defiled by burning plastic. He lifted the corpse free and carefully placed it on the wooden pyre, facedown.

Then he took out his knife and carefully cut open Trek's clothes, starting at his neck and slicing straight through his leather belt all the way down his right leg. Then he cut open the pants on the left leg. He peeled away the clothes so that they would burn under the body and not into the flesh.

Hinton felt a chill run down his back and into his scrotum. He thought about the fire searing the flesh off a face that would be looking directly into the flames. Hinton felt a strange kind of ecstasy. The burning was sexual and sensual and exciting to him.

Now Hinton knelt down to find the small gas jet that fed the pilot light. He reached around and felt for a spring button that would start the gas. He pressed the button, heard the hiss, and lit the flame.

He stood up and swung shut the heavy steel door. It would have been wonderful to see the flames lick and consume the body, but he didn't want to waste the sacrificial smoke. It must fly high up into the smokestack and be released into the air above, he told himself. It was best that way. The smell of the burning flesh would be for Chango alone.

He turned the gas on full and stepped back, imagining the flames igniting the wood, picturing the fire licking at the flesh, blistering it, then scorching and charring the skin, burning it away until the blood and muscles began to blacken. And he kept imagining until he felt the heat of the big steel box suffuse the entire front of his body, until he saw the first white streams of smoke emerge from the chimney, and until he saw in his mind the bones cracking and the skull popping and everything slowly turning into ash.

Hinton forced himself to turn and walk away. He wanted to be in his chapel, in front of the altar with the scent and heat and feelings that were in him now.

Hinton truly believed that the smoke that swirled above Hackney would be the catalyst that would spin a vortex of power to bring together the players in this game of death.

CHAPTER 24

WALDRON SIGNED IN with the receptionist at the Crown Prosecution Service, took a seat on the couch in the waiting area, rested his head on the wall behind him, and promptly fell asleep.

The voice of the receptionist woke him.

"Sir! Sir! Mr. McDermott will see you now."

Waldron rubbed his face to rouse himself and quickly stood up. This was no time to be sleepy and dull.

He walked past the reception desk to a set of double glass doors where a young black girl waited to escort him.

She handed him a plastic visitor's tag, smiled, and led Waldron through several turns in the maze of halls. She motioned for him to enter a nondescript office. It was about fifteen feet square, but it had a window which Waldron interpreted as a sign of some authority.

"Mr. McDermott will be right with you."

The office was unoccupied, but the desk was piled high with briefs, forms, folders, and papers.

Before Waldron could settle into a chair, a man entered the office. He seemed to be rushed. He was about thirty, balding, very thin, and just over six feet tall. He wore the expected white shirt, tie, and dark suit pants. The pants were baggy on him. Waldron figured the suit jacket was hanging behind the door. The man's identification card was pinned to his belt over his right hip. Sure enough, the name was McDermott. He looked more like an Ichabod Crane than a McDermott.

McDermott held out his hand. "You must be Milt Reisel's friend."

Waldron shook the outstretched hand.

"Right. James Waldron."

"You're with the Met?"

"Yes, Chief Inspector."

"I see. Well, Milton asked me for a favor, to put you at the top of the list this morning. So what can I do for you?"

Waldron had never heard Milt Reisel referred to as Milton, but that was beside the point.

"I have a witness I need to get into your program."

"That's what Milton said. When?"

"When?"

"Yes, when do you want her in the program? Does she realize what that means?"

"Yes, of course she realizes. I want her in now. Right now."

"That's not possible. It'll take at least three weeks to process her application. And there's no guarantee she'll be accepted. We're quite full at the moment."

"Can you lodge her temporarily while she's being processed?"

"Why the hurry?"

"She'll be dead in a matter of days if we don't."

"Where is she now?"

"Right now she's hiding somewhere out there, waiting for me to tell her she can come in."

"You know where she's hiding?"

"Not precisely, but I know how to contact her."

"Sounds like she doesn't trust you."

"She doesn't."

"Why?"

"It's rather complicated. What about getting her set up somewhere while she's being processed for the program?"

"Well, old man, I've got to insist that you know her whereabouts before I get involved. I'm not going to move mountains for her and find out she's hiding somewhere we can't find her."

After working for two days straight, and dealing with the pressures surrounding him, Waldron almost lashed out at McDermott's fussiness, but he held himself in check and resolved to negotiate until he got what he needed.

Waldron responded, "All right. I'll find out where she's hiding."

"Can I be assured of that?"

"Yes. Definitely. So you'll take her in?"

"We're still discussing it."

"What else do you need to know?"

"First of all, we are certainly not prepared to take care of her while we process her. Usually your people do that. What division are you with?"

"Tower Bridge. We're too small to take on witness protection jobs."

"Something temporary shouldn't need too many hands."

"I'm also worried about security problems. Information has been leaking to the wrong people."

"From your side?"

"Yes."

"That's why she doesn't trust you."

"Correct."

"Oh. Well. Bad luck, then."

"Yes. It's a difficult situation. Milton did tell you this was rather an emergency."

"Yes, but Milton has very little credibility. Everything is an emergency with him. What can this witness do for us? Is it going to end up in Crown courts?"

"Absolutely. I'd say this will be your biggest case this year. Maybe of your career."

"You sound sure of that."

"I am. Definitely."

Waldron opened his attaché case and extracted a folder. He laid two pages, one by one, in front of McDermott.

"These are quick summaries I've done on two crime groups. One is made up of Jamaican Yardies, a rather vicious gang of thugs who seem to be on the top of the crack-dealing pile at the moment. I spoke to the intelligence officer in Hackney this morning. He's sending me more information on them. We already know they are responsible for the rather gruesome murder of my witness's husband."

" 'Gruesome'?"

"They chopped his head off with a machete."

"Lovely."

"And Hackney intelligence believes they are involved in at least two other murders and several shooting incidents. Also a pair of stabbings. They are definitely bad people."

Waldron pointed to the second sheet of paper.

"This is what we know about a Yugoslavian group now based in London—in Soho, actually. We don't have much on them, but I assembled bits and pieces, plus what I know. It appears that they are intent on breaking into the drug trade. They are also dealing in prostitution and the sale of automatic weapons. They're laundering a considerable amount of money in The City at the moment. I don't think there's any doubt they intend to build a base here for rather extensive criminal operations. As I said, we don't know a great deal about them, but I estimate them to be far more dangerous than the Yardies. Yesterday morning they fired off over two hundred rounds of high-caliber bullets in an attempt to kill my witness and her bodyguard."

"We're talking about those bloody maniacs?"

"Yes."

McDermott's interest was now piqued. Waldron pushed on.

"Yes, those are the people we're dealing with. I think the matter has already gone up as far as the home secretary. It's going to be quite an opportunity. To make an impact, I mean."

"Yes, of course. It caused quite a stir yesterday."

"It's only the beginning. The worst part is, these two groups of villains have joined forces at the moment."

"Gawd."

"Mmm. Afraid so."

"Uh, what was that you said about a bodyguard? This woman has a bodyguard?"

"Yes. As I said, her husband was killed by the Yardies. She has since hired a man to provide security. An American, actually. Has rather extensive credentials."

"He must know his business if they shot two hundred rounds at her and she's still alive. How did he pull that off?"

"I'll send you the report if you're interested."

"What's her connection to the two crime groups?"

"Drugs. Her husband was dealing cocaine with the Yardies. He, in fact, was a middleman supplying to the Yugoslavs. My assumption is that the Yugoslavs will now deal directly with our Yard brethren. They have the money. And I'd make a fair wager that guns are involved as part of their payments for drugs. I don't fancy it will do anybody much good to arm the Yardies with AK-47s."

"Quite."

"My witness will be very instrumental in putting as many of them away as we can catch."

"She'll stand up?"

"I think she realizes it's her only hope of staying alive."

"I see."

Waldron watched McDermott think it over. He had laid the bait. Waldron waited. McDermott made his decision. He bit.

"Of course, I'd have to meet her. I'd want to see what I'm paying for."

"She'll make a very convincing witness."

Again, McDermott looked over the pages Waldron had placed in front of him.

"What do you want to charge them with?"

"Murder, conspiracy to murder, drug dealing, weapons possession, attempted murder—you can choose from quite a list."

"She's not going to be enough to make all those cases."

Waldron felt McDermott squirming on the hook.

"She's the key. We start with her and go forward. They killed her husband. They tried to kill her. And, by the way, she has a six-year-old child who they tried to kill yesterday, too."

"Isn't that lovely. What the hell did she do to them?"

"I don't know that she did anything. Her husband cheated the Yardies. It's not at all unusual for these types to go in and kill the whole family. Tends to discourage others from cheating them, too. I suppose the Yugoslavs have to go along with their new business partners to prove their loyalties."

"What other investigations are going on with these villains?"

Waldron laid another folder on McDermott's desk.

"I haven't had time yet this morning to pull it all together, but within one half hour on the computer system I found sixteen references specific to these two groups. I'll start coordinating whatever information is out there today."

"You're walking into a mess here."

"Of course. But I want these people off our streets."

"Yes. Quite right. The whole thing is a bit dicey, though, isn't it? Where are you going to start?"

"By arresting the Yugoslav. His name is Ivan Mislovic. I know where his headquarters are located. I'll bring him in for attempted murder and whatever else I can find on his premises. I've already got warrants in the works. She'll testify against him. As will her American bodyguard."

"Sounds like you're about to go on an extended fishing expedition."

"Maybe. But I've got my hook, and it's this woman. I'll take down the Yugoslav and whomever I can around him. Maybe if we're lucky we get the Yardies, too."

McDermott suddenly sat up straight, elbows and forearms on his desk.

"All right. You've convinced me. It's worth a shot. But I wasn't exaggerating about being full up. I'll have to do a bit of pushing. And I can't guarantee access yet. And the best I can do is get her into Stage One. She'll have to go to a safe house. Really not much better than being in prison, except the child will stay with her. And she'll have to stay there until the trial starts. No new name. No documentation. No new residence until after conviction. No employment. Just bare-bones stuff, I'm afraid."

"Fine. As long as it runs through your end. When can I bring her in?"

"I'm afraid I'm going to have to insist that it be after you arrest this Mislovic character."

Waldron would have preferred to be free of that requirement, but he knew he was going to have to arrest Mislovic before Devlin would bring in the woman, so he didn't argue.

"Same day I make my arrest?"

"I'll say the day after to be safe."

"All right. Done. We have an agreement?"

McDermott handed a card to Waldron.

"Yes. Stay in touch. Do your paperwork correctly, please, and follow procedures. I don't want my cases tainted at your end."

"Right. Exactly. Don't worry about that. Thanks."

McDermott was already on to the next task as Waldron walked out the door. But just as he was leaving, McDermott stopped him. Waldron gritted his teeth. Something was still sticking in McDermott's craw.

"Chief Waldron."

"Yes?"

"Exactly who is this bodyguard you were talking about?"

"I'll send you background information on him. Used to be a New York cop, then went into the military. Spent time with the U.S. Secret Service."

"Interesting. A professional."

"Yes, absolutely."

"What is a legitimate woman doing hiring her own professional security operative? How can she afford that? Don't bring me a witness who's up to her ears in dope dealing. I don't need a criminal testifying for me. People tend not to believe them."

"This woman is no criminal. It was her husband who was dirty. The Yugoslav is a relative of his. She's never been arrested, never been accused of a crime. She's a victim here. A citizen. A widow with a kid in school. Judges and juries will love her. She's a mother, for God's sake."

"So was Ma Barker."

"Don't worry. The American happens to be an old friend of hers. I don't think she's even paying him."

"Okay, Waldron, just don't lead me down the garden path on this. I don't like surprises. I'll start the wheels moving. You get your criminal and your witnesses and we'll do business."

"Done."

Waldron bolted out the door before McDermott changed his mind.

Mislovic had just about finished reading his *Times* when the call came in at Marla's. It was Dragan's bodyguard, a man named Tesich. Mislovic had once seen Tesich punch a man in the face for refusing to answer one of Dragan's questions. He had hit the man with so much force that he had broken his jaw, his cheekbone, and his neck. Tesich made even Zenko nervous.

They met in the bar at the Park Lane Hotel. Whenever Dragan came to London, he took a suite at one of London's four-star hotels. This time it was the Park Lane.

Dragan was seated in a banquette at the far end of the room. It was three o'clock. The bar was deserted except for a bartender and a waiter.

Dragan was a big man who had recently lost a great deal of weight due to a heart ailment. He was suffering from chronic arrhythmia. For some unknown reason his heart decided to beat faster than it should. Constantly. The doctors told him they could control it, but never cure it. Unfortunately, the medicine they gave him made him nauseous. He couldn't eat. After seventy-three years of being overweight, the pounds fell off him. Now he looked like a man who had been given a size-52 bag of skin to cover a size-42 body. Dragan had taken to wearing turtlenecks to cover some of the loose jowls of flesh that hung from his neck.

He extended his still-meaty hand to Mislovic and shook Mislovic's hand without much warmth. Mislovic sat across from him and declined when the waiter asked him if he wanted to order a drink. Dragan waved off the waiter and turned to Mislovic. Both men spoke in Croatian.

"Talk to me, Ivan."

Mislovic updated Dragan. He didn't exaggerate. He didn't minimize. And he didn't leave anything out.

During Mislovic's monologue Dragan nodded once or twice. His most animated response to the information was to bend his head slightly toward Mislovic.

When Mislovic finished, Dragan asked a few questions which seemingly had nothing to do with the latest events. He asked about their finances and how smoothly goods were being shipped into and out of their various London locations.

Then he asked, "How close are you to finding your niece and the American?"

"I would assume she'll have to contact the police in the next couple of days. Then we should know where she is."

"All right, let the blacks take care of them. Give them the information. Then step back. Concentrate on your deal. Buy the drugs."

"Do we give them guns?"

"Give them two; the rest of your payment should be in the form of money. We don't want to arm these pigs. Make an excuse."

"All right."

"Go through with the first buy. Continue dealing with the scum until we move up to their suppliers. Then kill their chief and as many of his people as you can."

"That's it?"

"That's it."

"Okay."

Dragan sat silently, his hands resting on the table in front of him. Mislovic waited, knowing the meeting wasn't over. He gathered a few nuts from the dish in front of him and popped them into his mouth. They were oily and warm, and very good.

Finally, Dragan spoke. "I'm sure he'll want to kill you sometime, Ivan. You're not one of his."

"I know. I've let him think that he can."

Slowly, the older man turned and stared at Mislovic. "Very good. Deal with them for now, Ivan. Be patient. And then we will clean them out like a cancer."

"Yes, sir."

"Keep in touch. Give them the girl, then send our condolences to your sister."

CHAPTER 25

ON THE WAY to Cambridge Devlin made one more stop, in Bishops Stotford. He drove to the airport, returned the minivan to Budget, and rented a yellow Ford Sierra station wagon from Avis. It confused Annie and Elizabeth and made the trip longer, but switching cars was the kind of precaution that had become second nature to Devlin.

When they arrived in the Cambridge area, Devlin followed Annie's directions to the farmhouse.

He found himself driving down narrow roads with barely enough room for one car, much less two. Some stretches were bounded on each side by hedgerows that obscured any view of cars that might be coming around the bend. It did not make him comfortable, but by the time he arrived at the farmhouse the roads had opened up. And the setup at the farm satisfied him. Empty fields—fens—surrounded the house on all sides. The field to the east was intersected by the M11 Motorway about a half mile away. To the north and west it was open for about a mile before other houses or farm structures could be seen. To the south there was a rolling hill that led down to the River Cam about three hundred meters away. On the other side of the narrow river were more open fields.

Devlin was pleased. If anybody came for them, he and the others would be able to see them from a good distance.

Once again, Devlin confused Annie and Elizabeth by circling around the farmhouse and then pulling back onto the road and driving away.

"Where's the closest town?" he asked.

"I guess Barton over to the east, or Trumpington over west. Trumpington is a bit closer."

Devlin headed west, driving over local roads until he reached the first houses on the outskirts of Trumpington.

"What are you looking for now?" Annie asked.

"A nice quiet little B and B where I can rent a room."

"Aren't we staying at the farmhouse?"

"Yes, but I need another location for the police."

"Why?"

"They're going to want to know where we are. I've got to give them something or they might not continue to cooperate."

Annie didn't quite know what Devlin was talking about, but she decided she didn't really care. She sat back and resolved to let him do whatever he was going to do.

After fifteen minutes of cruising around the area, Devlin spotted what he was looking for. He pulled into the car park of a small hotel. He told the others to wait and went inside the hotel carrying the package he had purchased during the stop in Harlow.

In fifteen minutes he returned to the car.

A small voice from the backseat asked, "What did you do, sir?"

Devlin turned around and saw Elizabeth staring at him. It was the first time she had ever spoken directly to him, and Devlin didn't quite know what to say. As if to help him, she asked again.

"Why did you go in there, sir?"

"Oh, I just wanted to see what it was like."

"What happened to your package?"

"I left it in one of the rooms."

"Did you mean to?"

"Yes."

Elizabeth looked as if she wanted to ask more questions, but she didn't. Devlin had the feeling she refrained because she wanted to be polite. He also realized the little girl was taking in more than he had thought.

They drove back to the farmhouse in silence. It gave Devlin time to think about his odds of keeping Annie and Elizabeth alive.

Right now he was banking on the police. If Waldron didn't come through in the next day or two, he would have to run far and fast. Devlin started planning his escape even as they pulled into the front yard of the quiet farmhouse.

While Elizabeth waited out front with Devlin and Ben, Annie located the key under the porch and opened the back door, walked through to the front door of the old stone farmhouse and let them in. Elizabeth had stayed right next to Ben while they waited.

Annie quickly set about putting food away, opening windows, and setting the place up for a stay. She enlisted Elizabeth's help, and the child fell into the work quite happily.

The main part of the house consisted of a fairly large living room, a dining area, and a kitchen. The back door of the kitchen opened onto a wooden deck that overlooked the fen. A few of the farthest-off fields were dotted with large rolled bales of alfalfa or with cows grazing about aimlessly.

On the same floor was an extension that had been added to the east end of the original structure. It housed three bedrooms and a bathroom.

Ben disappeared into the farthest bedroom and dropped his satchel on the floor. He pulled out the Mossberg and checked it over. He loaded a Colt Python .357 long-barrel pistol, set up a row of six shells of three different types for the shotgun, took out a small .22-caliber Beretta and loaded it. Devlin had dumped the Yugoslavs' Grendel before he walked into Heathrow, so Ben pulled out a 9-mm Glock 17 for him and made sure the magazine was full.

Devlin found the phone in the kitchen and dialed the number for the Tower Bridge Division. He asked for Waldron and waited for the operator to transfer his call.

Waldron's extension rang. A bony hand snatched a phone off the cradle and punched in Waldron's line.

"Tower Bridge Division."

"Chief Inspector Waldron, please."

"Who's calling?" asked Patrick Reilly.

"Jack Devlin."

"Just a minute."

Reilly placed the call on hold and thought furiously. Waldron was still out. Reilly was desperate to turn this call to his advantage.

"Chief Inspector Waldron isn't in. Give me a number and I'll have him call you."

"When do you expect him?"

"Any minute. Let me have a number where he can reach you."

Devlin hung up the phone without another word.

"Shit!" Reilly slammed the phone down. He sat brooding about Devlin. He seemed so close, but how could he find him? Reilly wanted to unleash the killers on Devlin so badly that there was a sour, coppery taste in his mouth.

Reilly heard someone greet Waldron and looked up as the tired chief inspector walked into the squad room. He walked through without even looking at Reilly, adding to the well of resentment in the bitter man.

Waldron's desk was partitioned off from the squad room by three-quarter-high panels. His space occupied the far corner of the room. The panels created a cubicle of semiprivacy. It was one of the few privileges Waldron enjoyed as the highest-ranking patrol officer in the division.

Reilly watched Waldron disappear into his corner and waited for him to read his messages, two of which were from Superintendent Fenton.

Reilly grinned to himself. He had already peeked at Waldron's messages. Fenton was demanding to know Devlin's whereabouts and ordering Waldron to report to him in person. Too bad Waldron had just missed the man's phone call.

When he calculated that Waldron had gotten to Fenton's second message saying that he wanted to see him, Reilly left his desk and walked over to the chief inspector's corner.

Reilly took another small bit of enjoyment on seeing Waldron's condition. He looked like hell: unshaven, disheveled, haggard.

"Fenton wants to see you."

Waldron looked up. "Go tell your boss that I'll be right in."

"He's your boss as much as mine, Chief."

"No he's not."

"I daresay he is, unless someone made a change of command I don't know about."

"There's lots you don't know about, Reilly."

"Well, here's a piece of advice on something I do know about. You buck Fenton, and he'll bury you."

Waldron started to answer Reilly, but stifled his response.

He didn't want to give the bitter old cop the enjoyment of seeing him rise to the bait.

Instead, he told him, "Get out of here, Reilly, I've got work to do."

Just then, Waldron's phone rang. He snatched it up.

"Waldron."

The voice at the other end answered, "Devlin."

Suddenly Waldron was no longer tired.

"Devlin, where the hell are you?"

Reilly stood where he was. If he could have forced his ears to grow another two inches, he would have. He bent forward toward Waldron's phone, straining to hear Devlin's voice through the earpiece.

Waldron stared at him, but Reilly wouldn't move. Waldron motioned him to leave. Reilly walked out of the corner cubicle, but stood just on the other side of the partition, still straining to hear. Waldron was holding the phone just a bit away from his still-puffy ear, and Reilly could almost make out Devlin's end of the conversation. He heard him ask something about Mislovic.

Waldron answered, "No. I've got his place staked out and I'm just waiting for warrants to be delivered here in the next hour or so. Then we'll get him."

Reilly couldn't quite make out Devlin's response, but he heard Waldron say, "I've already taken care of that. She can go right into the Crown Prosecution witness program. She'll be completely safe."

Reilly picked out the words "time frame" at the other end of the phone, and heard Waldron answer, "I'll get Mislovic this afternoon. Or tomorrow."

Devlin responded, "Call me when you have Mislovic. That's the deal."

"Wait a minute," said Waldron. "Don't hang up. I have to know where you are. Crown Prosecution won't deal unless they are assured you haven't run off somewhere."

"We're three hours outside of London. I don't want to see any cops looking for us, Waldron, or the deal is off."

"You have to give me a number where you can be reached."

"Call me at 0223-679111 extension 211."

"What's that? A hotel?"

"Yes."

Reilly edged around the corner and watched Waldron write down the number. Then he heard him say, "Devlin. Devlin. Are you there?"

He stepped back into Waldron's cubicle as the chief inspector banged the phone back into the cradle. Reilly moved closer so he could see the phone number Waldron had written on a pad near the phone. He had a clear view of it, and repeated it over and over to himself until he was sure he had the number memorized.

Before Waldron could tell him to leave again, Reilly asked, "Was that him? Was that Devlin?"

"Yes. You know goddamn well it was."

"Is he coming in?"

"Don't worry about it. Everything is under control."

Waldron ripped the top page of his pad off and stuck it in his pocket. He stood up and brushed past Reilly. Reilly watched him leave, then went to the message pad. He could still see the blank impression of the phone number Waldron had written. He lightly filled in the lines with the numbers he had memorized. They fit. Reilly smiled and said to himself, Go tell Fenton whatever lies you want, bucko—the man is dead.

Reilly walked back to his desk and picked up his phone. He dialed a special number at British Telecom. The service rep asked for his account number. He told her, "London Metropolitan Police." She asked for his name and badge number. He knew the names of other cops cleared for access, but he didn't know any other badge numbers, so he had to give his own name and number.

"Sergeant Constable Reilly. Badge MD1211."

The service rep asked him for the number he wanted checked, and he gave her the number Devlin had just recited.

The service rep punched the phone number into British Telecom's computer system and entered the access codes. In twelve seconds the computer listing produced the name and address of the phone's location. Reilly wrote everything down very carefully.

"The listing at that number is for the Hotel Monteague. Wingate Close. Cambridge Postal District 2, CB2."

"Thank you."

Reilly quickly hung up the phone and walked to the division's reference area on the second floor. He picked up the atlas that contained maps of Cambridge, England, and found the location. It was a small street between Trumpington and Cambridge off the A1309, a small highway with the local name High Street.

"I've got you now, you bloody bastard. You'll soon wish you'd never seen Patrick Reilly."

Reilly picked up the phone and dialed the bailiff in the Magistrate's Court. The network moved very fast. The word was sent to Mislovic's headquarters on Berwick Street. Everyone was alerted to pass the information quickly. Zenko was called on his cellular phone, then called Reilly.

"You sure?"

"Yes, goddammit," Reilly hissed. "Why are you calling me here?"

"You forget we work directly now."

"All right. Have you got it?"

Zenko repeated the address. Reilly added, "Room 211. Got it? It's a hotel. Don't shoot up the place. It's that room. Do your job this time. You won't get another chance from me. Good-bye."

Reilly never stopped to think that the "job" included killing a mother and child.

Waldron battled with Fenton for fifteen minutes, fending him off, guaranteeing him that not only would Devlin and the woman be in the division within the next twenty-four hours, but so would his prime suspects in the case. Fenton badgered him about stringing him along, and threatened him, but Waldron stubbornly stuck to his story. Devlin and the woman would be in. The criminals would be arrested. The case was being handled.

Waldron left Fenton's office knowing full well how far away he was from delivering anybody. He checked with the stakeout on Berwick. Nothing. He told his men to stay on it. He thought about calling Devlin, but he knew there was no point. Devlin would not come in without Mislovic under arrest. Suddenly, after twenty-six hours of continuous work, there was nothing to do except go home and sleep and call Devlin as soon as his team picked up Mislovic. If they picked up Mislovic.

CHAPTER 26

AFTER ZENKO GAVE Mislovic Reilly's information, the Yugoslav sat in Marla's cafe brooding. Helping Oliver, as if he worked for him, rankled Mislovic. And for the first time, he thought about the fact that he would be causing the death of someone related to him. He tested his feelings to see if the notion bothered him. It did, but not much. He hadn't seen his sister in so many years, he hardly remembered her. He'd never even seen Annie. All their dealings had been over the phone. No, the only thing that really bothered him was the possibility that Oliver would patronize him.

Then, of course, there was the child. Mislovic sipped his coffee and thought about that. It elicited a shrug, but not much more. How many women and children had Mislovic seen slaughtered in the brutal civil war at home? Hundreds? Thousands? Two more casualties wouldn't make a difference. Not to Mislovic. The father was already dead. The mother would be, too. Better the child not be an orphan. And better that bastard who had wrapped a chain around his neck and used him for a shield be dead, too. That was the most important thing: Devlin had to die.

Mislovic picked up Zenko's cellular phone. He didn't care who out there might hear his voice deliver a death sentence. He smiled. Dealing death still felt good.

The phone rang three times, and a woman answered. She gave him another phone number for Oliver. Mislovic dialed the number and reached the office in the warehouse. Oliver answered.

"Mr. Oliver, this is your friend in Soho."

Oliver smiled as he talked into the phone. The cocaine was like magic to him. It pulled the powerful as well as the weak to him. He loved this part of the game. He had it, and they wanted it.

The Yardie hunched over the phone and told Mislovic, "Yes, mon, I was expecting your call. Are we ready to get on wit' it den?"

"Yes. I have the information you need."

"Good, good."

"Do you have a pencil?"

"Go ahead."

Mislovic gave Oliver Reilly's information.

"I suggest you go quickly. I have no idea how long they will be there."

"I don' do notting slow, mon. Don't vex yourself. They already dead."

"Will you be ready to deliver the goods?"

"Yes, I'm ready at my end. You want'a deal now, or you wan' me to take care of dis?"

"Oh, taking care of this is part of the deal. You've got to do that first. Assuming you get this first part done, when do we pick up our shipment?"

"Tomorrow. Six o'clock in da evening."

"And where would that be?"

Oliver gave Mislovic the location of his warehouse. "Do you know where dat be?"

Mislovic answered, "Yes. Do you know where Cambridge is? I hear there's a lot of smart people there."

"Don' worry, fren', soon be a lot of dead people there."

Devlin and Annie sat quietly in the grassy field south of the farmhouse. About fifty yards off Ben stood near the bank of the River Cam. Elizabeth was a few feet away from Ben, picking clover and wildflowers. Ben held a ridiculously small wicker basket that Annie had found in the farmhouse. Whenever Elizabeth found a treasure she wanted to keep, she would run over to Ben. He would bend down and extend the basket. She would place her stem of grass or piece of clover or tiny flower into the growing pile. Once in a while, she would venture a little farther away than Ben wanted her to, and he would take the necessary steps to stay close.

Annie and Devlin watched the incongruous pair. Annie

couldn't help but smile at them, but Devlin found it difficult to enjoy the moment. He was not comfortable with them being out in the open. Annie had to almost beg him to let her take Elizabeth outside. The child hadn't walked or played outdoors in two days. Devlin had finally relented, but only for an hour. The hour was almost up. The sun was slowly sinking into the western horizon, casting a reddish golden glow over the fields and river.

It was a peaceful, lovely evening in the English countryside, but there was nothing charming about the fact that Ben carried a Colt Python .357 Magnum under his armpit or that Devlin had a Glock 17 shoved into his waist at the small of his back and Ben's .22-caliber Beretta in his right pants pocket.

Annie had overcome Devlin's reluctance to go outside, but now she worried about his silence. She was afraid that she had antagonized him. She did not want to do that. The night before had somehow brought them both closer together and further apart.

Finally, she asked, "Are you all right, Dev?"

Devlin turned and looked at her. It seemed to him a strange question.

"What's the matter? Are you angry because I asked to get out?"

"No. Not really."

"Then what is it?"

Devlin felt like shrugging off the question, but he didn't. He turned to answer her, then stopped for a moment to look at her. The setting sun cast Annie in such a warm, golden light, making her appear so vibrant and beautiful, that Devlin finally just said what was on his mind.

"What it is, is that I'm tired of keeping my distance from you. My separation. I know there's very good reason to, but I don't feel like it."

"I see."

"Sorry, but that's it."

"Don't be sorry."

"Well, I guess I'm not. I'm more pissed off than sorry."

"Maybe, Jack, when this is all over, when things get back to normal, we can sit down and think about it. You know, talk about it without all this shit hanging over our heads."

Devlin smiled.

"What?" she asked.

"I'm trying to remember what 'normal' is."

"Is your life that . . ."

"That what?"

"That . . . unusual?"

Devlin laughed. Annie had barely seen him smile since his arrival, and now his rich laugh seemed to fill the field.

"What?"

"Annie, 'unusual' is such a polite word. You're very nice."

"Well, I probably can't even imagine what your life has become. But maybe if we survive this, we should think about changing our lives. Maybe we deserve a second chance."

"Maybe."

"What do you think of Elizabeth?"

Devlin turned to look at the little girl.

"She's amazing. She seems like the child every man or woman would want."

"I don't think I could live with myself if anything happened to her."

Annie wanted Devlin to tell her that nothing would happen to the child, but he didn't.

"I know what you mean," he said.

Annie felt the panic coming on, and Devlin sensed it without even looking at her.

"Take it easy, Annie. She'll be all right. As long as Uncle Ben is around, I doubt very much is going to happen to her."

"That makes me feel a little better."

"Good."

"What are our chances, Dev? Really."

Devlin thought a moment before he answered.

"Years and years ago I was in a dojo with a black American karate instructor. He was a very tough guy. Very strong and understandably macho. You know, street-smart, tough black macho type, but he had come up through the karate ranks, and he had changed himself a great deal. He had become somewhat more contemplative. More thoughtful.

"But under it, of course, he was still the street survivor. Still instinctively tough, you know what I mean?"

"I think so."

"I learned a lot from him."

"Yes."

"So one day, way back when, he was demonstrating a technique to about five or six of us. We had formed a circle around him to see what he was trying to show us.

"It was a hand-to-hand thing, so he motioned us closer.

"Suddenly he looked up, and he saw himself surrounded. And he turned his head from side to side, checking us out, and he smiled. He decided to make a small lesson out of it, so he said, 'What would you all do if you were surrounded like this?'

"Well, the answer was obvious—get out, get away.

" 'But how?' he asked us.

"Well, he showed us an interesting technique."

Devlin stopped talking for a moment, remembering the day and the lesson he had learned. And then he brought himself back and continued.

"So he showed us this move, and then he said something very interesting. He said, 'Once you open the way, move fast, 'cuz one of them has the knife.' "

"I don't understand."

"For him, it was taken for granted that someone in that crowd around him would have a knife. No question. Nowadays, it would probably be a gun instead of a knife, but the point is he had no question about it. For him it was a fact. The lesson was, once you break out, you keep going. You move. Because whoever has that gun or that knife won't hesitate to use it. We smashed out once, Annie, but now we aren't moving. We're sitting here waiting for that cop to do his job. It might or might not be the right thing to do. Maybe it's the only thing to do. But we're not moving, and I don't like that."

"What should we do?"

Devlin smiled. "That's what I was thinking about. I can't figure out anything but this. Lay low until you get into that witness program. If it takes too long, or it doesn't work out, we'll move again. And we won't stop this time. We'll move fast and keep moving fast."

"Okay."

Devlin stood up and brushed his pants. The movement caught Ben's eye, and he watched Devlin help Annie to her feet. Annie took Devlin's arm. It was a spontaneous act, but one which quite naturally turned them into a couple. They walked arm-in-arm down toward the river, angling slightly away from Ben and Elizabeth. But Devlin made sure he was always in Ben's sight.

He finally allowed himself to relax slightly. It felt good having Annie on his arm, by his side. It was a beautiful evening in a very quiet and peaceful part of the world. Devlin knew that this moment was as good as it was going to get until the nightmare was over.

CHAPTER 27

FOUR MEN SAT around a makeshift table in Oliver's mezzanine office at the warehouse. On the table in front of them were two MAC-10 machine pistols. They were compact, deadly weapons, converted into fully automatic mode, capable of firing a twenty-round magazine of 9-mm bullets in seconds. The pistols had a squat coarseness about them, but each gun bore an undeniable elegance in its deadly efficient design.

There were also two semiautomatic handguns: a Ruger P89 with a fifteen-shot magazine, and a Smith & Wesson, also 9-mm, and also carrying a fifteen-shot magazine. All the guns were fully loaded, and there was an extra loaded magazine for each weapon.

Oliver sat at one end of the table. Behind him, his driver, Louis, leaned against the dirty green plaster wall. Two of the men at the table alternated between listening to Oliver and looking at the MAC-10s. They wanted to hold the machine pistols. The guns meant power to them. They had never shot fully automatic pistols, only handguns. But they did not dare reach out until Oliver told them to.

The fourth man, Hinton, didn't seem to listen to or look at anything. He had come directly from Lydia Cientro's altar. His eyes were glazed. He appeared to be deeply stoned on ganja, but there were no drugs in his blood. His only intoxicants were the murderous trance induced by his recent kill and the subsequent additional hours spent in front of the effigy of Chango.

Hinton had absolutely expected to be summoned by Oliver for this killing. He knew for certain that the time was drawing near. His entire concentration since burning the body of Trek had been on worshipping and waiting for his god Chango to send him to kill.

Now, his hands resting in his lap, Hinton sat quietly as Oliver talked about what he wanted done. With his right thumb, Hinton stroked the eight-inch switchblade that was always in his right pants pocket. A Hintonian form of masturbation. The switchblade had been honed to the sharpness of a surgical steel scalpel, and its point was so precise that the slightest touch would draw blood. Hinton enjoyed caressing the knife.

The other two men at the table were Dexter and his partner, Rockliffe. Dexter was a Rasta man. He wore his hair in long dreads stuffed up under a large cap knit from yarn the colors of the Ethiopian flag: green, black, and yellow, which went well with his very dark skin. Dexter was the quiet type. He tended to stare silently, boring into you with his cold, deep-set eyes.

Rockliffe was the opposite of his hard-sounding name and the opposite of Dexter. He was big, soft, and fat; almost six feet five and weighing just under 350 pounds. But his size made him powerful. And he had no trouble pulling a trigger, no matter at whom the gun was pointed. Rockliffe dressed entirely in black, in a futile attempt to look a bit slimmer.

This was the killing crew. Two teams. Oliver and Hinton. Dexter and Rockliffe. Louis would drive Oliver and Hinton. And a man named Elbert waited downstairs, ready to drive Dexter and Rockliffe.

Oliver had experienced less trouble rounding up the men and the weapons than he had trying to find a map of Cambridge. He had yelled and threatened until one of his men finally came up with a map of the United Kingdom and a guidebook to Cambridge. The large-scale map indicated the highway that would take them to Cambridge. The guidebook showed a few details of the town center and the famous college campuses scattered throughout the area. They would have to suffice. Oliver knew that once he arrived at Cambridge, he would find the Hotel Monteague, even if he had to shoot people to do so.

"Okay, me bredrin"—Oliver pointed to the compact machine guns—"Hinton and Rockliffe take da MACs. Dexter, take the Smith. I'll handle the Ruger. Be careful wit' my weapons. They cost me plenty. Keep your fingers off da triggers until we be there. And don' shoot at notting until we find dem. Understood?"

Hinton, Dexter, and Rockliffe each picked up a weapon. Oliver picked up the last one.

"They're in a hotel out near da damn college town, Cambridge. The plan is very simple. We drive to da place and kill all dem. Anybody get in our way, we kill dem too. You got a full clip in each pistol an' one extra for each of you. If you get to da second clip, you best be shooting into dead meat. Let's go."

The men picked up the extra magazines of ammunition and filed down the stairs to two cars waiting on the ground floor of the warehouse. One car was Oliver's black Mercedes 560 SEL. The other was a gray BMW 633i. Both cars were stolen. Oliver and Hinton got into the back of the Mercedes, with Louis driving. Dexter and Rockliffe climbed into the BMW. Elbert was already in the driver's seat.

One of Oliver's men hit the button on the electric winch, and the big steel corrugated door at the front of the warehouse started grinding up to reveal the dirty gray backstreet. The cars drove out quietly.

During the drive, Hinton did not say one word. He looked as if he were in deep meditation. Breathing lightly, he stared out the window of the car, his hand resting calmly on the MAC-10 lying in his lap.

Oliver didn't attempt to make conversation. He had seen this before, and couldn't shake the impression that Hinton was repeating some silent prayer to himself.

In the other car, the mood was quite different. Big Rockliffe joked and complained about how long the ride was taking without any beer or ganja in the car. He laid a big hand on the driver's seat and shook it, telling Elbert, "Hey, mon, cyan ya not stop and get us some cold pints, den? Some chips too, mon. We cyan make dis fucking trip wit'out some pints and a spliff or two."

Elbert looked in the rearview mirror and answered, "That's a good idea, big boy. We stop for brew, and I get to watch Oliver shoot off your balls when I tell him why."

"Aw, fuck Oliver, come on."

"You know, Rockliffe, I knew you would be a pain in the ass."

"If you knew, why din ya not get some beer, ya dumb son of a bitch?"

"Guess what, you fat fuck?"

"What?"

Elbert reached under the seat next to him and pulled out a brown paper bag filled with pint cans of Tennants Triple X.

"I got your fat ass covered, bwouy."

He passed the bag back to Rockliffe. The big man slapped Elbert on the shoulder and yelled, "Good work! Dat's a Yard mon for you now."

The two men whooped and hollered at each other. Dexter sat in the corner of the backseat and watched them carry on about the beer. He smiled, but didn't say anything.

Rockliffe opened a can and let the foam spray against the front seat. "You a beautiful lickle mon, aren't you den?"

"So give me one, too, Rockliffe."

Rockliffe took four huge swallows from his can, finishing half of it. He paused to open a can for Elbert, handed it to him, then finished his first pint. He crushed it and asked, "Dexter, you wan' one den?"

The small intense man flashed a quick smile at his partner and shook his head no.

By the time the cars arrived at the outskirts of Cambridge, the beer was long gone. It was almost five o'clock.

In the lead car, Oliver told Louis to pull into an Exxon station. The BMW with the others followed right behind, and both cars filled up with gas.

Oliver sent Louis out to ask for directions to High Street and Wingate Close.

Louis came back to the car very quickly. The directions were surprisingly simple.

They pulled back onto the highway, drove for about a mile, and made a right turn onto Wingate Close.

Oliver watched closely for the Hotel Monteague, but it would have been hard to miss. The hotel was a two-story, Tudor-style house made of gray stone, topped with an old thatched roof and fronted by a gravel car park with room for about five vehicles. Two double sets of floodlights set in the ground illuminated the front of the squat little building. The small hotel stood out distinctly in the evening twilight.

Both cars slowed down as they came abreast of the hotel. When Oliver saw the hotel's name clearly displayed on the sign swinging near the car park entrance, he felt a shock of anticipation. They were in there.

Hinton's attention peaked, too. His eyes narrowed as he tried to peer into the front windows of the small, quiet hotel. It was early evening, but the place looked empty and closed.

Oliver told Louis to turn left at the next corner and pull over. The BMW followed closely, and both cars parked under a large oak tree. The drivers killed their lights and engines. Everyone stayed in the cars. The only sound was the pinging of the sheet metal cooling in the chill November air.

None of the men were accustomed to such a quiet place. There was no room in the silence for Rockliffe's loud voice. Everyone in both cars stopped talking.

Dexter and Rockliffe picked up their guns and checked to make sure the safeties were off and the ammunition clips properly loaded. They pulled back the slides on the weapons, chambering the first bullets.

In the backseat of the black Mercedes, Oliver turned to Hinton. He knew that in his present state Hinton would not be able to accept anything that sounded like an order. All instructions would have to be suggestions.

"Okay, Hinton, I say you and I go to da front, Dexter and Rockliffe da back. You go in; Dexter go in. Me and Rockliffe follow and cover da doors so no one gets out. You and Dexter find da room an' unload first. It's room 211. Any more dan two of us in there shooting, and we'll kill ourselves. If anybody left standin' after you finish, I'll take 'em out. Sound okay?"

Hinton nodded, then said, "Tell Dexter and Rockliffe to be quiet when they go around back."

"Okay."

The two men stepped out of the big Mercedes, closing the doors but not completely shutting them. They went over to the second car. Dexter and Rockliffe got out, and all four men stood in the shadows of the quiet street. There were only a few houses visible in the neighborhood. Most of the them were set back from the road or behind tall hedges. There were no streetlights. The only illumination came from the twilight sky and a cloud-covered moon.

Oliver told the others the plan, reminded them of the room number they were looking for, and asked, "You got it?"

Dexter and Rockliffe both nodded. Oliver gave a final instruction to Dexter. "When you hear us go in da front, you go in da back. If dat door back there be locked, kick it open, shoot it open, just get in."

Dexter nodded. Rockliffe answered, "Okay, Don, we got ya."

The four men walked quickly, with their machine pistols and guns pointed down and held near their legs. In the dim light it was almost impossible to see the gunmetal gray weapons.

As they neared the front of the hotel, they veered off in pairs. Hinton took the lead toward the front door. The closer he got, the faster he moved. It was as if a huge magnet were drawing him to the hotel. For a moment, Oliver was afraid that Hinton might simply walk in and start shooting before Dexter and Rockliffe arrived in place at the back of the hotel.

He cautiously reached out and held the side of Hinton's arm. The man stopped, but did not take his eyes off the front entrance. Oliver whispered, "Wait for dem to get aroun' back, okay?"

A dog barked somewhere in the distance. Oliver gritted his teeth, but Hinton simply moved up closer to the front door. He took a position and pointed the machine gun at the front door lock. Oliver knew he would wait only a few more moments; the killing urge was about to overwhelm the Voodoo assassin. Oliver stepped around Hinton and tested the door to see if it was locked. The handle would not turn, but he stayed in front of the door, blocking the way so that Hinton could not shoot. Oliver wanted the second team ready to break inside before Hinton was let loose.

Dexter and Rockliffe reached the back of the hotel in less than half a minute. Dexter looked at the back door. It was a thick wooden door with glass panels. There was an aluminum storm door in front of it. Dexter cautiously opened the aluminum door and stepped inside it, holding it out of his way with his shoulder. He reached out to test the doorknob. It was locked. He pointed the Smith & Wesson and leaned back, pushing the storm door out of his way and positioning himself so he would have a clear shot at the lock and handle of the wooden door. He was waiting for the sounds of Oliver and Hinton breaking into the front before he opened fire, but instead he heard the unmistakable splattering sound of Rockliffe emptying his bladder on the scrubby lawn behind him.

Rockliffe whispered over his shoulder, "Too much goddamn beer, mon."

Despite himself, Dexter started to laugh. He had an urge to turn around and fire a shot at Rockliffe while he pissed, but just then he heard the ripping cracks of an automatic weapon discharging into the front door of the hotel. Hinton was blasting his way into the Hotel Monteague.

Dexter leaned a little farther back against the storm door, pointed his gun, shielded his face with his arm and shoulder, and squeezed the trigger. The door handle and frame exploded in a blast of splinters and tearing metal.

He squeezed one more shot into the door, then stepped back and kicked it. The door was jammed shut. The goddamn storm door was pushing back against him. It was in his way. He couldn't step back far enough to get a good kick into the thick wooden door. He could hear the sounds of Hinton firing in the front of the hotel. He reached out with is right hand to push the storm door back so he could get a good position to kick in the recalcitrant inner door, when suddenly the storm door was gone. Rockliffe had grabbed it and ripped it off its hinges. Dexter, now free from the encumbrance, kicked hard at the wooden door. It finally popped loose, banged against the jamb, and bounced back at him. Dexter shoved it aside and strode into the kitchen area of the hotel, ready to shoot anyone who appeared.

Behind him, Rockliffe said, "Go on, mon, I got da back here covered now."

Dexter hunched over and hustled toward the front. He could hear shouts and a far-off scream in front of him. He rushed forward, his finger on the trigger of the Smith & Wesson.

Rockliffe watched Dexter move off into the hotel. He walked slowly into the kitchen area, flipped on the lights, and covered the back door. All his boisterous play vanished. In battle he did exactly as he was told. Nobody would get out the back way without being shot.

Out front, Hinton had already moved through the foyer and past the reception area. Oliver stood in the reception area near the door to the manager's apartment, blocking any exit.

Hinton rushed up a short flight of stairs, quickly checking the numbers on doors, looking for room 211. A guest at the far end of the corridor looked out and Hinton sprayed his doorway. The bullets ripped upwards from the floor to the ceiling, just missing the guest's hand as he frantically ducked back, pulling his door shut.

Hinton strode down the hallway until he found 211. He hardly missed a step as he turned and fired into the door. The door shattered and bucked. Hinton kicked it open and stepped into a dark room. He shot at the bed to his left and the bed to his right, then sprayed bullets across the far wall of the room. The mattresses jumped and bucked. Windows shattered, walls ripped, fabric and stuffing tore apart and spewed into the room. The flashes from the MAC-10 illuminated the empty room, revealing in strobelike bursts that Hinton was shooting at nothing living. He stopped immediately, stepped back, and looked for a light switch.

Downstairs, Dexter had reached the reception area where Oliver stood. Oliver raised a hand and Dexter stayed where he was. Both men waited to hear the sounds of screaming and death. Suddenly, the small hotel was weirdly silent except for some muffled whimpering in a far-off room.

Oliver knew something was wrong. Something had been wrong from the minute they entered. The place was practically empty, as if it had been shut down after a summer tourist season. Nobody seemed to be there, much less Devlin and the woman.

He snarled at Dexter, "Check every room on dis floor. Get Rockliffe and pull out whoever you find and stand dem over here."

Oliver turned and ran up the short flight of stairs. Hinton was already kicking in doors and shooting up empty rooms.

There were four doors on the right side of the corridor. Hinton had kicked open all four and fired into them. Oliver peered into the rooms as he passed them. Each one looked as if a small bomb had gone off in it.

Oliver yelled at Hinton, "Stop."

There was one room still unopened at the far corner on the left. Oliver stepped in front of Hinton and kicked open the door. Inside, a middle-aged couple cringed in a corner. Oliver almost shot them out of pure anger and disgust. Instead, he turned out of the room and led Hinton back down the stairs.

In the cramped reception area, Dexter and Rockliffe were with a fat, balding man who was shaking so badly he could barely stand. He was the manager.

Oliver walked up to him and pressed the muzzle of the Ruger into his temple.

"How many people staying here?"

The man spluttered, "Three. The couple upstairs and a single gentleman."

"Any other woman?"

"No. No."

"Where's da single mon, den?"

"I don't know. I don't know. Out to dinner, maybe."

"No woman?"

"No. I swear. Check the register. I only have three in tonight. Please."

Oliver knew they had come to the right place. But it was clear that Devlin and the woman were not here. He stood still for a moment, fuming, wondering if he should turn to Hinton and tell him to kill all these people. But he decided not to give Hinton that order. He wanted to know why this place.

He turned to the manager.

"The single mon, was he tall? A big mon?"

"Yes. Yes."

Oliver turned and ran up the short flight to the room. He wanted to see if there were any clothes, any suitcases, any sign that Devlin might be coming back.

He looked around the room, and then he saw it. The answering machine. By luck, none of Hinton's bullets had smashed it.

He stepped up to the machine and saw the message light blinking. He pressed the button and listened as the incoming message tape whirred and reversed.

And then James Waldron's distinctly angry and distraught voice sounded throughout the ruined small hotel. "Devlin. Devlin, are you there? Answer me, Devlin. Dammit, man, you must call in. I need you to come in, now. Call me. Anytime at the division. Just call."

Oliver turned from the room and walked back down the stairs and straight out of the hotel. He didn't speak to or look at anyone. The rage inside him was so intense that if anyone had crossed him or questioned him, he would have shot him without hesitation.

The other men simply followed him out of the shattered front doorway.

Dexter knew that if he looked at Rockliffe and so much as raised an eyebrow, the fat man would start laughing, and then he would laugh, too. And then they would be dead. Oliver would turn his gun on them and shoot them until the clip ran out. Dexter kept his head down and followed Oliver toward the cars.

Even in their giddy mood, Dexter and Rockliffe, like Oliver, were pumped up and hot to kill. But Hinton, crazy Hinton, was ice cold. He held his machine pistol pointed toward the sky to keep the hot muzzle away from his body. He never said a word. He left the rage to Oliver. His faith was unaltered. He didn't question the ways of his god. He didn't understand, but he was convinced they were close to the woman. He felt it in his bones.

The four men climbed back into the cars. Oliver slammed his door shut and told Louis, "Get out of dis fucking town now! Stop at da first store ya see wit' liquor and buy a bottle of rum. Go!"

Oliver's rage was barely containable. If Devlin had intended to return to the room, he would never come near the place now. If it was just a location to receive messages, he wouldn't be back anyhow. In either case, Oliver had been called out for nothing.

Louis asked no questions. He turned the car around and retraced his route back toward the highway.

At the ravaged hotel on Wingate Close, the stunned manager and his two guests began to realize they were still alive. They were unable to comprehend what had just happened;

the shock of it all had made them numb. The manager wandered around the reception area, knowing he should call the police, but not sure exactly what to say. None of them had ever seen a gun fired, much less the havoc that automatic weapons could produce.

Suddenly, an incoming call came through the hotel's switchboard. The manager picked it up. When the voice asked for room 211, he automatically put the call through.

On the second ring, the answering machine upstairs came on. Devlin's recorded voice said, "Waldron, leave a number where and when I can reach you."

James Waldron sat on the edge of his bed. He had been just about to drop onto the bed and go to sleep, but he thought he'd try one more time. He listened to Devlin's outgoing message and waited for the tone. He looked at his watch. It read 6:20 P.M. After the tone sounded, he spoke in a resigned voice. "Waldron here, Devlin. Please call at the division. They'll ring me through at home if I'm still here. Thank you."

Waldron placed his phone in its cradle and lay back in his bed. He began to think about what he would do after Fenton was finished destroying his career. Waldron was not at all sure he wanted to have anything more to do with law enforcement. Maybe he could teach. Find a nice private school in the hinterlands and settle back into a quiet life of teaching. Perhaps history, he thought. Say ancient history up to the time of the Romans. That was about as close to the present as Waldron wanted to deal with.

CHAPTER 28

DEVLIN TURNED FROM the riverbank and headed toward the farmhouse.

Annie held him back for a moment and said, "Wait, Dev. Just a few more minutes. This is the best part of the day out here."

"It's getting late, Annie."

"Just a few more minutes."

He didn't agree, but he stopped and looked up at the sky, which was turning a deep purple-red, streaked with darkening clouds. Devlin stood where he was, amidst the tall grass of the fen, and looked at the sunset colors of the sky and listened to the gentle sound of the river lapping at its bank. He allowed himself to go deeper and deeper into the moment, until he was unaware of anything but the sight of the sky and the sound of the water.

And then he slowly pulled himself back and said quietly, "C'mon."

He waved at Ben to follow him back to the farmhouse. Annie walked slowly by his side, with Ben and Elizabeth following behind.

When they arrived in the front yard, Annie asked him if they could run into town and get some wine.

"And I need some milk for breakfast. Wouldn't mind picking up a newspaper, too."

She expected Devlin to say no, but he just said, "All right."

Devlin figured if they had to go to town, now would be a good time, when there would be fewer people on the street but the stores would still be open.

Devlin asked Ben to drive. The big man shoved himself behind the steering wheel of the yellow Ford station wagon.

Elizabeth, of course, climbed right into the front seat next to him. Devlin and Annie sat in the back.

Ben carefully buckled Elizabeth's seat belt, then fastened his. He started the car and drove along the narrow country roads until he reached the little business district of the nearest town. Most of the stores were clustered around a large playing field that made up the central square in the little town. Around the square were a newsagent, a small grocery, a post office, a petrol station, an estate agent, and, at the far north side of the square, a shop that sold wines and liquor where Devlin had found a very good red Bordeaux from St. Julien. He returned to the station wagon, and Ben drove to the south end of the square.

Thirty seconds later, Oliver's black Mercedes pulled up to the liquor store. The BMW was following close behind and stopped.

Nobody in the BMW knew why Oliver's car was stopping in this town, but as soon as Rockliffe saw they had passed a liquor store he announced that he was going in to buy beer. Dexter told him to be cool, but the fat man was not going to pass up a chance to get something to drink for the long drive home.

Louis was already stepping out of the Mercedes to enter the liquor store. Hinton was watching him. Dexter was holding Rockliffe's right arm so he couldn't get out of the car, but Rockliffe still managed to roll down the window and yell out a request to Louis.

"Get me some pints of stout, mon. I'll pay you."

Louis stopped and turned toward Rockliffe. Maybe it really was Chango. Or fate. Or karma. But as Rockliffe yelled at Louis, Hinton turned to look at him, and at just that moment, across the square, Devlin stepped out of the station wagon and walked into the newsagent store.

Oliver was watching Louis, anxious for him to get him his rum. Louis nodded at Rockliffe. And the others just sat in the cars, waiting. But not Hinton. Hinton was moving, and moving fast. He shouldered open the door of the Mercedes and hissed at Louis to get back in the car. Louis stopped and looked at Hinton. He was puzzled. He did not want to cross Oliver, but the look on Hinton's face stopped him.

When Louis stopped, Rockliffe yelled out, "Go on, mon."

Hinton told him, "Shut up," with such ferocity that Rockliffe jerked back into the car.

Oliver slid over toward the open door and asked Hinton, "What's happening, den, mon?"

But Hinton was galvanized. He was looking down at the other side of the square, waiting for Devlin to come out of the newsagent store, waiting to make sure he had seen what he thought he had seen.

Oliver persisted. "What, mon?"

Hinton spoke back into the car while keeping his eyes on the newsagent shop.

"He's here. He's over there."

Oliver slid across the backseat and opened the door on his side. He got out and stood on the street, looking. He saw the small Ford station wagon; he could tell there were people in it; but never having seen Devlin, he did not know whom he should be looking for.

"Where?"

Hinton didn't answer. He told Louis, "Get in."

The driver, seeing both men looking at something, hustled back to the car.

Now Oliver was seized by Hinton's intensity.

"Where? Where be da mon?"

Hinton pointed. "In that store. Wait and see if it him that come out. The others be in the yellow car."

Oliver yelled out, "Who? Where?"

"The woman and her bodyguard. In a yellow car. Watch the store."

And just as he said "store," Devlin emerged, heading for the station wagon.

Hinton immediately dropped into the backseat. He pushed the barrel of his MAC-10 into Louis's shoulder and yelled, "Follow the yellow car. Don't lose them."

Louis knew if he didn't move right now, Hinton would blow his head off and drive the car himself. Oliver wasn't sure if Hinton was hallucinating or not—maybe he had snapped under the pressure, maybe all that praying to his god had driven him over the edge, and maybe he was right. Oliver dropped back into his seat, along for the ride just like the others.

Louis quickly pulled away and roared after Devlin's car, which had already pulled around the bend leading back to the road that would take them to the farmhouse.

After Hinton had yelled at Louis, Elbert had started paying close attention. He shoved the BMW into gear and followed the big Mercedes.

Oliver watched Hinton stare out the windshield as they slid around the square in pursuit of the yellow station wagon. When they came around the bend, Devlin's car came into view.

"Are you sure it's dem?"

"Yes."

"You're sure?"

Hinton turned to Oliver and stared at him for a moment. "Don't ask me again. I'm sure."

Inside the yellow station wagon, Ben drove slowly toward the road that would connect them to the narrow unmarked lane that led back to the farmhouse. A car passed Ben from the opposite direction, and the beams from its headlights silhouetted the passengers in the station wagon for about three seconds. Oliver could make out the head of a man and woman in the backseat.

"Who's the driver?"

Hinton answered, "I figure it be his shooter."

Oliver had no reason to believe he'd gotten this lucky, but having seen the silhouettes, he simply suspended his confusion and disbelief and went along with what was happening.

Within a minute Devlin's car was past the few large houses that bordered the road leading into town. Ben was about to turn off onto the narrow road that led back to the farmhouse.

Oliver was pleased they were turning off the wide road, because whoever they were, they were about to die, and it would be better if it happened in a secluded area.

But then he realized that they must be heading toward a house of some sort. If they reached the protection of a house, it would make things more difficult.

Oliver made an instant, instinctive decision.

"Louis, take them. Now. Go!"

Louis didn't argue. He pushed down on the accelerator and the big Mercedes engine kicked in. The surge in speed and the sound of the engine caught Ben's attention. He looked into the rearview mirror and saw the headlights of the car behind him coming at them fast. Without a second's hesitation, he shoved the accelerator to the floor, and the station wagon roared forward.

Ben's instant response was enough to finally convince Oliver that somehow his crazy assassin had found the prey. It was hard to believe, but he didn't bother to try to figure out how it could have happened. It didn't matter now. He pulled back the slide on his Ruger, leaned out the window, pointed it at the fleeing station wagon, and pulled off four shots.

The shots bounced high and wide, but one of Oliver's bullets walloped against the sheet metal of the station wagon. It sounded like a huge rock had smacked into the car.

Ben had already released Elizabeth's seat belt and pushed her gently to the floor. He covered her head with his big right hand and steered the car with his left hand. Devlin shoved Annie down onto the rear seat below window level.

Just then the rear window blew out and everyone was showered with particles of tempered safety glass.

Devlin pulled out the Glock 17 Ben had given him and turned to fire back out the hole where the rear window had been. He squeezed off three quick shots, but the road was rough and Ben was weaving back and forth so they would make a harder target, and Devlin had no chance to aim. His shots went wide of the Mercedes, but Louis saw the bursts from the muzzle and hunkered down behind the wheel.

Annie had let out an involuntary scream at the sound of the gunfire, but Devlin couldn't let it bother him. He braced himself between the roof of the Ford and the backseat and squeezed off two more blasts. Annie winced under the twin explosions.

One of Devlin's shots smacked into a headlight of the Mercedes, putting it out, but Louis didn't slow down. He was intent on following the red taillights of the station wagon. Oliver was still leaning out the passenger window, but the jouncing on the rough road was slamming him up and down against the window frame, so he pulled back into the car. Hinton had not even tried to shoot at the fleeing station wagon. He had shoved a fresh magazine into the MAC-10 and was coiled in his seat, waiting for the Mercedes to close in on the car that held his prey.

In the BMW, Rockliffe and Dexter saw Oliver firing at the fleeing car. Dexter had wasted only three shots blasting open the back door of the hotel. Rockliffe's MAC-10 was fully loaded. They had no chance to fire with the Mercedes in front of them, so they waited. Between them, they had plenty of firepower left.

Rockliffe narrowed his eyes, trying to better see what was happening ahead of them, but he couldn't distinguish much. He sat bouncing around, staring into the darkness with the weapon in his right hand, wishing he had a pint can of beer in the left. He was waiting patiently, much like Hinton, until he was near enough to something or somebody he could shoot at.

In Devlin's car, the panic and confusion were mounting. This time Annie and Elizabeth weren't on the floor of a van out of sight of the action. Annie had seen the gunfire from the pursuing car. Elizabeth, still crouching down on the floor under Ben's hand, could clearly hear the noise of the gunfire and feel the car slamming down the road.

Going from a tranquil sunset to another ride in hell was almost too much for Annie to take. She found it difficult to breathe. If she'd had more air in her lungs, she would have been screaming.

To make it worse, the station wagon was bouncing so much on the rough road that it was impossible for Devlin to shoot back. He was afraid he might smash his head on the roof and jam his neck. Ben, however, was in no way letting up. He kept the speed up until they were actually extending the distance between themselves and their pursuers.

He half turned his head to Devlin in the backseat and yelled, "Get them ready to get out."

They were on a section of the road bordered by tall hedges on both sides. There was barely room to make it in one direction. Devlin knew that if an oncoming car were to appear, there'd be no way to avoid a head-on collision.

Devlin didn't have time to argue. He knew immediately what Ben was going to do, and he couldn't stop it. He pulled the .22-caliber Beretta out and pushed it against Ben's chest.

Ben grabbed the gun. Devlin reached over and lifted Annie up. He yelled, "Follow me when he stops."

Ben made a sharp right turn around a bend, pitching the car up on two wheels. When the car slammed down onto the road, he hit the brakes. The station wagon slid on the dirt road. Devlin was pitched forward against the front bench seat, but he fought the tremendous momentum and reached over to pull open his door.

Before the car skidded to a complete halt, Devlin was out of the door, hoping Annie was right behind him. He immediately pulled open the front passenger door, grabbed little Elizabeth around the waist, and lifted her out of the car. The poor terrified little girl clutched at the air in front of her, trying to grab on to Ben's hand. "Ben! Ben!" she cried.

The big man turned and yelled to her, "Go with them, honey. Go on."

Ben turned to see if Annie was out of the backseat. She was. He took one last look to see that Elizabeth was in Devlin's arms, then floored the accelerator.

The rush forward slammed shut both open doors. Devlin grabbed Annie's arm and carried Elizabeth as they plunged through the hedges into the tall fen grass to get out of sight. He made it into the fen just before the Mercedes came roaring around the bend. Louis had tried to take the turn too quickly, and the heavy car spun out slightly, losing traction. The big car slammed into a hedge on the driver's side. The left rear wheel slid off the road and dug into the soft boggy earth of the fen. The wheel spun. Earth, mud, and grass sprayed fifty feet from the churning back wheel, but the big engine on the Mercedes created so much torque that the tire didn't stick.

The right rear wheel was still on the narrow road. Just as the Mercedes was clawing its way out of the fen, the BMW roared around the bend. Elbert braked, but too late. The big car slammed into the rear right panel of the Mercedes.

All the occupants of both cars were shaken up, the BMW grille was cracked and the hood bent, and the driver-side air bag exploded into Elbert's face. The impact had knocked the Mercedes back into the soft earth. But both drivers were now caught up in a crazed desire to catch the fleeing station wagon. Elbert had to restart the BMW's engine. Louis floored the Mercedes and the big car lurched onto the road and roared after Ben, the BMW close behind.

Ben had gained back almost all the ground he had lost stopping to let the others out of the car. He had turned off his lights so that the pursuers could no longer clearly see him. During the confusion, Devlin had dragged Annie and Elizabeth farther into the cover of the marshland. The tall reeds were almost seven feet high right by the road, and didn't break until the wetland bog started about a hundred yards in.

Inside Oliver's car, Hinton was growling with frustration. It was taking too long to catch the yellow car. He thought he could see the car up ahead, but couldn't explain why there were no taillights.

He barked at Louis to go faster and peered into the darkness to try to find the yellow car. Hinton knew there was nothing he could do until they caught it.

Devlin was helpless in his way, too. He couldn't leave Annie and Elizabeth; he had no idea how to get them to safety; and he had left Ben alone to escape or face the pursuers without him.

Ben kept staring into the dark night. There was just enough moonlight to make the road visible in front of him. He drove as fast as he could, determined to draw the pursuers as far away from Elizabeth as possible. He reached down and grabbed the top handle of the Mossberg, lifted it off the floor, and placed it on the seat next to him. The shotgun was fully loaded. He reached under his armpit and checked the Colt Python .357 and shoved the powerful revolver deep into the holster under his armpit. The Beretta Devlin had given him was shoved in his belt under his stomach.

He had enough firepower to stop just about anything, but he had no idea how many men were after him, or how well armed they were. Whoever they are, thought Ben, some of them are going to die.

The big man grabbed the lap strap on his seat belt and tightened it even more. He leaned back and with the back of his head felt for the headrest. He reached behind him and lifted it until it was directly behind his head. Then he made his move.

At a section of the road that widened near a turn, he wrenched the compact station wagon into a sliding 180-degree turn and slued the car around so that it was facing in the opposite direction. Then he floored the accelerator and roared right back at the oncoming Mercedes. He could see the single headlight of the Mercedes, and when he calculated he was close enough he turned on his lights and hit the brights.

Louis was completely blinded by the glare from the station wagon, and in the next moment he felt the shuddering impact as Ben slammed head-on into the black Mercedes.

Oliver flew from the backseat into the front windshield and smashed his arm and shoulder against the thick glass. The windshield blossomed into a network of concentric cracks.

Louis was saved from serious injury when the Mercedes' steering wheel restraint bag instantly inflated upon impact. Hinton had somehow been able to twist his body and duck quickly enough so that he slammed into the cushioned back of the front seat. He survived serious damage, but his rib cage was compressed, so violently that his right lung was bruised, and three ribs cracked.

But that was just the first impact. Within a split second, the oncoming BMW slammed directly into the back of the stopped Mercedes. Unfortunately for Louis, the self-restraint air bag had deflated almost as quickly as it inflated, and because he didn't have his seat belt on the force of the second impact whiplashed his head viciously and then sent it slamming into the windshield on the rebound. The thick glass had already been cracked by Oliver's body, but now Louis's head hit it with such force that it broke completely. His skull was smashed at the point of impact, with fractures radiating out in six directions. His neck was cracked and his face was slashed from his forehead to his cheek, including the left eye. He died within minutes from massive brain hemorrhaging.

The rear collision crumpled the trunk of the Mercedes into an accordion, and gave Hinton another brutal shock.

The passengers in the second car were thoroughly scrambled, but no one was injured seriously. Elbert had already been saved once by his air bag, but this time his seat belt kept him from smashing his head. He did, however, crack his nose against the steering wheel, and the seat belt applied such pressure that he couldn't breathe for a few moments.

The sound of the double impact echoed down the road. Devlin heard it way back in his hiding place. For three or four seconds, nothing stirred but the dirt and dust that had been thrown into the air when the cars collided.

In the station wagon, Ben recovered quickly from the shock of the crash. His air bag had absorbed much of the impact, but his left arm was numb from the seat belt harness, and the entire safety belt reel mechanism was torn from the side door post.

The headlights on all three cars had been smashed, so the area was dark except for the faint glow of moonlight. Ben released his seat belt and bent over to pick up his shotgun, which had been thrown to the floor. The move saved his life, because, amazingly, Hinton had already made his way out of the Mercedes and now opened fire into the windshield of the station wagon.

But as soon as the burst from the MAC-10 stopped, Ben sat up and shot two blasts out of his shattered open windshield into the area where the shots had come from. Hinton dropped to the ground, then scrambled back behind the BMW for cover.

In the station wagon, Ben slid to the opposite side of the bench seat and tried to open the passenger door. It was jammed shut; the frame of the car had compressed around it. Ben swung his feet around and kicked at the door. The first blow loosened it. The second prodigious kick popped it open.

By now, Rockliffe and Dexter had managed to get out of the BMW and were on either side of the car. Elbert was still in a state of shock. He sat bleeding from his broken nose, clutching the bent steering wheel.

Both Rockliffe and Dexter were ready for action. They scrambled behind the BMW with Hinton and immediately started firing at the station wagon.

Ben managed to crawl to the rear of the wagon. He sat on the ground, his back propped against the bumper, using the car as a shield. His plan was to stay protected and keep shooting for as long as possible, but there were so many high-velocity bullets smashing into the station wagon that the car was actually bouncing up and down from the impact. It was being torn apart.

Both Rockliffe and Dexter had been aching to shoot their weapons, and now they were delivering a withering barrage of bullets. They assumed their rapid fire would keep Ben pinned down so that they could simply advance on him and shoot him down. But they underestimated Ben's courage.

When Dexter paused to reload the Smith & Wesson, Ben spun to the left, out from behind the station wagon, dropped into a prone position, and let fire two more quick blasts from the Mossberg. One blast took out Dexter's right knee, the second caught the right side of his head and ripped off a gruesome, bloody chunk. Dexter flew backwards and bounced off the BMW. He was dead before he hit the ground.

Hinton jumped up from behind the rear left of the BMW, flipped the MAC-10 to semiautomatic, and returned rapid single shots at the area where Ben was shooting from. He didn't waste his ammunition as Dexter and Rockliffe had.

A bullet slammed into Ben's left shoulder and spun him counterclockwise. Ben grunted with the impact. Rockliffe opened up again and emptied the remains of his clip, but his shots were too high. Ben rolled back behind the station wagon.

A searing pain from the bullet wound in his shoulder began, and Ben's entire left arm became numb. He fought off the shock and nausea and managed to get up on one knee. He propped the barrel of the Mossberg on his left knee and, by sheer force of will, gripped the handle and trigger with his numb left hand. He had to stop them. He knew their next move would be to come out of cover and advance.

With the shotgun ready, he dug out the Colt Python with his right hand. He step-crawled to the right side of the station wagon and opened fire. He pulled off another two blasts from the Mossberg, then alternated shots from the Python to each side. He shot slightly above and to the left of the flares coming out of the muzzles aimed at him.

He had six shots in the Python and alternated two shots right, two shots left until the big Magnum pistol was empty.

Nothing hit Hinton, but one bullet tore a section of metal and trim off the roof of the BMW, and the shrieking steel slapped into the right side of Rockliffe's face, knocking his head back and ripping into his right eye and forehead.

Hinton crouched down out of the line of Ben's fire. Rockliffe fell back, but even half blind and in pain he managed to pull out the second magazine for the MAC-10 then tried to load the machine pistol.

Ben realized that although he had stopped their advance, he now faced the problem of reloading the handgun. He had two more shells left in the Mossberg.

At the lull in the fight, the front passenger door of the Mercedes was kicked open, and Oliver rolled out onto the dirt of the dark road. His upper back and shoulder ached fiercely, but he was breathing and still in one piece. Oliver's anger raised him up, and he started to fire in Ben's direction.

Ben holstered the Python, then grabbed the barrel of the Mossberg with his numb left hand and the butt with his right. He stood up and leveled the Mossberg at the new set of muzzle flashes. He squeezed the trigger, and a burst of shot flew out toward Oliver. Unfortunately, Ben's grip on the shotgun wasn't strong enough, so most of the shot flew wide of his target, but enough pellets smacked into Oliver's right hip to spin him around and knock him down.

Now it was Rockliffe's turn to recover. Ben was standing out in the open. Rockliffe, half blinded but concentrating fiercely, let out three short bursts from the MAC-10.

One bullet hit Ben's right thigh, piercing the flesh and smashing the big femur bone. Another slug buried itself just below Ben's left collarbone.

But Ben didn't go down, and he was able to get off a final burst from the Mossberg, hitting Rockliffe in the left shoulder, knocking him off his feet and back over the rear fender of the BMW. He landed hard behind the car.

Suddenly, Hinton broke out from behind the BMW and ran toward the crumpled yellow station wagon. Ben pulled out the Beretta and fired two shots at Hinton, but missed the moving target. Hinton was not shooting back, so Ben held his fire to preserve his ammunition. Hinton wasn't interested in Ben. He had realized, even before Oliver joined the gun battle, that all the shots coming at them were being fired from one source. When he got close enough to see inside the car wreck, and saw that there was no one else there, he immediately turned and started running back down the road in the direction he and the others had come from.

Oliver saw him go and realized he was after the woman and the American. He could see they were not in the car. Oliver was able to crawl. He made it behind the BMW and saw that Rockliffe was still breathing. Dexter was dead. Hinton was gone. Let him get the others, Oliver thought; he himself was determined to kill whoever had done this to them.

He reached over and slapped Rockliffe.

"Get up, goddamn ya, get up."

Rockliffe moaned, then snarled, rolled over, and pulled himself into a sitting position. He still held the MAC-10 in his right hand.

Ben was leaning against the far side of the station wagon. He'd dropped the shotgun. It was empty, and he couldn't have shot it anymore even if it hadn't been. He shoved the Beretta back in his belt and pulled out the Python, which he laid on the roof of the Ford. He gritted his teeth against the pain, standing on one foot, concentrating on sliding bullets into the gun's cylinder. He managed to load four, expecting his enemies to come firing at him any second.

He wanted the long-barreled Python with six Magnum bullets for his last stand. He didn't believe he'd have time to use whatever was left in the Beretta. Even with a useless left arm, difficulty breathing, and a broken right leg, he was determined to stand and shoot until the Colt was empty.

Oliver pulled the magazine from his machine pistol and shoved it into Rockliffe's MAC-10. Then he pulled out his second full clip and shoved it into his gun.

He yelled up into the sky, "You're dead, you. I'm comin' to kill ya now."

Ben yelled back, "Come on then. Let me see your bloody face."

Oliver turned to Rockliffe. "You can stand, then, cyan ya not?"

"Yeah."

"All right. You take that side, I'll take this. You get up and you walk and you shoot until he be dead or us."

Ben slapped shut the cylinder of the Python. He gripped

the gun, eyes on the BMW. His best angle was to his left. He wanted his first shot from the big gun to hit flesh. Then he could unload on whomever was left.

Back down the road, Devlin had succeeded in making his way about fifty yards into the fen with Annie and Elizabeth. They had come to a point where they couldn't walk any farther without sinking into muck. They were well hidden by the tall reeds and grass.

Devlin settled them down amidst the reeds. Annie held Elizabeth in her arms. The little girl wouldn't stop asking about Ben. Annie tried to tell her that Ben would be all right, but her words were punctuated by the sound of gunfire in the distance. Devlin was torn between staying with the two of them and running down the road to help Ben. But at some point, he knew, they would realize Ben was alone, if they hadn't already, and they'd be coming back for Annie, Elizabeth, and him.

The dark night and the insanity of the situation infuriated Devlin. Elizabeth would not stop pleading with her mother about Ben. The usually quiet little girl was becoming more and more hysterical.

"Mummy, Mummy, where's Ben? Where is he, where is he, where is he?"

The pleading question came out in wracking sobs.

Finally, Devlin snarled at her, "Elizabeth, be quiet!"

The little girl stopped and looked at him.

"Stay here with your mother. Don't make a sound. I'll get Ben."

Devlin decided there was no way he'd wait and hide while Ben was fighting. And if they were coming back for him, he'd meet his enemies head-on.

Devlin pushed Annie down deeper into the reeds. "Stay here. Just stay right here, and don't move. Keep her quiet. I'll come back for you. Don't move, and don't make a sound."

All Annie could do was nod. She was terrified of being left alone in the dark, suffocating marsh, but she realized what Devlin was doing, and she knew it was the right thing. She clutched Elizabeth's head to her chest and held on to the child as Devlin disappeared into the black night.

Devlin cursed the dark and whatever perverse fate had led

his enemies to him and trapped Ben somewhere on this godforsaken road. He hoped against any rational reasoning that if he could get behind whoever was shooting at Ben, maybe they could trap them in a cross fire and drive them off. Drive them off, or kill them.

Devlin spat out the curse to himself. "Goddammit!" Killing. To save Ben, to survive, to keep Annie and Elizabeth alive, he would have to kill again.

And then, all thoughts left his mind as he burst out of the tall reeds onto the road and saw Hinton coming around the bend.

Hinton was perhaps more startled than Devlin. He jerked the MAC-10 up and sent out a spray of bullets, but it was too late. Devlin had already dived back into the cover of the tall grass.

Devlin rolled and crouched low, his Glock ready, expecting Hinton to come charging in after him, but the insane assassin completely ignored him. He entered the fen up the road from Devlin and plunged into the marshland intent on only one thing—finding and killing the woman.

Hinton instinctively knew that the woman had to be hidden in the grassy fen somewhere farther in. His crazed brain analyzed an incalculable array of information: smells, sounds, the sight of crushed reeds, the route Devlin must have taken out to reach the road. Despite the fact that the only light came from a sliver of the moon, Hinton was able to see, to fathom somehow the path Devlin had taken to hide Annie. He knew the object of his killing lust was near, and he was moving unerringly toward her.

Devlin waited for the next barrage of bullets to come streaking at him, waited to see the muzzle flash so he could shoot back. Kill or be killed. Just like always. It would never change. Never. The moment he had read that message from Annie and determined to get on that plane in Los Angeles, he should have known that it would come to kill or be killed.

The anger boiled through him. And it turned to rage. The rage became a kind of insanity of its own, pitted against the insanity of Hinton. The thought of anyone killing that beautiful woman whom he knew he loved, whom he had loved all these years, and her innocent baby girl, rolled over him and filled him and mixed with the blackness of the night and the stench of the marsh, and Devlin stood up.

He stood up with his gun at his side and walked forward to where he assumed Hinton was crouched, waiting to fire at him.

And just then he heard the scream, and he realized that Hinton had gone in after Annie.

He ran toward the spot where he had left them. Every muscle and fiber of the man was filled with the extraordinary power that adrenaline and rage can produce. The reeds slapped him in the face and his feet slipped on the unsure ground, but he moved with amazing speed and agility.

And suddenly he burst into the small clearing where he had left Annie for her killer to find her.

Hinton had a handful of Annie's hair. He had her head bent back, exposing her slim white neck. His eyes were closed, his razor-sharp knife was poised at her neck, ready for the slash. He was murmuring some insane prayer of offering to his god.

Devlin imagined he actually saw the carotid artery pulse in Annie's neck. Elizabeth was reaching for her mother's face. Everything seemed to move in slow motion.

Devlin never broke stride, never stopped in his dash toward Hinton. Just as the madman started to pull the knife across her throat, Devlin launched himself. Devlin smashed into Hinton with such impact that the killer was bent back over Devlin and his body was violently shoved away from Annie.

Hinton's sharp blade still caught the tip of Annie's ear and the side of her head.

As the two bodies collided, Annie instinctively rolled into a ball over Elizabeth.

Devlin hit the ground hard after the impact but Hinton used the momentum of Devlin's blow to bounce back and bring his right hand over in order to plunge the knife straight into Devlin's back.

Devlin just managed to twist away from the thrust. The tip of the stiletto still caught the top of his shoulder and sliced an eight-inch gash from his triceps to his elbow. The blade continued down, hit the butt of the Glock, and sliced the gun out of Devlin's hand.

Hinton stood trying to suck air into his lungs. He had ribs cracked on both sides of his chest. Devlin's diving blow had completely surprised him, knocking him out of his moment of ecstasy as he was about to finally kill his most desired victim. But the pain and impact were nothing to him. His fury at being thwarted was so intense that he did not even feel the scream he roared at the black sky.

Devlin came up on his feet. Hinton scrambled backwards, waiting for Devlin to shoot at him, but the shot never came. Hinton's MAC-10 was back in the grass near Annie. Devlin's Glock was somewhere nearby on the soggy ground, but he didn't dare look down for it.

Both men were now on their feet.

Devlin didn't feel the pain of the cut, but he felt the wetness that covered his arm from elbow to hand. Fortunately, the tear wasn't too deep, and he could still use the arm.

Hinton now realized Devlin's gun was gone. He grimaced, sucked in more air despite the tearing pain in his sides, and gritted his teeth.

He had the knife. His enemy had nothing. Hinton was sure that he could kill Devlin, but even so, he still ached to run and find the woman and cut her throat. He wanted to get to her so badly . . . but no. He knew he would have to kill this one first. Yes, he told himself, it was right that he kill this one first. Then he would have more time for the woman.

Devlin stared at the dark-skinned man and allowed himself to feel the almost overwhelming rage pulsing through him, energizing him, focusing him on his attacker. His whole being was concentrated with quivering intensity on the goal of disarming this killer, on beating, breaking, and maiming him.

Devlin felt loose and sure, and the anger, instead of blinding him, worked like a hot internal oil that made his moves fluid and lethal.

But Devlin did not realize that he was not fighting a man anymore. Somehow, Hinton had become an inhuman tool of hate and evil incarnate. The first thrust of the knife came with amazing quickness. Devlin saw it coming, moved back, and still was slashed across his chest.

He was quick enough to smash a blow into Hinton's face with a crossing left fist, but the blow not only didn't knock the man down, it left him with enough strength to slash back and up, cutting Devlin across his right forearm and cheek.

Devlin stepped back, amazed. No one had ever moved so quickly and so lethally against him. How many more slashes could he endure before he stopped this crazed beast in front of him? He had to get the knife, at all costs.

Again Hinton came at him, this time with a quick, short overhand stab aimed at his jugular, but now Devlin changed from defense to offense. Instead of stepping back, Devlin moved into the arc of the thrust and blocked the knife with a hard, sweeping move, smashing his left forearm into Hinton's downward-plunging wrist. The pain on both men's bones was instant, but Devlin's move gained him a fraction of a second's edge, and he managed to follow the left arm sweep with a short, vicious right hook into Hinton's ribs.

Still, Hinton wouldn't stop. He absorbed the blow and let it spin him around, then slammed his left elbow into Devlin's back. As Devlin was shoved forward under the blow, Hinton spun back and tried to punch the knife between his ribs, but Devlin anticipated the move and curved away from the attempt.

Hinton missed completely and fell to one knee. Devlin side-kicked Hinton in the head and scrambled away from him on hands and knees.

In seconds, Devlin was up and coming at the dazed Hinton, but the knife fighter still had enough power to keep him away with a wide slash at Devlin's leg. The blade missed, but it stopped Devlin.

Hinton gained the time he needed to get back on his feet. Once again, the fighters faced each other.

The fight had lasted barely more than a minute, but both men knew that it could not go on much longer.

Devlin was covered with his own blood. His pants were soaked in it. His shirt was ripped open, his face, arm, and chest were all cut. But he stood absolutely immovable, waiting for Hinton's last move.

Either he would wrest the blade from Hinton this time, or he would die.

Hinton smiled at Devlin. This would be the killing moment. He straightened up to his full height. He was a long, lean specter of a man, completely ready now to land the final blow. And he knew exactly how to do it. He deftly turned the knife upside down in his hand, hiding the blade behind his right forearm. The knife had disappeared, and Devlin knew that he might never see it again.

Devlin also knew what was coming next. He had seen it before. Hinton was about to attempt the deadliest of shell games. Even if you knew the next moves—and Devlin knew them—you could never know for sure which hand the knife would end up in. It would only be a fifty-fifty guess, and you had to back up your guess with a perfectly timed counter-move.

Then it started. Hinton placed both hands behind his back. He would either keep the knife in the hand it was in, or switch it. There was no way to know.

The mad Yard man gathered himself, pulling more air in past his broken ribs, and extended both arms straight out from the shoulders. He came straight at Devlin, windmilling his arms as he moved, turning in a series of graceful spins, coming faster and faster toward his target. Even now, as Hinton gathered speed, the knife could change hands. Devlin had to choose. Now.

As the two arms of the man came whirling toward him, Devlin timed his move to catch the left arm as it plunged toward his face. If the knife were now in that hand, he would live. If it was in the other hand, he would die.

He caught the left wrist overhead, not with a block this time but with an iron grip that clamped his right hand on to Hinton's left wrist. Still holding Hinton's left arm in the air, he stepped to Hinton's left, giving Devlin a slight chance to survive the stab that would be coming from below if the knife was in the right hand.

Hinton's right fist punched at Devlin's ribs, and Devlin smiled, because it was a fist that hit him, not the point of Hinton's deadly stiletto. Now it was Devlin's turn.

His first punch was into Hinton's armpit—a hard, brutal left hook, delivered with such force that it separated Hinton's shoulder from its socket. Hinton roared with pain and anger and frustration.

The physical pain was enormous. The psychic pain was

greater. His god had abandoned him. His arm was dead. His knife was useless, and his enemy was going to win.

Devlin maintained his iron grip on Hinton's wrist, holding him up, causing more pain to the ruined shoulder socket, as well as preventing Hinton from collapsing. Now it was Devlin's turn to hurt, to damage, to kill if he chose to.

He spun into Hinton so that his back was against Hinton's chest. He slammed his free hand into Hinton's crotch, rupturing the man's testicles. He smashed his head back into Hinton's face, breaking his nose. Then he slammed Hinton's wrist down across his right knee, breaking the wrist and sending the killer's knife into the marsh. Hinton was defenseless now, hovering in the twilight blackness between consciousness and unconsciousness. Devlin dropped Hinton's left wrist, spun back around to face him, and grabbed Hinton's throat.

They were inches apart now, face-to-face. Hinton's skin seemed to burn under Devlin's hand. Devlin suddenly felt connected to something so evil and vile that a wave of revulsion swept over him. Part of Devlin wanted to press his thumb hard into Hinton's trachea, crushing it, breaking Hinton and killing off this living evil once and for all. But he resisted the killing urge and, instead, he gripped Hinton's belt buckle, held on to Hinton's throat and lifted the assassin off his feet. With every bit of force he could summon, with his tendons straining, his muscles almost tearing, Devlin arched forward and slammed Hinton onto the ground with such force that the air was smashed out of Hinton's lungs and he was concussed into a deep, dark state of unconsciousness.

Devlin looked at the crumpled and broken man for only a moment, then turned to find his gun. He found both the handgun and Hinton's machine pistol and picked them up.

He looked around until he saw Annie and Elizabeth. Annie was still crouching a ways off in the reeds, holding the girl.

Devlin was far from coming down from the frenzied high of the battle. He tromped his way over to Annie and shoved the Glock into her hand. Then he pulled back the slide and pointed Annie's hand at Hinton.

"If he moves before I get back, shoot him. But don't kill him unless you have to."

Annie looked at him with a glazed, distracted glance. He shouted at her, "Do you hear me?"

Annie couldn't speak, but he waited until she nodded with comprehension.

"Don't kill him unless you have to. Wait for me."

Devlin didn't expect Hinton to move for a long time. Perhaps ever. If Annie shot the man while he lay there, so be it. Let her be the killer. He had to help Ben.

Once he was on the road, he gripped the MAC-10 and started running.

Oliver and Rockliffe had both struggled to their feet and gathered their strength for a final assault. They were going to move on Ben and keep shooting until they killed him. Ben knew they were coming and resolved to meet death standing and fighting. He knew there were two of them. And he also knew he wasn't going to wait for the bastards to come to him. Ben braced himself against the Ford and hobbled forward past the roof of the car until he was leaning against the front fender. He wanted a clear shot.

All three men moved out at almost the same time. But Rockliffe and Oliver had not expected to see Ben moving toward them. Rockliffe hesitated for just a moment and Ben fired the .357 Magnum bullet right into the center of his face. The entire back of Rockcliffe's head blew out and the fat man slammed down dead on the ground, but his finger locked on the MAC-10, and a ragged line of bullets ripped straight up in an arc that missed Ben by three inches. Ben was already turning to fire at Oliver who was saved only because his wounded hip gave out. Oliver fell back to the ground, and Ben's first two shots missed. But Oliver was a fighter, too. He cradled the MAC-10 and held the trigger down, trying to steady his aim at the big man. Ben got off one more shot from the Python before three high-velocity bullets slammed into his torso, sending him down for a final time.

Oliver struggled to his feet and limped forward to the Mercedes. Louis was dead. Hinton was gone. Dexter was dead. Rockliffe was dead. It was unbelievable to him that one man could have done all this to them. He hobbled back to the BMW and saw Elbert still sitting behind the wheel, still clutching it in shock. He was the one man among them who had not fought that big bastard and his guns.

Oliver pulled open the driver's door, stuck the muzzle of the MAC-10 against Elbert's temple, and pulled the trigger. The man's head exploded inside the car, instantly covering the interior with gore. Oliver pulled the carcass out onto the road and spit on it. Then he threw his still-smoking machine pistol onto the front seat and climbed into the driver's seat. His hip was bloody and painful, his shoulder and back ached, but he knew nothing was broken. He had to grit his teeth in pain as he bent his hip to sit, but the pain kept him going.

He reached forward and ground the starter. The engine barked to life with a strange, clattering sound. He revved the engine, and it kept running. It was almost as if the car didn't dare not work. Oliver shoved the gear lever into reverse and kept gunning the engine until it finally ripped itself free from the back of the Mercedes.

He pushed the lever into drive and maneuvered his way around the two wrecks in front of him. Oliver knew that no matter how remote this location, the police would be coming soon. He had to get out of there.

By the time Devlin arrived at the scene, Oliver had already driven the wobbly BMW around the wrecks and was accelerating off into the night.

Even Devlin was stunned at the carnage. He desperately looked around for Ben. He couldn't believe that Ben had survived this, but when he spotted the big man, flat on his back, his broken left leg bent awkwardly underneath him, he could see that his chest was heaving. He ran to him. Not far off he could hear the two-toned bray of police sirens. He cradled Ben's head in his lap, feeling for bullet wounds. It was too dark to see clearly. There was too much blood of his own and Ben's to tell how badly Ben was wounded.

He yelled, "Don't you fucking die on me, Ben! Goddammit, don't you die!"

CHAPTER 29

IT WAS FIFTEEN minutes after midnight when the insistent ringing of his alarm clock penetrated Waldron's deep, exhausted sleep. The noise seemed to be coming from the end of a long dark tunnel. Reflexively, his hand moved out and hit the off button.

Waldron had set the alarm so he could check in with the midnight-to-eight team staking out Mislovic, but for almost ten seconds after he shut off the alarm, Waldron could not remember where he was or what day it was.

"Oh, God," he muttered to himself.

The next task was to swing his feet to the floor and sit up. He had to sit up now, or he would fall asleep. He had too much to do. He couldn't sleep. He forced himself awake, and it all came flooding back into his consciousness: the stakeout, calling Devlin again, checking with the Transport Police, finding Mislovic.

He had to get up, get his damn feet on the floor. He jackknifed himself up into a sitting position, as if the sudden move could eradicate the fatigue. The covers fell away and the cold midnight air hit his body.

He swung his legs over the side of the bed to get his feet on the floor, and as his head and upper body twisted around following his legs, his face banged into something hard. Instinctively he jerked his head away from it. He couldn't even begin to figure out what had hit him.

He looked back and saw the barrel of a 9-mm Glock one inch from his right eye.

"God won't help you now, Waldron."

Waldron made a gagging sound and jerked back from the gun. Now he was fully awake. His heart was pounding furiously, and he had difficulty breathing. Jack Devlin was sitting calmly in a chair, pointing the automatic at Waldron's head.

"Jesus, man! What are you doing? How on earth did you get in here?"

"I didn't want to shoot you while you slept. I wanted you to know it was me. I wanted you to know that your murderers didn't kill me, Waldron. And they didn't kill Annie or Elizabeth."

Devlin stood up from the chair he had been sitting on and stepped toward Waldron, who had scrambled farther back on his bed.

Waldron was in too much shock to really hear what Devlin was telling him.

"How did you get in here?"

"The lock on your doors are a joke."

"What are you doing? How did you know to come here?"

"You're in the goddamn phone book, Waldron. You're not hard to find."

"Why are you pointing that gun at me?"

Devlin yelled, "Shut up!"

Waldron instinctively put his hands in front of his face. He thought Devlin was going to shoot him.

"Wait! Please. Devlin, stop. What happened? What did you just say?"

"I said your murderers didn't kill us, Waldron. At least not all of us."

"What happened?"

Waldron's mind was racing, but he had recovered enough from the initial shock to look at Devlin and realize what was going on. Devlin looked and sounded as if he had been through a terrible slaughter of some kind. His face, his arm, his hands were covered in dried blood. More blood had soaked through his shirt. Even the top of his pants was stained with blood. The dried blood stank, and fresh blood was still oozing from the deeper cuts on his body.

Waldron tried to imagine the possibilities. "What happened to you, Devlin? Tell me what happened."

"No, Waldron. It's *you* who are going to answer *my* questions. And I don't have time for any more of your bullshit. I'm going to start shooting pieces of you, and I'll keep shooting until I have all the answers."

Devlin studied Waldron as if to pick out the best place to start.

"Devlin! Stop it. This is crazy."

Devlin kept the gun trained on Waldron and talked while looking at parts of the chief inspector's body. "You haven't seen crazy yet."

"Don't do this. I had nothing to do with what happened to you. I've been killing myself for two days trying to help you. I've got it set up for the woman to come in. I'm ready to take out Mislovic. We're almost there. Why are you doing this?"

Devlin decided on Waldron's right foot. He would shoot the middle of the foot, but he knew the bones would probably shatter right up into the ankle.

Waldron saw Devlin aiming and scrambled back farther.

"You better not pass out on me, Waldron."

"Goddammit, Devlin, stop this. I'm trying to help you. I had nothing to do with hurting you. For God's sake, I've been sleeping here in this bed since seven o'clock."

Devlin stopped aiming and looked at Waldron. Waldron took it as an opportunity to keep talking.

"And you don't have to fucking shoot me to get an answer to a question. Ask!"

"You do keep surprising me, Waldron. I don't know too many men who could sleep while they're waiting for a slaughter to be carried out. But you could be one of them."

"I'm not."

Devlin looked closely at Waldron for a few more moments and seemed to decide that he was telling him the truth. He lowered the Glock, but kept the gun in his hand.

"The Jamaicans attacked us just as we were driving back to the safe house. If it hadn't been for my partner drawing them off, they would have gotten all of us. As it was, they shot him to hell out there on that empty road."

"Is he dead?"

"I stayed with him until the police arrived and they got him into an ambulance. He was still alive, but unless there's an emergency room team of doctors who know how to handle gunshot wounds out there in the sticks, my friend is dead."

"You were near Cambridge."

"That's what I told you. What did you do, send the bad guys to look for us? Did you tail me after our meeting? Were you just lucky? How'd you do it, Waldron?"

"Shit!"

Waldron moved to the edge of the bed and leaned toward Devlin. The gun was still pointed at him, but Waldron talked as if it weren't there.

"Listen to me, Devlin. You know I'm not the enemy. I am not the goddamn enemy. I don't know how they did it. I know who the leak is from my side, but I have no idea how he found out where you were, or if it was actually him. *I* didn't even know where you were, for God's sake. I have no idea how they found you."

"Waldron, before this night is over I'm going to know exactly how it was done and who did it."

"Good. If you don't, I will. But it wasn't me. I wasn't even looking for you. I took you at your word. I didn't tail you. Christ, man, I don't have that kind of manpower. I just managed to scrape together enough men who owe me to set up a bare-bones stakeout on Mislovic. The last time I saw you was in Piccadilly."

Devlin stared at Waldron, gauging the truth of his words.

"All I had was that phone number, and you weren't even there. It was a goddamn answering machine, and you never returned my call. I was about to call you again, hoping you'd be there. Hoping you'd come in with the woman. Where's the woman?"

"She's safe."

"And she still isn't anywhere I know of. You hung me out to dry, Devlin. I don't have shit. I don't have you. I don't have the woman. And I don't have Mislovic. In twenty-four hours my fifteen years on the force will amount to less than zero."

Devlin relaxed and rested his arm across his thigh. It was tiring holding up a 9-mm automatic.

"And you still don't have an answer to my question. How did they find us?"

Waldron looked Devlin right in the eye. "I don't know. I don't fucking know. But I sure as hell am going to find out. And the only way you're going to stop me is if you shoot me in the head right now. Otherwise, I suggest you put that bloody gun away and help me. I still want to nail these bastards."

Devlin sat back in his chair. "Well, I guess I'd better let you stay alive to do it."

"Good."

Waldron stood and started to walk toward the bathroom. Devlin's voice stopped him.

"Waldron."

"What?"

"If you want to stay alive, agree to one thing now."

"What?"

"When we find the answer, from that moment on, we do this my way."

"Your way?"

"Yes. The police can't stop this. You can't stop this. There's only one way out now."

"And what way is that?"

"Either we all die, or they all die."

"You're crazy."

"Right. Yes, or no?"

Waldron turned to face a man whom he realized lived in a world he could barely imagine. Waldron knew what bad men were like. He'd arrested plenty of them. Stood next to them while they were searched and booked and shoved into cells. Seen the damage they had done to their lives and homes and families. He had seen violence and despair. But from the moment he had seen the dead Yardie outside Annie's loft, this thing had spiraled out of control. He knew Devlin was right. It had gone too far. Something had invaded his city that was beyond him. He realized that he didn't know what to do. He didn't know how to stop it.

He looked at Devlin and said very quietly, "Yes. I'm afraid you're right."

Devlin nodded. Waldron's use of the word "afraid" might have been just a manner of speaking, but Devlin could see that Waldron was, in fact, dealing with a newly found awareness of fear.

"I'll do it your way, Devlin, but you must understand, this isn't me. I'll do what I can. But I'm not you. I'm not like you. If I can't do it anymore, I'll walk."

"All right."

"Will you put that gun away now?"

Devlin tucked the Glock behind his right hip. He did not want Waldron debilitated. He wanted him fighting, not acquiescing. The time for that had ended.

"Can you find out who led them to us?"

"I don't know."

"Yes you do. Don't punk out on me now, Waldron. You're a good cop. This is your town. You can't tell me you're going to let that piece of shit who did this get away with it."

Waldron looked at Devlin, but didn't respond.

"Are you, Waldron? Are you?"

And then the steel that was deep in the man began to emerge.

Waldron's voice was soft, but there was more energy in it now.

"No, as a matter of fact, I'm not going to let him get away with it. I think our traitor is a rather odious piece of humanity, and I made up my mind a while ago to take care of him. This last bit is the last treachery he'll ever commit."

"Good. Then let's get to work."

"Right, but I'd suggest a shower and fresh clothes for you. And a bit of a cleanup for me. I have some things here that will fit you. Approximately. My older brother's things, actually."

"He won't mind you lending them out?"

"No, actually—the poor chap died last year."

"Oh. Sorry."

"Not at all. Motorcycle accident. He wasn't a very careful person, my brother."

"Well, I'm sorry. Any other family still around?"

"You mean a wife and kiddies?"

"You're not married?"

"Divorced. For three years. She's still nearby. Still in Wembley, like me. About five streets over. I wanted to stay close to my girls."

"That's a good idea."

"Yes, much better that way."

Waldron started moving now, pushing away thoughts of a dead brother and a lost wife and murderers. Devlin watched him push himself. Watched him fall into a methodical get-on-with-it, get-it-done mode.

"You clean up," Waldron said over his shoulder. "I've got some calls to make. Then I'll take you somewhere you can get stitched up."

CHAPTER 30

WHILE DEVLIN SHOWERED, Waldron made coffee and warmed two large blueberry scones. Devlin came out of the bathroom with a towel wrapped around his waist. He had shoved his bloody clothes, including his blood-soaked underwear, into a plastic garbage bag Waldron had handed him before he went into the bathroom. Clean clothes were laid out on Waldron's bed—a pair of corduroy pants and a denim work shirt, but no underwear.

Devlin stepped into the pants. They were a bit short, but otherwise fit well, as did the shirt.

The aroma of the scones warming in the oven made Devlin's stomach rumble. Waldron pulled them out of the oven and poured coffee.

Devlin stepped over to a counter that separated the kitchen from the rest of the flat. He took a bite out of the scone and washed it down with black coffee.

Waldron said, "I have a jacket you can wear, too."

"Good. Thanks. I thought you'd have made tea."

"Don't like tea much. Prefer coffee."

"So who's going to stitch me up at two o'clock in the morning?"

"Yes. Quite so. Don't worry. I've a pretty good relationship with an emergency-room doctor at the hospital near the division."

"You mean he'll keep his mouth shut."

"*She* will."

"Ah."

"It's on the way. Eat up. I'll get showered and dressed and we'll be off. You're going to have some ragged scars if we don't get those cuts closed up."

"I've got enough as it is."

"Yes, I saw."

Waldron went off to shower and dress. Devlin looked around as he finished eating. Waldron's third-floor flat was meticulously well-kept. Devlin was not surprised. Waldron had impressed him as something of a plodder the first time he'd dealt with him. He wanted him to keep right on plodding. Devlin knew he needed him.

Guy's Hospital near the Tower Bridge Division police station reminded Devlin of every big, busy hospital he'd ever been in. The antiseptic smells, the hospital staff, the hurried pace. And room after room and floor after floor filled with suffering that varied from profound boredom to agonizing death.

They went straight to the emergency room. Waldron flashed his badge. They were shown to a curtained-off part of the examining area.

Waldron's doctor appeared in five minutes, examined Devlin, and went to work.

Devlin had been stitched up many times before, and decided within two minutes that this doctor was the best he'd ever had doing the job.

The job went on for just under an hour. The name on the hospital ID said Dr. Sonnenschein—a rather long name for someone who made such short work of zippering Devlin's wounds with just under a hundred stitches.

At the risk of being sexist, Devlin kept his opinion to himself that the young woman working so quickly and efficiently was so good at it *because* she was a woman.

She was a slim, intense, dark-haired woman who squinted through her round wire-framed glasses but worked quickly and precisely, without any wasted moves.

Devlin realized that the doctor thought he was a cop, and that she assumed something out of the ordinary had happened, and as a result didn't ask questions and seemed to be working extra-diligently. Devlin did nothing to correct her assumption.

He sat on an examining table, stripped to the waist, enduring the prick and pull of the stitching. She had made him sit up instead of lie down so his skin would not pull, but sitting made the experience more tedious. Devlin spent some time absorbing his surroundings: the smell of alcohol and antiseptic, the dazzle of white linens under the examining lamp, the surgical steel needle, and the black stitching thread. He let his mind drift free from the work being done on his body, allowing the pain to keep him sharp while he planned his next moves. He was about to enter a very deadly endgame.

After the doctor finished sewing Devlin together, she carefully bandaged each wound, including the minor cuts that hadn't required sutures.

"If you take it easy and don't pull anything apart, these should heal into nice long lines."

"Okay."

The slim young woman stepped back and looked at Devlin's face for the first time. Devlin knew she wanted to ask him something, but wasn't sure if she should, so he asked her.

"What?"

"Oh. I was wondering what he cut you with. They're very clean edges on the wounds."

"A stiletto."

"It must have had a very fine point and quite sharp edges."

"Yes."

She broke off her gaze and turned to open a drawer.

"Well. Your skin looks like it heals fairly well. That covering I used does a good job of reducing scarring. Keep it on for a week. Don't worry if it gets wet. You'd better have a doctor check you in a week. Sooner if anything feels hot or infected."

She rummaged around in the drawer until she found what she was looking for, turned, and handed Devlin several sample packs of tetracycline. "Are you allergic to any antibiotics?"

"No."

"This is tetracycline. It's good for this type of thing. Take three for ten days. Don't drink milk or take any dairy products with them. Restrict alcohol consumption."

"Is it necessary?"

"What? Not drinking, or the tetracycline?"

"The tetracycline."

"Yes. Your wounds were open for quite some time. If they become infected, it will be a problem."

Devlin put the pills in his shirt pocket. "Okay. Thanks, Doc. You do very good work."

"I see you've had some experience with it."

Devlin stood up and stretched a little to test the pull of the stitches.

"Yes. I have."

"Right. Good luck. I'm off. Good to see you again, James." She went one way. Devlin and Waldron went another.

On the drive to the division house, Waldron announced, "I think I know how he did it."

"You looked like you were sleeping in there, but it sounds like you were thinking."

"I was."

"How did he do it?"

"I'll have to check a couple of things before I know for sure. It won't take long."

Waldron parked behind the police division house and led Devlin inside. There was a single cop behind a reception desk. He buzzed in Waldron and Devlin without comment. Waldron led Devlin up three flights of stairs to the top floor of the old building. They walked down a narrow corridor and entered a room that was surprisingly bright and modern. It was packed with high-tech equipment. There were five consoles, each with a computer display screen, keyboard, and bank of switches. Three of the consoles were occupied by women wearing headsets. None of them were busy at the moment, although a call came in just as Waldron and Devlin entered the room.

Waldron said to Devlin, "This our telephone switching station. All calls come in and go out through here."

A chunky West Indian woman put down her copy of *The Star* and smiled at Waldron.

"Esther, could you do me a favor?"

"Certainly, Mr. Chief Inspector, sir. What can I do for you?"

"Can you find any calls made to the British Telecom tracking service from this division in the last twenty-four hours?"

"What's that number, dear?"

"Of the tracking service?"

"Yes, dear."

Waldron recited it for her, she punched it into the system,

and in ten seconds the display screen listed the call, which phone it was made from, the time of day, and length of conversation. Waldron squinted at the screen and wrote down the information he needed.

Waldron thanked the operator and motioned for Devlin to follow him.

They tramped back downstairs and ended up in another room, this one filled with more computerized communication equipment. There were two uniformed police constables manning the equipment.

Waldron said, "This is our CAD system—Computer Aided Dispatch," but he didn't explain any further.

He went to a file cabinet and opened it. Inside was a computer printout of all the personnel in the division, with names, phone numbers, and badge numbers. Waldron wrote down more information. Devlin let him work.

Next, they walked to Waldron's cubicle in his squad room. Waldron picked up the phone, called British Telecom, and after ten minutes of prodding confirmed that a call had been made asking for an address match to the Cambridge area phone number Devlin had given Waldron.

From start to finish, it had taken Waldron twenty minutes. He turned to Devlin and laid down his original notepad page with the Hotel Monteague's phone number on it.

"Okay. Here's the number you gave me."

He laid more pages down for Devlin to examine.

"Yesterday, a call was made to British Telecom matching this number with this address at a time which was consistent with when the attack was made on you. In fact, it was only minutes after I got the number from you."

"And who made the inquiry?"

"One of ours. A Sergeant Patrick Reilly. His badge number and name were given to British Telecom. He's the leak. Now I have the proof. He passed the information. They went after you."

"Only one problem, Waldron."

"What?"

"I wasn't at that location."

"No?"

"No. I was about two miles west of that address. I had to

give you a number where you thought I might be, but it was just a cutout. A place to put an answering machine. I wasn't there."

Waldron looked slightly deflated, but said, "Well, we know whom to start with."

"Your Sergeant Reilly."

"Exactly."

"Okay, you've gotten us this far. Now it's my turn."

"Meaning?"

"Meaning we do this my way from here on. Does Reilly know you suspect him?"

"Perhaps. But he's so bloody sure of himself he's not going to let it get in his way."

"Good. Can you get him to accompany you somewhere?"

"He damn well better. I'm still chief inspector here, aren't I?"

"Yeah. All right. I've got one more thing to do first. What time does he start duty?"

"Nine."

"Is he coming in here?"

Waldron reached behind and pulled a clipboard with an assignment roster off a peg near his desk. He scanned it and told Devlin, "Yes. I don't see any notices that he's not."

"All right. Bring him to the Draycott at ten o'clock. Room 12."

"You're at the Draycott?"

"Yeah."

"Last time I asked, you told me the Connaught."

"I lied."

"I know. Does this mean you actually trust me?"

"We're getting there. But you don't know the name I checked in with, do you?"

"Ah, yes. Another cutout. Where's the woman?"

"Safe."

"So what happens in room 12 at the Draycott?"

"When you arrive the door will be unlocked. Knock, and I'll tell you to come in. Make sure you walk in first."

"All right."

"Until then, you're on your own."

"I have things to do."

"What?"

"I still want to find Mislovic."

"I would assume Reilly knows you're trying to arrest Mislovic?"

"Yes."

"Then you can forget about Mislovic ever showing up at Berwick Street."

Waldron realized with some chagrin that Devlin was right.

"Yes. I suppose he won't."

Devlin watched Waldron frown.

"What's the matter?"

"I just realized that I suddenly have nothing to do."

"Then grab some sleep. You're going to need it."

Devlin stood up to leave, but Waldron stopped him with a question.

"Devlin."

"What?"

"Would you have actually shot me if I hadn't answered your questions?"

Devlin walked out. Over his shoulder he said, "Don't forget what I said about coming through the door first."

CHAPTER 31

THE CHARTER CLINIC didn't look at all like a psychiatric clinic. Which was exactly the point. Even a resident Londoner could stroll along posh King's Road, pass by Radnor Walk, and never notice it. The clinic, with its base of plain concrete facing topped by two stories of neat brown brick, looked like a nondescript apartment house. It was, however, a world-famous center that treated society's elite for a range of psychiatric problems and addictions.

Devlin had chosen it because the security was excellent, the staff was competent to treat both Annie and Elizabeth for the traumas they had suffered, and it was within walking distance of the Draycott.

Annie sat next to Elizabeth's bed. Her child was sleeping the deep peaceful sleep induced by just the right amount of tranquilizer for her age and body weight.

Annie had refused any medication. She had dozed intermittently in her chair, but she knew that this was no time to be impaired by drugs. Even friendly drugs. Her life was on the line, as was Elizabeth's. The terrible night in the fen had steeled her. She wasn't exactly sure what she would do now, but she resolved to do something other than run away from people shooting at her.

And yet it was difficult not to succumb to the quiet and peace of the clinic room. It seemed like such a protected oasis, continents away from the terrible dark marshland where she had waited for Devlin's return. One minute they were on their way to the farmhouse, and the next there seemed to be blood everywhere and she was squatting in a cold wet marsh holding a gun pointed at the comatose figure of that animal. Hinton had become the bogeyman incarnate, a devil who appeared anywhere, anytime, ready to cut her throat. It had taken great force of will not to empty the gun into his body. But Devlin had been so fierce and so focused that she knew she had to follow his command to not kill him. She began shivering so violently in the cold night air and on the wet boggy ground that she became afraid that she might pull the trigger involuntarily. And then she began to worry that she was shaking so much that she wouldn't be able to tell if the demon moved.

She had almost lost it out there, but two things saved her. Elizabeth had held her. And Devlin had reappeared. He had returned to the farmhouse, running through the fields. He had changed into a shirt that wasn't torn apart by Hinton's blade, grabbed clean clothes for Annie and Elizabeth, and taken the old Volvo that was parked in the farmhouse garage. He then drove back to the spot where he had left them, came back into the marsh, and led them out to the car.

He put Annie and Elizabeth in the backseat with a blanket he had taken from one of the beds. Police sirens were sounding around them, and Annie had the feeling that somewhere not too far off they were converging on one area. But for the moment, sitting in the warm car, huddled in the woolen blanket from the farmhouse, Annie felt invisible, hidden, completely apart from what had happened less than half a mile up the road. She felt separated from her past life, her dead husband, her family. Her only attachment was to Elizabeth.

Devlin disappeared into the marsh one more time. He found Hinton, lifted him onto his shoulder, and brought him back out to the car.

He dumped Hinton into the trunk while Annie watched from the backseat. She didn't know if the devil was dead or alive, but she sincerely hoped he was dead.

Devlin got behind the wheel of the car. It was then that Annie handed the gun back to him, and finally closed her eyes.

Devlin drove out of the area quickly, not turning on his lights until they were back on a main road leading to the motorway that would take them to London.

They passed two police cars racing toward the fight scene and crash, but they were not stopped.

Devlin drove without speaking a word to her. Neither of them spoke about Ben.

As soon as they were out on the M11, Devlin told Annie he was taking them to a hospital. Shortly thereafter, he pulled into a rest stop and stood at a pay phone, making calls. When they arrived at Charter, the intake nurse was ready for them. She called the attending child psychiatrist, a woman doctor who spoke softly in a slight German accent. She was trim, in her early fifties, with soft brown hair cut short.

Elizabeth was examined carefully and admitted. Annie was seen by a doctor who cleaned and treated her knife wounds, which were not severe. Devlin had not even entered the clinic. Annie was too exhausted to resist or question him. She allowed herself to be led along by the staff. By the time they took her to Elizabeth's room, the child was asleep in a clean white bed.

Annie sat next to her in a large high-backed chair covered in green fabric. Someone put a blanket over Annie and, for the moment, the nightmare was over.

At one point, sometime in the early hours before dawn, Annie woke to find a very fit-looking woman sitting in the room with her. The woman appeared to be about thirty years old. She wore her hair drawn back into a tight ponytail and was dressed in a pair of dark slacks and a simple white blouse. There was a holstered can of Mace and a walkie-talkie at the woman's waist.

The woman told Annie, "I am part of a security team that will stay with you and your child. We're under Mr. Devlin's orders. He specifically asked that we assure you he is all right, and you should not worry."

There was no further explanation. The woman emphasized that Annie should stay in the hospital room until further notice.

Annie slipped back into a half-sleep state until a ringing phone ruptured the cocoonlike atmosphere of the room.

She watched the woman security agent answer the phone. After speaking for a few moments, she handed the phone to Annie.

"It's Mr. Devlin."

Annie struggled to become alert as she took the receiver.

"Hello?"

"Annie, it's Jack. Are you all right?"

"Yes."

"Good. I want you to go downstairs and wait at the front entrance. Just stand in the lobby. When you see me pull up, get in the car. I'll be there in fifteen minutes. That's eight o'clock. I need you. Can you do it?"

Annie had no time to think before she answered, "Yes."

"Good. Fifteen minutes."

Devlin broke the connection. The first thing Annie thought of was that she had better get to the bathroom fast.

She splashed water on her face and took deep breaths. The trauma of the night before, the fear, the lack of sleep hung on her, but she felt quite focused.

At exactly eight o'clock Devlin drove up to the clinic in the same car he had borrowed from the farmhouse, an old blue Volvo sedan.

Three stone steps under a green awning led past a potted plant to the glass doors of the clinic entrance. Devlin leaned out the side window so Annie could see his face. She was at the door waiting for him. When she saw him, she came out quickly and got into the car, and Devlin drove off without looking at her or speaking to her.

Annie sensed that Devlin was operating on a different level than he had been. He was more intense. There was no small talk, no distraction, no wasted moves.

Devlin drove through the quiet Chelsea neighborhood until he found an empty curbside space near a small garden park. He pulled the car over, turned off the engine, and faced Annie. He opened a white paper bag and pulled out two cups of coffee. He handed one to Annie and said, "We have to talk."

Annie grimaced as she opened the coffee.

"God, that sounds like 'Get ready 'cause here it comes, bad girl.'"

"Yeah. Get ready."

"What, Jack? What now?"

"Now we drop all the bullshit, Annie. This is dead-or-alive time. I need your help. I need the truth. Or we won't make it. We've got very few cards to play in this game."

Annie swallowed the hot coffee, breathing in the fumes,

feeling the caffeine clear her head and energize her. She brushed her hair away from her face, leaned back against the car door to face Devlin, and looked straight at him.

"Well, I guess it's about time then. I've been scared shitless through most of this, but I never did quite enjoy being the damsel in distress. So how much have you figured out?"

"Mainly that Ivan Mislovic is *your* uncle, not your husband's. That, of course, leads to a series of assumptions. I don't want to operate on assumptions."

"How'd you find out? I mean, you weren't just guessing, were you?"

"It could have easily passed me by. I knew you as Anne Turino. I assumed your mother was Italian, too. But if Mislovic was your husband's uncle it didn't seem quite right that your husband would cheat a member of his family right from the start."

"You got that right. Johnny cheated him on the first transaction."

"So I made a few phone calls. It turned out to be more difficult than I thought it would be—confirming that your mother's maiden name was Mislovic."

"But you did."

"It's my business."

"So now what?"

"So now I want the truth."

"The truth?"

"Yeah."

"Okay. It will be. What do you want to know?"

"Is it true your husband was connecting Mislovic to the Yardie gang? Or were you behind that, too?"

"No. Johnny knew King Oliver, not me. Knew him from way back."

"In what context?"

"They lived in the same neighborhood. Notting Hill, before it became chic. A lot of West Indian families came into that area in the fifties. Oliver sort of stayed around longer than most. I think he and Johnny met in a bar or something. They were mostly acquaintances. Johnny used to buy reefer from him, but nothing unusual."

"And so Johnny became the middleman. You weren't connected to the Jamaicans."

"Yes. Johnny was the middleman. I never dealt with the Jamaicans at all."

"But you knew about your husband's connection to the Yardies, and you used him to get the drugs for your uncle."

"Pretty much. Believe me, Johnny didn't take much persuading. Failed artists don't make a lot of money, Jack, but Johnny wanted the successful artist's life. My uncle contacted me shortly after he arrived in London. It was a family thing. You know, the displaced distant relative getting to the West and asking for help."

"What kind of help?"

"Mostly just information. When I first heard from him, by phone, I was afraid this old impoverished guy would show up at my door looking for money or a job. I was totally wrong. Uncle Frank, as he called himself, was smooth, confident, aggressive. He only contacted me by phone. I never saw him. At first, he asked me about London in general. Places to live. How things worked. The usual.

"Then he slipped in a few questions about the drug scene. You know, along with questions about clothing stores and bars. Like it was for his personal use. By then we had talked a few times, so I just volunteered to get him what he needed. I had Johnny buy him a couple of grams of coke."

Annie had a look of reminiscence as she thought about it.

"Funny, I remember I was surprised he wanted so much. You know, a couple of grams. I had this picture of him supplying coke to this little group of avant-garde Yugoslav immigrants."

"That was just the beginning, I presume."

"I'll say. I think good old Uncle Frank wants to supply all of Eastern Europe."

"So it built up?"

"Yes. And fairly quickly. Johnny was such a pig. He even skimmed from those first little purchases. But Uncle Frank, or Ivan, he moved right along. Took me into his confidence. Said he wanted to build a business. Not here. In Eastern Europe, Russia. Maybe the U.S. Like I cared. He was talking cocaine. It seemed so far removed from me. All I had to do was say,

'Johnny, can you get such and such and bring it to Uncle Frank?' The next thing I knew, Johnny always had cash in his pocket. Not a lot. But I saw the potential."

"Why?"

"I let Frank think he was running me, running the show. But I saw where he was headed. Long before Johnny did. I saw that he'd be moving up to major purchases pretty quickly."

"And that didn't worry you?"

"If it did, I didn't let it stop me. It was easy. I just kept pushing Johnny and kept talking to Uncle Frank. I knew it was going to get bigger. I knew what Frank was doing. And I knew what Johnny was doing. But I didn't care. I figured everybody knew what was going on. If Frank had a problem with Johnny's skimming, he could tell him to stop it. I just kept pushing and hoarding cash and hoping I could get the hell out before anything happened."

"It's not that kind of business."

"No. It's not."

"The Yardies didn't take kindly to Johnny skimming off a piece for himself."

"They chopped his head off with a machete, for God's sake."

"Because he cheated at the other end?"

"I'm not lying, Jack. As far as I know, that was it. I assume somewhere along the line, my uncle complained about the weight or the purity of what was coming through, but he never said anything to me about it."

"Why did they come after you?"

"Because they considered what Johnny took for himself as money taken from them. They got paid by Mislovic, but that didn't matter. Somebody was earning extra money from their drug and their reputation. And I guess they assumed I had it. I don't think they wanted to kill me as much as they wanted to terrify me into giving them money."

"How much was there?"

"I don't know exactly. I was pretty good at grilling Johnny about how much he was taking out, but it's hard for me to know how much he sold. And although he wasn't selfish, he always spent what he had. I pulled out as much cash as I could. And I saved every penny, Dev, because I never knew when it would end. I wanted to keep Elizabeth in school, even if the extra money dried up."

"How much did you hoard?"

"Maybe I've got three thousand saved. About that. It's stuffed in a shoe box in my closet. Pretty pathetic, huh? Three thousand pounds for all this."

"Why did you lie to me?"

" 'Lie.' How much was outright lying, and how much was just not telling you all of it?"

"Stop it, Annie. I told you we don't have time for any more bullshit."

"What was I supposed to say? 'Oh, Jack, I know I haven't seen you in years, but I've been kind of dealing cocaine on the side with my husband and this shady uncle of mine who's just escaped from some war zone in Yugoslavia, and it's gotten a little out of hand. They killed my husband and now they want to kill me. Can you sort of come over to England and help me out?' "

"Is this easier than that?"

"No. No it's not. You're right: I should have been honest with you. But I really never imagined it would be like this."

"Then don't make it harder. Both of us have already made too many mistakes."

"What mistakes have you made?"

"Going to your uncle not knowing his real relationship to you or the Jamaicans. Not getting you out of the country. Letting the police try to do my dirty work for me. Cooperating with them. Believing you without question."

"All right, all right. I'm sorry. What else can I tell you?"

"Do you know how to reach Mislovic?"

"Yes. I think so. I have a phone number where he gets messages. And I have a cellular phone number for him."

"Okay. Now, we know he's working with the Yardies. I'm sure he's buying directly from them. Do you have any idea how much he intends on dealing?"

"My opinion is that he's going to buy as much as the Yardies can sell him."

"Any ideas how much that is?"

"Kilos. I don't know if it's ten or a hundred. I don't know how big the drug trade is here."

"Okay. Now, this is the most important question: Do you think you can contact Mislovic and bluff him, threaten to ruin his deal with the Yardies?"

"What do you mean?"

"You should be dead. You're not. You call him. You tell him you're sick of running for your life. Threaten to go to the police. Tell him the police already know about him. Tell him you want your cut of his deal with the Yardies or you'll go to the police and blow it wide open. Tell him you're on your own now. Tell him I'm dead. Tell him you want your cut, or *he's* dead."

"What does he get if he agrees?"

"Your silence. And you'll agree to leave the country and disappear. Tell him that's why you need the money. Tell him the Jamaicans are going to kill you if you don't get somewhere safe and start over."

"Wouldn't that be nice."

"Make him believe it."

"I can try. Though I don't know how well he'll respond to a threat."

"Do it the way you think will work, then. And do it in such a way that we might to able to find out how close he is to his next buy from the Yardies."

"Maybe I'll just act like I know he has a deal going down."

"And see if he denies it?"

"Yes."

Devlin thought for a moment, then said, "Okay. Try it that way. It's an assumption you could easily make."

"Anything else?"

"Yes. Get him pissed off about the Yardies. Tell him they screwed up the job of killing you, and now you're alive and you're going to get even at all costs unless he pays you off."

"And I'll tell him it has to be done fast. Now. So I have the money to get away."

"Right. Good."

"Funny, isn't it?"

"What?"

"You want me to tell you the truth and lie to him."

"Yeah. Lie through your teeth, but make him believe every word you say."

"I can see you have a very high opinion of me, Jack."

"That's not what matters now."

"You make me feel like . . ."

"Like what?"

"Like some manipulative bitch."

Devlin didn't respond. Annie didn't force it.

"So where does this leave us?"

Devlin looked at Annie before he answered.

"It leaves us with a chance to stay alive if you succeed."

"That's not what I was asking."

"No?"

"No. Or are you the only one who can ask questions now?"

"So what are you trying to ask me?"

"If you still care about me. If you still . . ."

"Love you?"

"Yes. Do you?"

"Do I what?"

"Do you still love me?"

Devlin turned away from her and started the Volvo's engine. He turned back to Annie.

"Right now it doesn't matter. Not if we die, or end up in jail."

"No. I guess not."

"So let's go make your phone call."

Devlin drove back across King's Road and headed toward the Draycott. He checked his watch. There was still plenty of time before Waldron was to meet him. He spotted a bank of pay phones just off Cadogan Square. He pulled the car over and turned to Annie.

"Okay, kid. You're on."

She stepped out of the car and walked to the nearest phone. She seemed angry, which was the way Devlin wanted her to be. He watched her go into the booth and dial. She listened for a moment, hung up, and dialed another number. While she waited for the call to connect, he watched her ripping down cards stuck on the walls of the phone booth which advertised prostitution services: "Busty Blonde Bombshell"; "Beautiful Thai Masseuse"; "Petite Indian Beauty"; "Bondage"; "Discipline"; "Water Sports"; "Diaper Training"; "S&M"; "Service for All Needs"; "Greek Training." One by one she ripped them off and let them fall to the floor. She was angry. Mad. Outraged. Good, thought Devlin. Good. It was an emotion he knew would make her sound real. She started talking into the phone. Devlin could see there was no hesitation. She was doing most of the talking. Now she was pointing with her index finger. Jabbing it in the air in front of her. Something stopped her, and she stood listening. Devlin could almost hear her yelling now. Devlin was afraid she might be going too far, afraid that her only option would be to hang up. But she stayed with it. Calming down. Coming down slowly. Bringing Mislovic along.

She talked for another minute, but Devlin knew she had won. Another half minute and it was over. When she came out of the booth, she was smiling.

She got into the car, still flush from her effort.

"Tomorrow. He'll have five thousand pounds for me tomorrow. I'm to call him and find out where to go get it."

"Good, Annie. Very good."

"If he's agreeing to give me that much, his next deal with the Yardies must be a pretty big one."

"I'd say so."

"Too bad I'll never see the money."

"Nope. Not unless you want to get shot."

After Annie hung up on Mislovic, the Yugoslav sat and brooded. The call had come to his flat in Dorset Square. He had just emerged from the bathroom after his morning shower and shave. He hadn't even begun the day, and it was ruined already. The buzzer sounded downstairs. Mislovic walked to the intercom and let Zenko in.

When Zenko entered the living room, Mislovic was sitting in his underwear, still trying to figure out what to do.

Zenko took one look at him and asked, "What's the matter?"

"Those stupid fucking Yardie animals cannot kill one stupid fucking woman."

"What happened?"

"Never mind."

"Did they get the American?"

"Yes, but she's still alive. And she's the real problem. We have too many goddamn loose ends to take care of. Enough with these black bastards. We do this ourselves."

Mislovic had decided. Zenko watched the energy and determination come over him. This was the commander he admired. Mislovic was taking matters into his own hands. Zenko sat and waited for orders.

Mislovic stood up and paced the room. He spoke as he walked back and forth, dressed only in his socks, his striped shorts, and his old-fashioned tank top undershirt.

"All right, Z, listen to me. We have a lot to do."

"Okay."

"That cop you use, he's burned."

"You sure?"

"If not, he will be soon. They'll find the leak now. He has to be disposed of. But we can use him before we get rid of him."

"How?"

"We have to get cash for our deal tonight. And we need some money to set up the woman. We'll use the cop. The extra security at the bank will help. And we'll use him to lure her in for her money. Getting it from a cop might make her feel safe enough to come out. Then we kill them both. Can you get in touch with him?"

"Yes. I think so."

"Good. Get on the phone with your people. Find out where he is and call him. Tell him to meet us at the bank. Tell him we need him to make a pickup and delivery. Tell him we're going to pay him for his services from this money. And that then we'll need him for another job."

"What time?"

"Noon."

"Okay. What else?"

"Did you get Jake to check out the Yardies' warehouse?"

"Yes. He should be back with information this afternoon."

"Good. I'll need it. Come on, let's go. I got to get dressed. Find your cop and get him lined up."

Sergeant Patrick Reilly sat in his underwear, too, at a small wooden table stuck against the wall of a small kitchen. He was home in Barking, sitting in a cramped, one-bedroom flat stuck in a line of dismal row houses on a dingy street. Just where Patrick Reilly belonged.

He smoked his first unfiltered cigarette of the day and nursed a cup of light and sweet coffee that had been sitting under the automatic coffeemaker for too long.

The coffee tasted lousy, but his wife refused to make it any other way. It represented the one scrap of luxury in her bitter life. She could lie in bed and know that something was being done without her having to do it herself. Reilly had taken the coffeemaker from a ten-year-old West Indian boy selling them to passing cars on Electric Avenue in Brixton. Reilly hadn't paid for it, except by not arresting the youth for selling stolen merchandise. It ended up as a gift to Mrs. Reilly, and she was loath to give up any of the few convenience appliances Reilly provided.

Neither the cigarette nor the coffee helped Reilly's fierce hangover. He had made the circuit of pubs he frequented, playing the big man by buying drinks for assorted alcoholic cronies. He had eighty-seven pounds left from the two hundred Zenko had stuffed in his pocket.

A cigarette cough wracked his scrawny chest and his mouth filled with yellow phlegm. Just as he stood up to spit into the kitchen sink, the phone rang.

It kept ringing while he spit out the yellow gob. He didn't bother to rinse it down before he grabbed the insistent phone. He could look away from the mess in the sink, but he couldn't stop the annoying phone unless he answered it.

"Yeah."

"Reilly, Zenko."

"How'd you get this number?"

"From your friend at the court."

"He's not supposed to give you this."

"Why not? We work together now, right?"

"I decide that."

"Okay, you want to get paid today for your information and make some more?"

"First tell me you took care of our friend?"

"Yes. It should be all done by now."

"Good. Good."

"Now we got other business to do. Are you in? Can you work with us?"

"Doing what?"

"Doing like a cop. Help us with a little extra security."

"Doing what?"

"Pick up and deliver money."

"When?"

"Noon. Barclays Bank. Moorgate Street."

Reilly took a drag from his cigarette and thought it over. The money he had been given just last night was more than half gone. He had an urge to replace it quickly, and this time he wouldn't spend it on Irish whiskey and pints for useless friends who would never stand him to a drink.

"All right. If I don't get hung up at work with something else, I'll be there."

"Take the late lunch. We need you for only one hour."

"How much are we talking about?"

"Don't worry. You'll be happy. Okay?"

"All right, then."

Zenko hung up before Reilly could get a chance to make any excuses.

The tired cop turned to the sink to try to wash down his phlegm. It was stuck now to the porcelain. He tried to direct the water over it with his hand, got his cigarette wet in the process, cursed, and finally pushed the gob down the drain with his nicotine-stained finger. He didn't want the old lady screaming at him when she came into the kitchen.

He was thinking about calling in sick so he could be sure of being available for Zenko, but then he decided he didn't want to miss seeing Waldron's face when the news came in about the death of his star witness.

If they got them last night, it should be on the bulletins this morning. Reilly decided he'd be to work on time.

Twelve hours earlier, as he steered the battered BMW away from the scene of the slaughter, Oliver was seething with rage. He told himself he wasn't going to wait to kill Mislovic. Whatever game that fuck was playing with him, it was over. To hell with using the Yugoslav to expand. He told himself he had all the business he could handle right now. So to hell wit' all of dem. Take da Yugoslav's money, shoot da bastard, and sell his coke to his regular customers. This big shipment would take care of business for a long time.

And where was crazy Hinton? He went back to kill the woman and her bodyguard. Crazy fuck. Like a dog after a bitch in heat. Smart, though. Why waste time shooting it out with dat big bastard? The job was to kill the American and the woman. Oliver was sure Hinton had succeeded. He hoped Hinton could somehow find his way back to the warehouse so he could help with Mislovic.

He thought with satisfaction that killing Mislovic would finish the whole business nicely. And the ten assault rifles and hundred thousand pounds Mislovic was bringing for the ten kilos would be a nice piece of change for all the trouble.

He pushed the battered BMW out of the town streets and north to the motorway that led back to London. Sirens were still sounding off in the distance. Oliver laughed and told himself, Those small-town cops nevah see any shit like dat before. An' nevah will again.

He tried to count up the dead. Man, he thought, everybody is shot up back there except me and Hinton. Plus that big guy. Like to have that one on my side. The man had balls.

The BMW's engine was grinding worse now. Steam was coming out of the radiator. The car had overheated. And to make matters worse, Oliver was not sure at all where he was or what direction he was heading in.

He knew the first thing he had to do was get rid of the wrecked BMW and get another car.

Just at the outskirts of Cambridge, he pulled over opposite a newsagent shop and a small grocery and cut the ignition on the dying BMW.

Within five minutes a man drove up, parked a late-model Rover in front of the grocery store, and walked in. He was middle-aged and balding, with a slight paunch. He wore khaki pants and a green windbreaker. He happened to be a professor of physics at the university.

Oliver pushed open the door of the BMW, forced his aching hip to bend, and climbed into the backseat of the Rover. Once in, he laid down. He stared up through the rear window and tried to see some stars in the black night. His left side burned from the shotgun pellets. He was worn out from the murderous fight and flight. For a moment, he thought about just going to sleep. The seat felt very comfortable. He was coming down from the body-wracking adrenaline rush of the gun battle.

Just as he was about to doze off, the man returned with a small bag of groceries. The sound of the open door surprised Oliver, and his finger almost squeezed the trigger of the MAC-10. He figured he had five or six shots left in the thirty-round magazine.

The owner of the car placed his bag on the seat next to him, started the engine, and pulled away from the curb.

Oliver waited until he had stopped at a traffic light, then he sat up and placed the barrel of the MAC-10 under the man's right ear.

The man flinched, turned around, and shouted, "Bloody hell!"

"Don' move or I shoot you. Head for da motorway dat goes to London. Do what I tell you an' I won't hurt you. I just need a ride to da motorway."

"What are you talking about?"

Oliver was in no mood to repeat himself. Or to be asked any questions in an outraged tone. He smashed the side of the man's head with the barrel of the MAC-10 and spit in the professor's face.

He snarled, "Don' vex me, old mon. Get goin' or I shoot you and do it myself."

The man's sense of outrage and defiance disappeared. He wasn't dealing with a university student's prank. He lost control of his bladder for enough time to wet himself thoroughly and soak the seat.

He managed to get the Rover turned toward the motorway, but he was so terrified he could barely talk. Oliver said nothing more, but kept the muzzle of the machine pistol pressed hard against the man's head. The muzzle was still uncomfortably warm.

Oliver watched the road until he got his bearings. He recognized the area they were passing through. As soon as he was sure he was headed toward the motorway that led back to

London, he began looking for a good place to get rid of the driver.

Just before the motorway he saw a large building that appeared to be some sort of barn or storage area. There was a gravel lot surrounding the building. The only light was from a single bulb in a shaded fixture attached above the wide double doors on the front of the building.

He punched the muzzle of the gun into the man's head again and told him, "Pull in dere. Go aroun' to da side."

The man did as he was told, but he had had time to gather his wits, and he started to plead.

"Listen, I'm sure you have reason to be doing this, but you don't need that gun. If you want money, that's fine. Take it. Just don't do anything you'll regret."

"Shut up, ya old fool. I regret notting."

Oliver's thick West Indian accent confused the man. Someone like Oliver simply did not belong in his community. But whoever, or whatever, he was, the professor had always heard that the thing to do is just give them your money. He looked into the rearview mirror and saw Oliver just sitting there. He didn't understand what the man was waiting for. He reached into his back pocket and took out his wallet.

It was a mistake. He should have sat motionless. Oliver was trying to decide whether or not to force this man to drive him to Hackney. Then he could lie back and relax. Besides, he wasn't exactly sure how to get back.

Then the professor thrust his wallet at Oliver.

"Go on, take it."

The officiousness of the man infuriated Oliver. Nobody gave Oliver orders.

He yelled, "Shut up!" and pulled the trigger of the MAC-10. The machine pistol was capable of firing over a thousand rounds per minute. In the few seconds it erupted, enough bullets entered the man's head to explode bones and brain matter over the entire front area of the car.

Oliver was furious. He got out of the backseat, cursing constantly. The sudden movement sent jolts of burning pain through his left hip. He wrenched open the driver's door, dragged the body out from behind the wheel, and dumped it on the gravel lot.

The front area of the car was a mess. He yanked off the man's windbreaker and tried to wipe the blood and brain matter off the windshield. But the jacket only smeared the gore across the glass and made it nearly impossible to see through.

Oliver's fury erupted, and he kicked and spat on the body. He had been angered that the man had shoved his wallet at him and tried to tell him what to do. Now he was even angrier because of the mess the man had caused him to make.

He grabbed the bag of groceries and pulled it toward him to see if it contained anything that would help him clean up. There was a liter bottle of mineral water. Oliver took it and uncapped it. He placed his thumb over the opening and shook it until he could direct the foaming spray at the windshield and dashboard.

The spraying water did a good job of cleaning off the windshield. Oliver was proud of his inventiveness, and some of his anger washed away along with the human mess.

Now that he was able to see out the windshield, Oliver struggled to get in behind the wheel and put the car in gear. The driver's door was still open, and he reached down and grabbed the cuff of the man's pants. Gripping the pants leg, he slowly drove the car farther into the dark, around behind the barn, dragging the body across the gravel until he came to the far edge of the lot. He dropped the body there, at the end of a wet, bloody smear.

Just then, he realized the seat he was sitting in was wet. He thought for a moment that it was the club soda. Then he realized the source of the dampness. He looked between the man's legs to be sure, and when he saw the wet stain his anger boiled up all over again. Oliver's fuse was down to nothing. He drove a little distance away from the body, turned the car around, and aimed his left front wheel right at the man's crotch. Then he revved the engine and drove straight at the body. The right wheel hit the space between the dead man's legs with a thump. He continued straight across the body, the front wheel running right over the face of the corpse, crushing what was left of the skull.

Oliver smiled when the back wheel bounced down off the corpse.

During the drive back to Hackney, he occupied himself with

planning the ambush he would set for Mislovic. Everything would have to be in place by tonight. He could get at least a dozen of his own men, plus as many armed Yardie bad bwouys as time would allow. He'd trade crack, use threats, and pay money to get them there, ready to kill. It would be a slaughter. Just what he was in the mood for.

Oliver looked at his watch. He'd be back before dawn. Plenty of time to set things up, get his hip cleaned by Momma Cientro, find Hinton, and maybe even catch some sleep. When Mislovic came for his drug buy, it would be the last time he ever did business with anyone.

CHAPTER 32

REILLY WALKED INTO the division a little after nine. Waldron was in his cubicle. Superintendent Fenton hadn't yet arrived. Everything appeared normal. Too normal. Apparently there was no word yet that Waldron's witnesses were dead. Before he could wonder why, Waldron came out into the squad room and walked straight toward him. Reilly's head still ached from his hangover, and he needed sleep. Seeing Waldron made him wish he had called in sick.

"Reilly, come with me."

Not even a "good morning" out of the officious bastard, thought Reilly.

"Yes sir. What's up?"

"I think we've got a break on Devlin's whereabouts. Let's go."

Reilly squinted in confusion. What the hell was going on now?

Waldron had a white unmarked police car waiting for them in the small car park in the back of the station. Nothing fancy this time. Just a plain Ford Escort. They drove in silence to the Draycott Hotel, double-parked the unmarked sedan, and put an "Official Police Business" card on the dashboard.

Waldron flashed his badge and told the hotel manager sitting behind the reception desk, "Police business. Please give me directions to room 12."

"Are you expected, sir?"

"Yes. No need to ring."

The manager gave directions, and Waldron led Reilly up and down the various staircases leading to Devlin's room.

Reilly finally ventured to ask, "What's going on?"

Waldron gave him a terse answer. "You'll see. Just stay alert and do what I tell you."

Reilly knew there was nothing he could do but follow along. Whatever was going on, he assumed it would be over by the time he had to meet Zenko. He looked at his watch. It was exactly 9:57.

When they reached the door of the room, Waldron knocked once and opened the door. He remembered to enter first.

There was a small foyer that led to the main room. Waldron walked under the archway, with Reilly following him. As Waldron entered the living room of the suite, his peripheral vision caught Devlin standing next to the archway with his back pressed against the wall.

When Reilly entered the room two steps later, Devlin dropped into a crouch and swung a tire iron directly into the skinny cop's shins.

The pain was so sudden and so excruciating that Reilly's scream sounded like a gagging choke. His legs were knocked out from under him. He pitched forward and fell onto the carpeted floor.

As soon as he hit the floor, Devlin was on him. He grabbed Reilly by the collar of his cheap blue blazer, lifted him up, and shoved him into a chair that had been positioned against the wall.

Waldron stood where he was, not moving, momentarily stunned by Devlin's ferocity.

As soon as Reilly fell into the chair, Devlin jammed the tire iron lengthwise across his throat and shoved back until Reilly's head was pinned against the wall and the man was struggling for air.

Devlin spoke over his shoulder to Waldron, never taking his eyes off Reilly. "Take out everything in his pockets."

Waldron moved quickly to comply.

Reilly was desperately grabbing with his fingers at the tire iron jammed against his throat. Waldron pulled out Reilly's wallet, badge, keys, cigarettes, money, and a lead sap from his right rear pocket.

Devlin snarled, "Frisk him."

Waldron felt up and down Reilly's legs and body, checking him for any other weapons, and Devlin finally pulled away the tire iron. Reilly pitched forward, retching to suck air through his damaged windpipe.

Devlin placed the tip of the tire iron into Reilly's nostril and carefully pushed his head back until the cop was looking up at him.

Devlin bent down and spoke quietly, inches from Reilly's face. "It's over, scum. You're not a cop anymore."

Reilly choked out a defiant reply. "The hell you say, you bloody bastard."

Devlin pulled away the tire iron, smashed Reilly's shins again, and jammed the bar back against his throat, choking off the screams of pain and anger. He pulled the bar off just as Reilly was about to black out and pushed his head back by shoving the tip into his nostril.

"Okay. We start again. You don't talk until I tell you. You don't say a fucking word. You've done all the talking you're going to do. No more squealing for killers, Reilly. You picked the wrong side, Reilly. You're going down for it, and for everything else you've done."

Devlin waited for him to answer back, but Reilly was cowed now. He kept his mouth tightly shut.

Devlin pushed him, "Go on. Answer me. Go on."

Reilly talked quietly, but with a hatred that fueled his defiance. "You're full of shit. You've got no proof of anything at all."

Waldron chimed in. "I've got all the proof I need, Patrick. I've got a record of your call to British Telecom. And I've had you followed since the ambush at Piccadilly. Jenkins, Parker, and Donaldson have been watching you. I know who you met with, when, and where. You're finished."

For a moment, Waldron's bluff seemed to hit Reilly almost as hard as Devlin's tire iron, but he recovered and showed enough mettle to stand up to Waldron.

"You've got nothing on me, Waldron. Everything I did, whoever I met with, was to investigate the case that you couldn't handle. Fenton will back me up. Go on, arrest me. You can't prove anything. I'll bury you by the time I'm done."

Devlin kicked Reilly's damaged shin. Reilly yelled. Devlin slapped him hard and snarled, "I don't need any fucking proof of anything. You're not going to be arrested. You turned against your own and you've killed innocent people. Now you're going to fucking pay."

Reilly sat clutching his shin. Nothing had ever hurt him as much as that blow.

"You can't do this. You can't do this to me. I'm a cop."

Devlin yelled, "You're not a cop. You're scum. You're a killer."

With that, Devlin grabbed the back of Reilly's head and forced it viciously down to the man's knees.

"You fucking dare to threaten us? You piece of shit!"

Devlin jammed his knee against the back of Reilly's head and forced it even farther down. Reilly felt as if his spine would crack. His muffled grunts of pain came out in gasps.

Then Devlin carefully placed the chiseled tip of the tire iron between two of the vertebrae at the top of Reilly's back, and pushed down hard. Waves of intense pain radiated through Reilly's body. Waldron, watching this, winced and began to feel nauseous. Reilly let out an agonizing growl.

Devlin yelled, "You're not going to be arrested. The law is too good for you. They don't even kill people like you in this country. But you're still going to pay for what you did. I'm going to kill your body, but keep you alive so you can feel it. I'm going to shove this through your spinal cord and turn you into a fucking vegetable from the neck down. But your head will be alive to live every minute of it. You're nothing but a rat who got caught. You're going to sit in a wheelchair pissing yourself and crying about your pension."

Reilly tried to grab and clutch Devlin's legs, but Devlin just pushed down harder with the tire iron, paralyzing the cop with pain and fear. Reilly's arms went limp. He gasped out a plea that was barely discernible. "Stop, stop. I'll do anything you want. Don't do this to me."

Even Waldron's loathing for Reilly wasn't strong enough to allow him to watch what Devlin was doing to him.

He grabbed Devlin's arm and yelled, "Wait. Let him talk!"

Devlin's arm was rock-hard. Waldron pulled on Devlin's arm and nothing moved. Devlin's entire body felt rock-hard. Waldron had no idea how to stop him. And then, suddenly, Devlin pushed himself off the crunched-over man and threw the tire iron onto the floor.

"Why," he said. "So you can hear more lies?"

Even though Devlin had stopped, Reilly was a broken man.

He remained bent over. He was sobbing now, but he didn't even have the wherewithal to cry.

Waldron took him by the shoulders and eased him back into the chair. He could see by the look in the man's eyes that he was truly terrified. Devlin had reached his core.

When he saw Waldron standing in front of him instead of Devlin, Reilly clutched the detective's arms and sobbed out in a rush of anguish, "Please, keep him away. I'll do anything you want. I'm sorry for it. I never told them nothing that they wouldn't find out themselves. I never squealed on you so's it would hurt you. I only played along with Fenton to keep my job. He had the goods on me for past things I did, Waldron. He threatened to force me out. To demote me. Cut my pension. I only have three more years and I'm out of the shit. Please don't do this to me."

Waldron let the man hold on to him. Pity mixed with disgust. "All right. All right. Maybe we can repair some of what you've done."

Devlin yelled, "He can't take the bullets out of my friend's body, goddammit."

Waldron turned to Devlin. He himself was shaken by Devlin's fury. Devlin was a big, angry man, capable of horrifying, crippling violence, and Waldron was beginning to fear he might be a target if he tried to stay between him and Reilly.

Reilly pleaded, "You can hurt me all you want, but it won't hurt the ones you should really be after. Why not let me at least help you get them."

"How?" asked Waldron.

This was what Devlin had been waiting for. He backed off and let Waldron take over.

"I know more than you think. I'll help you get them. I will. I know how."

"What do you know? How can you help us?"

Within a few minutes, Reilly had told them every possible thing he could think of regarding Zenko and Mislovic. He sold out his connection in the Magistrate's Court. He told them about the assignment he had to pick up money for the Yugoslavs, and told them it had to be for a drug deal with the Yardies.

Devlin let Waldron pump Reilly. He simply sat and stared

at the terrified police constable, silently reminding him by his presence and demeanor of what might happen if he lied. When Reilly could think of nothing more to say, he simply looked at Waldron for agreement or acceptance. But Devlin took away his hope.

He stood up and announced, "He's given you shit, Waldron. Big deal. You bust up a drug deal. They plead or bargain or whatever they do in your courts and maybe they get convicted and sentenced to a couple of years. That's not enough. Get out of here and let me take care of this scum."

Reilly grabbed Waldron's arm, clutching it, not allowing him to leave.

"No. No, don't leave. The drug deal is just the beginning. The Yugoslavs can lead you to those Yardie bastards. They're the ones who pulled the trigger on you and your friends, Mr. Devlin. We can get them for it. Mislovic will turn on them. You make him any kind of a deal, and he'll turn. You'll get them all. For murder. For attempted murder."

Waldron turned to Devlin. "Maybe he's right."

"Yeah, and maybe he's full of shit. You can't trust this weasel."

Waldron looked back at Reilly as if to say, Devlin makes sense. Prove him wrong.

Reilly started jabbering. "He's wrong. Give me a chance. I'll prove it. Stay with me until I help them get the money. Then I'll lead you to them and to the Yardies. We'll take them down, the whole lot of them, for all of it."

Waldron nodded, then turned to Devlin and said, "Can I talk to you for a second?"

Waldron stood up and led Devlin to the other side of the room. They stood with their back to Reilly and talked quietly so Reilly could not hear them, but he watched them carefully for some sign of salvation.

Waldron asked, "Are you serious? I can't tell if you're acting."

Devlin became calmer, but the answer was not as reassuring as Waldron had hoped it would be.

"Sometimes I'm not sure myself."

"Christ, man, you're scaring *me*."

"Good. But I'm done with this now. I think we have him

where we want him. Let him play this out the way he suggested. Can you get men to follow these bastards to the Yardies after they get their money?"

"Yes. Absolutely. I've got something solid now. I can requisition the men I need."

"Can you get it together by noon?"

"Yes."

"All right. Do it. But you'd better make sure Reilly doesn't double-cross you."

"I don't think he'd dare try that now. But I'm not going to leave him until this goes down."

"Good. Get your people together, and be ready. Once they have the money, it's going to move fast. I suggest you make whatever arrangements you need to get armed personnel on the alert. If you try to bust these guys, it could get nasty. You saw how much firepower they unleashed at me."

"You're right. I'll contact Special Operations now and have them on standby. Once we find out where the Yugoslavs are going with the money, we'll call them in."

"Can you get what you need?"

"I'll have to pull a few strings, but Thomas Creighton, the commander of that operation, is a mate of mine. We did foot patrols together for two years when we started. We've kept in fairly good touch over the years. He'll have his people stand down for me. The Trojan Units and Blue Berets are well trained. We can handle this if we have notice."

"How many men can you get?"

"As many as I need. We don't take kindly to villains running around with automatic weapons. We'll call out the military if we have to. We've got the best-trained urban fighters in the world."

"Yeah, twenty-five years of practice in Belfast."

"Exactly."

"All right. Convince Reilly you're going to let him help you, but you make sure he knows this is his last chance. Tell him if he crosses you, I swear, I will hunt him down and tear his fucking heart out of his mouth. Make him believe that."

"I don't think it will be too hard."

"It shouldn't. Because I will."

"Right."

"One more thing. While you're tracking the Yugoslavs, you'd better find out where this Yardie boss Oliver is, and have him watched. The more you know about what's going on at the other end, the better chance you have of nailing all these guys."

"The intelligence group in the Hackney Division knows most of his locales. The report I read said he works out of one of the older estates in that area. And I think I also saw something about a warehouse or used-car lot he owns up there, too. I'll find him. What else?"

"Just make sure you have good people at the bank. You've got to have enough guys to get on this Zenko and stay with him. I doubt if Mislovic will be there, but his man will lead you to him. And they should stay on the Yugoslavs until this deal goes down."

"You think the buy will go down today?"

"I guarantee you the Yugoslavs and Yardies will get together today."

"How do you know?"

"Because we're doing this my way, Waldron. Just get on these guys and stay with them. And have your armed personnel ready to move."

Waldron realized that Devlin wasn't telling him everything he knew. But he didn't push it. Devlin had already given him enough to justify his actions and, if he was lucky, survive Fenton.

"All right. So what are you going to do?"

"I'll be around. How can I keep in touch with you?"

"Call the division. They'll patch into me wherever I am. What about the woman? I'll still need her as a witness once I get these guys. And you."

"You'll have us both when you need us."

Devlin checked his watch. "I've got things to do. Make sure Reilly is where he's supposed to be."

Devlin told Waldron how he wanted Reilly to handle the pickup. Waldron simply nodded. He knew he was along for the ride. This was Devlin's show.

Waldron quickly but thoroughly instructed Reilly until he was satisfied the old reprobate cop was ready to play his part.

But first, Reilly had to get up out of his chair in Devlin's suite at the Draycott and walk. Waldron helped him to his feet and tried to convince him he could walk on split shinbones. Reilly tried, but crumpled almost immediately.

Waldron wondered if the poor bastard could do it. He told him to sit down and went into the bathroom to see if he could find something that would help.

Devlin's extra-large-size shaving kit was sitting on the sink. Waldron opened it and was happy to see it looked like the inside of a doctor's bag.

He rummaged around and found a large bottle of painkillers with codeine and a roll of one-inch adhesive tape.

Back in the living room, he gave one pill to the broken-down Reilly and ordered coffee from room service.

Then he took the roll of adhesive tape, pulled up Reilly's creaseless pants leg, and began tightly taping the man's skinny white legs from the knee to the ankle.

The coffee from room service came, and Waldron told Reilly to drink as much as he could. He didn't want Reilly to fade under the drowsiness the painkiller would soon bring on.

While Reilly drank coffee, Waldron got on the phone and started issuing orders. He looked at his watch. Time was running out. He shifted the stakeout team from Berwick Street and called in another team to find Oliver. And he left a message for Creighton at Special Ops.

At eleven-forty, Waldron had done all he could, and Reilly had drunk all the coffee he was going to hold down.

This was the moment of truth. The codeine from the painkiller had kicked in. Everything now depended on the battered legs of Reilly and whatever heart he had left.

Waldron stood in front of him and said, "This is it, Reilly. You walk out of here and do this with us, and I'll have a chance of protecting you. You don't, and I walk away."

Waldron watched as Reilly slid forward to the edge of the chair, preparing to stand. If this bastard doesn't make it, I'm dead too, thought Waldron.

But the combination of codeine, adhesive tape, coffee, and fear pulled Reilly onto his feet. He managed the first step, and his strength and confidence built each time he completed another. By the time he reached Waldron's police sedan, double-parked outside the hotel, he appeared almost normal.

Waldron raced across London and managed to get Waldron to the corner of London Wall and Moorgate at two minutes past noon.

Waldron slowly edged the unmarked police sedan around the corner and pulled to the end of a line of cabs waiting in a rank that ran right down the center of Moorgate Street. He was fairly well hidden, yet he had a clear view of the bank. Barclays was the last in a lineup of banks that occupied the entire block. It occupied the ground floor and second floor at the corner of Moorgate and South Place.

Waldron watched Reilly gamely walk to the entrance on Moorgate Street and stand outside waiting for Zenko. Before Reilly made it to the entrance, Waldron heard a tapping on his window. The detective who had helped him organize his stakeout at Berwick Street was standing on the curb. His name was Jimmy Rinaldi. He was about thirty years old, a compact, rugged Italian with close-cropped hair and a two-day growth of beard. Rinaldi was dressed in jeans, a brown cashmere sweater, and a black three-quarter-length leather jacket.

He opened the car door and slid in next to Waldron, then handed the chief inspector a two-way radio unit and told him, "We're parked across from the bank over there, ready to follow whoever you say. We're in the white van. If they go with the traffic, we'll pick them up. If they U-turn back that way, you can get them and keep us on it by radio."

"Right. Good. How long have I got you?"

"Me and Edwards are supposed to be investigating a burglary and rape by the wharf, but we slipped over here. We can hang in for a while. I'm supposed to meet a stoolie at four, but we're yours until then."

"Perfect. Are the radios on the same frequency?"

"Yes."

Both Waldron and Rinaldi spoke without taking their eyes off Reilly at the front entrance. Waldron wished he looked as if he could stand until the Yugoslavs showed up, but he didn't.

"Anything else?"

"I hear Fenton is looking for you."

"Bloody wanker."

"Yeah. Speaking of wankers, I hope you come up with something more than your dick in your hand on this one, mate."

"I will. Who's checking on the Yardies?"

"Witkowski and Johnson. I don't know who the third guy on their team is. I think he's in court today. It's just them. If your Yard boss is in either of those two places you mentioned, they should be able to find him without too much trouble. CAD will put you through to them."

"Okay, Jimmy. Thanks. I owe you."

"I hope you're around to make good. See ya."

The young detective opened the door of the tan sedan and slid out onto the street, heading quickly back to his van. Just then, a red Saab pulled up to the bank entrance on the Moorgate side.

Zenko was sitting in the backseat. Roland, the big guard from the Berwick Street headquarters, was behind the wheel. A bald block of a man was sitting in the front passenger seat. His name was Radic.

Reilly spotted them and walked painfully over to the car. Zenko rolled down the window and asked, "What happened to you, Reilly? You look like shit."

"I've got a hangover, if you don't mind."

"You Irish are all drunks, aren't you?"

"Anything you say, Zenko. Have you got my money?"

"It's in the bank. This is Radic. Go with him. Make the pickup. Bring the money here."

Zenko motioned for Radic to get out of the car. He climbed out, carrying a large leather salesman's case. It was shaped like a rectangular box and had a top that split open in the middle.

Zenko nodded, and Radic handed it to Reilly.

"Reilly, ask for Miss Reynolds. Show her your badge and identification. Get the money and bring it to me. I give you some, then you go, but keep in touch. We may need you for something tomorrow."

"Fine."

Reilly took the case and started walking toward the entrance. Zenko turned to Radic and spoke in Croatian. "Stay close to him. Fucker walks like he's got piles or something. Go on."

Radic followed Reilly into the building.

The ground floor held the commercial banking counters. One flight up was the Private Banking Division. Radic pointed to the escalator that led upstairs. Reilly stepped on it, grateful that he didn't have to deal with stairs. Radic followed. On the way up, Reilly suddenly felt his stomach cramping from the coffee, codeine, and fear.

They turned off the elevators, past more teller windows, through a set of offices, and down a short corridor to a set of double glass doors. A receptionist buzzed them in and greeted them.

Reilly told her, "We're here to see Miss Reynolds."

Behind the receptionist was an open area surrounded by small offices. The receptionist called Miss Reynolds, and within a minute she appeared holding a key marked with the number seven on a large ring.

She was dressed in a gray business-suit jacket and skirt with a white blouse and red bow. She seemed to combine the right mix of cordiality and efficiency.

She checked Reilly's identification and said, "Good morning, gentlemen, you'll be in office number seven. We have everything ready for you."

Reilly took the key and handed it to Radic. "Where's the toilet, missy?"

"Missy" didn't make it with the young lady. She frowned to indicate her displeasure and added the proper chill to her voice.

"Just back in the hallway and around to the left."

The receptionist opened her drawer and pulled out yet another key on a ring. Reilly took it and told Zenko's man, "I'll be back in a second."

The young bank executive led Radic to the small office. Reilly shuffled off to the men's room.

Once there he quickly took an empty stall and released his watery bowels into the bowl. The relief was almost instant. Waldron had given him an extra pill, and Reilly fished it out of his shirt pocket. He picked the lint off it and swallowed it without water.

When he was finished, he had to grip the toilet paper dispenser to get back on his feet. His shins ached, and his throat hurt terribly from the tire iron Devlin had jammed against it.

By the time he got to the small office the bank provided for private transactions, the last stacks of hundred-pound notes were being placed on the desk in front of Radic. Zenko's man sat stolidly watching the piles of money grow. The bank teller walked out of the small office and closed the door behind him.

Reilly and Radic sat together in a room with a hundred and five thousand pounds. Reilly had never seen so much money in one place, and yet the stacks didn't take up very much room at all. The case Zenko had given him was much too large.

Reilly wondered if the amount was correct. He asked Radic, "Do we have to count it?"

"Yes."

It was the first word he had spoken.

There were twenty-one stacks. They each picked up a stack and counted fifty hundred-pound notes. They each counted all twenty-one stacks. Reilly couldn't have cared less, but he went through the motions. It took longer than he expected.

"Right then. Let's take it to your boss."

Radic had already signed for the cash. Out on Moorgate, Waldron sat patiently in his unmarked car. In the Saab, Roland turned and asked Zenko, "How long it take to get some money?"

Zenko gave his usual shrug in lieu of an answer and said, "Put your gun in your lap and be ready when they come out."

The Private Banking offices exited down into the main lobby of the office building that housed the bank. The only way down to the lobby floor was via a spiral staircase. Nobody paid much attention to the man who was standing near the building directory, half hidden by the staircase. He was reading a copy of the *London Times.* He wore dark slacks, a bright green pullover sweater, and black leather gloves.

The sweater reached below his waist and covered the Glock 17 automatic stuck behind his right hip. It was Devlin.

Back up in the small office, Radic and Reilly had finished placing the twenty-one stacks of hundred-pound notes into the leather case. Radic watched Reilly grab the handle of the case. It was just heavy enough to make Reilly afraid his aching legs would not be able to stand the load.

Radic opened the door for Reilly. The beat-up Irishman took a deep breath, stood up, and started walking. The last codeine pill was kicking in, and the pain of his split shins was becoming bearable.

Radic was a chunk of a man. Bald-headed, scowling, wearing a suit that was too tight, he looked intimidating enough to keep everyone at a good distance. Being in charge of a considerable amount of money made him even more threatening.

When Reilly saw the spiral staircase, he grimaced. More bloody pain, he told himself. The hell with it. It would be over soon.

Reilly's hesitation gave Devlin a chance to see them before they started down. He maneuvered into position just behind the staircase. He put down his newspaper, and as they reached the lobby floor, he fell into step behind them. He didn't have much time before they'd reach the exit door. Neither Reilly nor Radic noticed Devlin closing in on them. They both were concentrating on getting to the exit.

As they approached the door that led to the street, Devlin reached into his back pocket and slid Reilly's lead-weighted sap into the palm of his hand. He knew he would have to time this perfectly. Reilly's busted-up legs didn't have much strength left in them. He lagged behind the scowling gangster. Radic avoided the revolving doors and stepped to the swinging door at his right. He placed his hand on the door and turned to look for Reilly. He leaned over and opened the door for him, letting Reilly pass out onto the street first.

Just as Radic moved into the doorway after Reilly passed, Devlin grabbed him by the collar, pulled him back into the lobby, and brought the blackjack down hard on the side of his head.

The blow knocked the heavy man to his knees. He was still conscious, but he had no control over his legs. He fumbled for his gun under his armpit, then crashed over onto his side.

Reilly continued walking out the door. He hesitated for a moment, confused as to which direction he should walk to get to the Saab. He looked for Radic, but now it was Devlin who was behind him, not Radic.

From his vantage point in the front seat of the Saab, Roland hadn't seen what had happened to Radic, but now he saw a man with a black ski mask pulled down over his face coming out of the lobby close behind Reilly. He immediately started to get out of the car.

At the same moment, Devlin smacked Reilly in the back of his head, avoiding the tender area of the temple. Reilly went down, but before he hit the sidewalk Devlin had wrenched the case out of his hand and was off and running.

Roland was out of the car now, running to the sidewalk, his gun already in hand. He was trying to get an angle on Devlin so he could shoot at him. Zenko was out on the street side. He had a better angle, but he was still pulling his gun out. Roland fired first. Three shots. None of them even came close to Devlin.

It had all happened so quickly that Waldron barely had time to react, much less figure out what was going down. When he heard the first gunshots, he frantically punched the call button on his radio to tell his stakeout team, "Hold your position! Don't call in. I'll take care of it. Hold your position and be ready to follow the Saab."

Waldron gripped the two-way radio unit and waited for a response. It finally crackled over the small speaker, "Roger. Holding our position."

Waldron had no intention of calling for an armed response. He wanted the Yugoslavs to get away so they would lead him to Mislovic.

Devlin was almost at the corner of Moorgate and South Place when Zenko finally got off his first shot. It, too, missed. Roland was running after Devlin now, trying to get close to him for a better shot. Devlin whipped the Glock from his waistband, dropped into a perfect shooter's crouch, and turned to fire.

In a fraction of a second he saw every possible target: Roland running toward him; Zenko moving toward him, aiming his gun; and from the corner of his eye, Radic staggering out of the building lobby.

The gunfire had every pedestrian in the area running or crouching down to the ground. Devlin had a clear shot at Roland, who was the closest target. He took careful aim and put a bullet right into Roland's left thigh. The leg was blown out from under him so quickly that the big man fell forward on his face.

Devlin didn't waste time shooting at Radic, because the man could still hardly walk straight with the concussion he had given him.

Zenko got off one more shot that missed. Devlin spun around, grabbed the case, and turned the corner onto South Place which became Eldon Street after one block. Now he was out of sight. Zenko ran after him, but he was far behind.

South Place/Eldon Street was a wide thoroughfare. Traffic was light. The west side of the street was almost free of parked cars, since it bordered a construction site. The east side was filled with cars parked bumper-to-bumper. Devlin ran right down the middle of the street, not bothering to dodge pedestrians on the sidewalk.

Around the corner on Moorgate, Zenko came after Devlin as fast as he could.

Midway up the block, the blue Volvo was double-parked. Annie was in the driver's seat waiting, watching in the rearview mirror. Devlin had told her exactly what to do, and she was determined to do it. She had heard the gunfire clearly, but her mind was so focused on what she had to do that the bullets had lost their ability to terrorize her.

When Devlin was about fifteen feet from the car, Annie leaned back and unlatched the back passenger door on the street side, put her foot on the brake, and shoved the gearshift into drive.

Devlin ran to the trunk, dropped the case on the street, and pushed the release latch. Inside, curled into an inert fetal position, was Hinton. Hinton should have been dead. He was beaten, bruised, and broken. He had been jammed in the trunk for hours, trying to breathe. His nose had been smashed so badly that he had to suck air in through his teeth. He should have been dead. But he wasn't. He was waiting for one last chance to kill, and when Devlin opened the trunk, Hinton grabbed his throat like a cobra striking.

Devlin was almost as quick. He jammed the muzzle of the Glock straight into Hinton's sternum and pulled the trigger, one time.

The bullet tore through Hinton's heart and blew a hole out his back as big as a fist.

With his free hand, Devlin pulled Hinton's body straight out of the trunk and dropped it faceup on the street.

Devlin had turned him into just another piece of dead meat. Another life sacrificed to the gods of death. The moment had been coming ever since he had returned to Annie. Ever since he had read her letter in Los Angeles. Ever since he had seen her that first night so many years ago in Billy Budd's.

And it had all taken less than five seconds.

Devlin turned back toward Moorgate and saw Zenko rounding the corner. He aimed and fired a shot over Zenko's head. Zenko ducked. Devlin threw the money-filled case into the trunk, slammed it, and turned back standing straight up, aiming at Zenko. Zenko fired first. Devlin flew back, banged into the trunk, and fell down out of sight.

Zenko was half a block away, but running hard toward the car that held his money.

Now Devlin made his final move. Zenko's shot had missed him. Devlin had bet his life that Zenko wouldn't be able to hit him on the run, a half block away. With most, that would have been a safe bet. Devlin never knew how close Zenko's shot had come to hitting his head.

The back door of the sedan was open. Devlin was still down on the street, out of Zenko's view. From that position, he pulled off his ski mask and shoved it over Hinton's head and face, then scrambled into the backseat of the Volvo.

As soon as he was in, Devlin yelled, "Go!" and Annie floored the accelerator. The Volvo screeched up Eldon Street. Zenko ran after the car and tried to get off a shot, but it was too late. He ran about ten more yards to the corpse that was bleeding all over the street. The body was dressed in dark pants, bright green pullover sweater, black ski mask. Except for the black gloves, it was the exact outfit Devlin had worn.

Zenko looked at the body, proud of the center shot that had killed the man who had robbed them.

He reached down and pulled the black ski mask off the face. It was Hinton.

Zenko lost whatever control he had left. The rage roared

out of him in a stream of Croatian curses. Zenko aimed his gun at the body and pulled the trigger again and again until there were no more bullets. He kicked the face of the dead Yardie, but it barely satiated his rage.

Zenko shoved his gun into a pocket and turned to go back to his car. He would have preferred to stay and mutilate Hinton's body, but he didn't want to be arrested by the police, who he knew would surely be flooding the area.

When he turned the corner at Moorgate, he saw Radic leaning with one hand on the wall of the bank building, bent over and throwing up—a reaction to the concussion he had sustained.

A small crowd had gathered around Reilly, who was still on the ground.

Zenko gripped Radic by the back of the neck and shook him gently. "Radic! Get in the car. Can you make it?"

Radic looked up at him and nodded weakly. His face was drained of blood, and he was in a cold sweat, but he managed to stagger off toward the car. Zenko started to push his way through the crowd around Reilly.

Waldron sat in his car, still watching the red Saab. He monitored the police calls on his radio, waiting to see when the Trojan Units would be dispatched. He hadn't called them, because even though he had been appalled at what had just transpired, he knew that he would never be able to adequately explain his presence or his actions. Devlin's Yardie clothes and ski mask hadn't fooled him. He knew it was Devlin who had just caused another gun battle on the streets of London.

He cursed the American. What the hell was he doing? Was it possible that he was just going for the money so he could have it himself? Or for the woman? Waldron slammed his hand against the steering wheel in frustration. How the hell are the Yugoslavs going to do the drug deal now? It didn't matter. He had no choice but to follow them and execute Devlin's plan. Hopefully, Rinaldi and his partner would stay with the assignment. Now the main problem was whether or not the Yugoslavs could get the hell out of the area before the Armed Response Vehicles poured in and trapped them in a hail of gunfire.

Luckily, no one from the bank had called. Apparently, they

were unaware that a client of theirs had been robbed in their own lobby. Now finally the first call was coming in. It was a woman's voice. She sounded hysterical. She identified herself as a clerk at the Marks & Spenser store across the street from the bank. He listened as the police emergency operator tried to sort out the information.

Waldron knew the Trojan Units assigned to this sector were fairly close, he estimated no more than five or six minutes away. The Yugoslavs had about three minutes before they'd be trapped in the area. He knew they would not surrender without a gunfight. And he knew the highly trained Special Ops marksmen and their deadly Heckler & Koch MP5 carbines would win. Then any hope of redeeming himself would be over. Waldron realized he was in the strange position of rooting for the bad guys to get away.

Zenko was through the crowd now, pulling the semiconscious Reilly onto his feet. He half carried him to the Saab, still parked in the same spot next to the curb. A well-meaning businessman in a pinstriped brown suit helped him get Reilly into the car.

Zenko thanked the man with a grunt.

Roland was already behind the wheel, fighting off the shock and pain of a shattered bone in his leg. His right leg wasn't damaged. He had the engine running and he was ready to drive.

Zenko shoved Reilly over to the other side of the backseat and climbed in next to him. They had loaded up fairly quickly, and for a second Zenko thought about going after the car with his money, but he realized it was hopeless. His anger boiled up all over again. He slammed the back door of the car shut and yelled, "Go."

A crowd had gathered around the area. Traffic was stopped. Police sirens could be heard braying in the distance. Roland revved the engine, leaned on the horn, and bulled his way into traffic.

Waldron was already in the flow of traffic, heading in the right direction. He positioned himself behind the red Saab and followed it up Moorgate. The backup team was in touch with him by radio and was maneuvering around so it could follow.

Inside the Saab, Zenko turned and grabbed a handful of Reilly's stringy hair and shook the man's head until the pain brought him fully conscious.

Zenko started screaming, "Who did this, you fuck? Who did it?"

Reilly answered in pain, "I don't know. I didn't see anything."

"Liar! You tell Yardies."

Zenko pulled out his gun and pressed it to Reilly's head.

"No one know about pickup except you. You fucking whore. How did Oliver get to you? Answer me."

"He didn't. I swear to God."

"Liar!"

He shoved his gun into Reilly's left eye and pulled the trigger. Waldron was only one car length behind the Saab and could see Zenko shoving his gun into Reilly's eye. As much as he despised the man, Waldron could not watch him be murdered. But he had no gun, no idea how to stop it. He was about to ram into the back of the Saab, when he realized that although Zenko was pulling the trigger on his gun, nothing was happening. The gun was empty.

Zenko threw the gun down in disgust and screamed at Radic to give him his gun.

Radic had a concussion, but he still had his wits about him.

"Wait a second, Z, don't kill him. He's the only one who knows where that money is. Frank will want to talk to him. Keep him alive."

Zenko yelled, "Fuck!" and smashed Reilly across the mouth with the back of his fist. Reilly's battered head hit the window post, and he crashed back into unconsciousness.

"You right, Radic. But he not live for long."

Waldron concentrated on the car in front of him. He gripped the steering wheel tightly and tried not to notice how much his heart was pounding.

CHAPTER 33

BACK IN THE Volvo, Annie drove as quickly as the traffic would allow. Devlin sat in the backseat pulling and wrestling out of the green sweater.

He told her, "All right, slow down. Drive normally. It's over."

Annie had been angling to skirt the lane of traffic ahead of her, but now she slowed down and proceeded at the same pace as the other cars. The street had narrowed down to two lanes. A few yards ahead, traffic had stopped for a red light. She wanted to turn and talk to Devlin, but she didn't dare take her eyes off the road.

Devlin spoke to her calmly. "When you get to the next corner, take a right and let me out."

"You killed him, Jack."

"Yes. I killed him. That's what you wanted, wasn't it?"

"Yes. But I'm sorry you had to do it."

"No you're not."

"I would've done it, Jack. I would've gladly pulled that trigger."

"Only the first time, Annie. Only the first time."

The traffic started up, and Annie fell silent as she continued toward the next intersection. Devlin had taken a change of clothes from the Draycott. He was now out of the dark slacks. He maneuvered around in the backseat until he was wearing a pair of fine wool olive-colored slacks and a cashmere sienna blazer. Under the green sweater he had worn a cream-colored linen shirt. He was now dressed completely different from any person who'd been at the crime scene. The change had taken less than three minutes.

He told Annie, "When you make the turn, pull over and let me out. Keep on driving out of this area. Get as far as you can in fifteen minutes and put this car in a garage somewhere. Then take a taxi and go back to the clinic. If you get stuck in traffic, just dump the car, jump on the Tube or in a taxi, and get out of the area."

"All right."

"Go back to the clinic and stay with Elizabeth."

"You're letting me go by myself?"

"They won't be looking for you now."

"Why not?"

"You're not at the top of the kill list anymore."

She stopped at the corner. Devlin stepped out quickly and retrieved the leather case from the trunk. He stuffed the pants and sweater into it and walked to the driver-side window.

"Just in case, don't leave anything in the car. If they do find it, your friend will just say it was stolen. Otherwise you can drive it back to Cambridge when this is all over."

"All right."

Annie had tried to be tough in the face of Devlin's hard manner, but suddenly, rather surprisingly, she could feel the tears welling up. She didn't trust herself to speak. Devlin could see it, but wasn't giving an inch.

"Stay at the clinic until I call you."

Without another word, he turned and walked away.

As Annie drove off, she inventoried her feelings. With Devlin gone, the urge to cry left her. Why did he make her feel that way? Because he had been so cold to her? She wasn't accustomed to men being that way with her. And then she realized she was not accustomed to caring very much at all what men did, unless there was something she wanted them to do for her. And wasn't Devlin doing what she wanted him to do? So why cry about it? she told herself.

Why not cry over being an accomplice to murder? she asked herself. Yes, the murder of an animal, but a murder nonetheless. She checked her feelings about that. No, there was nothing. No guilt. If anything, what she felt was relief. Maybe she was a little worried about getting caught, but that was it. Even though she had been so close to the killing the sound of the gun had made her flinch, even though she'd felt Hinton's body slam back into the car, even though she still seemed to smell the smoke from Devlin's gun, she realized she couldn't have cared less that Devlin had killed him. The only thing that made her feel any pain, any remorse, was the thought that she might never see Jack Devlin again.

When he left Annie, Devlin had headed directly for the rear entrance of the Liverpool train station. It was a quick walk back up Liverpool Station Street to a small plaza, past a huge iron sculpture piece that looked like elongated girders standing on end, and into a long corridor that led to the main terminal area. The walkway was crowded with displays and merchandise and bordered by neatly arranged shops behind glass walls.

Liverpool station was a major junction for both trains and the Underground. It was all glass and ceramic walls and marble floors. The only parts of the station that seemed old were the ornate girders that arched above the main terminal and joined to form the huge vaulted glass ceiling which covered the terminus.

As he walked toward the main concourse, Devlin looked for a luggage check. He had to ask two people before he was directed back toward the rear entrance. The left luggage room was obscured by a kiosk selling hats. The room was discreetly tucked into an area away from the main terminal, probably to avoid any extensive damage to the rail lines and ticket booths if someone chose to use it as a place to stow a bomb.

Devlin purchased a copy of the *London Times* and a British edition of *Vogue* magazine and placed them on top of the neat stacks of money at the bottom of the case. On top of that he placed the clothes he had worn at the bank. He bent into the case and sniffed them. The faint odor of gunpowder still lingered on the sweater. He shoved that to the very bottom and hoped the smell didn't make whoever manned the left luggage room think of explosives. The contents just about filled the case.

Since the IRA declaration of peace, the personnel who normally checked bags for bombs had relaxed somewhat. The short, bald man working the left luggage room gave Devlin's leather case just enough of an inspection to verify that there wasn't anything obviously dangerous inside.

After verifying that the left luggage facility would be open until nine o'clock, Devlin blended back into the flow of people moving toward the main concourse. Even in the middle of the day, there was a good number of travelers moving through the station. Devlin had no trouble disappearing into the crowd.

He walked almost the entire length of the concourse and found a bank of pay phones near the entrance to the Underground. He picked up the phone and started to dial a number, wondering how many people would be dead by the time the left luggage room closed.

Once Zenko decided not to shoot Reilly, Waldron was able to relax and follow the red Saab. The tailing went smoothly. Rinaldi and Edwards were experienced enough to follow a car across London without being spotted and without losing it. They kept in touch by radio and deftly hopscotched back and forth in front of and behind the Saab.

Waldron knew he could trust Rinaldi to keep his mouth shut about this rather irregular assignment. Edwards would follow his partner's lead. Rinaldi disliked Superintendent Fenton almost as much as Waldron did. Which was one of the reasons Waldron had picked him. But no amount of dislike for Fenton would make Rinaldi keep quiet about a police sergeant getting his brains blown out in the back of a car he was tailing. That would be a bit too irregular.

For the moment, Waldron stuck to the Saab, deciding to follow Devlin's plan, even though he was not at all sure what Devlin was up to. If Devlin had done all this so he could abscond with the Yugoslavs' drug money, Waldron decided, he would hunt him down and shoot him himself.

Zenko's driver, Roland, was making the cops' job easy. He drove with the flow and did nothing to lose anyone who might be following. The heavy London traffic kept the procession at a relatively slow pace, also making it easier to follow the red Saab.

They were heading west, staying on local streets. Since they hadn't slipped onto a motorway, Waldron assumed they were staying in town.

Waldron kept in touch with his team by radio, but they kept their transmissions short and cryptic so that other police personnel would not pick up on their conversations.

Despite the excruciating pain and considerable loss of blood, Roland made it back to Marla's restaurant off Portobello Road. Waldron stopped his car well in back of the Saab. Rinaldi continued on, passing the Saab and stopping farther up the street. The Saab was bracketed.

Radic got out of the car and went into the restaurant. A moment later, two busboys came out, accompanied by a dark, heavyset man, Czmenceau, who carried a stack of bar towels and a cook's apron. He helped cover Roland's bloody leg with the apron and directed the busboys to take Roland into the restaurant. They half-carried the wounded man while Czmenceau used the bar towels to wipe up the considerable amount of blood on the front seat area. Zenko talked to him from the backseat while he worked, and Radic followed Roland into the restaurant. When the blood was cleaned up sufficiently, Czmenceau laid clean towels on the driver's seat and got behind the wheel. He drove off, and this time Waldron let the white van fall in behind first.

The red Saab headed back in the direction they had come from. Waldron and the team in the white van hung in and found themselves driving through the City, only blocks from Barclays Bank. Waldron found it hard to believe that they would drive the same car into the crime area, but they saw no cops and no one stopped the Yugoslavs. After struggling through a little bit of congested traffic, the Saab headed for the large commercial area known as Spitalfields. The sprawling market was housed in a series of high-ceilinged buildings. During the early-morning hours it was teeming with commerce. Some establishments had permanent offices and shops that were open throughout the day. But now it was mostly empty. And Waldron knew that if he tried to follow the Saab into the maze of streets and alleyways that wound through the market, he would be spotted immediately.

Rinaldi pulled his white van into a parking lot near Lamb Street as the Saab turned right onto one of the narrow streets that coursed through the market. Luckily, the Saab parked within sight. Waldron pulled into the same lot, keeping his distance from the van. He watched Zenko, Czmenceau, and Reilly exit into a storage building or warehouse located on the corner of the market area. The entrance was about twenty feet in from the street, but clearly visible from the parking lot.

Waldron's radio crackled, and he heard Edwards's voice.

"Looks like they've landed."

Waldron responded, "Let's wait a few minutes. If they don't come out, you two stay here and keep an eye on the place."

"Roger."

"I've got to find a phone. I'll be back in a few minutes. If they move, call me."

Waldron got out of his car and headed for a pay phone back toward Liverpool station. As he walked, he realized that the location made sense. It was close to the bank, yet secluded. Any traffic going in and out wouldn't be noticed. And if the Yugoslavs wanted to distribute merchandise from the area, whether it be drugs or weapons or flowers, it could be done without attracting any attention at all.

About ten minutes later, Rinaldi and Edwards watched as Zenko came out of the warehouse with two other men. They walked farther into the market. About five minutes later a Fiat pulled up next to the Saab. Zenko gave the two men instructions and they set about taking things out of the Saab's trunk and changing the license plates on the front and back.

While this was going on, Waldron was on a pay phone talking to one of his men, who had taken a message from Devlin that he could be reached at his room at the Draycott. He also received a report from the detectives up in Hackney that they had found Oliver in his warehouse and phoned in the location. Waldron wrote it down. Then he dialed the Draycott.

Devlin picked up the phone on the first ring. "Yes."

"It's Waldron. Is that what you mean by doing this your way? Bloody hell, man, what are you trying to do?"

"How much of it did you see?"

"Everything until you made it around the corner. I wasn't sure you didn't get shot."

"I didn't. Where are you?"

"Right back near that damn bank. Spitalfields Market. We tailed the Yugoslavs all over town, and they ended up here. Looks like they have a small building right on the outside edge of the market."

"Where's Spitalfields Market?"

"A few blocks away from Liverpool station."

Devlin said, "That's interesting."

"Why?"

"Never mind. Is Mislovic there?"

"I haven't seen him, but I would assume he's probably here. They took Reilly in there with them. I suppose they'll want to know where their money went."

"I suppose so."

"Why did you do that? How much was it?"

"I didn't count it."

"Was it sufficient to purchase kilos of cocaine?"

"Yes."

"Why did you take it? How are they going to do their deal with the Yardies now? What exactly are you playing at?"

"Just watch and see. It should be pretty obvious fairly soon."

"What should be obvious?"

"What's going to happen next."

Waldron could tell Devlin wasn't going to be more specific. He asked, "What about Reilly?"

Devlin asked back, "What about him?"

"We can't just leave him in there."

"Why not? It's where he goddamn belongs."

Waldron thought that over for a moment and couldn't disagree. He told Devlin, "I wouldn't bet on him coming out of there."

"So much the better. Do you care, Waldron?"

"I only care if they ask me why I didn't bust in there and get him out."

"If I were you, I wouldn't know anything about him being there. If I were you, when they ask, I'd tell them you got a call from Reilly saying he'd be at that location and asking you to meet him there."

"So here I am. Doing nothing."

"You're waiting for Reilly."

"Meaning I didn't really know if he was in there or not."

"Sounds like it's a big place. How are you supposed to know where the hell he is?"

"Right."

"Did you locate Oliver?"

"Yes. He's at a warehouse in Hackney, near the River Lea."

"A river?"

"More like a canal, actually. I'm not too familiar with the area. Do you mind telling me exactly what you're doing, Devlin?"

"Why do you need to know?"

"Because I'm involved."

"Not so's it'll do you any harm."

"How can you say that?"

"Look, Waldron, I told you there's only one way out of this. You're going to have to suck it up and play your part."

"My part in what?"

"In the final battle. I took that money to make the Yugoslavs think the Yardies stole it."

"What!?"

"You heard me."

"Why the hell did you do that? How did you do it?"

"It doesn't matter. Just realize that the drug deal is now secondary. Look for the Yugoslavs to go after the Yardies. I'd suggest you have your people ready to handle that."

"Why do they believe the Yardies did it?"

Devlin raised his voice. He knew Waldron wouldn't stop asking questions until he got an answer.

"Because they think Oliver's killer did the snatch. His body is riddled with their bullets and lying around the corner from the bank. He was wearing a black ski mask, green sweater, and dark pants."

"Good Lord, Devlin, how did you pull that off?"

"Just barely."

"Who killed him?"

"Ask Mislovic's guy. The one that looks like a bulldog in a brown suit."

"He's here."

"And you know where I am, so stop worrying. Keep track of both sets of bad guys. Get your troops ready. The ones with the guns. You should soon be making enough arrests to satisfy everybody on your ass. You play this right and you'll be a hero."

"Bullshit. I'm the goat no matter what happens. If I'm lucky I get to stay a cop. What are you going to do now?"

"Sleep. Call me if Oliver or Mislovic makes a move."

Devlin hung up without further words. Waldron was still trying to sort things out as he walked back to the van. He tapped twice on the door and Edwards let him in.

"Anything happen over there?"

"Not much. They cleaned up the Saab and switched license plates, but that's it so far."

Waldron sat thinking about how to cover himself if Reilly never came out of the Yugoslavs' warehouse. It didn't take him long to realize that Devlin's advice was close to the mark.

"All right, fellows, this could be a bit of a sticky wicket, as I'm sure you can already tell. Our main problem at the moment is Sergeant Reilly. I want to be quite clear on this matter. I don't want you blamed for anything if he doesn't come out of there, so here's exactly what happened.

"You were on the stakeout on Berwick Street, just like you were supposed to be. I received a call from Reilly regarding a man named Mislovic. Reilly told me to meet him here. I called you at the stakeout on Berwick Street. But not until one-fifteen. About a half hour ago. And you didn't get called to Barclays in the City, you were told to meet me in this car park near the market. When you arrived here, I told you that I had spoken to Reilly and that he was supposed to meet me here. He was going to tell us—me—if Mislovic was here. Then we would go in and arrest him. Understood?"

Both detectives nodded. Waldron gave Rinaldi time to think of any holes in the story.

"Okay?"

Rinaldi frowned, thought it over for a few more moments, then nodded.

"We got it. If that's the way you want to play it, Chief, we got it. But if it unravels, it's every man for himself."

"Understood."

"Just between us, what are Reilly's chances of coming out of there? I've never liked the old bastard, but he is a cop."

"*Was* a cop. He's been providing information to the Yugoslavs. I suspect he's been dirty for quite a while. Fenton knows he's dirty. So it won't seem far-fetched that this time he got in over his head. If he doesn't come out of there, he'll only be getting what he deserves."

"What was all that shit that went down by the bank?"

"Did you see what happened around the corner? I couldn't."

"Not all of it. Traffic was in the way. One of 'em shot some guy running around the corner with a leather case. Maybe wounded him. Then he went over and emptied his gun into him."

Waldron knew that Devlin had taken the money from Reilly. He knew he had the leather case. But who was it the Yugoslav shot? It obviously wasn't Devlin.

"What happened to the leather case?"

Edwards answered. "I saw him toss it into the trunk of his getaway car. A blue Volvo. The car took off, but he didn't. What was in the case?"

"They were using Reilly to pick up cash for them. For a drug buy. I wanted to tail them to wherever they were going after they got their money and then tail them to the drugs. Unfortunately, somebody must have known about the pickup and jumped on it. Whoever it was, I think they've got the Yugoslavs' money. I imagine Reilly is going to get blamed for it. For all I know, he might have set up the double cross."

"Nasty old bugger. Didn't think he had it in him to pull off something like that."

"I'm just guessing. But as far as you two are concerned, you don't know anything about that. If what Reilly was playing at comes out, he'll have to answer for it, but I'm not going to inform on him. If Reilly walks out of there alive, he'll have enough explaining to do. If he doesn't, like I said, he gets what he deserves. All we know is, I got a call from Reilly to be here, I called you two, and we're still trying to find Mislovic. We'll wait here for a while longer and see what happens."

Both detectives sat and privately evaluated the odds of getting away with the story Waldron had outlined. In the end, it amounted to following the unwritten rule that stood the world over: Cops cover for each other. Both Rinaldi and Edwards knew they were too far along to turn back. If Reilly was killed, there'd be a major investigation. There was no alternative except to agree on a story and stick to it as long as they could.

Rinaldi asked, "How long do we hang in here?"

Waldron replied, "I don't know."

They didn't have to wait long. Within ten minutes, cars and taxicabs began appearing. Out of each car climbed one or two men. The call had gone out, and the hirelings were responding.

Having made it to the West, most of the men who were arriving at Spitalfields Market in ones and twos were working in various criminal enterprises at the lowest echelon. Some worked directly for Mislovic, others for the shadowy network of Eastern European gangsters and criminals who had begun to establish their presence and enterprises in various Western European cities. But all of them took Mislovic's call as an opportunity to increase their value and prove their loyalty to a burgeoning organized crime group that might promote them to the next level of power and prosperity. If they had to kill someone to get to that level, so be it. For most of them, a call to war was a time for glory. An excuse to kill was something they lived for.

Inside the market building, Zenko was on the phone sending out the word for various men to assemble. Nothing explicit was said, just enough to get the men to the market. Once they arrived he would give face-to-face orders on whatever he wanted done.

In a back room at the far end of the market building, Mislovic was sitting with Reilly. Zenko had explained what occurred at the bank, but Mislovic was determined to find out why.

The small back room was brightly illuminated by a set of bare fluorescent tubes suspended from the ceiling. The floor was concrete and the walls were unfinished corrugated steel.

In the middle of the room was an old, square oak table that was surprisingly ornate and impressive. It looked as if it should have been in the dining room of an eighteenth-century town house in one of London's better neighborhoods, instead of in a storage warehouse on the edge of Spitalfields Market. Mislovic sat with Reilly facing him on the same side of the table, close on his left.

At the other end of the small room sat a man who was capable of breaking any bone in Reilly's body without using any instruments. He was George Antone, the older brother of Dragan's bodyguard, Tesich. George sat without moving or making any sound at all. He was hunched over, elbows on knees, like an old heavyweight boxer ready to shuffle into the ring.

Reilly was a mess. The painkillers had worn off. Every spot where Devlin had hit him throbbed fiercely. His head was splitting from the slap of the blackjack and his nose was cracked from Zenko's blow. He was absolutely miserable.

Mislovic had not yet said a word to Reilly. He was sipping coffee and staring at him. Finally, he spoke.

"So, you're Zenko's police friend."

Mislovic's tone of voice sounded cordial, almost sympathetic. A small spark of hope flashed somewhere in Reilly's brain.

"Yes, sir. I am. I've been trying to help Mr. Zenko with . . . with information and such."

"Well, you weren't much help today, my friend. What happened?"

"I don't know, sir. I swear I don't. Whoever it was jumped me from behind."

"You have no idea?"

"No. Not really."

"Not really?"

"No."

Mislovic nodded thoughtfully and looked up toward the ceiling. He breathed in deeply, as if he were preparing himself for a particularly difficult task.

"I don't have the time or desire to ask you these questions more than once."

Reilly didn't know what to say to that. Mislovic turned toward the big man, who was waiting patiently.

"Do an arm, George."

The big man got up off his chair, shuffled over to Reilly, and grabbed Reilly's right wrist. He did it so quickly that Reilly had no chance to avoid his grasp. Reilly instinctively pulled away, but against George's massive strength, nothing moved very much. There was no reaction at all from the big man, except that his next move might have been just a little faster than if Reilly had not resisted. George quickly, but carefully, gripped Reilly's arm just beneath the elbow. Then, without a hint of warning or hesitation, he slammed Reilly's forearm down across his knee. This one quick, brutal move caused both bones in the forearm to crack completely in two. It sounded more like a muffled pop than a crack. Reilly's forearm bulged momentarily as the broken ends of the bone pushed outward from inside the skin. Reilly gasped. Whatever color was left drained from his face, and he passed out.

Even Mislovic grimaced at the sound and sight of an arm snapping so quickly and brutally.

George let go of the arm so the broken ends of the bones wouldn't poke through the skin as Reilly fell back. Then he shuffled over to a set of shelves attached to the opposite wall of the brightly lit room and reached down to pick up a quart jug of ammonia.

In the same deliverate, shuffling walk, he came back to the table, unscrewed the cap, and placed the mouth of the jug directly under Reilly's nose.

The miserable Irishman woke with a start and coughed at the acrid smell. There was surprisingly little pain in his broken arm, but he was breaking out in a cold clammy sweat from shock. The thought of what they were going to do to him if he lied caused black spots to swirl behind his closed eyes.

He heard Mislovic's soft voice through the haze of nausea that forced bile up into his throat.

"All right, let's start again. What happened?"

Reilly cradled his broken arm in his lap and started to speak, but something had broken deep inside the bitter man. Devlin had terrified him, but Waldron had offered him some sliver of hope. Mislovic had now taken that away. He answered without artifice or guile or energy. It came out like a bitter, rueful comment on the futility of his life.

"They knew I was in with you. The great Chief Inspector Waldron. He knew after you missed them in Piccadilly that it was me. You might as well have put a sign on me. He had me tailed. Tapped my phone. He and that bastard Devlin took a tire iron to me for fun. But they knew everything anyhow. They just wanted to make sure I'd do the bank job with you."

"Devlin?"

"Yeah. He's the one."

"He's supposed to be dead."

"Well, he isn't. Seems like you people just can't kill him, no matter how much information I give you. I'm working with idiots here."

Mislovic bristled, but did not comment.

Reilly pulled up his pants leg to show Mislovic the bandages.

"They took a tire iron to me. Threatened to cripple me. Paralyze my spine. They were after you. They wanted to know where to find you and the others, but I didn't know where you were."

"But they knew about the job at the bank?"

"They had a tap on my phone. They knew everything."

"They knew you were going to pick up money for us?"

"Yes. Waldron told me to go and get it, turn it over, and that was all. They were supposed to tail you, then follow you to your drug deal."

"They were?"

"That's what they told me, but it was all bullshit. They just wanted the money. They're just thieves, no better than any of us. They set me up. They got me as I was coming out."

"Who?"

"Devlin."

"You're sure."

Reilly shrugged. "Who else?"

Mislovic said no more. He was playing out different possibilities in his mind. He drained his cup, smiled once at Reilly as if to congratulate him, and walked out of the room. George Antone already knew what he was to do. At the doorway, Mislovic turned and nodded to the executioner.

George rose from his chair and walked toward Reilly, stopping a few feet away.

The old heavyweight asked him, "You want a drink?"

At that moment, Reilly thought there might have never been a time in his life when he wanted one more than now.

"Yes. Yes. Whiskey, if you have it."

He watched the big man walk over to the shelves on the opposite wall. George came back with a water glass and a bottle of Dewar's. He poured Reilly two fingers and set the bottle on the table.

Reilly took the drink down in one swallow, relishing the

burning woody taste as the whiskey made its way down to warm his stomach.

He looked hopefully at George and was rewarded with another two fingers of Scotch. He thought about taking the drink a little more slowly this time, but was too eager for the whiskey to soften his pain. Maybe this big dumb bloke would just keep pouring them. As he bent his head back to drain the glass, George Antone pressed a small revolver to his temple and shot him.

Reilly's head jerked away from the glass. He died spilling whiskey all over his dingy white shirt.

Now came the real work. George would carry the body downstairs to another room and lay it on a long, stainless-steel worktable. Then he would put on a large rubber apron that covered him from just under his neck to just above his shoes.

By the time he was done cutting, almost all of the blood and fluids would be drained out of the body. George would hose down the area and push most of the gore into a drain in the middle of the floor. The rest of the job consisted of patiently grinding the parts in a large industrial meat grinder.

The paste of flesh and bones would then be stuffed into heavy-gauge thirty-gallon plastic bags. George would tape the bags shut with duct tape.

Sometime later that night, George would drive a battered van into the market and load the bags up. Nobody would notice. Or if they did, it would not seem at all out of the ordinary. Early in the morning, before the London traffic piled up, George would drive to an industrial waste-processing plant outside London, where the contents of his plastic bags would be incinerated.

By the time he was done, the shooting of Patrick Reilly in the head would be almost forgotten. It wasn't the killing that tired George Antone. It was the same thing that exhausted many enterprises throughout the world: getting rid of the waste.

CHAPTER 34

WHEN MISLOVIC WALKED into the main section of the storage building, he was surprised at how many men Zenko had gathered in such a short time. Zenko had found the right outlet for his rage: preparing for war. Several of the men were already unpacking the crates of AK-47s.

Mislovic motioned for his disheveled second in command to come talk to him.

"Z, let me ask you a couple of questions."

"Yah?"

"You said the one who jumped Reilly and Radic was that same black devil who came to Berwick Street to get Devlin."

"Right. Tall, skinny, mean-looking. I shoot him right after he throw the case in his car."

"He had a mask on?"

"Yah. Knit cap pulled down. With eyeholes."

"You shot him?"

"After he throw the money in the trunk."

Mislovic was still trying to sort out the information.

"It almost makes sense."

"What?"

Then he seemed to understand it all.

"Oliver doesn't know this happened."

"What?"

"The robbery. He doesn't know they took the money."

"What you mean?"

"About an hour before you got here, he called to confirm the buy tonight: time and place. Reminded me of the terms. Guns and money. The whole deal."

"So what? That's just a smoke screen to make you think he wasn't in on it."

"No, no, Z. Why should he steal the cash when he can get it

for the cocaine? And then do business for that much and more. It doesn't make sense to steal from me now and ruin the future. Why should he make an enemy of me now?"

"Who says these animals make sense? He got our money and he can still sell the drugs to someone else. He make double."

"No. He's not that stupid. It doesn't make sense. But with Reilly's story it does. He told me his boss, some cop named Waldron, and Devlin found out he was our informant. Waldron tailed him. Tapped his phone. Knew everything. They beat him up to make sure he would come get the money with us. They told him they wanted to follow us to the drug buy."

"Maybe they did."

"No. You send some guys out to look around later, but you won't find any cops out there. They don't want us. They wanted the money."

"The cops?"

"Why? Is that something new? Cops stealing drug money for themselves?"

"So where does the dead black come in?"

"They must have turned that crazy bastard and got him to make the grab. Make him take the risk."

Zenko frowned in concentration as he tried to sort out what had happened.

"How?"

Mislovic ran it down for him.

"Follow me, Z. The old cop in there was not lying to me. He tells me the cops and Devlin were in on the rip-off. He even thinks Devlin stole the money. But you shot Oliver's man throwing our money into the trunk of his getaway car. So the black, the cops in charge, and Devlin were all in on it together."

"The blacks were supposed to kill Devlin and the woman last night."

"But Devlin is alive. The woman is alive, too. She said Devlin was dead, but she must have been lying. I spoke to her this morning."

"So what happened, goddammit? Did Oliver tell you they were dead?"

"He said it was all taken care of. Maybe he thinks it was."

"But it's not."

"Right. Put it together, Z. The cops were onto Reilly since you went after the American in Piccadilly. So they knew Reilly passed on the information about where Devlin was hiding."

"So you think they warn him?"

"Yes. Of course. They must have warned Devlin. Oliver sends that maniac to kill them. The cops are ready for him and grab him."

Zenko filled in the rest. "They got him for trying to kill the woman and all."

"Exactly."

"For all the shooting and murder tries."

"Right," said Mislovic. "Then they hear on Reilly's tapped phone about the money."

"The next morning."

"Yes. They've got that black devil, Hinton, and they convince him to rob for them."

"He double-cross Oliver and go with cops and Devlin."

"Yeah. And thanks to you, ends up dead on the street. But the cops and Devlin get our money."

"Ivan, everyone fuck everyone else around here."

"Welcome to the West. What the hell do you think the drug business is?"

"Yah. So Oliver don't know anything yet."

"Maybe he's looking around for his dead black, but that's not stopping him from trying to complete his drug deal with us."

"So Oliver still thinks we do business?"

"Yes."

"So now what?"

"Now all these bastards pay."

"Good."

"I get my damn cocaine, and this Oliver gets nothing but a bullet. He's useless. He can't kill one woman. He was supposed to clean up that mess. His man steals my money. That woman is still alive, threatening me. Oliver is a dead man. That's it. And we kill every one of those black Yardie cockroaches. I don't want any of them alive to bother me."

"You tell Dragan about this?"

"I'm calling him now. With a hundred thousand gone, there

will be no way he will try to hold me back. Get the rest of your men in here."

"Okay. When do we move?"

"We move on him an hour before the pickup is scheduled."

"When is that?"

"Six o'clock tonight at Oliver's warehouse. So we show up at five."

For the first time in days, Zenko smiled. The image of his men shooting down the Yardies with their AK-47s was a picture that brought joy to him.

Up in Hackney, Oliver had a similar vision.

Every Yard man in London who owed him a favor or wanted to be part of his crew was showing up at the warehouse, armed and ready to kill. From Hackney, Stoke Newington, Brixton, they filtered in with revolvers, automatics, rifles, shotguns, machetes, and homemade weapons like spiked chains and long knives. A man named Roach showed up with an Uzi and two full clips of ammunition. Before long it looked as if some wild modern West Indian tribe had shown up for war. The rolling papers and bags of ganja were dumped onto the old wooden table down on the warehouse floor. The bwouys were toking on big spliffs and pouring down pint cans of stout and lager. Someone lit a crack pipe and was passing it around. Before long there were more than twenty hard-core Yard men fueling up for war.

Oliver came down from his office in the mezzanine of the warehouse. He had washed, sat through Momma Cientro's bandaging and prayers, changed his clothes, and snorted up four fat lines of coke. He used the drug only rarely. But he knew he was going to need the cocaine to keep him going through the pain in his hip and the fatigue of last night's battle. And through the killing that was soon to come.

When he saw so many armed men standing on the floor of his warehouse, brandishing weapons, talking of shooting and killing, his blood stirred. He had never seen so many Yard men in one place at one time, ready to war. For a moment, he worried that there were too many of them. A group had started a particularly raucous game of dominoes. The players yelled and slapped down the tiles. Money was being wagered.

Boasts and threats were made. It was a situation ripe for violence. He realized that the coked-up, stoned army in front of him could easily start to riot and decide to take over his warehouse. Only six of the men in the warehouse were members of his own crew. The fact that the Yugoslavs would soon be dropping ten Kalashnikovs into the mix only added to his worry. He had more cocaine on the premises than he'd ever had in his life. And soon there would be a small fortune in cash money on the scene. He was playing a dangerous game. But within the crystal intensity of the cocaine sparkling in his head, Oliver found that he really didn't give a damn.

Oliver stepped onto the floor, all eyes on him. He tried to pick out his own men scattered around the warehouse. Some of them weren't even armed. Where the hell was Hinton? If Hinton were here, he knew that whatever happened, he would at least have the satisfaction of knowing Hinton would kill a good number of them before they looted him.

One of the men, Johnny Trumball, a handsome, light-skinned black who wore his hair in glistening soft curls, took off his black shades and swaggered over to Oliver, offering him a high five.

"Respect, Don."

Trumball was a potential rival. A dangerous man who had pieced together a violent little crew. Trumball was a regular buyer from Oliver, but Oliver knew full well he was sitting vigilantly on the sidelines of the Yardie world, making small deals, waiting for the right opportunity to hook up with a more powerful crew, or to gather enough men of his own to become the next Don himself.

Oliver met the false friendship with an equal dose of his own and slapped Trumball's hand. He wrapped an arm around the taller man's shoulders and guided him off to the side of the warehouse floor.

He talked quietly to Trumball.

"Lissen, brother, I need your help. We got too many of these bad bwouys in here. We cyan set dis up wit' everybody inside. We be soon shooting ourselves wit' so many guns concentrated in here."

"Yeah, man. Plus I bet you got lots a valuable t'ings in here that need lookin' after. Be too hard to do dat with all da trouble soon happenin'. Maybe I make my regular buy now and take a lickle extra out of here for ya."

"Cool now, Johnny. We cyan be dealin' and fussin' wit' dat now. We got other business. I take care of you later. Don' vex me now 'bout anyt'ing else. I want you to take some of dese bwouys outside and set up on the street. Dat way, whatever come in here, don' get out. Are you wit' me?"

Trumball give him a dazzling smile. It could have been the prelude to a shot in the stomach or an agreement. Either way, Oliver had to pay. Oliver now owed Trumball, and Trumball knew it.

"Okay, Don, I cover da outside for ya. We settle up later."

Trumball gathered up six of the Yard men and headed outside. Oliver didn't care what they did, as long as they were out of the warehouse. Twenty minutes after Trumball left, Leon Kingsmen showed up with his posse. They numbered eight. All of them were stoned, all wearing their balloonlike knit caps that gathered and covered up their long dreadlocks. Kingsmen and his followers were hard-core Rasta men. When Leon stepped inside, he pulled off his cap and displayed his dreadlock mane for all to see. It was huge.

Kingsmen wore a silk suit, an open-neck shirt, and soft leather shoes. He had one gold chain around his neck and one gold front tooth. He held up two 9-mm handguns and yelled out something about the power and protection of Jah. If there ever was a Rasta warrior, it was Kingsmen. Even Oliver had to smile.

Kingsmen's troops themselves were a ragtag bunch, but Oliver knew they would stand and shoot until the last one died. Something had happened long ago to the brains of these men and nothing seemed to penetrate them any longer. Standing and talking or standing and shooting—it didn't seem to matter very much.

At three-thirty, Oliver began the delicate process of checking everyone's weapons and assigning each person a place to stand for the ambush.

Kingsmen, for all his laid-back Rasta ways, was sharp. He wanted his men to fight outside, which would obviously be safer than fighting inside. Oliver relented after Kingsmen agreed to leave two of his warriors inside. Oliver told him to work it out with Trumball as to how the men would block off the street once the Yugoslavs arrived. Outside there were about a dozen buildings standing, interspersed with empty plots of overgrown land. Most of the buildings were either in ruins or abandoned. There were plenty of places for the outside men to disappear into doorways, or down in the overgrown lots. Oliver could only hope they would all find places to hide and stay out of sight until the Yugoslavs were inside his warehouse.

Oliver began to worry less about the Yugoslavs and more about what would happen after the slaughter. There would be money, and Kalashnikovs, amidst a pack of wild Yard men whose blood would be boiling after the kill. Oliver realized he and his crew could easily become their next target. He had stashed his coke in a safe hidden behind a brick alcove in the basement of the warehouse, but at this point he wished it wasn't even in the building. Where the hell was Hinton?

The detectives from the Hackney Division, whom Waldron had asked to locate Oliver, were watching the warehouse from about four blocks away. They had never seen so many Yardies converge on one spot. It was obvious that the situation was becoming extremely dangerous. They called in, and Witkowski was patched in directly to Waldron, sitting in the van with Rinaldi and Edwards.

His message was clear: The Yardies were getting ready for a war. There were at least thirty men in the warehouse. Witkowski was insisting now that they call their division chief superintendent and alert him to the situation. Waldron told them to go ahead and notify him and then to get the hell out of there. He had already put in three calls to Creighton at Special Operations. Waldron didn't quite know how Devlin had done it, but he now knew he had no choice. The London Metropolitan Police were about to gear up for a small war. Waldron knew Mislovic was doing the same thing Oliver was. They had counted twenty-seven different individuals who had come in and out of the warehouse across the street. Whatever Devlin had started was about to explode out of his control.

Waldron told Rinaldi and Edwards, "Okay. I've seen enough. You two get out of here. Go find your burglary informant. My advice is, you were not involved in this."

Rinaldi didn't have to be told twice.

"You got it. We're gone. Good luck then."

By the time Waldron reached his car, his personal radio crackled with the voice of Special Operations Commander Thomas Creighton.

"Creighton here."

"Yes, sir. James Waldron."

"Waldron, what can I do for you?"

Waldron knew his entire police career was now squarely on the line. The next words he spoke, and every communication from this moment on, would be recorded at Scotland Yard. The senior territorial commanders would be involved in the operation. The chief superintendents of the Hackney and City Divisions would be notified. Creighton would notify the assistant commissioner, who would in turn alert the chief commissioner. Before the day was out, the commissioner of the Metropolitan Police would almost certainly be monitoring the operation that James Waldron was about to unleash.

Waldron had thought it through up to this point and a bit further on. His cover story would work only if Patrick Reilly was dead, and would probably make Reilly a posthumous hero, but Waldron was willing to bet on the former and live with the latter.

"Sir, are you familiar with the Eastern European gang situation we've been dealing with these past couple of days?"

"Yes. Nasty shoot-ups over in your division. We've had another dustup in the City. Is this related?"

"Yes. To the trouble in my division. I'm afraid the situation has escalated rather severely."

"Go ahead."

"One of my sergeants has tracked down a location where they have a cache of automatic weapons."

"Go on."

"Unfortunately, there's a good chance they've taken him captive. I was to meet him here, but there's no sign of him."

"What's your assessment?"

"I think he's been taken captive by them."

"Why?"

"In a moment, but that's not my main problem."

"What is?"

"I've got about thirty Eastern Europeans who look like they're about to launch an attack."

"An attack on whom?"

"A gang of Yardies up in Hackney."

"Waldron, where are you now?"

"Sitting outside the Spitalfields Market."

"When did all this happen?"

"In the last hour. My information was that the Eastern Europeans were going to meet their Yardie colleagues in a warehouse near the River Lea in Hackney. Place set back from Homerton Road. It was supposed to be a drug buy, but it looks to me like they're preparing for some kind of raid on the place. If their past behavior is any indication, I'd look for them to be heavily armed."

"And what about your sergeant?"

"Don't know. I'm staying here until he comes out or they come out with him."

"How many men did you say?"

"I estimate thirty at this end. Heavily armed. I've been informed the Yard boys in Hackney have a good amount of weapons, too. I'm afraid Special Ops has got to be involved."

"I daresay, Waldron, if I didn't know you personally I think I'd have a hard time believing all this."

"Yes, well, unfortunately it's all true."

"What's your request, then?"

"I think this one needs an all-out mobilization. If it were me, I'd pull out everything I have. Estimate dealing with up to sixty heavily armed men. Many with automatic weapons. I wouldn't recommend staging a raid on the market here—I have no idea how many civilians may be working in there."

"Don't think that's an option. We've already got units trying to calm things down near there. Is that these people?"

"Don't know, sir. Could be."

There was a pause, then Creighton came back on.

"I'm looking at maps of the area in Hackney. More like Hackney Wick."

"I haven't checked a map."

"Homerton Road, you say."

"Yes."

"How do you know this location?"

"It's in our files. I've been tracking this thing for the last few days."

"All right, Waldron, I'm taking this completely on your request. You confirm that you are observing thirty armed IC1 individuals whom you report will be traveling en masse to attack a group of IC3s numbering approximately thirty. Is that your report?"

"Yes sir."

"All right. S.O. Command will take over now. I'm calling out two divisions of T.O. 19 riot squad troops, all Trojan Units, and all available Blue Beret squads. Your location is exactly where?"

"I'm in the parking lot inside the market area, on Spital Square, just east of the Flower Market building. I'm in a tan Ford Sierra, license L711FXD."

"Check. Maintain your position. Under no circumstances are you to intervene. We will be dispatching an ARV, unmarked, and a tracking team. Police helicopter is now being dispatched to maintain aerial observation. Stand by there, James, and wait for my orders."

"Yes sir."

Waldron could tell that Creighton was covering himself, but also launching a full-scale operation. If Waldron was right, Special Operations was about to score a major coup. Creighton's career would be forever enhanced. If Waldron was wrong, Creighton had the taped conversation, and would be covered.

Waldron fidgeted in the front seat of the car. Inside the market area, it seemed as if there was very little movement. In fact, things seemed so extraordinarily quiet that Waldron wondered for a moment if all of this was a vast exaggeration that he had concocted simply because Devlin told him there was going to be a confrontation. But no, the gunshots at Barclays Bank were real. The number of men he had seen going into the warehouse was real. And Witkowski's report from Hackney was real.

And the amount of armed men and equipment that Creighton was calling out was definitely real. The T.O. 19 riot squad troops were basically thugs, the biggest, toughest police in the force of thirty-odd-thousand men and women. They were generally armed with only truncheons and shields. Their purpose was riot control. They would be used to seal off the entire area around the warehouse. If any of the West Indian neighbors from the nearby estates or houses became agitated because of a gun battle in their midst, the riot squads would keep them under control and away from the trouble.

The three-man Trojan Units would be used for backup and specific attack points, based on commands from their tactical advisers.

The main attack would be handled by the Blue Beret squads. These men were the closest thing to a paramilitary unit within the Met. All highly trained, all heavily armed with Heckler & Koch MP5 carbines, and all ready to shoot dead on target and kill on sight. The Blue Berets no longer wore the paramilitary cloth berets; now they wore caps with checkered bands to increase their visibility. But the name "Blue Berets" had stuck. They worked in twelve-man squads. Waldron had no idea how many squads Creighton could summon, nor did he know the full extent of the arms and weapons at their disposal. What he did know was that Creighton would follow one rule: Employ a massive, overwhelming response. For all he knew, Creighton might be coordinating with Scotland Yard to call out the army.

Hell was about to burst forth in Hackney, and Waldron wanted to talk once more to the man who had unleashed it, Devlin. He left his car, carrying his radio with him, and went to a nearby phone booth.

It took three rings this time. And Devlin answered already knowing who it was.

"Waldron."

"Right. Were you sleeping?"

"Yeah."

"Well, you'd better wake up. This thing is about to explode."

"Tell me exactly."

"Exactly? Mislovic has assembled a small army out here. I've counted twenty-seven so far. God help us if he has automatic weapons for all of them. The Yardies are up in Hackney doing the same thing."

"At that warehouse address you gave me?"

"Yes."

"Okay."

Devlin looked at his watch. It was a little before four o'clock. He stared out the French doors of his suite and looked at the private garden behind the Draycott. The sky was already dark, and Devlin could tell by the gusting wind that a cold breeze would probably soon be bringing a biting rain.

"Waldron, did you notify your people?"

"Yes."

"I'd say you have less than two hours before this goes down. What's their strategy?"

"Keep track of the Yugoslavs. Let them go to Hackney. It's a much more isolated area up there. We'll have a better chance of containing it and taking them all down at once."

"Sounds right. See you when it's over, Chief Inspector. You've done a good job."

"What are you going to do?"

"Do you really want to know?"

There was a pause. "No."

Waldron hung up the pay phone.

Devlin had awakened feeling unusually refreshed and extremely hungry. He called room service and ordered a Caesar salad, a grilled chicken sandwich with chips, and a pot of coffee.

While he waited for the food, he checked the Glock and was reminded of Ben. He had already set an operation in motion through Pacific Rim to track down Ben. Devlin still didn't know if he was alive or dead.

The magazine in the Glock had only three bullets left, and Devlin didn't have the time to find more. It would have to do. Devlin knew that if he needed a weapon, there would be plenty of them up in Hackney.

Next he went through his inventory of necessary items, laying each of them carefully on his bed.

After leaving Liverpool station, he had shopped quickly at a few stores near Sloane Square. He had the largest-size *A to Z* street map published for London, a sixty-foot coil of nylon rope favored by mountain climbers, a small crowbar, and a pair of compact binoculars. In addition he laid out his Manriki chain and a set of brass knuckles he had concealed in his luggage.

By the time he finished dressing in black denim jeans, a black T-shirt, a dark wool shirt, and a pair of black rubber-soled shoes, the kind favored by soccer players who competed on artificial grass, Draycott room service reaffirmed its reputation for excellence and delivered Devlin's food hot and fresh.

Devlin ate slowly, monitoring his breathing and concentrating on envisioning what was about to happen.

He finished the coffee, feeling the caffeine powering his wakefulness.

He sat in the chair that Reilly had suffered in and closed his eyes. He cleared his mind of everything and carefully went over all his preparations.

Then he sat at the hotel room desk and studied the *A to Z* map of the area. It oriented him, and showed all the streets and open spaces in the area, but it did not show him any of the buildings. Devlin would find that out only when he arrived.

It was time. He tore out the *A to Z* page of the area and placed it in his shirt pocket. He stood up and slipped on a dark brown leather jacket, then carefully placed each item laid out on his bed into some pocket of his clothing. Looking at the large man, no one would have guessed how many tools of his trade he carried.

Devlin had now reached the dead-calm state he needed to finish this job. He estimated it would take two more moves, each of which would end in death. Then he stood up and took five steps out the door.

CHAPTER 35

It was almost four o'clock when Devlin walked out of the Draycott and headed over to Sloane Street to hail a cab. The sky was dark now, and the chill winds brought a mist of rain. It was typical London fall weather. A gust of wind blew past, shuffling leaves from one side of the street to the other.

Devlin pulled up the collar of his leather jacket. A taxi came by and Devlin stepped in. He gave the driver a location near the warehouse, but on a main road. The cabbie didn't ask where it was or how to get there. He had "the knowledge." Devlin sat back and enjoyed the civilized ride in the spacious taxi, glad that London was a town where the cabbies still had to study for their profession and knew how to do their jobs.

For the most part, the driver stuck to main thoroughfares as he wended his way out of central London and north to Hackney.

Devlin watched the neighborhoods change, slowly but surely. Hackney was nothing like the desperate, segregated urban slums that were part of American cities like New York, Detroit, and Chicago, but it was clearly different from prosperous central London. There were many buildings in disrepair, quite a few empty stores, and the businesses that were usually found in poor neighborhoods: junkyards, car repair garages, secondhand stores.

Many of the faces on the street were black. But like most of London's poorer areas, Hackney held many white faces, too.

When the driver started to head north toward the river, the area turned decidedly grim. There were many large public housing estates, some quite run-down, as were many of the cramped two-story flats jammed side by side along narrow, twisting streets. It was an area well suited to breeding the kind of criminals called Yardies.

By the time they arrived at the spot Devlin had selected, he found himself in a mostly industrial area. The rain was coming down more steadily, and all the light had gone out of the chilly November sky. There were large open tracts of land on both sides of the narrow barge canal. On the far side of the river were gas works, truck and rail terminals, depots, warehouses, and freight terminals. There was also a caravan park and empty recreation fields that looked seldom used.

Devlin paid the taxi fare and headed across the Lea Bridge to find access down to the canal. He oriented himself on the map and estimated how far up the canal he would have to walk before he reached the rear of Oliver's warehouse.

He found a dirt track that ran alongside a run-down pub just on the near side of the canal. There was very little light, which was fine with Devlin. He walked down a short incline until he reached the bank of the waterway. Within a few paces, he was absolutely isolated and hidden as he carefully picked his way along the overgrown, rutted bank. On the other side of the canal was a towpath cleared for walking. But on his side, it was hard going.

The dim light from the pub behind him disappeared almost immediately. The open area gave full range to the bitter wind gusting along the waterway. The chill rain made it even more uncomfortable, but it also decreased visibility, which suited Devlin's purpose.

After a ten-minute walk, he found himself behind what he estimated to be Oliver's warehouse. The back of the warehouse was obscured by brush, grass, and a scraggly tree, but Devlin was just able to make out the narrow path that led to the back door.

Now that he had located the warehouse, Devlin was looking for something else. It didn't take him long to find it. There was only one possibility. Farther ahead, just past a small footbridge that crossed the canal over to the towpath, was a massive, fortresslike building that had the shape of a squat L lying on its long side. From Devlin's view, the structure was all concrete and solid brick. There were no windows facing the canal. Devlin estimated the building to be about one hundred meters long, but only about twenty meters wide. He walked until he was directly behind it. Access was blocked by a ten-foot-high Cyclone fence, but there was no barbed wire or razor wire topping it, so Devlin was able to easily scale it.

At the far end of the structure—what would be the top of the L—Devlin saw a fire escape that led to the roof, which was where Devlin wanted to be.

When he reached the area under the fire escape, Devlin saw that the last platform hung almost twenty feet above ground. Devlin took out his nylon rope. He carefully coiled about twenty feet of rope on the ground, then wrapped the other end around and around until it took on the shape of a small football. He stood back and threw the wrapped end into the air. It arched over the fire escape platform and dropped back down on the other side. Devlin had wrapped the end of the rope in such a way that when the single strand came down on the fire escape platform, it jarred loose the coil and twenty-five feet of rope fell back toward Devlin.

With his climbing rope now positioned over the fire escape, Devlin simply fashioned a sling for himself at one end and hauled himself up by pulling down on the other end. He grabbed the bottom platform of the fire escape and climbed onto it. In two minutes Devlin had ascended the iron stairs to the roof.

He quietly walked to the opposite side and peered down. He had thought the fortresslike building might be abandoned. But when he looked down he saw a large paved parking area and signs that indicated he was standing on top of a power plant. A few cars and trucks were parked in front. Devlin pulled his head back, walked to the side of the roof facing Oliver's warehouse, and surveyed the area. He had a clear, bird's-eye view. Directly to the north, about two hundred feet away, Oliver's squat, ugly warehouse sat with its back to the sluggish waterway.

Devlin pulled out his powerful binoculars and surveyed the street in front of the warehouse. There was a man standing outside, seemingly guarding the front door. Most of the other buildings on the block seemed closed up. A small truck rolled past on the darkening street, illuminating the area as it went.

Devlin visualized the neat, clean two-dimensional image of

the street map he had studied. It had shown white streets surrounded by pink and green areas veined with cool blue waterways. The real streets were dark, dirty, and cold.

From his vantage point, Devlin could also see over the warehouse to the overgrown area behind it and the dark, still waters of the barge canal.

There was no other activity on the street, but Devlin noticed that high in the sky a police helicopter was slowly circling. It was so high up he could barely hear the sound of its engines. He stepped into the cold shadows at the corner of the roof's parapet. He was sure they hadn't spotted him, but he was also sure that they had enough surveillance equipment to have picked him out if they had been looking for him.

It appeared that Waldron had done his part so far. The presence of the police helicopter told him that they were assembling their forces.

There was nothing more he could do now. He leaned back in the shadows and waited.

CHAPTER 36

THE WAITING WAS over for Mislovic. Out of the men who came, Mislovic selected twenty-five. Each was armed with an AK-47 and a full thirty-round magazine. All of the men were familiar with the assault rifle; it was widely used in its various versions throughout the Eastern Bloc. At six hundred rounds per minute and with its smaller, lighter bullets, the AK was the perfect weapon for the close-in assault that Mislovic was planning.

Mislovic had already received a report on the warehouse from the man Zenko had sent to scout it. He knew the layout and he had formulated a plan of attack. He kept his orders to the men very simple. Experience had taught him that the simpler the order, the greater the chance of it being carried out once a battle started.

Zenko repeated the order to each of the men: "When you get the word, go in and shoot anybody who is black until they all stop moving. Don't get in front of each other's line of fire. Don't shoot each other."

Zenko divided the men up into five cars, while he and Mislovic rode in the red Saab Oliver had given them.

They had two passengers with them: the idiot from Berwick Street, Bobby, and a wiry Irishman dressed in black overalls whom hardly anyone had noticed. He wore round steel-framed glasses, had his hair cut to a short bristle, and gave the impression of being some sort of mechanic. He spoke to no one and during the entire time men had been assembling he had confined himself to working on the Saab. No one but Mislovic knew his name, and he only knew the man's first name, Liam.

Zenko had no idea of what Mislovic needed the idiot for, and only a vague idea of what the Irishman was going to do.

Czmenceau drove the Saab. He didn't seem to care about either of them.

On the way to Hackney, the conversations in the various cars ranged from boisterous banter to a few nervous comments.

At the warehouse, Oliver had instructed his men to construct a makeshift table using a large slab of half-inch plywood laid across concrete blocks. On the rough plywood board was a gleaming Haliburton aluminum case filled with what looked like ten kilos of cocaine. Two men stood on either side of the table guarding it with Oliver's last two Ingram MAC-10s. Only one of the guns had a full clip.

Oliver stepped back and viewed the scene. It looked perfect. Just like in the movies. He expected the Yugoslav to be very impressed.

It was nothing more than a distraction. The plastic-wrapped kilos were sugar. They were meant to capture the Yugoslavs' attention so they wouldn't see the men that Oliver had carefully placed throughout the warehouse. Ten were up in the mezzanine, positioned so that they could shoot clearly down onto the floor of the warehouse in deadly crisscrossing lines of fire.

Ten more were on the main floor, concealed on the far sides. One man guarded the street door entrance. The big rolling steel door was firmly shut.

Outside a dozen men hid in doorways and shadows at the north and south ends of the street.

Oliver knew Mislovic would walk in with an armed guard. But there was no way any of them would walk out.

Back at Spitalfields, Waldron saw the first of Mislovic's cars pull out from the warehouse. Each car carried five armed men. He called in to Special Ops and Creighton answered immediately. He told Waldron that his teams would be tailing Mislovic's cars and that Waldron should drive over to the street that ran along the west side of the Liverpool station train yards. He would meet Waldron there with one of the Met's four on-call helicopters and fly to the warehouse site in Hackney.

Waldron drove quickly through the streets. The train yards

were less than half a mile from his location, and he didn't waste any time, but the big police helicopter was already there. The noise of its thundering engine was much louder than he'd have imagined. A Special Ops constable led him to an area set off from the train traffic. Creighton was sitting strapped in his seat, a huge grin on his face. He wore the checkered cap of the Blue Berets and a NATO-style sweater with epaulets bearing full insignia of his rank. Underneath the sweater were his officer's white shirt and tie. He looked more like a military man than a police official. And he looked as if he were enjoying every minute of the crisis.

He yelled over the engine, "James! Get in. We want to get there ahead of them."

As he climbed into the ungainly aircraft, Waldron realized why Creighton appeared to be so enthralled. The call to arms had come so quickly that there hadn't been time for other police officials to become involved. Creighton was heading up the largest armed operation in the history of the Met, and he was in command. Success would ensure his place in Met history. Waldron didn't want to even think about what failure would do to both of their careers.

The seat next to Creighton was empty. An aide sat in the seat behind Creighton. He was a young man in civilian clothes. His police ID was on a beaded chain which he wore around his neck. He was extremely thin and appeared to be so nervous that he was shaking slightly, but Waldron couldn't be completely sure the shaking wasn't caused by the reverberations of the helicopter's powerful engine. Waldron finally decided the young man didn't want to be there either.

Creighton yelled over the noise of the engine, "By seventeen-thirty hours I'll have in excess of two hundred men assembled up there." He turned to his aide. "Give me the map, William."

The assistant handed him an enlarged photocopy of a street map, already folded to reveal the area around the warehouse.

Creighton's beefy forefinger mashed down onto a red circle on the map. "Here's the warehouse, if you've got the address right. You have got it right, haven't you, James?"

"I have."

"Over here, on the other side of the canal, is a large recreational field. You can't see it from the warehouse. The last teams should be assembling there now. We'll be out of sight, but close enough to move in and surround this place when we need to."

Waldron pointed to spots on the map and shouted back, "The men are going to have to get across Eastway. Can they do it quickly enough to close down these intersections?"

Creighton pointed to an area to the north, "We'll have enough over on Wick Field Recreation Ground to do that."

"Why not take a contingent over to Mabley Green here. That way they can close off the front or back end of the warehouse, and shut down Homerton Road, too."

Creighton studied the map for a moment.

Waldron added, "The Yugoslavs will probably come over on Lea Bridge. They won't see you if you stay south and west."

Creighton followed Waldron's finger and decided to agree. "Good idea. Then we'll box them in here, here, and here. The canal will keep them from going anywhere east."

Creighton turned to his aide. "Are we in touch with the teams following them?"

"Yes, sir. We can put it over your headset anytime."

"Are they headed for Hackney?"

"Yes, sir."

Creighton tapped the shoulder of the pilot and told him, "Okay, let's go."

While Creighton was busy checking with other police officers, Waldron turned his attention back to the map.

He pointed to the river that ran behind the block where the warehouse was located and asked Creighton, "What about the canal?"

"What about it? They can't get across. If they go along the bank, we'll catch them at either end. We can track them from the air. I've got an observation helicopter up there right now. We have to find some roof or high point on the ground. Whatever we can't see, the helicopters can. They'll inform us of everything that happens on the street."

Waldron saw that Creighton wasn't going to take any more suggestions, so he let it drop.

The copilot turned and announced, "The control tower has

us cleared. Hackney Division says the first groups are in place inside the park."

Waldron spoke up. "You've got time to move them."

Creighton didn't answer him. Instead he told the copilot, "Patch me in to Jones at Lippet Hill."

Waldron sat and stared out the window while Creighton gave orders to move half their men into position on Mabley Green. Waldron realized that not only had Creighton taken his word on what was about to happen, he had also taken his advice.

Creighton yelled over the engine noise.

"James."

"Yes?"

"My posterior is hanging out quite a ways on this one."

"Yes, sir."

"I'm not going to be disappointed, am I?"

"No sir. You're not."

"Good."

For whom? thought Waldron.

The police helicopter rose slowly off the ground, then quickly gained altitude and banked left. All of London was suddenly at their feet. There was no turning back now, thought Waldron. Unless I want to jump out of this thing.

The cold rain had eased off a bit, but as the chopper plowed through the night sky, Waldron watched streaks of moisture slide across his window. It seemed quite cold inside the cabin. By the time the helicopter slowly settled onto the grassy field in Hackney, Waldron was chilled to the bone. He had to clench his teeth to keep them from chattering. He wondered if that was only because of the cold.

Creighton jumped out of the cabin, full of command energy. He didn't seem fazed by the cold evening air or the slight mist of rain. He strode across the field to a knot of men waiting for him. Waldron followed behind, not sure of what he was supposed to do at this point. He knew he had now become useless. He had played his part—his part according to Devlin. He had half a mind to slink off to the nearest pub and sip whiskey until this was over.

Waldron checked his watch. It was ten minutes to five. He

calculated that they didn't have much time to get in place before Mislovic arrived by car.

Creighton was met by the chief superintendent of the Hackney Division, the Special Ops chief tactical adviser, and a three-man team of Blue Berets in bulletproof vests. Two of the Blue Berets carried H&K carbines, the other a menacing ARWEN—ENfield Anti-Riot Weapon.

Within five minutes, Creighton had issued orders to everyone who needed them and was running off to an unmarked van that would take him, his aide, the chief tactical adviser, and their three-man bodyguard team to their observation post.

Creighton ran by Waldron and told him, "Come on."

Too late to slink into the night now, thought Waldron.

Creighton and his entourage made the same choice Devlin had. They, however, didn't need to climb the fire escape. They walked right into the building and up an internal staircase that led to the roof. Devlin barely had time to jump over the parapet and back to the fire escape before they burst onto the roof.

Devlin silently descended two levels and crouched against the wall of the building. In his dark clothes, half hidden by the metalwork of the fire escape, he could hardly be seen, even if the men above him were to look directly down toward him. Devlin was actually happy they had decided to perch above him. Because they were keyed up for the coming battle and because they were outside, the men on the roof above naturally spoke in loud voices. Devlin could hear almost every word. They had spotted Mislovic's cars pulling into the streets north of the warehouse. Devlin peered through his binoculars and counted six cars. The armed caravan stopped and filled most of the street one block north of the warehouse. Devlin thought it looked like a funeral cortege that had lost its way.

Up on the roof, Creighton was shouting orders into a cellular phone to begin moving his force into the area. First would come the Trojan Units, which were more mobile, to seal off key intersections surrounding the warehouse. Then the Blue Berets would move in on foot. Finally, the riot squad police would form a third outer ring to seal off the area from outsiders coming in, and from insiders getting out if they made it past the Blue Berets and Trojan Units.

Down on the street, Zenko was the first one out of the red Saab. He walked over to each of the five cars loaded with Mislovic's men. He gave the drivers careful instructions. Three cars drove off. Creighton, the observation helicopters, and Devlin watched the cars wend their way through the quiet narrow streets and take a position at the south end of the street where the warehouse was located. The Saab and other two cars remained north of the warehouse. It was obvious Mislovic wanted to attack from two sides.

Zenko returned to the Saab and drove it to the intersection just around the corner from Oliver's warehouse. The other two cars followed and parked behind him.

The only other cars moving in the area were Creighton's Trojan Units, which were driven by top-class drivers, men who had trained for months. From his elevated view, Devlin caught glimpses of the powerful Rovers tearing through the backstreets of Hackney, converging from several points on intersections circling the warehouse. They were taking up positions far away from where the actual fighting might occur, but would effectively seal off any exit from the area.

As each ARV arrived at its designated position, the three-man units quickly turned their cars into bulletproof barricades. They draped their vehicles with Kevlar blankets and set up bulletproof shields to provide additional cover. Finally, they placed powerful searchlights where they would do the most good in illuminating the dark streets at the right moment.

But for now, everything was being done in the dark. Devlin could not clearly see any of the Blue Beret troops filtering into the area. The only noises discernible were Creighton's voice and the occasional crackle of static on personal radio sets.

Behind the scenes, at Scotland Yard, at Special Ops headquarters on Old Street, and at their training center in Lippet Hill, it was much different. A flood of communications was pouring in from dozens of transmissions. A bank of senior officers in each location were answering questions and monitoring the operations. No one quite understood how chaotic the situation could easily become. Over two hundred heavily armed men, nerves taut, were moving around in dark fields and streets in an area where no one had much familiarity.

Somewhere, far off in the dark night, a police siren suddenly hee-hawed for a few seconds, then fell silent. Devlin imagined the men above him grinding their teeth in frustration waiting for the siren to fall silent. He smiled. Someone was getting his ass chewed out. But he was glad the siren had sounded. It had been too quiet in the area. As if someone dangerous walking through a jungle had silenced the birds. A sudden burst of noise that was common to urban areas was needed. In a strange way, it broke the tension and allowed Devlin to relax and focus. He settled back against the dark, wet brick wall and watched, and listened.

He heard Creighton checking off a number of locations, and assumed they were spots that were now manned by his troops. Devlin estimated that soon the areas north, west, and south would be closed off. That left only the east side of the warehouse, which was bordered by the canal. He wondered if the Met had any police boats. They could be used to patrol the waterway and prevent escape in that direction. In fact, the Met did have police boats, but they had been thought of a bit too late. They mostly patrolled the Thames, and two of them were now gamely navigating their way through the maze of waterways that would eventually take them into Hackney.

Devlin spotted movement at the head of the street where Mislovic was parked in the red Saab. He watched Mislovic get out of the car with a small man dressed in dirty blue jeans and a sweater striped in white and blue. Devlin focused his binoculars and saw that the small man was carrying a bright yellow canvas bag slung over his shoulder bearing the name and logo of the Cycle Messenger Service. It was Bobby, the idiot from Mislovic's Soho headquarters.

Bobby nodded constantly while Mislovic spoke to him. Devlin watched as Mislovic gently turned him toward the street entrance door of the warehouse, patted him on the back, and sent him on his way.

Zenko turned to Mislovic. "I can't believe we're leaving this up to a nitwit."

"Shut up. He's perfect."

Mislovic, Zenko, Creighton, Waldron, Oliver's Yard bwouys and Rastas, and several of Mislovic's crew watched as Bobby walked resolutely to the door, opened it, and went straight in. An eerie calm and quiet descended on the street as the boy disappeared behind the closing door.

CHAPTER 37

DEVLIN HAD TO steel himself against the wet cold. The lack of movement didn't allow him to generate much body heat. With everything so silent forty feet below him, he felt as if he were all alone. Even the radios crackling on the roof above fell silent.

Mislovic's men waited in their cars with the engines idling. Creighton and over two hundred cops waited. The Yard men hidden at either end of the block waited. The only sign of their presence was the slight smell of burning marijuana as one of the Rastas fed his high.

Oliver had posted only a single guard outside the warehouse so as not to alarm Mislovic. He stood alone, looking as if he wished he weren't there.

Inside the warehouse it was also rather quiet, but much brighter than out on the street. Oliver had turned on banks of exposed fluorescent lighting fixtures that hung at odd spots around the ceiling. He wanted his men to have a clear view of their intended victims.

When Bobby had arrived at the warehouse, he had told the man outside he had a delivery for Mr. Oliver. Because he looked to be so harmless, Bobby was allowed to enter. He was so thin and gangly and odd-looking that no one considered him at all threatening. He stood on the main floor of the warehouse and looked around. There were two guards near the door. One of them held a hand on Bobby's chest while the other looked through his messenger bag and frisked him. After he was done he told Bobby, "Gimme the package."

Bobby handed him a small padded envelope that had been stapled and taped on all four sides. He held out a clipboard with a form and told the man, "You have to sign, you have to sign."

The guard ignored him and walked toward Oliver with the envelope. Bobby followed him, holding out the clipboard. "Mister, you have to sign for it."

Bobby's pleas attracted Oliver's attention. He saw his man with a package and Bobby following him. They were in the middle of the floor. Oliver yelled, "Get dat guy out of here."

The guard with the package turned and told Bobby, "You. Out. Now!"

Bobby stopped. The yell surprised him. The whole thing confused him. Then he suddenly turned and started walking for the door. He decided to forget about the clipboard and concentrate on the thing Mr. Mislovic said was most important.

He walked back in the direction he had come in. Oliver's man watched him for a moment and then turned back to bring the small padded envelope to Oliver.

Nobody else paid any attention to Bobby. No one noticed that he turned away from the street door where he had entered. Now he was walking straight for the big steel rolling door that sealed the entire front of the warehouse.

Oliver ignored Bobby, too. He was concerned about the envelope in his man's hand, and snatched it from him. While he was looking for a return address, Bobby kept on walking. As he approached the big door, he was muttering something to himself. He was concentrating so hard he had his head down. He was saying to himself over and over again, "The green one, the green one."

Outside, Creighton was still on the roof observing everything that happened on the entire block in front of the warehouse. He knew that Mislovic had arrived with cars filled with men. He knew something was going to happen here. But absolutely nothing had occurred of any importance.

Just then Devlin spotted movement up the street. He looked through his binoculars and saw the red Saab turn the corner and continue slowly to the front of the warehouse. When it reached a spot parallel to the warehouse, the driver stopped the car and backed up into a Y-turn, then pulled forward so that the car pointed directly at the big warehouse door.

Devlin watched the maneuver. The car stopped about ten

yards from the warehouse. At first, Devlin thought it might be getting ready to ram open the door, but there wasn't nearly enough room to gain sufficient speed.

A small man got out of the Saab and stood next to it with the driver's door open. It was the Irishman, Liam. He leaned into the car and seemed to be making some sort of adjustment to the seat.

If Devlin could have seen the inside the car, Mislovic's plan would have become more obvious. Liam had changed a few things on Oliver's gift. The ignition lock had been removed from the steering column so no keys were needed. A steering wheel lock had been installed. Liam now squatted down and slid home the hook on the lock so that the steering wheel could not be turned. The car's front wheels were pointed straight ahead.

Liam's crudest addition to the Saab was sitting on the front seat. It was a cinder block. He took the heavy block and placed it on the accelerator. It pushed the pedal right down to the floor. The idling engine revved to thirty thousand rpm's.

Inside the warehouse, Bobby was almost to the big door. Outside, the guard started to walk toward the red Saab pointed at his warehouse with its engine screaming. He was convinced they were going to ram his door with the car.

Liam straightened up and closed the door of the car. He smiled at the guard as if to say, Yes, come on over and help me with this crazy car. The guard was confused. Then he noticed that Liam was holding a broomstick in his hand, and he became even more befuddled. He drew his gun and came slowly toward Liam.

Inside the warehouse, one of the guards finally noticed Bobby and yelled at him, "No! Over there, stupid. The other door."

Bobby had often been called stupid. He didn't like it the first time it had happened, and he didn't like it now. He concentrated harder. He was going to do this. He kept walking until he was standing in front of a rectangular switch box mounted on the wall next to the steel door. The box had two large buttons on it. One button was red, the other black. Bobby was thinking. He was exerting the maximum amount of brainpower he could muster. For perhaps the only time in his life, he was about to make a conclusion based on deductive logic. Mislovic had told him to press a green button. But there was no green button. There was only a black button and a red button. Which one should he press? Bobby stood staring at the two buttons. He squinted his eyes. He furrowed his brow. He thought furiously. Finally, something came to him. He knew that red meant stop. So probably, he figured, he shouldn't touch the red. It must be the black. He mashed his thumb against the black button just as Oliver finally managed to tear the taped and stapled envelope open.

The big electric motor that turned the winch that rolled open the big door kicked into life.

Inside the envelope was a set of car keys wrapped in newspaper. A note attached to the keys said, *I'm giving you back your car.*

Oliver had no idea what the message meant. And then in the split second that he realized the message was from Mislovic, his attention was grabbed by the sound of his warehouse door grinding open.

He looked up just as Bobby scooted under the door.

Then everything seemed to happen at once.

Oliver yelled, "Shut da fucking door."

Outside, the guard who had been walking toward the red Saab turned around at the sound of the opening door. As he turned his head Liam casually raised the hand that had been hidden behind his back and shot him in the left ear. The inside of his head exploded, and he went down.

Oliver's yell sent two men running for the door switch. The door was already more than halfway up.

Mislovic stood at the north end of the block screaming, "Let it go, let it go."

Bobby was running as fast as he could toward Zenko, who waved furiously at him to come on.

Liam implacably stood his ground by the roaring engine of the Saab. Perhaps he couldn't hear Mislovic's yelling. But he was a patient, methodical man. He was merely waiting for the door to be fully open.

Finally, one of Oliver's men made it to the switch box. He slammed his hand against the red button. The door halted in mid-flight for a split second, and then with a *chunk* reversed direction.

Mislovic was screaming, "Do it!"

Liam saw the door reverse direction and immediately leaned into the car and used the broomstick to shove the gearshift from neutral to drive. The Saab's transmission almost cracked apart as the engine's enormous power and torque were transferred to the gears. The car's wheels spun just long enough for Liam to pull his arm back out of the window before the tire rubber gripped and the car bolted forward.

The rear end fishtailed and wobbled, but the lock held the steering wheel in place, and the car raced toward the warehouse.

Three men looked out from under the closing door. The car was racing forward, right at them. One of them had enough time to slide a cartridge into his handgun and pull the trigger. It didn't make a bit of difference to the three thousand pounds of car racing forward.

Just as the steel warehouse door lowered to the height of the car roof, the Saab slammed into it. The collision was impressive. The warehouse door was smashed off its rollers and stuck. The entire roof of the Saab peeled back like the lid of a sardine can.

Liam was an IRA bomb specialist who hadn't worked at his trade since the cease-fire declaration. He'd been anxious to work on this job and had spared no effort. His plan was for Oliver's Saab to smash into the back wall of the warehouse, which would detonate seventy-five kilos of high velocity dynamite placed behind the car's grille. That in turn would ignite four incendiary bombs that were placed in the hollows of all four doors. The objective was to cause a huge, fiery explosion.

But Liam didn't know that Oliver had set up a gauntlet of weapons inside the warehouse. Mislovic had said nothing about an ambush. As the car screamed into the warehouse, a hail of gunfire poured down on it from the men in the mezzanine, and into it from the men on the main floor.

The Yardies thought they were shooting at whoever was in the car. They had no idea they were shooting at a moving bomb. The red-hot bullets ignited the incendiary bombs before the car made it halfway into the warehouse.

Walls of flame shot from both sides of the car, ballooning out and up in a floor-to-ceiling blossom of flame. The front of the Saab slammed into the back wall of the warehouse. Instead of exploding *before* the incendiary bombs, the dynamite exploded a few seconds after. The massive concussion that ensued blew the air inside the warehouse in all directions so quickly that the flames were pushed outward and snuffed against the inside walls and ceiling of the structure.

The effect was to burn everyone directly in its path for a few seconds, and then slam them with deadly force until they hit something solid.

Most of the men on the floor of the warehouse were killed. The shooters on the mezzanine were spared some of the blast and flames, but almost all were burned and knocked senseless. Blood ran from their noses and ears. Skulls cracked, eyes were charred in their sockets, bones were crushed.

In the back of the warehouse, Oliver had been facing the car, so he was spared some of the flames. And because he was running toward the back when the car skidded into the warehouse, the blast did not kill him. But it did lift him off his feet and slam him into a reinforced glass window at the back wall. The force of his body and the explosion shattered the window, and he was blown out of the building. He flew ten feet in the air and landed hard amidst the weeds and rubble of the ground near the canal. He looked like a big, broken, and burned rag doll.

Out on the street, the explosion sounded like a huge suppressed *whump*. The ground shook, shock waves reverberated, and a frightening billow of dark greasy flames plumed out under the half-closed steel door.

From his position on the roof, Creighton jerked his head back so quickly from the blast that he pulled a muscle in his neck. "Jesus God Almighty," he muttered.

As soon as Mislovic's men heard the explosion, they shoved their cars into gear and came careening around the corners at both ends of the street. They screeched to a halt in front of the warehouse.

The power of the blast and the scope of the destruction

shocked everyone, especially Waldron. He had never seen anything like it, and now Mislovic's men were pouring out of their cars, AK-47 assault rifles in hand, taking up positions to fire into the warehouse.

Devlin watched intently, struggling to pick out Mislovic from the confusion of cars and men that had converged in front of the warehouse.

Burned and battered men came reeling outside. Some of them were shooting as they came out, but in their condition, they were easy targets for Mislovic's men.

The Eastern Europeans simply opened fire on the battered, outgunned Yardies. The AKs laid down a merciless barrage. The first men out were shredded by the high-velocity bullets.

Up on the roof of the power station, Creighton was screaming into his cellular phone. He was ordering all troops to converge on the warehouse.

The suddenness and surprise of Mislovic's attack had stunned everyone. But now it was Mislovic's turn to be surprised.

From both ends of the block, the men hidden outside by Oliver opened fire on the Yugoslavs. At first, Mislovic's men had no idea where the shooting was coming from. Many of them were behind cars, which sheltered them from the warehouse but left them exposed to the shooters at both ends of the street. The twelve surviving Yardies outside were firing everything they had into the knot of men grouped in front of the warehouse. Mislovic's killers were caught in a deadly cross fire. They were so tightly gathered that most of the Yardie bullets found their targets. Blood splattered, glass flew in all directions, the sheet metal of the cars was ripped and punctured. Five of Mislovic's men were killed within seconds.

By the time the Yugoslavs realized where the shots were coming from, more of them had been hit.

Amidst the screaming and yelling, Zenko began pulling the men near him away from the cover of the cars. He pushed and shoved and kicked them in the direction of the Yardies shooting from the north. Zenko fired his handgun at the Yardies, and the others finally started laying down bursts from the AKs. Most of the Yardies had good cover, so only one of them was hit. They stayed under cover and shot back. Many of the

Yugoslavs had emptied their thirty-shot magazines. They had to scramble to retrieve loaded weapons from their fallen comrades. Suddenly, the battle had turned.

Zenko grabbed the man next to him and stepped out from behind the cars. He ran toward his attackers, snarling and yelling for the men to follow him. Two came with him and he shoved a third forward, who was so panicked to be out in the open he emptied his AK in seconds. The others hung back, but Zenko charged ahead up the street. One of Kingsmen's Rastas casually leaned out of a doorway and shot Zenko five times in the chest and face.

Creighton continued to shout into his phone for the police to "close in, close in," but the unit commanders were not eager to bring their men into a raging gun battle, so they advanced slowly and carefully.

The few survivors of the explosion had regrouped inside the warehouse and started shooting out at the Yugoslavs. Now Mislovic's men were under fire from three sides.

Waldron and the others watched the new wave of slaughter. They were far enough removed so that they could safely view the entire battle, but near enough to clearly hear the gunshots and see men hit by bullets. It seemed too horrible to be real. But it was real. Waldron began to scream for them to stop. But the Yardies were not going to stop shooting from their protected positions. And the Yugoslavs could not stop. It seemed to Waldron that they had all lost their minds. One of the Yardies charged out of the warehouse firing his automatic. Two of Mislovic's fighters were so enraged, they jumped out from behind the cars and ran at him, firing their AKs on full automatic. The Yardie shot one of them dead before he was ripped apart by bullets. Two more men had died in a matter of seconds. Waldron wanted to turn away, to stop looking, but he couldn't. He could not refuse to bear witness to something he had been so instrumental in causing.

The full impact and dimension of Devlin's plan was finally and terribly clear to him. Which made it even more impossible for Waldron to bear the sight of it. Waldron had seen victims of a shooting, but he had never seen anyone shot. Now he was witnessing a carnage so sudden and so savage, he knew that the images of blood and savagery and death would be burned forever in his memory.

The first police sirens were finally approaching. The Trojan Units had been called up, and screeched to a halt near the north and south corners of the blocks, almost directly behind the Yardies. Their Rover headlights and powerful searchlights illuminated the area. Voices came over loudspeakers yelling for the men to stop firing their weapons.

Mislovic stood amidst his men evaluating what had happened. He had not expected Oliver to be armed and ready for any kind of a fight. He had certainly not expected him to have men outside the warehouse. With the police fast approaching, he knew the situation was untenable.

Devlin had picked out Mislovic's steel gray hair early on and now kept him in sight through his compact binoculars. He saw Mislovic suddenly run out from the cover of the cars and head away from the warehouse. Mislovic was smart. He ran hunched over, moving fast to make himself a difficult target. He ran straight for the building just north of the warehouse, hugging close to the walls so that he would be out of sight and covered from most of the Yardie fire.

Seconds after Mislovic made his break, Devlin was moving. He could not allow Mislovic to escape.

Devlin slid down the handrails of the fire escape and landed with a thud on the platform one story down. The thundering sound attracted the attention of the cops on the roof. Waldron looked over the parapet, as did Creighton and the others.

They saw Devlin quickly make his way to the bottom landing of the fire escape.

Down on the street, Mislovic stayed close to the cover of the buildings on the east side and made his way up the block. He ducked in and out of doorways to avoid being shot.

When Creighton saw Devlin heading down the fire escape, he bellowed, "Who the hell is that?"

Waldron answered, "I don't know," and wished he really did not.

They watched as Devlin jumped down to ground level, rolled, and came up on his feet. Without missing a step, he was racing toward the warehouse.

Creighton asked again, "Who the hell is that?"

This time Waldron didn't answer. He wondered what Devlin was going to do now. It looked as if his enemies would certainly die in the horrible scene on the street. If they didn't kill each other, they would be shot or arrested by the police. Why was he running into the battle? Why was he risking getting shot?

By now dozens of police were massing at either end of the block. Commands were repeated over the loudspeakers: "Cease fire. This is the police. Put down your weapons."

It was too late. Whatever men were still alive weren't going to surrender to anyone. Somebody unleashed a spray of bullets at the police. The Blue Berets had maintained discipline and control and had resisted firing on the armed men in front of them, but now that restraint vanished. The highly trained marksmen at both ends of the block opened fire. It was terrifying. Hundreds of bullets turned into thousands. Most of the surviving men out on the street were cut down in the brutal barrage.

Creighton seemed powerless. He yelled into his cellular phone, "Cease fire! Cease fire!" Nothing stopped it. He threw the phone down, turned, and stormed toward the door that led down from the roof.

Devlin had to dive into a doorway to avoid being cut down by the police barrage, but he continued to scan the area until he spotted Mislovic furiously kicking and pounding at a door about thirty yards up the street to the north.

Mislovic aimed the gun in his hand at the door lock and started shooting. He still couldn't get it open.

Now an announcement came over several loudspeakers ordering the police to cease fire. The shooting stopped within five seconds. The din of gunfire had suddenly ceased from all sides. Now the horrid sound of wounded and dying men could be heard.

The shock of the police assault had numbed everyone, even the highly trained police personnel. But not Devlin. He used the lull to dash across the street just as Mislovic managed to finally break open the door and disappear into the building. Devlin ran toward the open door.

Waldron had remained on the roof watching Devlin while Creighton left to take command on the street. When he saw

Devlin moving very fast up the street and into the building, he turned and ran toward the exit door that led off the roof.

The police were starting to organize themselves for a slow, careful advance on the warehouse. The outside ring of riot troops was encircling the area, sealing it off completely. Communications were crackling over the personal radios and headsets. Creighton was now conferring with the command center at Scotland Yard. Nobody had seen Mislovic escape. And nobody had noticed Devlin disappear after him, except Waldron.

Mislovic made it to the back of a ground-floor hallway. He kicked open another door which led to a small room cluttered with junk. At the back of the room was a metal door locked from the inside by a heavy iron bar. Mislovic pulled off the bar, pushed open the door, and stepped out into the rubble-strewn grassy area that bordered the canal. The smoldering warehouse building was about fifty yards to the south. There was black smoke rising from the roof of the warehouse, but no flames. The heat from the blast had started fires inside the walls of the warehouse that were just about to burst into a full-blown inferno.

Mislovic couldn't see any movement behind the warehouse. He looked to his left and saw that the bank of the river ran almost as far as he could see. About fifty yards farther north was a small walkway that crossed the canal and connected with the towpath on the other side. It was clear that his best chance of escape was to get on the towpath, move fast along it and look for a way out of the area.

Mislovic could see police personnel and vehicles assembled in the recreation field far off to the east, but he was sure they would not see him if he could get to the walkway and head back south on the other side.

He started to run/walk through the trash and rubble that lined the bank of the waterway.

Out on the street of blood, at either end of the block, the police had formed two phalanxes, one behind a huge emergency service truck, the other behind an armored personnel vehicle. Both ranks of armed Blue Berets walked slowly toward the middle of the street. Any men who weren't dead were either bleeding or in so much shock that they had given up.

Devlin ran quickly through the building, following Mislovic's trail to the open door in the back. He pulled out the Glock, held it pointed up, and stepped outside.

He immediately looked to his left and saw that Mislovic had reached the base of the walkway that traversed the canal. However, Mislovic's progress was blocked by a Cyclone fence about six feet high, topped with razor wire, that prevented access to the walkway. Mislovic reached down and grabbed the bottom of the fence. He tried to pull it up enough so that he could crawl under it. He had the strength that desperation provides and managed to pull the bottom of the fence out of the ground, but no matter how hard he tried, he couldn't bend the fence back far enough to give himself room to crawl under.

Devlin watched him carefully as he quickly closed the distance between them.

As desperate as he was, Mislovic gave up trying to pull up and bend back the fence. He was caught between deciding whether to climb over the top and face the razor wire or to plunge into the scummy canal water and try to swim to the other side. He started moving to his right, imagining the cold, wet stench of the river surrounding him, when he heard the voice of Devlin.

"Stop!"

Mislovic had shoved his gun into a holster when he'd attempted to pry up the fence, but the sound of Devlin's voice was enough to make him grab the gun, spin around, and fire.

The shot went wide, but it should have forced whoever was after him to at least duck. Devlin didn't even flinch. He was completely focused. From less than twenty feet away, Devlin squeezed off a shot aimed directly at Mislovic's right biceps.

Mislovic's arm was bent to hold the gun in firing position. If someone had drawn an X on the skin at the exact center of Mislovic's slightly flexed biceps, Devlin's bullet would have penetrated at the point where the lines crossed.

The muscle was split apart and the arm was shattered. Mislovic was spun around and bounced against the fence. Amazingly, Mislovic still held on to the gun, but there was no way he could pull the trigger.

He lay against the fence, helpless. The shock of the bullet short-circuited his brain. He couldn't get his legs under him to stand up and run. He couldn't fire back. Devlin calmly walked the rest of the distance to him, grabbed him by the throat, and pulled the man to his feet, shoving him back against the fence. He kept him pinned to the fence while he snatched the gun out of his hand. It was a Russian Makarov.

There was still enough hate and fight left in Mislovic for him to snarl at Devlin and grab at his wrist.

Devlin pulled him off the fence and shoved him back against it.

"You're going back. Now!"

Mislovic screamed, "Fuck you!"

"You're going down with the others."

Mislovic struggled to get control of himself. "Wait. Wait a minute. Don't do this. I'm worth ten times more to you alive than dead or in jail. Don't be stupid. Think about what you're doing. You think that a lousy hundred thousand split with crooked cops is some kind of score? I can give you millions. I can guarantee safety for the woman and her child."

"Shut up!"

Devlin spun Mislovic around and shoved him back toward the warehouse.

Mislovic walked slowly, clutching his arm, but talking all the time.

"What are you trying to do? You have the money. You think it's going to make a difference if the cops arrest me here? If they arrest me, so what? I do a few years in your soft jails and I'm out again."

Devlin didn't respond.

"Why do you insist on playing the hero? That bitch niece of mine used you just like she used everybody else, including her husband."

Mislovic turned to see Devlin's reaction. There was none.

"You hear what I said? I'm *her* uncle, not her stupid husband's. She lied to you when she told you her husband was my nephew. None of this would have happened if it wasn't for her."

Still Devlin didn't respond.

"She ran the scheme. She used me to find out if her husband's source could get large amounts. She pushed hard. Right from the beginning."

Devlin shouted, "Walk."

Mislovic turned to face him, walking backwards, but still talking.

"She ran that pathetic husband, and she's running you. He got himself killed for her. You almost did, too. She tried to get me to call off the Yardies, but I wouldn't, so she called you in."

Mislovic stopped walking. He faced Devlin. His confidence and his air of command had returned.

"So tell me. What good is this going to do?"

Devlin's response was to raise the Glock and point it at Mislovic's head.

"Mr. Mills, don't you think I know that your sister's name is Mislovic? Don't you think I knew Annie was involved in this drug business up to her neck?"

"You knew she lied to you?"

"Yes."

"So why did you risk your life for a woman who was lying to you?"

"Because I loved her. Because you and these other savages don't have the right to kill her. Because her daughter doesn't deserve to die. Because I got too involved. Because things happened too fast. Because I didn't want to die. Because I still stare at her whenever I see her face."

Mislovic sneered at Devlin. "You're a fool. Pull the damn trigger and get it over with. My arm hurts like hell."

Devlin lowered the Glock. He stared at Mislovic for a moment and said, "You're not worth one of my bullets."

Mislovic screamed at him, "You don't have the guts to do it. Go get the cops, you worm. You'll be looking over your shoulder the rest of your life."

Just then, something moving behind Mislovic caught Devlin's attention. From the burned rubble and mess behind the warehouse, about ten yards away, a figure was staggering toward them. It was Oliver. The skin on the left side of his body was blistered and burned. His clothes were seared into his raw red flesh. His left eye was sealed shut. His face and body had been deeply torn and cut by the thick window glass. Internal injuries were sending fires of pain through him, but the fires of his hatred burned even more intensely. He recognized Mislovic, even from behind, and continued to take his painful, wretched steps to get to him.

Devlin watched as Oliver struggled to close the distance. He looked back at Mislovic and said, "No. You look over your own damn shoulder."

Mislovic turned. For a few moments, he had no idea who it was coming toward him, and then in amazement he muttered, "Oliver."

Devlin said, "So that's him."

Mislovic nodded. "Yes. What's left of him."

Mislovic could not take his eyes off the mutilated specter moving toward him.

Devlin pointed the Glock toward the canal and fired one round into the black water. He handed the gun to Mislovic.

"You've got one bullet in there."

Mislovic eagerly took the gun in his left hand. His left-handed accuracy was shaky so he started to step toward Oliver to close the distance between them, but Devlin pushed him aside and walked toward Oliver first.

Mislovic regained his balance and tried to aim, but now Devlin blocked his shot. He had to wait for Devlin to walk past Oliver, which gave Devlin the opportunity to calmly hand Mislovic's gun to Oliver.

Oliver stood where he was, exerting every ounce of his concentration in order to grip the gun Devlin had given him and aim it at Mislovic.

Devlin continued walking. He didn't even look back when the shooting started. He never knew who shot first, but Oliver and Mislovic were less than six feet apart when the guns went off. They died within seconds of each other.

Annie unlocked the makeshift plywood door to her apartment. It was two days after the warehouse massacre.

Devlin and Elizabeth stood behind her. As soon as the door opened, the little girl ran past them to see her room.

Annie and Devlin entered the apartment after her, and stood together in the empty living room. The last time they had been in the room was taken up with the rush to get out before Hinton, Mislovic, and the others trapped them. It seemed to Annie as if weeks had passed since that day.

On the way from the clinic, they hadn't spoken very much at all. Partly because they didn't want Elizabeth to hear anything more about the nightmare they had lived through, partly because Devlin didn't feel much like explaining anything.

Finally, Devlin broke the awkward silence.

"What did the doctors say about Elizabeth?"

Annie turned to him and answered, "They said kids are resilient. But they want her to come in for some more tests. And then they'll probably recommend therapy for the foreseeable future."

"I see."

"She still doesn't even know her father's dead. And she keeps asking about Ben."

"Ben is alive."

"Thank God."

"We found him in a hospital near Cambridge. Luckily there was a doctor on staff who had worked in Belfast. He knew enough about treating gunshot wounds to save him."

"How bad was he hurt?"

"Bad. But he should make it back. I had him flown to a place in Geneva where he can get the treatment he needs."

"Maybe someday Elizabeth can see him again."

"I don't know."

Annie nodded, thinking about the implications of that last statement.

"It's just beginning to dawn on me that we can stay here."

"Yes. Your enemies are all dead now."

Something in her stiffened.

"Are you waiting for me to say I'm sorry about that?" she asked.

"No."

"All of them?"

"All that I know of."

"So now what?"

"Now I go, and you stay."

"There's no chance for us?"

Devlin didn't answer.

"How much do you know, Dev?"

"Everything. Nothing. Sometimes I think the truth isn't much more than a point of view."

Annie reached out and grabbed Devlin's wrist.

"No matter what I had to do, no matter what I did wrong, I loved you fifteen years ago and I still love you, Jack."

Devlin stood very still. Annie waited for a response that wasn't coming, then let him go as suddenly as she had grabbed him. She pushed her hair back and wiped her eyes.

"So you're going."

"The police don't want me in London."

Devlin reached into the inside pocket of his sport coat and pulled out a thick envelope. It held the last of Mislovic's money.

"I used most of it for Ben's care, but I thought you should have some of this. Help with Elizabeth's school."

Annie took the envelope without comment.

Devlin turned from Annie and walked toward the hallway. He walked back to Elizabeth's bedroom and gently called for the child. She came out slowly and looked up at him.

"Elizabeth?"

"Yes?"

"I want to say good-bye."

"Are you going where Ben is?"

"Not right now. But I'll tell him you're home safe, and that everything is all right."

"Will I see him again?"

"Well, Ben is a very special person. Now that everything is all right, Ben's going to be busy helping other people for a while. But maybe."

The small girl nodded.

Suddenly Devlin bent down and picked her up. She felt almost weightless. He held her face in front of his and told her, "You're a good girl, Elizabeth." Then he kissed her on the forehead and set her down.

Devlin turned to find Annie standing behind him. He walked to her, touched her face, and left.

When Devlin returned to the Draycott, Waldron was waiting for him in the lobby. Devlin's suitcase was with him.

Devlin asked, "Are you my escort?"

"Exactly."

Waldron drove to Heathrow. Neither man spoke for a long time. As they approached the airport, Waldron finally broke the silence.

"I keep thinking about it. I'd like to believe it couldn't have turned out any other way."

Devlin didn't bother to comment.

Waldron gave up looking for verification, and his voice hardened.

"I'm to make it clear to you that you are not wanted in London. I would be thinking in terms of years before you try to come back here."

"All right."

"The only reason you got away with it was because there were enough guns to justify what happened. And enough drugs in the basement of that warehouse to provide some reason for it. And no cops got hurt. Except for perhaps Reilly, but they still haven't found the body. Some are speculating he's in hiding somewhere."

"How about you, James? What are they going to do with you?"

"I'm afraid they don't know what to do with me. I'm somewhere between being a hero and a somebody they'd rather not see again. The fact is, they won't. I'm getting out."

"Oh?"

"I've been debriefing and writing reports for two days, and I still can't believe it. Or understand it. I just know I don't want to be part of it anymore."

Devlin spoke softly. "Give yourself a little time before you do anything, James."

"Is that what you do? Is that how you do it?"

Devlin didn't answer.

But as they pulled into the parking garage at Heathrow, Devlin began talking.

"I can't explain how so much hate and insanity can exist. I can't explain why men would kill each other for the money that drugs can bring them. How do you measure that, James? In dollars? Pounds? Tons? You can't quantify the evil."

Waldron pulled into a parking slot.

"It's not going to stop, is it?"

Devlin shook his head. "No. Somehow you've managed to keep much of it out of your part of the world. But no, it's not going to stop."

"I'm supposed to take you to your plane and make sure you get on it, but I'd rather not."

"You don't have to."

"Where are you going?"

"I have some healing to do. I'm going someplace warm and quiet."

"Right."

Waldron offered his hand, and Devlin shook it.

"You're a good man, Chief Inspector. Thank you."

Waldron nodded. Devlin got out of the car. Waldron watched him until he was out of sight.

Devlin entered the terminal building and headed for the first-class check-in counter. Out of the corner of his eye, he saw someone approaching him.

He stopped and turned to face whoever it was. He found himself staring at a beautiful blonde woman whom he recognized immediately. It was the woman he had met on the plane.

She said, "My God, what happened to your face?"

There were purple bruises on Devlin's cheekbone and above his right eye where Hinton's head had banged into him. He still wore a bandage to cover the slash on his cheek.

Devlin said, "It's a long story."

"Are you heading back to L.A.? You can tell me about it."

"No, Joan. What happened to the modeling career?"

"It didn't work out. You don't look like you made out too well either."

"I survived."

"So you're not going back to L.A.?"

"No, I'm going on a little vacation."

"Where?"

"I was thinking of Bermuda. British civilization in a better climate."

"Sounds good."

"You want to come?"

"Don't ask me twice, I might take you up on it."

"You want to come?"

The blonde paused, gauging whether or not Devlin was serious.

"Are you serious? Don't kid around. I don't have to be back in L.A. for a week."

"Give me the ticket, Joan. I'm making it easy on you."

"What do you mean?"

"Mr. Chow wants you to keep track of me, doesn't he?"

Suddenly the big sexy smile faded, replaced by a scowl.

"You know!" She stamped her foot. "Was I that easy to spot?"

"Not at all. You were very good."

Devlin took her arm and led her to the ticket counter.

"I wasn't sure at first. I asked Mrs. Banks to check on you, and she didn't get back to me. Mrs. Banks never lets a request like that slide. I figured it was because she didn't want to lie about it, so that proved it to me. It wasn't your fault.

"Of course, having you show up a second time is pushing it a bit, don't you think?"

"Yes. That's what I said, but they told me they didn't have anyone else who could do it." She paused, then said, "But I'll bet Mr. Chow figured I was burned anyhow, so why not push it."

The glamorous actress/model Joan disappeared. Now she was a relaxed, natural beauty who was worried about doing a good job.

"Mr. Devlin, you know Mr. Chow is very concerned about you. I'm supposed to make sure you get back to L.A."

"I will. Eventually. But just think how many points you'll score with William by sticking with me."

"You think so?"

"Yes."

Now she held on to Devlin's arm.

"You really want me along?"

"How are you at removing stitches?"

"Actually, pretty good. I have a degree in nursing."

"No kidding."

"I wouldn't kid about that."

"Great. I hate taking them out myself."

"I can do that."

"Fine. Then I really want you to come. On one condition."

The blonde frowned a bit and looked at Devlin.

"What's that?"

"Be anybody you want except Joan Cunningham. She's not my type."

A bright smile lit up the tall woman's face and she said, "No problem. She's not really my type either. Let's go."

"Good."

She leaned into Devlin as they approached the ticket counter and said, "You know, Mr. Devlin, you really do look like you need a vacation."

"I do."

"And someone to nurse you a little."

"Yes."

"Some things are best done by a woman."

"Absolutely."

Five days later, another tall woman, this one with dark hair, walked into the opulent bar of the Grosvenor House hotel. She strode to the table where an aging Eastern European man sat. He had lost another three pounds and looked quite tired.

Annie Turino Petchek sat across from him and smiled quickly.

"Thank you for agreeing to see me."

"What do you want?"

"I understand you have an opening for someone to manage your affairs in London. I assure you I can do it better than the last person did."

Dragan frowned. He stared at Annie. She stared back, not afraid of the silence, waiting for his answer.